GUNSWIFT

Owen rested his hands against the boulder, waiting. The riders were mounting the trail. He heard voices, the crack of gear, the nearing clatter of iron on rock. He could not see them yet for the overhang. When the drift of noise grew directly beneath, he looked down and saw the first rider draw into view.

He gripped the boulder, lifted it, so suddenly that its mass tumbled outward, he lost balance and had to scramble back. He heard it strike; a horse screamed and plunged off the ledge; the thin, wailing cry of its rider died away into the gulf. The boulder made a falling crash that drowned all other sound—a thinning rattle of gravel, silence.

RAMROD RIDER

Trevannon palmed open the door and stepped into the murky hallway. He instantly froze as the bobbing flare of a lantern appeared in the stairwell, filling the corridor with its diffused glare. Trevannon's hand brushed his holster, reaching for the gun Treat had taken, before he remembered. He stopped dead, facing the stone-faced giant coming up the stairs with a lantern in one hamlike fist, a leveled gun in the other. Jans Vandermeer had caught up at last. And crowding behind the sheriff's bulk was the grinning face of Bill Treat....

T.V. OLSEN

GUNSWIFT
&
RAMROD
RIDER

LEISURE BOOKS　◧　**NEW YORK CITY**

A LEISURE BOOK®

March 1996

Published by special arrangement with
Golden West Literary Agency.

Dorchester Publishing Co., Inc.
276 Fifth Avenue
New York, NY 10001

GUNSWIFT Copyright © 1960 by T.V. Olsen

RAMROD RIDER Copyright © 1961 by T.V. Olsen

Printed in the United States of America.

GUNSWIFT

wed
we have moving

ONE

A chill wind had dipped off the peaks, and Owen reached automatically for the long-gone buttons of his tattered sheepskin, and then remembering, dropped his hand back to the rifle across his knees. He hunched his chin into his collar and settled back on his heels, patient again. He was crouched in the heavy timber that mantled the slope shouldering steeply above the dry wash below. The camp down there was silent and deserted, as it had remained throughout this long afternoon of waiting.

Owen reflected for the hundredth time on the personality of the unseen camper. It was a small, Spartanly furnished outfit. Gear was piled neatly to one side, the embers of the dead fire had been carefully trod into the earth. An efficient man, no doubt a cautious one. Owen would have to set this up carefully in any case; he wanted his man alive.

He lifted his gaze to the opposite slope. Also heavily wooded, it afforded good cover for Abner. Two hours before, Owen had watched Ab take a position behind a screen of brush a few yards above the wash, had seen no movement from there since. These were two patient men who had traveled too long and far, on a quest that had settled into plodding habit, to come this near and lose their quarry. From far up the wash Owen heard the steady, monotonous creak of the sluice box. The sun had westered beyond the peaks; even the long afterlight was dimming. Garvey would soon quit for the day and return to camp.

The plan was simple. Owen and Abner had devised it

when they'd arrived here at midafternoon and spotted the layout. Without catching sight of Garvey, they picked out the sound of his workings, evidently on a running stream that branched off about this dry lower wash. The old man in the village had told them that Garvey was jumpy and spark-tempered; he'd struck a rich gold vein here a month ago, had shot at several people who'd ventured too near his claim. Garvey carried a revolver and rifle at all times, could use both.

"Friends of his?" the old man had asked; "We know him," had been Owen's meager reply. He smiled grimly now. They knew him . . . though only Abner had set eyes on him—that once and briefly, seven years ago. They knew his place and year of birth, his detailed description, his several occupations; they almost knew the hour of his death, Owen thought savagely. He considered that with merciless detachment: the thought was part of a pattern instilled in his mind.

Any chance sound in stealing up on the man would give them away; with his nerves at hair-trigger, Garvey would surely panic and begin shooting. With two of them in cover when Garvey returned to his camp, they could catch him close and between them, giving time for one to wing him if he cut down on the other. Owen hoped the man would have the sense to stand steady when he gave the order. . . .

Abruptly Owen's senses sharpened, straining to alertness. The wooden squeak of the sluice box had ceased. He cocked his head, listening, watching upwash through the dappling of foliage that concealed him.

Soon Garvey swung into view from around a crook in the steep banks. Now at close range, Owen gave him a raking scrutiny. A small and bearded man with faded eyes in a face as bland and unassuming as a tired sheep's, he wore filth-ingrained butternut pants and a sweat-clinging linsey-woolsey shirt, slouch hat pulled low. His narrow shoulders were stooped from his cramped labors. In one hand swung a rifle; in the other an elk-hide gold pouch.

He walked to the dead fire, bent to lay the pouch on

the ground and lean the rifle across it. He reached for a tier of stacked brush to start his supper fire. Owen stirred to ease his cramped legs muscles, then started to rise, hauling in breath to call sharp warning.

He froze with knees bent as Garvey suddenly stood. Watched, breath held, as the man raised his arms in a tremendous yawn and at the same time slowly turned to face the slope. For a moment Garvey's gaze swung and held on the spot where Owen crouched; then it moved idly on. Owen watched narrowly as the man bent again. But it was only to pick up his rifle and a bucket, then turn and tramp unhurriedly back up the wash beyond sight.

Owen sank down, his muscles trembling. A trickle of sweat cut raggedly down his ribs beneath his shirt. *Damn, he couldn't have seen me. Or did he? He'd started to lay a fire. . . . No, he needs water is all. Coffee.* Yet he wished he hadn't hesitated, that he had laid down his warning at once while Garvey's rifle was on the ground.

Seconds dragged into minutes, touching a wary unease to Owen's spine. The stream was only around the bend yonder. *Maybe he saw you then. Can't chance he'll run out.*

Owen unbent to slow erectness, scanning the wash and the silent flanking forest. Standing, he was a man of well above six feet, muscled like a blacksmith, his great-shouldered frame made bulkier by the heavy sheepskin. The hamlike hands gripping the rifle were scarred at the knuckles; his face was broad through the cheekbones with a nose twice broken, a face battered without being brutal—legacy of the fights and brawls that gravitated to a big, prideful man in this raw country. His shaggy hair sworled into a short chestnut beard that slurred the sharp angles of the lower part of his face. His eyes redeemed an allover roughness, being a clear, wide-open gray, yet mature and watchful to soberness.

About to call softly to Abner, he checked himself at a crackling of brush upslope, perhaps fifty yards to his rear. The noise abruptly stilled, as though the stalker had alarmed himself. *That was no animal,* Owen thought. *He saw me, must think I'm here to deadfall him for his poke. He won't run, leave that dust. He's circling behind to get a shot.* Motionless, he listened. For another telltale sound. When it came—the sharp snap of a foot-pressed twig—Owen left cover and went up the steep incline, toes digging hard at loam. Yet his great body moved with catfooted silence between the crowding tree boles.

He caught a glimpse of Garvey's narrow figure coming downslope, head lowered as he ducked through swatches of brush. Owen hugged a thick pine trunk, barely exposing his face as Garvey beat his way closer. Then the man spotted him, froze in his tracks.

Owen hauled in breath, released it in a shout: "Throw your guns away, Garvey. I don't want your dust, only—"

Garvey gave a sharp, shrinking cry, brought up his rifle with the quickness of thought. Its roar buffeted echoes from trees and rocks. The slug cascaded dead bark from the pine six feet above Owen's head and whined off at an angle. Garvey pivoted and lunged up the slope and Owen bounded after him, crashing like an angry bull through the thickets. He'd had a clear aim there, but no time for a wing shot. The desperate need to take Garvey alive burned in his chest like a bitter prayer.

The slope sheered to an ever-mounting pitch. Pine and brush growth ended just ahead, where Garvey was scrambling up a broken shale escarpment, leaping from one shattered boulder to the next in a goatlike desperation. Then the man lost balance, spun on his heel to grab at a splintered protuberance. He recovered footing, but lost his rifle. It slid and clattered down the facerock, and fell at Owen's feet as he broke from brush and halted at the base, head tipped back. Garvey clung to the jut of the rock. He gibbered unintelligible curses.

"Come off there, Garvey!"

For answer Garvey reached a trembling hand to his pistol. Owen drew a breath and held it as he swung up his rifle and steadied a bead. He squeezed off the shot as Garvey's gun cleared leather. Garvey howled and sank down on his haunches, cradling his shattered arm. He let out a kind of wailing moan and subsided to frightened silence as Owen began swinging up the escarpment. He stepped carefully from one rock to the next, working his way at a cautious angle. He wanted to circle above Garvey and down to him.

But the prospector saw his intention. He scrambled higher, the panicked drive of his legs rattling down a small avalanche. Owen cursed once under his breath. Then he climbed, doggedly and furiously, to take advantage of every seam and outthrust on the escarpment's upper height. Garvey needed both hands; one was useless. His panting sobs drifted down to Owen, steadily closing the distance between them.

Garvey achieved a narrow ledge, his pain-drawn face peering over its brink. Then he ducked back. Owen halted, hearing Garvey's straining gasps and the grate of rock on rock. No time to move aside, time for nothing but to shrink helplessly against the cliffside as a huge chunk of shale toppled over the ledge rimrock. Deflected by a bulge, it veered aside and bounded past Owen by a full yard.

Pebbles and rock dust sifted over Owen; he coughed and choked back a momentary paralysis. Leaning out far as he dared, he gripped a fissured crack in the wall. He caught sight of a fresh foothold and swung himself sidelong to safety from well beneath the ledge.

Garvey appeared on the brink, a hefty piece of rock in his hand. He heaved it wildly and it harmlessly lobbed far out. He picked up another. The second throw shattered against rock so near Owen's body he felt the explosion of rotted shale bite into his sheepskin.

Owen had left his rifle below. He slipped out his Colt and fired. The slug burst the rimrock like a miniature grenade. Garvey faded quickly back from view. Owen sheathed the Colt and resumed climbing. Hot breath rasped in his throat and he was drenched with sweat. Pain needled his side.

Inside of a minute he reached a point horizontal with the ledge, then worked carefully toward it. Garvey sank on his haunches, holding his useless arm, and apathetically watched Owen's progress. Then he dropped his gaze to a point between his knees and did not look up until the big man dropped onto the ledge.

Owen caught him by the scruff of the neck, and with an effortless twist, brought him to his feet. His face shoved close to Garvey's sweat-shining one.

"Look at my face. You've seen it."

Against the choking grip Garvey stirred his head in dull negation. "No . . . never saw you. Never done you dirt."

"You've seen it." To his own ears, Owen's words were a dogged chant. "There were four others somewhat like it . . . a man, a woman . . . two girls not out of their teens. Think back . . . seven years ago . . . the blue-grass country outside Lexington. A big farm. You were with Tierney's Raiders. Only five of you left, rest wiped out by Morgan's Rifles. The war was a week over. . . ." He paused, seeing the pale terror mottle Garvey's blood-choked face. But the man's look was blank, half-comprehending.

"Or wouldn't you remember?" Owen went on softly. "There must have been a lot of burned farms . . . a lot of butchered women and children before the war's end, and after—for you and Tierney, eh? This was the Rutledge place. I'm Owen Rutledge. Those four people . . . my mother, my father, *my sisters, Garvey!*"

On the heel of his teeth-ground words, Owen's arm lifted and flung the man against the cliffwall. Garvey dropped to his hands and knees. His eyes glittered up through the lank hair falling over his eyes. "You . . ." he whispered, "you follered me all these years . . . all this way—"

"You're not finished till I am," Owen said tonelessly. "Two of the other raiders were killed, shot down by Federal troops. That left three—you, a lieutenant called Sykes, and Tierney himself. The three of you escaped to Texas and broke up." Owen towered above the man, his fists closing and unclosing. "Where are they, Garvey? Where are Tierney and Sykes, damn you!"

"Listen," Garvey pleaded hoarsely. "I tell you—we'll make a bargain—"

Owen bent and caught him by the throat, shaking him like a rat. "Slow or fast, Garvey. It's all one to me. Not to you." He let up the pressure of his thumbs to let Garvey suck wind into his bruised throat. He had to bend low to catch the ragged gasp: "Blanco. Blanco town . . . Blanco Basin. Both—of them."

Owen let go of him and stood, breathing heavily with the quick drain of tension. Seven years, he thought. Seven years . . . and now. . . . Strange how revenge thoughts grew to habit so dulled that a man could not yet be aware of the sharp exultance of journey's end. As though its end were the end of everything . . .

A deep voice hailed from below. Owen's back was toward the rimrock and he half-turned to glance down. He saw Abner at the cliff base, looking up with questioning concern. Owen waved an arm in reassurance.

He sensed rather than heard Garvey's sudden shift of movement, and swung back even as Garvey, rearing up on his knees in a burst of vitality, thrust his palm against Owen's middle and threw his weight behind it. The shove was a little thing to a man of Owen Rutledge's bulk —but with less than a foot of rimrock at his heels he could not step back for balance. For a moment he teetered wildly, tried to swing his weight to crash on his side. But most of his body plunged over the drop-off.

His fingers taloned against the rotted shale, caught his full weight with a violence that almost ripped his nails out. Rock crumbled beneath his fingers. They took fresh hold and he hung straight-armed, clinging along the outer ledge with his upper body hugging the rough rock, legs dangling free. He swung them inward for foothold and found none.

Garvey laughed hysterically. His boots rasped across the ledge. Owen flung back his head, saw the man above raise a boot to heel down on his hands.

The rifle made a clean, splitting report.

Garvey jerked and turned slowly in mid-stride with an arching grace. He pitched out over the rim in a twenty-foot free fall before his body crashed against the cliff's slow incline. Limply he rolled and bounded downward and was brought up, twisted and broken, across a base boulder.

Craning his head over his shoulder, Owen looked down. Abner lowered his rifle. "You got to hang on a bit there!" he boomed.

"A minute," Owen gasped. "No . . . longer . . . Ab."

He heard the quick shuffle and rattle of Abner's ascent. *He's coming too slow,* Owen thought almost detachedly, *but how fast can a man climb?* His arms numbed into his shoulders against his pendant weight, but shot into his fingers with raw pain where they curved into the ledge. He bent his head against the rock, eyes squeezed shut. Sparks flailed behind his lids. He knew his fingers were unbending. Then powerful hands fastened on his wrists.

He strained his neck backward, staring into Abner's mahogany-brown face. "Can't help you . . . no footing."

"You got to help me, Mars' Owen." The big Negro's voice held a positive calm. "Can't git no great leverage this way. I kin pull you a foot or so. You gits yore legs up far enough to dig in yore toes, I kin reach further, git a better grip. You ready?"

Owen jerked his head.

Abner heaved backward, squatted on the rim with his heels set. Owen felt his body rasp a foot upward along the rough shale. He flexed his knees, doubling his legs till he could hook his toes in a crevice against the ledge's underside.

"Got it," he panted.

Abner released one of his wrists, reached down long fingers to close on Owen's arm at the elbow. When his grip was firm he took like hold on the other arm. "Now you climb, man!"

Abner threw back his weight on his straining arms and Owen scrambled up the rimrock, toppled onto the ledge across Abner's legs. Then they lay, drawing great breaths.

Abner climbed to his feet and helped Owen up. "All right, Mars' Owen?"

Owen massaged his arms and shoulders, nodded numbly.

"He say anythin'?"

"Blanco . . . Blanco Basin."

"Which 'un?"

"Both. Tierney and Sykes. Both of them."

For a moment they simply stood looking into each other's faces. They had come a long way together—two men of two races with a single purpose. Watching the Negro with quiet affection, Owen thought of the marks these years and far driftings had left on them both. Abner was thirty-five—only six years Owen's senior—but the tight-kinked hair already lay gray and grizzled against his round head. They were equally thick-bodied, solid men in soiled, well-worn clothes, but Owen stood a full head taller than his companion.

Abner's deep, rich bass put into words their common, sobering thought. "Mighta lied, this Garvey-man. Cornered like you had him. Might not a knowed their whereabouts a-tall."

"Only one way to learn that," Owen said grimly.

Abner nodded once more, and gravely. "Best we see now to gittin' us off this rock, Mars' Owen."

TWO

Trouble, O Lawd! Nothin' but trouble
In de land o' Canaan—

Abner song-chanted softly as they rode between the slopes of a deep saddle between two mountain flanks. The pass bore the sign of old wagon passage and should bring them into Blanco Basin by nightfall.

"Very apt selection," Owen observed. "Got your juju, I hope?"

Abner's fist dipped inside his shirt collar and reappeared, holding up a bare-worn and desiccated rabbit's foot on a rawhide thong. "I been rubbin' her smart enough to drive Satan offn his hearth."

"You had her smoking for sure," Owen smiled.

Abner's broad palm cradled the rabbit's foot tenderly. "Best *gris-gris* in Kentucky. Sure-hell best in this lowdown West. Got it from Tante Marie day you was born, Mars' Owen."

Owen gave a sober and expectant nod, though he'd heard the story many times. Tante Marie had been his mother's personal maid and his own nurse for many years—an ancient, tiny Negress regarded by the blackfolk as the best voodoo woman in the country.

Abner went on distantly, "She say that day, 'You gwine be this white boy's bodyservant, little Ab. He be born to trouble, this little 'un. This *gris-gris* gwine protect you both. Day it's broken'll be day you die. Take care you never let it off your person.'"

Owen grinned, letting the old memories relax his taut senses. Memories of good days . . . yet Tante Marie had been right and he'd been born to trouble. Trouble that had begun for the South with that first shell on Sumter, that had never ended for him.

He and Abner had buried Garvey where they had caught up with him, rock-shoring the shallow grave against predators, and lashing two sticks crosswise for an anonymous marker. A week's travel northward had brought them below the broken dragon-spine of a minor arm of the Sangre de Cristo peaks, beyond which lay Blanco Basin. By this midafternoon, they were high on the south slopes of the saddle pass.

Abner called attention to the bleak, low-banked clouds scudding the north horizon. "They be on us in a couple hours, Mars' Owen. Be one hell of a big blow. We best take to shelter 'fore then."

"No shelter here. We'll push on. Land dips off from here. Make the low country before dark . . . if the storm holds off."

Abner nodded his tacit understanding of the other's bitter impatience. Strange, Owen reflected, how the pattern of seven years' quest became part of a man's very marrow, till many times it seemed a life-purpose in itself, at other times an insidious poison he knew he should shake for his own good . . . yet through it all, he'd kept an iron patience. Now, with the end in sight, he chafed against even a few hours' delay.

The first dip of land was gradual, the terrain bland enough to allow a fine-controlled clip. They paused often to blow their horses in this high, thin air. Blanco Basin's sprawling acreage grew to view below, a great grazing bowl tucked in a wild off-pocket of the Sangres. Here an outpost of civilization, a well-settled cattle country, had developed and prospered during two hundred years of Spanish and American rule, preserved by natural insulation from the brawling frontier outside. From this height through the amazingly clear and wine-sharp air, they made out the tidy sprawl of the town of Blanco far below.

The storm did not hit till they came off the pass into the first gentle foothills beneath, the pre-storm murk mingling with early dusk. Then it began, shortly buffeting men and horses in torrential sheets. Owen and Abner rode hugging the base of a high ridge, hoping for a cave or ledge that would afford shelter. They entered a cottonwood grove which broke the force of wind and rain as they headed into its murky aisles.

The forest floor was brush-free, so they caught the ruddy glow of a fire ahead while they were still a good fifty yards from it. Neither man said a word, nor slackened his pace. They'd faced too many dangers in harness for need of words. Though few would turn away a traveler on this wet and miserable night, the fire might belong to friend or foe. Owen knew the Negro's thought would be as his; Abner's silent action as he un-buttoned his mackinaw and loosened his Bowie knife in its sheath was expected. He carried no pistol, but he could throw or close-wield that heavy blade with equal dexterity.

Nearing the fire, Owen saw it situated back beneath a granite shelf protruding from the ridge face. Now a man stepped to the rim of firelight and peered through the rain-lashed dimness. His sharp call was razored with warning:

"Name yourselves, you out there!"

"Friends," Owen answered.

"Move in slow, friends."

Owen paced the bay into the tawny glow, reining in just beneath the overhang. He swung down and threw reins. The narrow man silhouetted against the fire was faceless as he stood hands on hips. He whistled, head tilting up and down to take Owen in. "Gawd, what a big ugly stud. All right, walk on in."

Owen came to the fire with a stiff-legged gait, giving only a glance and a nod to the other men sitting back against the rock wall, bending then to spread his chilled hands to the fire.

"A black stud, too. We're in fine company, Missou."

This from the narrow man. Owen turned to see him regarding Abner's dismount. The man glanced back at Owen, flamelight catching full on his face. He was hatless, his hair of flaxen paleness. His thin face was satyr-like, the eyebrows lighter than its sun-boiled ruddiness. Eyes of a deceptively weak and faded blue didn't lessen an impression of viciousness in leash. A low-thonged gun was strapped over his denims. *A pure-quill bad actor,* Owen thought.

The other man rose to his feet with the fluid grace of youth. "Couldn't expect a lowdown pilgrim that travels with his like to have the decency not to come to a white folks' camp."

Owen met the boy's challenging stare with unblinking calm. He was of middle height, sturdy of build in well-worn range clothes, his gaunt young face topped by black, curly hair, lending a certain rakishness that yet held no self-conscious swagger. The rash challenge in his words blended with a touchy pride of upbringing. The kid had seen enough of life to be self-sufficient without false cockiness, Owen guessed, but a streak of untempered wildness held him short of maturity.

"An ugly night," Owen said mildly. "We're cold and wet and obliged to you."

His moderate reply seemed to disconcert the boy; he glanced uncertainly at Abner, then at the narrow man who thinly smiled and shrugged one shoulder.

Abner broke the afterdrift of sudden silence: "I'll offsaddle, Mars' Owen, then rustle up more dry wood."

The boy's tense pose relaxed. He laughed. "Your man, eh? That's different. Good old-fashioned darky, are you, uncle?"

Abner had swung to Owen's horse; his hands halted on the latigo. He lazily glanced at the kid, his deep voice softly slurred: "Whose brother is I, boy? Mammy's or Pappy's?"

The kid made a choking sound. His hand moved; not quite touching the holster of his sidearm. Abner's right hand went under his coat to the unseen knife. Both were motionless, stare fixing stare. Owen stepped quietly back to stand by the narrow man, clearing the space between. He and Abner had been through this situation many times; however it went, he knew Abner would handle it for the best. He wouldn't take a hand unless the kid's companion did.

The narrow man sized this up with the tough, shrewd caution of an old hand. "Kid," he said tonelessly. "I'd let it ride."

Firelight flashed against the boy's eyes. He said, "A-a-h-h-" with a fathomless disgust and flung himself back on his blankets. *He's not afraid and he has good sense,* Owen thought. And knew a sudden perverse liking for this boy just as, at first sight, he'd instinctively disliked the narrow man. Owen made swift first judgments, and rarely had cause to regret them.

Abner toted their saddles and gear to the sheltered rear of the overhang, ground-haltered the horses to one side. Then he vanished in the outer darkness. Owen stood by the fire and shed his drenched clothes. The narrow man stared at his great-muscled height and laughed. "Damn, I never did see such a big ugly stud."

Owen unwrapped his sugans and spread his ground tarp out against the rock face where the fire's reflected heat made a comfortable aura. He wrapped himself in his two blankets and settled with back to the wall where he could watch both men. The narrow one sauntered over, grinning down at him.

"Name's North. They call me Ivy. The kid is Missou Holbrook—of Clay County, Missouri. Related to Jesse James, so he says."

"Owen Rutledge."

North's flaxen brows pinched. He squatted down, his lean satyr's face bemused. "Well. Well." He picked up a handful of sand and sifted it between his fingers. "They say you can use a gun. They said it in El Paso. And far north as Cheyenne. They *said* you was a big stud."

Owen nodded and yawned, aware of an aching drowsiness. Such stories were currency across a frontier where men must make their own entertainment, stories passed by mouth during long evening hours in cattle town, mining camp, bunkhouse, and range camp. Tales which lost nothing through many recountings, he thought wryly.

He'd heard of Ivy North too . . . a Rio border gunswift tied into deals of many shades and always shady . . . nothing to pin down. Missou Holbrook was evidently a newcomer—but there was an easy, yet hard-won, competence to the way the boy carried himself. A pity he was siding North . . . Owen sensed that this youth had clean stuff—his righteous, naïve wrath at Abner's presence —but he was traveling in company that would fast bring him to a forking of the road.

Abner returned bearing an armload of dry, crumbling punk which he must have kicked out of a rotten deadfall. He dropped his burden, threw a sizeable chunk on the fire. A flurry of tinder-dust ignited like a hundred fireflies and the flames flared higher.

"Better get out of those wet clothes," Owen advised Abner.

"I never seen such a pair of studs," said North.

The kid Missou stood up, idly lifted his dragoon pistol from holster, spun its fluted cylinder. He glanced around, his gaze stopping on an empty tomato can laying on the bare ground off from the fire. He brought the gun level, took easy and unhurried aim and fired. The can bounded high. It bounced a good dozen feet away. The kid aimed again. A slug sent the can spinning into the outer darkness. Missou had not fired the second shot; his dark, defiant stare swung to Ivy North.

North sheathed his gun, chuckling. "Got to hold your target faster, kid. Suppose that was big stud Rutledge and not a can?"

Owen sleepily closed his eyes. The kid's defiant exhibition became, in North, a cheap bravura. He opened his eyes as Abner jogged his elbow, silently extending dried beef and hardtack from their saddlebags. Owen chewed slowly, washed it down with swallows from his canteen. Afterward he reached for his gunbelt and unholstered the gun. It was a cedar-gripped Navy Colt converted to take metal cartridges. North and Missou watched expectantly, but seeing him proceed to clean it, North smiled thinly and the kid snorted his disgust.

Abner stretched out in his blankets, keeping his eyes open till Owen gave him a nod. He grunted softly, closed his eyes and went to sleep almost at once. Owen smiled faintly. Admittedly their relationship was a strange one, and an inner intuition had warned him not to analyze it too closely. He remembered how once, long after the war and end of slavery, he, with embarrassed roughness, had told Abner to drop the "Mars'." Abner had flashed one of his rare grins and continued with the old address as though nothing had been said. Since Abner had an independent pride of his own, Owen guessed that this was the only token of respect and loyalty that a black man raised in the South could show to a white. On their common quest, Abner recognized him as leader; otherwise, he wore his freedom with the same dignity he had slavery. . . .

Those had been good ones, their youthful days . . . hunting, fishing, swimming, riding, always inseparable.

As far back as memory reached, there had always been Abner, watching over him through boyhood's golden trials with the protective pride of six years' seniority, accepting the white boy's occasionally cruel assumptions of superiority with calm, never obsequious, diffidence. That Abner had been his father's slave was a fact which neither ever forgot . . . then or since. Both had listened to Owen's big, burly father bellow that if that damned monkey Lincoln were elected, war was inevitable.

And so Owen Rutledge at eighteen had marched off with Morgan's gray videttes, bearing on his youthful shoulders the full honor of home and family, the only son. He had soon acquitted himself with a lieutenant's commission, with his shed blood (a slight, romantically unserious wound), but always with honor. It had all been an exercise in honor at first, full of dashing skirmishes, visits home, and parade-ground pageantry.

But Kentucky had been a state divided. The independent and poor-proud peoples of the mountains gave loyalty to the Union; to the Confederacy went the pride of the wealthy slaveowners of the bluegrass plains. Not in Boone's day had Kentucky been a darker or bloodier ground than those four years when a man in the frenzy of battle might unknowingly take the life of father or brother. From this borderline sympathy had grown borderline factions: guerrilla bands who switched loyalties overnight till they degenerated into loyalty to nothing. They donned blue or gray and raided as immediate profit demanded.

One such band had been Cushing Tierney's Raiders. Tierney had begun as the scion of one of Kentucky's finest families, while the sum of his band consisted of inbred hill trash. By 1863 the Confederacy was so scandalized by his repeated turn-coating and attendant massacre, pillaging and rape that Jefferson Davis had officially outlawed him. By early spring of '65 his depredations became so brutal that Morgan's Rifles had been ordered into Tierney's mountain stronghold to run him to ground. Lieutenant Rutledge, now a grimly seasoned veteran, had played a major hand in the bloody battle that had exterminated all but the five raiders, including Cushing Tierney, who escaped and fled down into the bluegrass country.

A month later, Owen Rutledge, weary of war, sickened by defeat of his cause, had returned to his father's isolated farm. He had found house and buildings reduced to cold ashes, fields and meadows a charred and blackened waste. He found mutilated bodies—his father's, his mother's, their slaves. He did not find his two sisters. He found Abner in a thicket where he had crawled with three bullets in him. A spark of life still hung on in the big vital body, and Owen had nourished it carefully.

Later, Abner, sweating from broken fever, had weakly whispered the story. Three days before, five ragged, wild-looking men had come, demanding money of Owen's father. The old man had responded typically. They had shot him and Owen's mother, dragged the screaming girls from the house. They'd rounded up the slaves at rifle point and systematically proceeded to slaughter them. Abner recalled nothing more, except lunging at one of the men, struggling with him for his rifle . . . then the shots. But what of Owen's sisters? "Must've taken 'em both along, Mars' Owen."

Owen left food and water with Abner, then hopelessly picked up a cold trail. It led to the nearest farm, miles away. Only that morning while ditching his fields, the head of the house told him, he had found the two girls' bodies near a spot where some men had evidently camped and gone on. Owen brought the bodies back to the Rutledge farm and interred them with his parents and seven slaves in the family plot.

"I'll stay with you till you're on your feet, Ab," he had told Abner. "Then it's goodbye," to which the big Negro said simply, "Reckon I got to go with you, Mars' Owen."

"The law says I got to pay you now, Ab. There's nothing left."

"I'll ride alongside. Seein's I'm free now, man'll be ridin' where his fancy goes." A shudder had run through him; his voice broke. "My woman Saph is lyin' by your family, Mars' Owen."

That, Owen reflected now, was as much as either had spoken directly then or since of their single-minded mission. At first it had seemed short-lived. Tierney had left a trail of bloody carnage, swinging westward. Then the Federal provost-marshal ordered occupation troops to shoot any of the five outlaws on sight. Two were killed holding up a bank in Lexington. The other three were hunted out of the state. Working west on a thin-clued trail, Owen and Abner found a dead end on the plains of Texas.

The long years that followed ran to pattern. They confined an aimless search to the Southwest, their only reasoned guide being that a man who wished to lose himself would do so on a brawling frontier. They systematically covered a piece of territory, worked when money ran low, drifted to new country, bought drinks for strangers, asked guarded questions, searched a thousand new faces. Crowding strangers who turned out to be the wrong men tempered them to quick danger.

At last the search broke by pure chance. One morning in a little mining town, the name of Yeager Garvey was casually dropped by an old man in a saloon. Owen bought him drinks, plied him with questions. Garvey was prospecting in the hills above the village . . . and now Garvey was dead, leaving them with one slender lead: Blanco Basin.

Owen stared out savagely, unseeingly, at the rain running off the sheltering overhang. Blanco Basin—that was all. Had Cushing Tierney and "Red John" Sykes, his lieutenant, changed their names? Likely enough, for they'd been the big fish; Garvey was a minor member of the gang. Where—and who—might they be now? How much might their appearances have changed in nearly seven years? They might be earning a living as respected merchants or thirty-a-month ranchhands. . . .

"Thinkin', stud?"

Owen looked at North squatting a few feet away, eyes squinted against smoke from the cigarette in his teeth-set grin. "You and the black boy bound for Blanco town? We'll ride in with you."

"Pleasure," Owen said dryly, adding: "We're strangers to the basin."

"Hell, my first time here too . . . looking for a job, by chance?"

Owen shook his head in negation. "You got one here, maybe?"

"Just maybe." North's grin held as he rose and heel-ground his cigarette. "Got to see a man . . . he might have something for you. I'll put in a word if you want."

He tramped across to his bedroll by Missou who was already snoring softly, pulled off his boots and stretched out, sighing out his breath deeply. Owen remained as he was, sitting with chin on knees, his cleaned and loaded gun in his fist beneath his blanket. He stared into the outer darkness, disregarding the dying fire from long habit. A man who stared into fire and then into darkness would be momentarily blinded when his life might depend on clear sight. Despite his marrow-deep exhaustion he sleepily decided to hold wakefulness . . . no telling about Ivy North's stripe. Then within a minute his muscles were lax, his head tilted, and he slept.

THREE

The settlement of Blanco had been one of the northern-most outposts of New Spain, important enough to bring plodding *conductas* up from old Mexico deep into the Sangre de Cristos. Mule trains laden with abundant supplies and rich furnishings for the feudal household of the *hacendados* Rivera, the family whose New World grant from His Catholic Majesty had comprised a good two-thirds of the great Blanco Basin for nearly two centuries.

The last of the Rivera line had been assassinated by one of Armijo's agents during the Mexican War. Ceding of the southwest to the United States had brought only a mild cultural transition to the Blanco Basin; its wealth of rolling grasslands was the key to the continuing prosperity of the American ranchers here. Self-governed almost lawlessly, it was nevertheless so peaceful that officials in the county seat beyond the mountain arm ignored it. Federal, territorial, and county lawmen had no occasion to visit.

Owen Rutledge's knack for storing up scattered fragments of information let him automatically reassess these facts; he bleakly reflected on his need for many more as he and Abner trailed into the main street of Blanco, Ivy North and Missou Holbrook riding ahead. If the basin held the end of his search, he had to bend all he could learn toward that end.

The mid-morning sun picked out stately old adobe and fieldstone buildings whose Andalusian *exótica* contrasted with the interlarding of square, clapboarded frame buildings of a more recent frontier. The night's heavy rain stood in glassy pools along the rut-channeled street, an oozing mire thickly churned by their mounts' hoofs. Ivy North drew rein in front of a dual saloon and store with a one-word legend, CLAIBORNE'S, across its false front.

North wrapped his reins around the tie rail, squinting up at Owen. "Step down. Have one drink on me, anyway."

Owen dismounted. Abner reached down to take his reins. "I'll be a minute, Ab."

"All right, Mars' Owen."

North remarked as they tramped inside with Missou, "Your boy there knows his place for all his sass."

"He's no fool," Owen answered dryly. "Around the border and below we both go in a Mexican cantina . . . but up here colored men have been shot for as much."

The barroom was long, vaulted, and smoke-free this early in the morning. The mahogany bar was innocent of customers. A yeasty tang of beer hung pleasantly in the stale air. Owen ordered a beer; North and Missou took whiskey.

"Here's to sin," North said, tossing off his drink. To the thick-bodied bartender: "I'm North, Ivy North. Claiborne'll be expecting me."

The man paused in the act of mopping at a bar stain. He looked North over carefully, nodded once and in the same motion tilted his head toward a rear door. "Office back there."

"Give my friends another," North said. He tossed a double-eagle on the bar. "Suppose you hold your horses, Rutledge. The man might want to see you . . . might change your mind about working for him."

"Don't bother," Owen murmured.

"No bother." North grinned and sauntered the bar's length to the rear door. He went through it uninvited.

Owen brooded into the schooner, turning it barely tasted between his big hands. He wished Missou weren't here . . . he wanted to ask the bartender a few questions privately. Barmen were always the first to know the most. He shrugged, lifted his glass and drained it. He'd swung from the bar to leave when the office door opened and Ivy North called, "Oh, Rutledge—slow down."

A man stepped out past North and came across the room. A rawboned man who towered above even Owen, his face nearly hidden by a huge beard which spilled like dark hoarfrost over his pleated white shirtfront. His gaunt head with its high, bulging brow had a kind of hungry melancholy in keeping with the conservative black broadcloth he wore like any small merchant. But his skin was deeply sunburned, eye corners meshed with fine wrinkles . . . eyes that were colorless and ceaselessly darting and strangely chill. His age might have been anywhere from thirty-five to fifty-five.

"This here's Matthew Claiborne," North said laconically. "Owen Rutledge."

Claiborne extended a large bony hand, sizing up Owen in a flicking glance. He nodded as if with approval. "Pleasure, sir," he rumbled in a voice soft, yet rich and rolling. Unlike most lofty, loose-jointed men, he was not stooped; he carried himself with an erect military bearing. This, with his name, jolted an echo of recognition in Owen's mind.

"Not General Claiborne? Bloody—"

"Yes, Mr. Rutledge," Claiborne cut in gently. " 'Bloody Matt' Claiborne. My reputation has preceded me, as usual. Will you have a drink with me?"

Owen automatically nodded, held by curiosity. Major-General Matthew Claiborne had been the South's infamous spearhead in the Tennessee border campaigns. Efficient, quick-thinking, always a good officer, never a martinet, he'd yet inspired no love in the troops who had dubbed him "Bloody Matt," this man who'd been willing to coolly sacrifice any number of men to gain or hold a foot of enemy ground. A glory-hunter, they'd called him. . . . Yet, seeing him now, Owen's quick intuition sensed that the man had probably cared nothing for the opinions of his men or his superiors or the Confederacy itself. Claiborne would need to feel himself a power in his own eyes alone, and would have used any cause, any human life, to that end. Now he was uprooted and cast on a strange beach like much other flotsam of the war. Owen guessed that whatever his business here, it would run true to his character.

Claiborne snapped his fingers. "My private bottle, George. Three glasses."

"Four," Ivy North suggested. "Missou Holbrook here's with me."

Claiborne settled his brief, restless glance on young Holbrook. He said with a peculiar flatness, "A kid, Mr. North. A green hand. Besides, you'll be handling this job alone."

Missou met the darting stare levelly, saying, "Even a kid learns by watching, sir."

Claiborne's beard parted in a noiseless laugh. "Why that's the only way, my boy. Set one out for the man-to-be, George."

Owen downed the dark, fiery liquor, let its heat flood through his veins and set down his glass to find Claiborne appraising him. "Mr. Rutledge, I have hold of a

large thing here," he announced without preliminary.
"I've already gathered some men. Riffraff, a cross-dog
outfit. Now I need some special ones . . . of which Mr.
North here is the first. I want at least one more."

One crook to another, Owen thought wryly, but Clai-.
borne's unquestioning interpretation of his hard look,
seedy tramp's appearance, and generally tough name was
a common one. *All right, play it that way awhile;
you'll need to learn all you can of the basin situation.*
"What's your proposition?"

Claiborne said smilingly, "My business. Unless and
until it becomes yours. Suffice it to say I need one man
who can lead a few others by the nose. You look like
him. How would—"

The sound of a wagon rattling down the street drew
Claiborne's attention. He walked quickly to the batwing
doors and looked over them. He glanced back and jerked
his head at Ivy North who came to stand by him.

"There's Colonel M'Kandless now," Bloody Matt said,
and lowered his voice to speak in a rapid whisper. North
asked a question or two, listened, nodded. Then he pushed
open the swingdoors and stepped onto the porch.

Owen and Missou stepped over beside Claiborne.
Looking out above his shoulder, Owen saw a dark-haired
girl in her teens being assisted down from a fringe-
topped rig by an elderly man. The rig was drawn up
before a store downstreet and across from the saloon at
a sharp angle.

"That'd be North's job?" he asked casually. "That
old man?"

Claiborne's sharp sideglance searched his face with
faint suspicion which relaxed with his confiding smile.
"That's right. Colonel Amos M'Kandless, owner of Lionclaw—biggest ranch in the basin, and heart of the old
Rivera grant."

"North won't take him here . . . broad daylight, the
middle of town?"

"The more witnesses, the better. It'll be a fair—" Claiborne chuckled mildly— "a fair fight. I told North to
touch that hot-blooded Kentucky pride of the good colo-

nel's. The colonel won't suspect the way of the provocation, since North is a stranger here. This is an opportunity we can't let pass—the colonel in town with his daughter and none of his crew. I hadn't expected it to come off this easily."

Owen watched the elderly man as he bent to check one of the team's forehoofs. The colonel moved slowly and with a severe limp, yet holding himself erect with a painful and iron pride. He was slight, almost frail-seeming, but his thin features seemed hewn from brown granite. White mustaches bristled like sabers above a thin, incisive mouth; deep humor lines saved his face from cold austerity.

"Like shooting a fish in a rain barrel," Owen said softly.

"Yes, exactly; the beauty of it." Bloody Matt smiled thinly.

Owen brushed swiftly past him through the doors just as Ivy North stepped off the walk and began his catlike saunter across the street. Behind him, Owen heard the stunned disbelief in Missou Holbrook's voice: "Mr. Claiborne, you mean to say . . . you sent for him to kill that crippled old man?"

"What kind of sugar pap were you weaned on, boy?" Matthew Claiborne said irritably. "You know what North is, you came in his company."

"Never thought about this," Missou said in a voice soft and dazed. "Never thought about crowding a crippled old man . . . no fair fight."

"You should have thought of that earlier."

"But that girl—she's in line!"

The boy was teetering on a thin edge of indecision . . . he was a possible ally, but Owen could not wait. He stepped down from the walk. Claiborne's voice crackled behind him: "Stay out of it, Mr. Rutledge. He doesn't need your help."

"*You* stay out of it," Owen said softly.

"What!"

"The kid was right—it's too heavy a hand to load against the old man. I'm going to stop it."

Claiborne hauled in a wrathful breath, but before he could speak, Missou Holbrook pulled his dragoon pistol in a fluid movement, cocked it, and rammed it into Claiborne's ribs. "Go ahead, mister." The kid had made his decision; his voice hardened with it. "Stop it."

Owen nodded, pivoted and stepped off the boardwalk, heading after North. He gave Abner a quick shake of his head that said, *This is my affair*, as he passed him.

North had halted a dozen paces from the old man. "Oh, Pappy." He whistled. "You there."

Colonel M'Kandless lowered the horse's hoof, turned with a slow, painful dignity. He said icily, "Did you speak to me, sir?"

"Why you old pone-and-sweet-tater bastard, I meant none other."

Deep crimson mounted to the colonel's face. He brushed back the coat of his white tropical suit with a veined and trembling hand, exposing a belted pistol. His soft drawl thickened. "I am not an unreasonable man. I will hear the meaning of your words, then an apology."

"If you ain't the cockiest old sonuvabitch!"

"Pa," the girl said. It left her as a soft scream. "Pa, don't . . ."

"Cissie, get off out of the way. Hurry."

"North."

Owen had reached street's center, halting in the ankle-deep mud. Then he spoke. North looked at him lazily but did not turn. "Stud, I had just a feeling we might strike sparks. Why I figured on keeping you around. I'll look for'ard to another time. Right now—"

"Right now," Owen said flatly, "you better turn around."

North swung one foot back and made a half-turn, coming motionless with legs braced. His faded eyes were alight, amused. "I'm gonna stomp you, big stud . . . *now!*"

Owen felt the smooth smack of the gun butt against his palm, and as the Navy Colt came level, the whole scene froze in iron clarity. Then the gun blasts merged. Owen brought one foot sideways—a small movement;

North's slug passed between his arm and body. A giant blow wrenched North's head and he fell with his arms and legs splayed from his body. A thin pool of muck splashed with his impact and washed back against his body.

Owen walked to him. He started to bend and saw the back of North's head where his bullet had emerged and straightened. He swallowed against a roiling sickness. A man could get a reputation in all manner of brawls . . . but few bullets killed at once. A man shot in any number of vital spots could live for days. This was his first known killing . . . but North was the real killer and he knew he must hold to that thought and not think of the rest.

He drew an arm across his clammy face and looked at Colonel M'Kandless. The old man faced him stiffly. "I did not ask your help."

"I know you didn't, sir," Owen heard himself say.

"Unfortunately you've placed me in your debt . . ."

"Yes, thank you." Cissie M'Kandless moved close to her father. She was tall, slim in a rangy, colt-lithe way, not pretty; the thin, too-sharp features of her father lay on her face, strained to paleness beneath its Indian-tan. "Thank you from the bottom of my heart. He would have been killed—"

"Cissie," the colonel reprimanded stiffly.

"Oh, you know it's true!" she said passionately.

Owen nodded and touched his hat, then slogged back to the porch, his face iron-hard as he tramped across it to face Claiborne. "Want my answer now?" he asked thinly.

"Why, I have it," Matthew Claiborne said. "You're a purple fool."

"My own, though."

"Well, that may be important to you. But I will advise you to ride on. If you do not, and cross me again in this basin, it will be for the last time."

"Now," Owen said, feeling the backwash of violence grip his body with its trembling reaction, "now you have me shaking."

Missou Holbrook holstered his dragoon as Claiborne gave him a long, measuring look. "You pulled a gun on me, boy. You drift. You could just be shot on sight and no one would care."

Missou's dark eyes moved to the sprawled form of North, and he shook his head slowly, once. Then he slapped open the batwings and went off the porch to his horse. He mounted, reined about and started into a rough canter down the street.

Claiborne took a cheroot from his vest pocket, bit off the end with a savage twist and spat it at Owen's feet. Without a word he turned and walked back to his office.

FOUR

Owen stepped down to the tie rail and untied his bay. "We'll take the horses to the livery stable. I'll put up at the hotel, the livery owner will likely let out his loft to you."

Abner nodded, crossing his hands on his pommel. It was their usual way in a white man's town. "Mars' Owen, that Genril 'Bloody Matt' Claiborne himself?"

Owen swung into his saddle. "The same man. Same kind of man. Got big ideas, warned me to keep out of his way."

"Heard him. Reckon we can handle that, too?"

"No choice as to that now." They kneed their horses down the street toward the big livery barn at its north end. Owen felt an odd pleasure at Missou Holbrook's reaction when the chips were down, confirming his first judgment. Likely he'd not see the kid again, but at least Missou was pointed off from Ivy North's lead.

Meanwhile Owen Rutledge had turned one acquaintance into an enemy to pose an ever-present threat while he remained in the basin. As was his way, Owen had helped Colonel M'Kandless without checking wherefores, and he knew no regret. If he'd made an enemy, he'd also helped a boy and saved an old man's life.

"Please."

They were reining past the mercantile store. Owen glanced absently at the woman standing on the porch as she spoke; then he looked away. "Please," she said again, a little louder, and he realized she'd addressed him.

He ranged over by the porch, touching his hat. "Yes'm?"

"I saw what happened. I'd like to talk to you."

He regarded her wonderingly from the top of her primly coiffed head to the hem of her plain black dress. She was small and in her mid-twenties, with a placid little face rescued from plainness by its pert, tip-tilted nose and vivid blue eyes. A sprinkling of girlish freckles countered its prim, high-chinned poise. Realizing he was staring, Owen said in some embarrassment, "You must be mistaken, ma'am."

"No. You shot a man in front of that saloon."

This laconic directness disconcerted him more; he nodded mutely.

"It's rather private. If you come to my house, I'll tell you my proposal. You may find it a valuable one. . . . I'm Virginia Gilchrist."

Her voice held a twangy New England accent almost alien to his ears, yet with a pleasant crispness. Curiosity alone impelled his slow nod of agreement. "Ab, take the horses on to the stable—"

Abruptly and sharply the girl cut him off. "He is welcome in my house. At least as welcome as you."

Oh Lord, another rabid Abolitionist, Owen thought wearily. Southern-born and bred, he'd met these people rarely, but their attitude left both him and Abner cold. They could not explain a relationship which simply was, which had always been. "If that's your pleasure," he said quietly. "But our horses have to be watered and grained. They've carried us a far way without proper care."

"I see," Miss Gilchrist said primly. "Mister—Ab, my house is the small white one at the very south end of town. When you've finished . . ."

Abner soberly touched the down-furled brim of his ancient slouch hat and took Owen's reins as he stepped down. Owen set off down the boardwalk by the girl, accommodating his long stride to her small, brisk steps. He held a puzzled silence which she did not break.

They turned up the gravel path of a square adobe building on the outskirts, set off from the others. It might have been a Mexican laborer's shanty, now furnished with a heavy coat of whitewash, a white picket fence, and a grassy lawn with geometrically parallel flower beds, all bearing out the personality of an orderly and feminine tenant.

She unlocked the door with a key from her reticule and stepped in, holding the door for him. He jerked off his hat and ducked his head beneath the low jamb. She nodded him to a sagging, battered divan with a faded-rose pattern on which he gingerly settled his bulk, knees drawn uncomfortably high.

"In Boston I would serve tea at this time of day," she observed with the faintest smile. "But you've come a distance, and in this country . . . coffee?"

"Yes'm, please."

She disappeared through a rear doorway, and he gave the small front room a careful attention. The worn rug and few pieces of furniture was spared shabbiness by precise, balanced placement and spotless cleanliness. A shelf on the wall held a number of fragile crystal pieces . . . dishes and figurines. Her only display heirlooms, he supposed. With a sudden poignancy he remembered his mother's pride, the tasteful parlor where she had entertained. . . .

Virginia Gilchrist returned bearing a tray with a small coffeepot which she set on a taboret facing the divan. She filled two china cups. "No cream, I'm afraid. Sugar, Mr.—?"

"Rutledge, Owen Rutledge. No thank you."

He lifted the steaming brew, sipped it as she drew up a straight-backed cane-bottomed chair, sat, and folded her hands on her lap. "Now, Mr. Rutledge, to business. . . . You're a stranger here, but have you heard of the Rivera family?"

"Clan of Spaniards that used to hold this basin on a king's grant, yes, ma'am."

She cocked her head slightly, vivid eyes measuring him coolly. "You haven't heard, probably, that the original charter granted by the Spanish Crown to Don Felipe Rivera is—was in my possession?"

"News to me."

"As it was to me when I learned of it nine months ago on my father's death. We were quite poor; his will bequeathed me little more than his strongbox holding a few papers, mostly of indebtedness, and a sealed envelope containing the charter and a letter of explanation. It seems that I, as my father's only child, am the legal heiress to all the property stipulated in the old grant."

Owen caught himself leaning forward with interest and now he straightened casually, his words tinged with a shade of doubt: "Your father was a poor man . . . and you hadn't heard of this before?"

She stiffened a little. "He was, and I had not. But the story, as related in his letter, explained a strange situation."

In 1792, she went on, her great-grandfather, a Boston merchant named Samuel Gilchrist, had been supercargo of a ship with goods consigned for Monterey. There his native and cultured charm had ingratiated him with *Californio* high society . . . with the grandees Rivera, who had come from the eastward territory to visit relatives. He later married the current family-head's only daughter and returned with her to Boston. After the Mexican War and transferral of southwestern properties to the United States, the disentangling of numerous documents resulted in the dispatch of the original Spanish charter for Blanco Basin to Samuel Gilchrist's eldest son. But John Gilchrist was a cautious, well-to-do merchant with no desire to risk money in a long-drawn legal battle with other claimants; the question of southwestern property right was still vague and unsettled. The charter was passed to his son, Virginia's father, a frail invalid under whose hand the family business had decayed. His only remaining possession of value was an ancient document which might prove the key to fortune—but it lay useless in his sick, timid, poverty-stricken hands.

" 'I did not have the courage or the means to use it,' " Virginia softly quoted her father's letter. " 'You have the courage, daughter, and the wit and the will, and you may find a way.' So I sold our house, Mr. Rutledge, and came out here to see . . . if there was a way."

Owen was silent a moment, scowling into his empty cup. Doubt still shaded his voice: "You mentioned that you *had* it."

"The charter was stolen from me only yesterday."

"How?"

"I had it wrapped in an oilcloth and locked in my trunk, stored beneath a cupboard in the kitchen. Someone stole in while I was at work, forced the lock, and took only the document."

"You tell anyone where it was?"

"No. . . ." She sounded doubtful, then added emphatically, "No."

So somebody knew and she's not saying, Owen thought sardonically, and went on: "Then who do you think stole it?"

"Colonel Amos M'Kandless," she said unhesitatingly, and then, quickly: "Yes, you saved his life . . . he must have appeared the very soul of the Southern gentleman. So he may be, but not where his property is concerned. . . . Lionclaw, his ranch, is the heart of the old Rivera grant. When I learned of this on my arrival at Blanco, I went to see him. He greeted me courteously and heard my story. He mocked it politely at first, but when I was insistent he grew angry—said I was a cheap fraud trying to perpetrate a large-scale swindle."

"You show him the charter?"

"Of course. He pronounced it a clever forgery after

barely glancing at it . . . and my story, a fantastic hoax."

"A strange story, you'll own," Owen observed dryly.

"I told you it was," she said tartly. "Well, what could I do? I had enough money to buy this house, then learned that the local schoolhouse needed a teacher. So I have a job and very meager salary . . . hardly enough to contest a claim against the wealthy colonel. I have no ties back East. I could only stay on, hoping for . . ." she shrugged, looking down at her folded hands . . . "a miracle."

Owen frowned. Told in her direct and cool manner, the story had a ring of truth. If she was a fraud, she was an incredibly convincing one, who seemed what she appeared—a transplanted Boston schoolmistress. He stirred his feet uncomfortably. "This is interesting, ma'am. Very. But . . ."

"I want your services for a very simple reason. You're a stranger with no visible interest here. You saved a helpless old man by shooting an attempted assassin. That showed both competence and integrity. Our talk has also borne out your . . . moderate good breeding."

"Thank you. And you want me to rectify my mistake and shoot Colonel M'Kandless?" He immediately regretted his perverse response.

She said steadily and with no heat, "I do not. I want you to find the charter and return it to me. With its transferral to my family a matter of government record, it's useless to anyone but me, but plainly dangerous to anyone with an opposing claim."

"Are you certain," Owen said very slowly, "that nobody but Colonel M'Kandless has such a claim?"

She hesitated. "There is another—Matthew Claiborne. He came to the basin a month ago, ostensibly to buy a saloon, actually to force a claim of his own. Somehow he'd come into possession of a thirty-five-year-old Mexican grant laying claim to all the old Rivera land. It's made out, so I've heard, to one General Estevan Torres, evidently a reward for loyal service . . . and signed by Armijo, the last Mexican governor of New Mexico, I believe."

"A genuine claim?"

"I haven't seen the paper. I understand that Claiborne showed it to Colonel M'Kandless and they had hot words . . . the upshot being that the colonel threatened to shoot Claiborne on sight. Since then Claiborne has quietly hired several shiftless toughs. He doesn't have nearly enough money to fight his claim against the colonel's in court either; doubtless he intends to force him off Lionclaw and afterward deal from a more equal position."

"He tried to get M'Kandless killed today," Owen pointed out.

"That would be surer still. He would then have to deal with only the colonel's brother and the daughter, Cissie. I doubt if the colonel has any other heirs. The brother, I have heard, is not of the colonel's fiber, and Cissie is little more than a child. Probably he could bully and frighten them into giving him at least a large chunk of Lionclaw without difficulty."

"I've met Matthew Claiborne," Owen said, "and I'd put him down as the more likely to steal your charter—to remove another claimant."

"But only M'Kandless . . ." Again he noted her uncertain pause. . . . "Only M'Kandless knew of the charter; I spoke to him in private."

"If he did take it, he had no reason not to destroy it."

"I've thought of that. Still he might keep it if only till he ascertained its authenticity. I'm assuming that his righteous designation of me as a fraud was a fraud of his own. Actually he must have been alarmed. Such Spanish grants have been often given precedence in American courts, and—after all, what becomes of a gentleman who loses his estate?"

"You tell me."

She leaned forward earnestly. "Mr. Rutledge, you have given me some discourteous replies, and I understand your feelings. . . . You are—a tramp proficient with a gun. Isn't that it, bluntly? And you resent a woman who would ordinarily snub you on the street now stooping to ask your help when she needs it. You are right, of course, so let me put the proposition on a purely business basis. If you will investigate the theft of my charter, I'll pay you well. In my present occupation, I may be long accumulating the money. If you leave the basin before then, I will forward the money to whatever address you leave."

"This charter," he said thoughtfully. "A kind of life-line for you, isn't it, though you can't use it?"

"You need not consider that," she said stiffly. "How much do you want? I'll put it in writing."

"Fifty dollars, and that won't be necessary," he said roughly.

Her face cleared. "Why, that's more than reasonable."

He shrugged. "You're trusting me—and that's unreasonable. I might sell the charter for a lot more to either Claiborne or M'Kandless."

"I don't believe you would do that, Mr. Rutledge."

He smiled faintly. "Where do I begin?"

"You helped Colonel M'Kandless. In return he should be glad to give you employment. You're a resourceful man; you'll think of something. If you become convinced that he doesn't have the charter, I will forfeit the fifty dollars."

Owen stroked his chin absently. "How many men on the Lionclaw crew?"

"Oh . . . I should say twenty, not counting the Mexican tenants whom the colonel inherited when he bought the place. It's a thriving affair."

Why not? Owen thought. A man might help himself and this girl too. He would have to reconnoiter all of Blanco Basin to find his men, and Lionclaw's twenty-man crew was as good a place as any to begin.

"I'll do my best."

"Thank you." A warm wave of relief colored her face. She followed him to the door. Someone rapped at it briskly.

"That should be your friend," Virginia observed, opening it. ". . . . Oh, Charlie."

The young man who stood on the threshold smiled casually. "I didn't know you had company, Ginny."

"Mr. Rutledge, this is Charles McVey—Blanco's only lawyer. This is Owen Rutledge, Charlie."

McVey extended a firm hand. He was of medium height, about of an age with Owen, cutting a slim and elegant figure in his inexpensive black suit. His light blond hair was close-cropped above an oval cherub's face of fresh, ruddy color. Owen thought that McVey's most valuable asset as a lawyer must be his eyes—a wide, innocuous blue.

"You're new to the basin, sir," McVey said, as pleasantly as though encountering a big, rough-looking tramp in Virginia Gilchrist's parlor were an everyday matter. Owen said yes, as he shook hands.

"I don't want to intrude, Ginny. . . ."

"I was leaving." Owen clamped on his hat. "Day, ma'am, Mr. McVey."

"Goodbye, Mr. Rutledge," she said warmly, "and thank you."

That must be her beau, Owen thought as he tramped down the gravel path. An unbidden consideration struck him: was McVey the unmentioned party whom she'd told of the trunk-stored charter? Unusual for him, Owen could not make a quick judgment about the young lawyer: McVey had a perfectly-cultivated attorney's blandness which closeted his thoughts from the sharpest eye. It was a thing to keep in mind.

Turning onto the street, he saw Abner come from a store carrying a bulging flour sack, and went to meet him.

"Bought some noon grub, Mars' Owen. We kin walk out from town an' build us a cook fire."

They went down to the riverbank and Abner gathered brush while Owen scraped a hollow for the fire and told of the bargain with Virginia Gilchrist. "I think she rings true, Ab. We can find out what she wants to know and maybe what we want to know, same time."

Abner's dark face creased approvingly. "I liked the cut of that little lady, Mars' Owen. Lowdown 'bolition foolery an' all."

FIVE

Colonel Amos M'Kandless had made the ancient house of Rivera his own home. The main building was a huge block of whitewashed adobe, two stories high and set on a fieldstone foundation. The front veranda columns supported an iron-railinged gallery which ran around all four sides. Two new one-storied flanking wings were of hand-hewn pine timbers, green and still oozing pitch. A park of towering cottonwoods surrounded and shaded the house and its outbuildings, set well off from the main structure.

Owen and Abner caught their first sight of it at late afternoon, topping a rise nine miles east of Blanco town. The long slope rolled into the grassy flats where Lionclaw headquarters lay. "That's near big an' fine as any bluegrass plantation," Abner observed.

Owen nodded absently as he gigged his bay down the slope. It was a fine and peaceful old land, this basin, with a long-established, aristocratic Spanish culture which men like Colonel M'Kandless, himself of old Kentucky's finest, would have preserved and enhanced. Now another breed of man, a violent breed, like Ivy North and Matthew Claiborne *and Owen Rutledge,* he thought with wry honesty, were ready to disrupt it into bloody warfare for their own ends. His hired killer's failure to kill M'Kandless would hardly deter Claiborne. He would only change his mode of offense, and no telling how it would come.

They rode past a row of Mexican shanties where coffee-brown women and children stared curiously at Owen's companion, of a color far darker than theirs. Finally they turned up a gravel buggy drive which curved gracefully athwart the front of the big house.

At their approach three people on the wide veranda broke off conversation. Owen reined in his fiddlefooting bay by the steps, and touched his hat to Cissie M'Kandless who was sitting on the top step, slapping a riding crop against her palm. She wore a gray riding habit and was bareheaded. She smiled warm recognition and respectfully said nothing, waiting for her father to speak.

The colonel, a cool, distinguished figure in white flannels and a Panama hat, sat in a rocking chair, a glass of brandy in his hand. By him stood a tall, middle-aged man in worn range clothes whose leathery face, seamed with fine-grained lines, outshaded his pale brown eyes, eyes which laid a neutral, watchful gaze on Owen.

The colonel painfully uncrossed his legs and slowly rose. He stumbled as he took a short step forward. The tall man instinctively reached a hand, as quickly drew it back unnoticed when the proud old man recovered balance, limped slowly to the veranda edge. He nodded stiffly. "Good afternoon, sir. Will you step down?"

Owen swung to the ground and turned, lifting a foot to the bottom step. M'Kandless' courteous poise relaxed with his curious scrutiny of Owen's face. "There is something very familiar about you; I marked it this morning in town. What is your name?"

Owen told him.

"Rutledge, of course!" A warm smile broke the colonel's polite austerity; he held out a wasted and trembling hand which Owen took. "Young Owen . . . Harry Rutledge's boy. I served with your father in the Kentucky legislature, just before the war. He often spoke of his only son . . . a law student."

Owen smiled too. "You're *Senator* M'Kandless, sir? Your surname is one of Kentucky's oldest, of course . . . but we never met."

"I am proud to shake hands with Harry Rutledge's son before I die. And how is your father?"

"Dead, sir. The war," Owen said shortly.

"I'm genuinely sorry to hear it," the colonel said quietly. "He was a fine man . . . too forceful and outspoken—I should say too honest—to have lasted long in politics. During his brief tenure in the Senate, I came to respect him highly."

Owen smiled. "That was Pa."

"I've gotten out of touch," the colonel went on. "Rather than remain to watch the downfall of the Confederacy, my family and I came to New Mexico and this peaceful basin late in '64. Afterward we severed all ties in Kentucky. Too many painful memories."

"A good many Kentuckians can say as much, sir," Owen said quietly.

"Yes." The colonel's hawk eyes were intent. "You will forgive my seeming ingratitude of this morning, I hope? I had forgotten that a gentleman's honor must express itself in different ways in a different land. You gave that fellow his chance . . . and saved a sick and aging man." His mustaches twitched with his smile. "A fact I don't mind confessing to the son of Rutledge."

Owen knew a quick stab of shame, thinking of his purpose here—which he must conceal. "I will have to confess, sir, that I am here to ask for a job. Abner and I have worked cows."

"Abner?" The same bodyservant you had as a boy? Your father used to speak of him, too. . . . Of course there's a place for him on my crew. But I can offer you better, Owen. I have need of a man . . ." He coughed embarrassedly . . . "A sort of general secretary. I'm no hand at figures, and the ranch books are in a sorry state. Also, of late, certain questions have arisen about my legal ownership of this ranch and I need a legal advisor, one I can trust. You've studied law. . . ."

"Thank you, sir."

The colonel smiled broadly. "It's settled, then. Here, shake hands with my segundo, Paul Dirksen. Paul, show Abner to the bunkhouse—"

"If you don't mind," Owen interrupted, "I'll see him there."

"I understand," the colonel nodded wisely. "But there are Mexicans, a Ute wrangler, and two mulattoes on my crew. They work in team with the whites; there is no discord."

"Nevertheless I'd like to see the bunkhouse, Colonel."

The colonel laughed. "Your protective loyalty to your man is admirable, Owen. Very well . . . and look over the place, if you like. Be back at the house in time to clean up. We eat at six sharp."

Cissie got quickly to her feet and came down the steps. "I—I'd like to thank you again, Mr. Rutledge. For this morning."

She colored deeply as he spoke, and Owen realized her extreme shyness. She must be seventeen or eighteen, an age when Southern-bred belles were long-groomed to crinoline and cotillions. But she was a plain girl on a lonely ranch with a stern father, a combination which would have easily formed her withdrawn and tomboy manner. Her riding habit was well-worn and dusty, her nut-brown hair carelessly caught in a loose knot at the back of her neck. But her eyes were a light clear hazel that made him think of a poet's line about windows of the soul.

He removed his hat with careful courtesy, saying gently, "Glad I was there, Miss Cissie."

She blushed more furiously, and ducked her head. Owen smiled and picked up his mount's trailing reins. Abner stepped down, and he and Owen followed Paul Dirksen to the corral, leading their horses. Walking apace of Dirksen, Owen was aware of the man's sharp, shrewd sideglance, and he thought, *It'll come now, all the questions.* But Dirksen said only, in a deep musical drawl, "So the kunnel knew your pappy?" and Owen nodded, and that was all.

They turned their horses into the corral and carried their saddles to the harness shed. As Owen went inside close behind Abner, he said softly, "If we find one of our men in the bunkhouse and there's trouble . . . we don't start it, Ab. Not here."

"I know, Mars' Owen."

Owen's conscience was already smarting from this necessary subterfuge; he didn't intend to violate the colonel's generous confidence further with violence. They'd waited nearly seven years . . . could wait a while longer.

His real purpose in accompanying Abner to the bunk-house was to learn whether Tierney or Sykes were on the crew. There was a chance that either might recognize Abner, whose thick powerful body and strong-graven face were not easily forgotten; if so, there'd be immediate trouble. Only Abner could identify the pair positively; Owen had seen Cushing Tierney but once, briefly and at a distance, when Morgan's Rifles had crushed the guerrilla band. He remembered a wolf-gaunt form and a fierce, pinched face, nothing more.

Some of the crew were lined up at the wash bench in front of the low log building, waiting their turn to wash up for supper. Abner's passive stare fixed the face of each as they passed, and then they went through the doorway into the puncheon-floored room. Several men were resting on their bunks. Owen met the feisty stare of a thin, short man who was removing his brush chaps. His bushy black hair bristled over a thin and predatory face. He came at once to his feet, a man who evidently compensated for his lack of size with a bantam-cock strut and a fiercely assertive manner.

"What're you staring at, bucko?"

"Nothing," Owen said mildly, idly shifting his glance around the bare interior of the bunkroom. The man's flat challenge, this time to Abner, brought his eyes quickly back.

"Black boy, you see something interesting over here?"

"Simmer down, Fitz," Dirksen said. "The Negro's a new hand, and Rutledge here is a friend of the kunnel's." He added apologetically to Owen, "Fitz is always this way with newcomers, don't mind him any."

Fitz glowered and sank back on his bunk. At once his banjo eyes shuttled back to Abner. "Black boy, you keep starin' me over. I lived too long in Tennessee to take that off a—"

"You talk a lot," Owen said, and was sorry then. It was all Fitz had needed. He mouthed a soft, foul epithet as he lunged to his feet, spreading his wiry arms. *He's the kind wants to jump every big man he sees, and now he's got the excuse,* Owen thought. He glanced at

Dirksen, but the segundo said nothing, only looked on with that neutral, quiet gaze. In a few words, it had developed to a personal antagonism in which no seasoned frontiersman would interfere.

Owen felt a helpless, half-amused irritation as Fitz began circling him. *Should I step on him,* he wondered, *or just blow him over?* The faintest grin touched his lips and Fitz saw it and rushed in, face twisted with fury. His arms windmilled wildly. Owen cuffed them aside, grabbed him by the scruff of the neck and sent him stumbling away. Fitz pivoted back and bored in. A wild swing caught Owen on the nose. In the blaze of pain, he forgot restraint. He fisted his hand in the little man's shirtfront and carried him back to slam him hard against an upper bunk. Fitz was lifted off the floor, legs flailing wildly; the sideboard caught him across the shoulders with a crash that snapped his head back. He gave an agonized yell. Owen's anger cleared at once and he released Fitz, who fell to the floor and lay rubbing his back, eyes blazing up undiluted hatred at Owen.

"You took a grizzly by the tail, Fitz," Dirksen observed with no sympathy, and to Owen with mild reproof: "Man your size can't afford to lose his temper, Rutledge."

"No," Owen agreed.

His sharp old eyes twinkling, the colonel reached the bottle of Madeira across the table to refill Owen's glass. He chuckled. "Quite a man, your father. I'll never forget the time when he announced before the entire State Senate that first seeing Abe Lincoln's picture had converted him to that Darwin fellow's new-fangled theory of evolution. Kentuckian sentiment divided as it was, his remark almost broke up the assembled distinguished gentlemen into fisticuffs."

Owen smiled perfunctorily. In him mounted an uneasiness compounded of impatience and quandary. There was a thing that had to be said, and he did not know how to break it. He let his gaze travel the dining room, taking in the two fine paintings and the tasteful antiques

—undoubted legacy of the M'Kandless ancestral home. The table was spread with white linen and gleaming silverware, centered by two hand-wrought candelabras. It stirred him nostalgically . . . casual refinement, gracious living, fine wine, good after-dinner conversation. It was as much a part of his past as of the colonel's. It would have been tempting to accept the offered position and forget the old mission. But a man could not live in the past; these things no longer belonged to his world.

He raised his glass and across its rim caught Cissie's eye. She sat opposite, wearing a bright frock, and the candlelight caught softly on her hair, now braided and wrapped in a shining corona around her head. He smiled and her freshly scrubbed face blushed quickly. She made a pleasant and healthy picture, and he wished fleetingly that he was ten years younger, a lifetime younger in experience. He sipped his wine and set the glass down to catch the colonel's measuring look.

"You have your father's size," M'Kandless observed. "Almost his spit'n' image . . . except your quiet manner. That's your mother's part, of course. I met her once, a most charming woman. Is she still living, perhaps?"

"No. The war didn't spare—"

"Can't we discuss something else?" the colonel's brother asked pettishly.

Owen's first thought on meeting Reed M'Kandless was that the family blood had run thin in the younger brother. Reed was only in his forties, but indoor confinement and lack of exercise had slackened and slumped his body and inclined him to stoutness. His dark hair was thinning, his precisely-clipped spade beard gray-shot. His face did not show the mottled floridness of an inveterate drinker, but his milky eyes were deeply pouched in the soft paleness of his cheeks. He had been introduced as handling most ranch affairs since the colonel had been thrown from a mettlesome bronc several years ago and his right leg permanently stiffened. But Owen had guessed that this was courtesy title to cover a shiftless and parasitical relative.

"War, I believe, is hardest on the women who wait for its end," the colonel observed soberly, misinterpreting Owen's broken statement. He added with a dry smile, "Reed is sensitive on subjects of violence," and switched the subject.

Owen toyed with his wine glass, only half-listening. Leaving the bunkhouse, he'd caught Abner's brief, negative shake of head to indicate that neither man they sought was on the Lionclaw crew. That finished Owen's own business, leaving only Virginia Gilchrist's.

From the moment of the colonel's cordial recognition of him, Owen had known increasing doubt that Amos M'Kandless had contrived to steal the Rivera charter. The half-hour of conversation they had shared during the meal had hardened doubt to conviction. Virginia had believed that he'd feigned his accusation of her, yet Owen knew there was not a shred of deceit in this old man's withered frame.

It was not a thing which Virginia Gilchrist, reared in a merchant family and used to sharp business practices, would easily understand. It was called honor, and it was the backbone of a life dead, war-shattered. An old-fashioned, antebellum, perhaps foolishly unrealistic integrity of character, but it had been the Southern aristocracy's greatness, of which this ailing, silver-maned lion of a man was a . . . relic? . . . rather a living testimonial. Owen Rutledge was the only deceiver here, and his impulsive pride impelled him to the truth.

"Colonel," he said slowly, "I met a young woman today. You know her . . . Virginia Gilchrist."

The colonel lifted his napkin, patted his lips. "Yes, Owen?"

"She said that she had shown you a document . . . a Spanish charter that fell into her family's possession after the Mexican War."

"That is true." The old man's tone had gained a testy edge.

Owen drew a deep breath, knowing he could still dissemble and keep this man's liking, knowing, too, that he would not. "Yesterday this charter was stolen from her house. She believes that you high-graded it."

"You believed her?"

Owen didn't answer directly. "I agreed to come here, ask you for a job, try to find out if the charter was in your possession. Believe me, sir, I did not intend to play on your friendship with my father to gain your confidences; then, I didn't know who you were."

The colonel crumpled his napkin and threw it in his plate. He stood hastily, knocked over his chair, stumbled and grasped at the table for support. Then he turned and slowly limped to a window, hands clasped behind his back. His slight frame was stiff with anger, his voice shaking slightly:

"Will you leave, sir?"

Owen let out a breath of resignation. "As you wish, Colonel."

"Pa!" Cissie's exclamation was shocked and objecting.

"You heard, daughter. This man is an errand-boy for that cheap woman . . . that lying fraud."

"That isn't fair," Cissie said exasperatedly. "If she tried to dupe you, she did no less to Mr. Rutledge. He's not to blame!"

"He came into my house, ate at my board, took advantage of my hospitality," the colonel said brittlely, "all under a deceitful guise."

"Pa, this isn't the bluegrass!"

"Changed circumstances do not soften the spine of a gentleman. You're young; you'll learn that many a blackguard wears a white fleece." The colonel swung a blue lightning gaze on Owen. "What was your price? Thirty pieces of silver?"

Owen felt his own hot flush. He knew how tawdry the answer would sound, knew the old man would take any explanation as evasive. He said quietly, "Fifty dollars."

"Your father would kill you with his own hands," the colonel said harshly.

Cissie looked speechlessly at her father, then at Owen; he gave her a slight, almost imperceptible shake of head. He rose, reached for his hat on the rack of staghorns by the door, and tramped around the table, heading for the parlor's connecting archway. Passing Reed M'Kandless, he glimpsed a faint, malignant pleasure in the man's face, and was puzzled, and then forgot it as he went through the parlor. He halted by the front door as Cissie's quick steps came up behind him, turned to face her.

"I . . . I feel so ashamed, Mr. Rutledge."

"You needn't, Miss Cissie. Not on my account, and surely not for your father."

"I—I don't. I understand him. And you, too." She laughed, shakily and in some confusion. "Why is life so puzzling? You must have been eighteen once."

"Believe it or not," he smiled.

"Oh you." She ducked her hotly blushing face and toed smilingly at the carpet. Then, soberly: "I hope you won't go too far. Pa won't listen now of course. But later he'll remember that you saved his life, that you told him why you came openly and of your own will. If he doesn't, I'll remind him."

"I wouldn't," Owen said quickly. "I have no reason to stay—now. Best to let the matter die."

She shook her head sadly. "I guess I still don't understand, not really. This foolish, foolish thing—honor. It's narrow, intolerant. And it's a man's thing, I believe, though perhaps," she added with sharp bitterness, "a woman would understand."

"You are a woman, Miss Cissie," Owen said gently. *A warm-hearted and gentle one and some man will be a lucky one,* he added silently. "You're right about honor. A man's thing. We have to live by it—to a woman's heartbreak, I suppose, but . . ." He shrugged, opened the door.

"I hope," Cissie M'Kandless said softly, "you find whatever it is you're trying to find, Mr. Rutledge. . . . Goodbye."

He headed for the bunkhouse, feeling a strong relief as he breathed deeply in the cool twilight. *Well, that's done.* With his regret at this harsh period to a brief friendship was mingled a curiosity about Reed M'Kand-

less . . . the sly, fleeting satisfaction that man had shown
as he left. *You're getting too damned suspicious,* Owen
thought. *His name is Reed M'Kandless, he's the colonel's brother, no mistaking that.* No doubt Reed was
pleased that there would after all be no addition to the
household, showing up Reed's sloth by his industry.

Reaching the bunkhouse, Owen fumbled for the latch,
swung the door wide. He blinked against the smoke-
hazed lamplight. The crew was sprawled in bunks, mending harness, reading, or talking. Activity broke off as he
stepped over the threshold. He caught Abner's eye, tilted
his head slightly backward, and Abner immediately
swung off his bunk and came over.

"Get your stuff," Owen murmured. "We're leaving."

Abner nodded, his stolid face unchanging, and tramped
back to his bunk. He pulled his warbag from beneath it
and began rolling up his sugans. Paul Dirksen came
lazily to his feet and sauntered to Owen.

"Leavin'?" There was puzzled curiosity in his drawl.
Owen nodded.

Dirksen put out a calloused hand and Owen took it.
"Sort of pleased when you hired on. Thought, 'Now the
kunnel'll have a man to look after his interests, not—' "
The segundo broke off, stoically. *Not his brother,* Owen
knew he'd begun to say. "Sorry. Anything I can do?"

Owen shook his head. "Thanks. And so long."

Owen's gear was still packed on his saddle, and in the
harness shed he waited as Abner fastened on his
own, quietly telling the Negro what had happened. "Then
what we do now, Mars' Owen?" Abner asked as they
trudged toward the corral, lugging their hulls.

"We go back to town," Owen said grimly. "We tell
Miss Gilchrist what I learned. Then we start looking.
You're going to take a sight at the face of every man
jack in this basin if we have to start a small war in the
doing."

SIX

Virginia sat on the cane-bottomed chair, her back straight, her small face placid and composed in the lamplight, bent above her work. At her feet was a crocheting bag full of afghan squares, and her fingers plied a needle with quick deftness, stitching these together. Charles McVey shifted his weight restlessly on the sagging divan, frowning faintly.

"You're quiet this evening, Ginny."

She looked up with a preoccupied smile. "Am I, Charlie?"

"Thinking about the big fellow . . . Rutledge?"

Her hands stilled on the material. "As a matter of fact, yes. I might have sent him into . . . anything."

He smiled. "We barely said hello, but I should say that there is a man who was weaned to hard fortune long ago. He'll take care of himself. He'll find your charter too, if M'Kandless has it."

Her fingers moved quickly again. "Don't you think he has it, Charlie?"

"I wouldn't say, Virginia," McVey said in a careful, neutral tone. "A lawyer's caution, you know."

After a moment's long silence, he said almost irritably, "You wouldn't have toyed with the thought that . . . perhaps that I . . . would you?"

Her gaze was very direct, and McVey flinched beneath his bland composure. "If I had thought so, Charlie, you would have heard so."

"Yes, of course," he murmured awkwardly. "But I was the only one you told of the charter's location . . . in your trunk. Naturally, if first suspicion is to be fixed—"

She smiled slowly. "Stop being the attorney. I told

you because I trusted you. I had to talk matters over with *someone*, and you were logical . . . a legal mind, as well as my only friend here. The person who stole the charter simply searched for it and found it."

"I imagine," he nodded, with no trace of the cynical disavowment he felt. When Virginia Gilchrist had first come to the basin, they had naturally gravitated together . . . two young people of similar interests—mostly business, law, and literature. Yet, where Virginia's inclinations were natural to one of her temperament and background, McVey, a poor farmer's son, had deliberately acquired a cultured veneer toward the furthering of his career. He was looking for a wife who would keep step with such a man.

But Virginia was full of her own ambition, otherwise cold to everything except her own genteel and insular existence. He could always look elsewhere; that bothered him less than his smarting ego. Women had always been easy marks for his bland charm . . . this plain little schoolteacher was not. Meanwhile, he thought with secret satisfaction, their brief friendship had already proved unexpectedly profitable. He must not break off his evening and week-end afternoon visits with her too quickly; it might arouse the suspicion that now, to his relief, she did not feel.

Watching her through half-lidded eyes, he wondered whether a man might someday break her composed restraint and find warmth beneath. He'd never really tried —always keeping their relations on the basis of the dispassionate personal friendship she'd established.

He rose now casually, circled behind her chair and stood a moment. She did not look up. He set his hands lightly on her shoulders. "Ginny—"

She gave a little twist and his hands fell away; she was stiffly motionless then, not looking at him. "Charlie," she said brittlely, "it's getting late."

Her response sparked his prideful temper. "Virginia, you can't lock yourself up forever. You're certainly intelligent and perceptive enough to know I haven't been

coming here these weeks only for *talk!* I'd hoped . . .
never mind. Someday you may be sorry."

"Perhaps," she said inflexibly. "But you may be even
sorrier in a moment, Charlie."

The inference was plain. He said with distinct dignity:
"Very well, Virginia. Good night."

"Good night."

She did not accompany him to the door, and he closed
it with just enough violence, and headed down the gravel
path. He halted beneath a spreading cottonwood whose
moon-caught branches struck black shadow-patterns
about him, pausing to pull out a cigar. He drew it alight
with a savage breath, thinking blackly, *Damned cold
little frump. As if I need her!* His temper cooled quickly
to a darkness-hidden smile. Hell, that was as good a way
as any to break it off . . . and save more evenings of talking about dead authors over tea. Besides, there was her
precious charter . . . if it was valuable. He'd meant to
check on that, and now was a good time.

He strode downstreet with long impatient strides to the
darkened business building where he had his office. He
loped up the rickety stairs and down a corridor. He
fumbled out his keys, let himself into his office, groped
for the lamp and lighted it. The sallow light spread to the
dingy corners of the little cubbyhole and he gave it a
single circling glance of distaste; in this peaceful valley,
shallow premium was placed on a lawyer's services. He
unlocked a drawer of his rolltop desk, drew out a manila
folder and removed from it an oilcloth-wrapped packet.

His cherubic features sharpened eagerly as he removed
the wrapping and with infinite care spread out the
browned and fragile document on his desk, his fingers
trembling. The charter was penned in the delicate hand of
a court secretary, the ink faded to near-illegibility; at the
bottom was the Spanish monarch's bold signature, and
beneath this the wax seal of the royal arms. The key to a
fortune . . . if he handled his cards right. Years shaved
off his goal of the state bench by a little judiciously applied semi-blackmail.

Matthew Claiborne, he had long decided, was the

man to watch in the forthcoming crisis between his and Colonel M'Kandless' land claims. Claiborne was shrewd and absolutely unscrupulous; in his hands would rest the future of Lionclaw ranch and Blanco Basin. M'Kandless, old and ailing, could not long hold the prize of Lionclaw's great acres. When Claiborne had the ranch and believed himself securely in possession—that was the time to present him with evidence of an older and more substantial claim that his own Mexican grant. McVey knew ways to make Claiborne pay through the nose for the document without danger to himself—on the threat of returning it to Virginia Gilchrist, in whose hands it might someday wreck Claiborne's whole victory.

McVey carefully rewrapped the parchment and slipped it into his coat pocket. As a hesitant afterthought, thinking of the dark road ahead, he drew a nickel-plated, double-barreled pocket pistol from the open desk drawer, dropped it in his pocket. He blew out the lamp, locked his office and left hurriedly for the livery stable. He ordered the hostler to saddle his short-coupled billy horse. Five minutes later he was riding south from town on a moon-flooded dirt road which wended along the riverbank.

Ahead presently he saw a sprinkling of oily lights which was Mextown, a shallow cluster of adobe shacks situated in the riverbottom. A cur picked him up and yapped furiously at the heels of his mount till he cursed it off. He rode down the narrow dirt street, irritably aware of the faces appearing at doors and windows to speculate on the night appearance here of a lone *gringo*. But they had seen him before and they watched with only sleepy and half-hostile interest as he dismounted before the Ortega adobe.

McVey threw reins and stepped to the low door, raising his knuckles. Before he could knock, the door was quickly opened, and, "Come in, Carlos," Abrana Ortega said, her voice hushed and breathless.

He stepped inside without removing his hat, giving the chili-hung walls, the small plaster shrine and hand-fashioned furniture, his sardonic glance. The girl closed the door and turned swiftly to face him, her dark full skirt swirling out from dainty tanned ankles. "This is the first time in a week, Carlos . . . still the pale *Yanqui* creature takes your nights, eh?"

McVey said mildly, "Where's the old one?"

She jerked her head at a closed door to her back, not taking her dark eyes from him. He started to move past her, but she struck angrily at his shoulder. "Regard me, Carlos. I have no need to be spare-time woman. There are plenty of men including *Americanos* who—"

"Shut up," he said gently, watching her.

Her hard, flippant expression softened; she whispered his name. He smiled and took her into his arms. His lips brushed her shut eyes, a cheek and ear, and the smooth joining of neck and shoulder. She threw back her head, lips parted. His mouth found hers, roughly, as he put the residue of his thwarted anger at Virginia Gilchrist into the kiss. Abrana drew back in his arms, her eyes smoky with pride and passion and her own anger.

"Don' toy with me, Carlos." She glanced at the side door to her parents' room, and lowered her voice. "If you don' want a greaser girl even spare time . . ."

"Did I say so? But I've business on my mind, *querida mía.*" He thought detachedly that she set a man's blood afire as a pleasant diversion, but he had drawn an iron line short of the mounting jealousy of Mextown's young males, angry at a gringo's success with their fairest. He'd had to confine his visits to the dark, when a sudden anonymous knife-thrust would be too easy . . . and a poor and ignorant Mexican wench had no place in his plans.

Yet her loveliness was undeniably fine-bred and delicate; old Ysidro Ortega boasted of pure Castilian descent, and his granddaughter, with her blue-black hair and ivory skin, seemed to bear it out. Above the low round neckline of her blouse, fitful lamplight turned the skin to tawny satin and laid soft shadow in the beginning hollow between the small, pointed breasts. But his face tightened at the sight of the small crucifix gleaming coldly against the warm flesh. In sudden rage he wanted to tear it from her neck.

It framed a cold, hard remembrance of his mother. After his father's death she'd enforced a religious regimen of morning prayers, evening prayers, graces before and after every meal, till the numb ache of his knees filled every interval. The tedious Sunday sermons were nothing by comparison, but the gaunt sobersides of a preacher came regularly for free suppers, afterward discussing for hours hellfire and last things till you wanted to retch. Some ingrained habit of duty had held him, but the war had come as a welcome relief, sending him off with a passing guerrilla band at seventeen and with his mother's blessing; he was leaving her to kill Yankees, devil's spawn.

"Carlos?" Abrana's soft wonderment straightened his bitterly twisted grin into a charming smile. He moved her gently aside. "Later."

McVey opened the door to old Ysidro Ortega's long, narrow alcove of a room, closed it behind him. A wall-bracketed candle thick as a man's wrist flickered long weird shadows against the rough clay walls. The only furniture was a half-log table with a single bench, and a low wooden bedframe criss crossed with a network of rawhide thongs for a mattress. Reclining on this was Ysidro Ortega, eyes closed, frail chest barely astir with his breathing. On the foot of the bed perched a large, beady-eyed raven. It ruffled its inky plumage as old Ysidro opened one eye, glanced at McVey.

"I want you to look at something, *viejo*." McVey drew the document from his pocket, unwrapped it, and laid it on the table. Old Ysidro swung very slowly to his feet, yawned prodigiously, scratched his wispy gray ruff of hair, and made an odd little "Ch, ch," in his throat. The raven flapped up to his shoulder as Ysidro came to the table, seated himself. "It is late to be rousing an old man's bones, Eugenio," he told the raven. His voice was the rustle of dry corn shucks.

McVey leaned his fists on the table. "That's supposed to be the original king's charter for the Rivera grant. Look it over."

"Yes, very late, Eugenio," the old man crooned. McVey bridled with impatience. Ysidro yawned again and reached under his dirty cotton shirt to scratch his ribs. He was diminutive and shrunken, with a wrinkled, wizened monkey's face, and he must be incredibly old, McVey thought. . . . It was said he'd been past sixty when he sired Abrana's father. Like other strange tales revolving around this ancient man, it must be true. It was certainly true that he had a wide and enormous range of experience backed by an infallible memory, and McVey badly wanted his judgement on this document.

Ysidro finally dropped his bright black eyes to the charter, scanned it carelessly, and smiled. His yellow teeth were all intact and sound. "Have I not told you, Eugenio, that my ancestors were *conquistadores,* not blood of *los Indios?* Have I not told you—"

"Will you quit talking to that damned crow!" McVey grated. "All I want to know is whether that's the Rivera charter."

"Have I not told you, Eugenio," the old man went imperturbably, "that this McVey is a rooster without spurs? His soft crowing turns young girls' soft heads. McVey is getting mad, *amigo mío.* But he is not such a bird as your noble cousin, the fighting cock, he has no spurs, and the head of *el viejo* is old and hard."

Ysidro rose and went back to his bed. The raven dropped onto the bedpost, Ysidro stretched comfortably out. He crossed his hands on his chest and closed his eyes. He looked like a mummified saint's corpse till one sly sparkling eye cocked open in his shriveled parchment face.

"By the way, Eugenio, have I told you that I was a retainer on the estate of Jaime Sanchez y Nahuatl y Bandara y Rivera in my youth, and that because of my Castilian blood I became his personal valet?" His eye slid drowsily shut. "Yes, yes," he murmured, "I saw many times the charter given by the Spanish monarch to his family . . . and do you know, Eugenio, that *pergamino* on the table is the very same one?"

"*Gracias,* Eugenio," said McVey dryly, hiding his welling exultance. He returned the charter to its wrappings and his pocket, and left the room.

Abrana was standing by the outer door as he started for it, and she stepped quickly across his path, smiling up with childlike expectancy. He said mock-wearily, "All right, all right," and held out his arms. She nestled against him with a little giggling sigh. After a minute he let her go and started to open the door.

"Vaya con Dios, Carlos," she whispered. "I will pray for you to Our Lady. . . ."

"Save your Hail Mary's for grandpa, *querida* . . . needs 'em worse."

"Abuelito believes in nothing, but I do pray for him, I pray for everyone; it makes a good feeling in me. I wish you would pray sometimes, Carlos. I think the good God may hear it a Protestant man's way, though it is wrong."

"Damn it," he said viciously, "I've told you I got a crawful of that stuff from my old lady, get off it, will you!"

Her eyes blurred and her chin sank with a little sob. Why are you cruel to me? I have killed my pride, lost the respect of my family and friends. I have given up everything. For you. . . ."

He felt a twinge of guilt which died as quickly as it came. He stroked her head and whispered a little and left her smiling through her tears. He mounted and jogged back toward Blanco, his head full of excited speculations. Through it burned a savage and bitter satisfaction. His old lady, always talking about storing up treasures for the kingdom of heaven . . . he would show her and all of them, Virginia, Abrana, *women,* what a man could do on this earth without any damned women, reforming or cold or cloying, around him.

As he neared the fork where the river route joined the town road, the sound of two horses approaching from the other fork made him draw cautiously off behind a thicket. No telling who might be riding this lonely road at such an hour. He strained his eyes to pick out the riders in the moonlight—a big, broad pair riding abreast. He couldn't distinguish their features, but he thought that the larger man was Owen Rutledge—no mistaking that height and shoulder-breadth.

McVey waited several minutes after they'd ridden on, then put his horse into motion. What had brought Rutledge back to town, and at this time of night? A cold finger of fear touched his spine. Could Rutledge have found out something from Colonel M'Kandless that would enable him to learn the identity of the real charter thief? *Hell, you're spooking yourself, what could he know?* Yet McVey waited a full five minutes till they had ridden on, before putting his billy horse into motion.

As he rode down the silent main street, McVey saw Rutledge again, alone now, walking upstreet from the livery barn . . . passing up the hotel. *He'll be going to see Virginia then,* McVey thought, knowing real panic now. This late visit must mean that Rutledge had learned something. Passing the man, he swerved deep into the shadows at the opposite side of the street. Breathing easier, he rode on to the livery.

He turned in at the arched entrance, rode down the runway, stepped down from his saddle. He glanced about to see the squat man who'd ridden in with Rutledge, his back to McVey as he hoisted a pair of hulls onto the saddle pole. The lawyer gave him a fleeting wary and curious glance, then looked for the night hostler who was not in sight. A lamp burned in the window of the little walled-in office at the back of the barn.

"Oh, Bill!" he called. "Come out and take my horse."

The squat man turned casually and then stiffened, and the light from the bull's-eye lantern hanging on a stall post caught full on his shining black face. He simply stared at McVey and did not move.

"What's the matter with you, fellow?" McVey said irritably.

"I knows you," the Negro said simply, "Mistuh Sykes."

Terror rose and clawed up McVey's throat as a thick gasp. No . . . not after all these years. It could not be happening.

The Negro advanced with his great bulk rolling, his

long arms spread a little. McVey had more courage than
most men, but in this moment he backed away till a stall
partition caught him in the back. His voice was a thin
squeak: "I don't know you. . . ."

"Why, you wouldn', Mistuh Sykes," the Negro said
with a slight, almost dreamy, smile playing on his wide
lips. "Been a good long time since I jumped on you after
you killed my woman Saph . . . an' your boys put all that
lead into me." His big hands lifted and caught McVey
by the lapels. McVey shrank against the boards, thinking that there was something terrifyingly familiar in the
Negro's words, and then the Negro said gently and
gravely: "Not yet, Mistuh Sykes. First Mars' Owen will
want—"

Owen, Rutledge—Rutledge! The name burst across
McVey's memory. A few days after the war . . . a big
farm with a family named Rutledge . . . this big black
man . . . it all came frighteningly clear.

In wild panic he struggled, kicked and clawed at this
captor. The Negro held him as if he were a child, forcing
him into the runway. Another, more immediate memory
coldly touched McVey's brain . . . he quit struggling,
slipped his hand into his right coat pocket till it closed
over the little pocket pistol. The Negro swung him face
to face. "That's wise, white trash. You come 'long quiet,
now—"

McVey tilted the pistol inside his pocket till it angled
up at the broad chest a foot away. The Negro's gaze
moved quickly to the bulging cloth, and then the gun
made its spiteful bark, point-blank.

The Negro shuddered, his fists wrenched convulsively
at McVey's lapels. He went down, hauling the lawyer
with him. McVey got his knees under him and shot
again, carefully, into the Negro's head.

"Sweet bleedin' Christ. . . ."

It was the hostler, standing in the entrance of his office, frozen by what he saw. McVey scrambled to his
feet and lunged stumbling toward his horse. He got a
toe in the stirrup and kicked the animal into a run before he was firmly in the saddle.

SEVEN

Leaving Abner to see to the horses, Owen headed for Virginia Gilchrist's little house. He saw lamplight in the front window, hesitated, unwilling at this late hour to interrupt her preparations for bed. *Get it over with,* he thought resignedly; *she won't like this any more than you do.* He went up the path and rapped solidly, twice, at the door. Virginia answered at once, framed in the open doorway—a slim and petite figure in an oft-washed skyblue dress which, he noticed, matched her vivid eyes.

"Why, Mr. Rutledge." She stepped aside and he entered, stiffly removing his hat. "Please have a chair. There's coffee—"

"No, ma'am," he said coolly, and added, "Thank you." He scowled down at his hat, looked up into her still, expectant face. "Miss Gilchrist, I've been to Lionclaw, and you can keep your fifty dollars."

She caught her lower lip in her teeth, her bewildered chagrin plain. "You've . . . changed your mind?"

"Yes'm. Colonel M'Kandless is no thief. You wouldn't understand, but—"

"No," she cut in coldly, "I don't understand. But your tone indicates plainly that your mind is made up. Very well." She stepped to the door and opened it, proudly waiting for him to leave.

He felt an abrupt respect for this girl's lonely, rock-ribbed poise. "Look—" He did not know what to say. Then words came with unintentional roughness. "Ma'am, how well do you know this McVey—the lawyer fellow?"

"That is quite clearly none of your business."

"No'm." He set his hat on and went out the door, turning on the threshold. "It's yours, though. And I advise you to think about that." He hesitated. "If you'll want to see me again, I'm taking a room at the hotel."

"And your friend? Abner? Is he sleeping at the hotel, too?"

The mocking scorn was in her words, not in their quiet tonelessness. He felt the blood crawl into his face. She was hurt, and she wanted to hurt back. He said matter-of-factly: "Abner will sleep in the stable. As he always does." Before she could counter, he said, "Good night," and headed swiftly down the path.

He heard the door close firmly on her parting mockery: "Good night, Mars' Rutledge."

His anger cooled to a rueful smile before he had reached the gate. She had an unexpected spirit behind that tart, prim front, he realized with a small, odd pleasure.

As he turned down the street, a gunshot brought Owen to a halt. A second shot cracked on its heel. A small caliber gun . . . and he placed its sharp reports near the livery barn. As he started into a long loping run, he saw a rider swerve out of the livery archway two blocks down. Low-bent in the saddle, lashing his horse north from town at an all-out run.

An unbidden fear took sharp hold on Owen. The breath tore in his chest as he lengthened stride. He ran breathlessly into the runway and there drew to a dead halt.

The lank hostler was bending over a sprawled form, and Owen ran to it, shoving the man aside. "Ab— *Abner*."

"Big man, this *negra's* dead," the hostler whispered in a low, awed way. ". . . Was back in the office. Heard the shot. Came out just as he pumped the second into his—"

Owen grabbed the man by the collar, twisted it savagely. "Who was it?"

"God's sake—man—chokin' me—" Owen released him, and the hostler rubbed his windpipe, eying him fearfully. "It was that shyster . . . McVey. Charlie McVey."

Owen dropped on his knees beside Abner, gently turn-

ing his head. His hand came away slippery . . . there
was little blood. Numbly he opened the Negro's shirt. The
first bullet had entered his chest squarely. It had, Owen
noticed obscurely, cut clean through the rabbit's foot
talisman, almost halving it. *It had to be broken that
way, didn't it?*

A scrape of bootsteps brought his glance slowly
around to the approaching gaunt and towering form of
Matthew Claiborne. Others crowding behind him. Claiborne frowned and took a twisted cheroot from his
bearded lips. "Your man Friday, eh? Well, I warned you
not to stay around the basin."

Owen came to his feet, weight set on his toes. Bloody
Matt, abruptly seeing a very real danger here, backed
off a step. "You wouldn't," Owen said, almost whispering it, "have put McVey up to this, would you?"

Claiborne drew quickly on his cigar, watching Owen
warily. "McVey the lawyer? . . . I've never met the fellow. Use your head, Rutledge. Would I set up a clumsy,
needless killing like this?"

Owen shook his head gently. "Not your way. Unless
you have some end I don't rightly see . . . yet."

"See here," Claiborne said uneasily. "I understand
your feelings, but you can't bull about wildly accus-
ing—"

Owen's violent swing-around broke him off. Owen bent
and carefully gathered Abner into his arms. He started
toward the archway, and Claiborne, with a soft oath,
barely stepped from his path in time. Owen did not look
at him or the others as they cleared his way. He turned
down the boardwalk and halted after a few steps. *What
now?* he thought emptily. *What next?*

There was a soft tap-tap of brisk steps coming . . .
halting before him. He dragged his stare up to Virginia
Gilchrist's face, white and wide-eyed in the feeble moonlight. "Oh, Owen . . . Owen. I'm sorry. He is—" She
said then very softly, "He will spend this night under my
roof. Come along."

She walked off a few paces, turned when he remained
unmoving. "Please," she said gently.

He followed her in silence, his eyes fixed on her small, shawl-wrapped shoulders. Inside her parlor he laid Abner on the divan. He stood there a long time till his mind began to numbly function, feeling this last link with his past broken.

He realized that she was speaking, hesitantly. "I— didn't know him, of course, but I think—he must have been a kind of symbol—of dignity—of not only his own race, but of men everywhere who face out their condition no matter how all odds are against them. He—he looked like that kind."

Her words seemed to trigger loose the blind wrathful grief in him. *These damned cold-fish idealists. They think a man's feelings are something to be tacked on display for philosophical analysis. Christ!* He stared at her bitterly. "Abner was my friend." The words came strangely to his lips, before he was aware of what he'd said.

"Why," Virginia said softly, "that is all there is to say."

His anger slowly ebbed; he hadn't meant to use her as its target. He realized she had spoken unwillingly, for the comfort her words might give. "I . . ." He stopped, tiredly reflecting a moment. "I will appreciate your making the proper arrangements for a burial. I will be gone a while." He rubbed his eyes and re-fixed his attention. "Were you coming after me . . . back there?"

She nodded somberly. "I wanted to tell you I was sorry for how I reacted. . . . I know you meant well . . . but you were wrong, too—I mean about Charlie—" She broke off at what she saw in his face, then whispered, "What is it?"

"McVey," he pronounced distantly, tonelessly. "Your very good friend McVey. The hostler saw him put a second bullet into Abner's head. I do not think that was an accident, do you, Miss Gilchrist?"

As she stood in shocked silence he tramped past her to the door and went out, not closing it. He heard her wild cry behind him. "But why? *Owen, why?*"

He had claimed his bay at the livery and was jogging

along the north road before his chaotic thoughts caught up with Virginia's last words. Why? Why should a young lawyer struggling to build a respectable practice destroy his future with a cold-blooded murder? Certainly he hadn't provoked the shooting, and Abner would have provoked it for one reason only.

Abner had recognized Tierney or Sykes.

Mechanically Owen superimposed the description of John Sykes on the smiling cherub's face of Charles McVey. Remove the bristling yellow beard sported by Tierney's lieutenant . . . add seven years of age and a cultivated elegance and diction, and you had Red John Sykes: guerrilla, thief, and murderer.

McVey reached Lionclaw headquarters by midnight, and pulled off the ranch road well short of the Mexican shanties on the west end of the layout, for fear of being picked up by their dogs. He swung wide on the moonlit grass flats to come in on the headquarters from the north side. He put the billy horse into a dense cotton-wood grove back of the hayshed and here dismounted, tethering the animal.

He ran his hand over its wet, trembling flank. The horse was shuddering and breathing brokenly; he'd almost killed it in his haste to get here. After McVey's first ungoverned terror and the crushing realization that the game was up here, he was reasoning coolly. The basin people probably would not hunt him, even have a dodger put out, for his killing a Negro . . . but the Negro was Rutledge's man, and Rutledge would follow him to hell and back. In this cold and utter certainty, he needed help, and now. He had only the thin clothes on his back, an empty gun, no food, and a horse that could take him no further.

He left the grove and widely skirted the corrals and outsheds, taking in the bunkhouse and main house. All windows were dark, except for a solitary light burning in a first floor window of the big house. *That's Reed's room,* he thought exultantly, and breathed easier as he crossed the lawn at a fast trot.

He sidled cautiously to the lighted window. Reed M'Kandless sat in an overstuffed chair pulled close to a roaring fireplace. He wore a quilted dressing gown and his iron-rimmed glasses. He was reading.

McVey tapped on a pane. Reed turned in his chair, frowning as he removed his glasses. Then he came to the window, his eyes widening in recognition of McVey; his lips formed an angry question. McVey curtly signaled him to open the window. Reed wrestled up the sash, and McVey snapped, "Out of the way, I'm coming in," as he slung a leg over the sill. He stepped inside, closed the window, glanced narrowly around the big room, at the oaken commode and four-poster bed.

"Got it soft, haven't you, Cush?"

"Damn you, don't ever call me that!" Reed hissed. He dragged in a deep breath and said more steadily, "I told you never to come see me here. It better be important."

"To me, it is. To you too. Better listen."

Reed paced slowly back to his chair and laid his book down, then went to lean an arm on the fireplace mantel as he listened with a deepening frown. When McVey had finished, Reed thoughtfully took out a silk handkerchief, blew on his glasses, and squinted at the lenses as he polished them. He said without looking at McVey, "That's hardly news. Rutledge's family and mine lived far apart in Kentucky. The colonel did serve with Rutledge's father in the Kentucky legislature; that is our only connection—fortunately. He didn't know me from Adam."

"But I just killed his nigger," McVey said impatiently.

"So you said," Reed observed coldly. "Why tell me, though?"

"I need some things—food, a gun, some heavy clothes, a fresh horse. And money."

"So," Reed said with a half-smile. "So far my neck's safe, Charlie; why should I risk it by helping you?"

McVey moved to the vacated armchair and sank back into it with a sigh. He leaned his elbows on his stomach and steepled his fingers, regarding Reed with arrogant confidence. "Here's the thing, Reed. Any number of men could answer to our basic descriptions . . . and we've both changed in seven years. But you've guessed by now that Rutledge might not have come to this basin by chance. He might have got a clue—might have caught up with Garvey."

"How could Garvey tell him where to find us?" Reed demanded waspishly.

"Garvey came to Blanco Basin a year ago—evidently, like me, in hopes of getting money from your—from Mrs. M'Kandless. He happened to spot me in town, and I had to satisfy his curiosity. Then I gave him a little money, told him to ride on, forget what he'd seen and heard. Garvey was straight in his way, wouldn't have talked unless Rutledge cornered him. However that may be, only the Negro could positively identify us. The hostler saw me shoot him, so Rutledge'll be breathing down my neck shortly. With the Negro dead, your hide will be safe . . . unless Rutledge should catch up with me. Then I'll have him breathing down your neck. Simple?"

Reed swung from the fireplace, his face twitching. "You baby-faced bastard," he whispered. "For two years I've regretted the day I stopped at your mother's farmhouse . . . and invited a snot-nosed kid to come off to the war with me. I should have shot you when you found me here —forced me to set you up for a law practice—"

"But you first met the snot-nosed kid eleven years ago," McVey observed, "and filled his empty head with the glories of the great cause. We both got cynical fast after that. You taught me a lot, Reed . . . I'm going to repay the favor by clearing out of your life for good. With enough gold to throw Rutledge off my trail and get me to Canada. . . ." He shrugged. "It's to your interest to see I escape. Or the two of us can wait here for Rutledge, as you like—"

Reed cursed him once, softly and viciously, then strode to the commode and jerked open a drawer. He drew out a small canvas bag, threw it on the floor with a musical jangle. "There's forty double-eagles in there. Here," he savagely yanked out a holstered revolver wrapped in its cartridge belt, "is your gun. I can't get grub; the cook has his cot in the pantry. But there's a place in the mountains about twenty miles east of here. . . ."

"Sunfire?" McVey asked, and when Reed nodded, he added flatly, "I've heard of it. A dead mining camp, with a store and bar kept in business by the long riders—rustlers, killers, what-not—drifting through."

"Why, those are our people," Reed observed dryly. "What better can you ask? You ought to make it in a day . . . a place to sleep, a hot meal, and every man in the place ready to lie about you to Rutledge, throw him off your trail."

McVey smiled thinly as he strapped on the gunbelt. "I need a heavy coat. It's cold in the high country."

"Just a minute." M'Kandless went to the door, opened it, looked warily up and down the corridor, then stepped out. In two minutes he returned with a frayed mackinaw over his arm. He chucked it at McVey.

"Thank you, Reed." The lawyer started to pull on the thick coat, but it bound around his shoulders. With a curse he shed it, shrugged out of his suitcoat, and afterward strained into the mackinaw.

"It's an old one of Cissie's," Reed M'Kandless said with an amused malice, "but you're not much bigger'n her."

Reed did not answer, buttoning the mackinaw to his neck. He picked up his suitcoat and transferred his pocket pistol to the mackinaw. He glanced quickly at Reed and hesitated before he drew the cloth-wrapped Rivera charter from the coat and hurriedly thrust it into his trousers pocket.

"What's that?"

McVey met the sly interest in Reed's tone with a sharp, "Nothing," between his teeth.

"You act damn chinchy about 'nothing'."

McVey hesitated again, thought with a smile, *why not?* "This is the Rivera charter. I borrowed it from Miss Virginia Gilchrist . . . for reasons which aren't important now. It just struck me that a man of your abilities might find a way to use it. How much would it be worth to you, Reed?"

"Not a damned thing, friend," Reed said with a laugh.

"The Gilchrist woman tried to take the trusting old colonel in with that thing . . . even he wasn't simple enough to fall for such an obvious fake."

"Fake?" McVey asked softly. "Have you heard of Ysidro Ortega?"

Reed frowned. "Who hasn't? Old fellow over in Mextown, old as Methuselah and nearly as wise. He's a local legend."

"I saw him tonight before the trouble. Ysidro spent years under this roof when it belonged to the Riveras . . . and he says that's the original king's charter."

"I see." Reed stroked his spade beard. "And you were going to use it to shake down the colonel—or another interested party?" McVey did not answer, watching Reed's face as he paced a slow circle, seeing it shade from thoughtfulness to calculation, and McVey thought: *He's still Cushing Tierney at heart.*

Reed abruptly turned to face him. "You have all my ready cash in those double eagles. But listen—"

"No notes, no promises," McVey said flatly. "I've got to clear out now, and I won't be back. . . . In that case, I'll hang on to the document—and take the chance that I may be able to use it someday. Now I want a horse."

Impatience was beginning to ride him as M'Kandless studied him for a cold, silent moment, and he derived only thin amusement from the leashed hatred in Reed's eyes. "All right," Reed said then. "You came here on one, I suppose?"

"Left him in the grove back of the hayshed, near windbroken."

Reed nodded curtly. "Get back there and wait. I'll try to get you a fresh one from the corrals without rousing anybody—"

"If you rouse anybody," McVey cut him off softly, "I'll have to break on a winded horse, in which case the federals learn where you are. You get that horse, and get him quiet—Cushing."

EIGHT

Owen came stiffly up off his haunches, shifting his shoulders against the sweaty cling of his calico shirt. The sun had broiled up over the east peaks an hour past, and his legs ached from many such stops to examine signs in the road still mud-roiled from the heavy rain two nights ago.

He wiped his sleeve across his face, let his arm drop, a tired gesture. Last night he had not gone far from Blanco town before coming to the first fork-off. He was no tracker; in vague moonlight it had been difficult picking out McVey's fresh trail at the proper turn. Lionclaw had its own maze of ancient range roads, with a number of turn-offs to the small ranches strung along the south basin. Thus he'd made slow headway till false dawn.

He had noted earlier that McVey's track seemed to make for Lionclaw along the straight-ruled route he and Abner had traveled, on directions from the livery hostler. But Lionclaw was surely not McVey's goal and he could have turned off anywhere. Daylight had found Owen deep in Lionclaw range, less than two miles from its headquarters, and still he moved at an inchmeal pace rather than risk losing McVey.

Now he mounted his bay after the last ground-check and went slowly on, leaning from his saddle to scan the road beneath. Strained eyes and muscles, lack of sleep, were taking their iron toll; with these, a weighted despair. It was evident that McVey had pushed his animal hard, and all the while and still, he was widening many hours' lead. *This is no good, should have asked for a posse of men who know the country. And where*, he thought sinkingly, *will you find a posse to run down a black*

70

man's killer? Besides—pride, rage, grief, call-it-what-you-might—goaded him to run down Abner's murderer alone. And he had time now, plenty of time; he had that much.

A brisk-pacing horse coming up from the long flats ahead caused him to slow and loosen the Navy Colt in its holster. Within five minutes Cissie M'Kandless reined in her sorrel by him stirrup to stirrup.

He touched his hat, saying distantly, "An early jaunt, Miss Cissie?"

The girl's face was deeply flushed; she wore the same gray riding habit she had yesterday, and the wind toiled with and loosened wisps of hair from beneath her narrow-brimmed hat. She removed the hat and dangled it from her hand by the chin-strap, avoiding his eyes in deep confusion. "I like to ride early in the morning. I usually do. That is—"

"Know McVey, the lawyer?"

Her head tipped up at his point-blank question. "Why, certainly . . . by sight."

"Seen him?"

"This morning, you mean? No-o . . . should I have?" Her direct gaze was puzzled.

Owen let out a heavy breath. "McVey killed Abner. Last night. I'm trying to find him."

"Killed—Abner? The Negro?" she asked disbelievingly, and when he nodded: "I—I'm sorry. But I don't understand. . . ."

"And no time to explain. Will you trust me?"

"I think," she said softly, "I would trust you for anything."

"McVey's tracks lead to your ranch. That makes no sense to me."

She shook her head with an emphatic, "He didn't come by our place, Mr. Rutledge."

"Then where would a man go, knowing he'd be followed?" His voice was edged with impatience.

She thought only a moment. "Sunfire. That's an old mining town back in the mountains, well past Lionclaw's boundaries. A flash-in-the-pan gold camp in the big rush of '68. I've heard the men say it's a hangout for all sorts

of drifting riffraff. A man named Bayliss runs a saloon
and store there—the only stopover for men going over
that arm of the mountains. Then, the only good trail
through goes past Sunfire. A man would almost certainly
stop . . ."

"And how would he get there?" Head bent, he listened
to her directions, said gravely, "Thank you, Miss Cissie."
He started to rein past her, and she reached and caught
his rein in a strong, slim hand; he saw her face pale beneath its tan.

"I'll talk to Pa—get some men to help. You can't go
there alone."

"That's how I've got to go."

She shook her head bitterly, straightened in the saddle.
"I'll never understand men. Well, then—"

His face relaxed with the faintest smile. "At least be
careful?"

"Yes," she said, and did not smile. "I think that—I
wish—" She bit her lip, watching him a still moment, her
eyes tender and worried. "Goodbye, Mr. Rutledge."

He rode on, the brief gentleness she'd touched in him
hardening again. What had she almost said? Perhaps that
she had fallen in love with him, he thought with a quiet
pity now. No doubt she thought so—with a stranger who
had saved her father's life and shown a gentle, brief
understanding of her confused youth. Maybe being lonely
and young and too-sheltered was worse in its way than
the bruising, bitter clashes with life which had drained
away his green years.

Toward sunset Owen rode over a hump of the rocky
pass he had followed from the low plains, and a bare mile
ahead saw a slapdash clutter of shacks that was Sunfire.
The town had been hastily thrown up, unpainted, neg-
lected, soon abandoned to the raw mountain elements.
The road crawled like a torpid snake down between the
buildings and onward.

On one side rose a mountain flank scarred with old
gold diggings that showed how quickly the camp had
birthed and died; opposite, a castellated bulge of lava

lifted majestically above the tawdry buildings, and Owen saw how Sunfire had taken its name. Some hardrock miner with a touch of poetry in his soul had come over this pass at sunset, just as the dying light crowned the lava bulge with orange fire and bled streamers of molten gold down its ribbed corrugations.

In fifteen minutes he dismounted in front of a clap-boarded building in sad disrepair, its weathered shakes flapping loosely in a hard wind that lashed eddies of dust up the deserted street. It was by far the most imposing structure still standing, wide and two-storied, with a crudely lettered sign—

GRUB LIKUR SUPLYS SLEEP—DOLER NITE

—above its sagging porch. Two horses, leaning hipshot to windward, were tied at the rail. Owen regarded them narrowly as he tied the bay . . . neither was the short-coupled horse the Blanco hostler, whom he'd questioned, had told him was McVey's.

He tramped up on the porch, skirted a gaping hole in the rotten planks, and pushed through the batwing doors. The bar was a pair of unplaned two-by-sixes nailed across a couple of beer barrels. Two ragged men turned from it and gave him their dirty, shifty stares as he came up beside them. He ignored them, looking across at the bartender. He was a tremendously fat old man wearing greasy leather pants supported by red galluses over his dirty cotton underwear. His frosty eyes glinted without expression above a tangled gray ambush of whiskers.

"You Bayliss?"

The cold eyes shifted sparely. "I'm Sam Bayliss." His voice grated like a rusty bucksaw. "Yours?"

"Feed, a stall for my horse. A meal. A bed."

"All right. Whiskey?"

Owen nodded. Bayliss set out a use-yellowed glass and took a labelless bottle from the two-by-six backbar. He poised it above the glass but didn't pour, his hard glance questioning. Owen sighed and laid a coin on the bar. The drink drained the bottle. Bayliss gave its bottom three hard raps against the wall. He turned to meet Owen's narrow look with a toneless, "Tellin' my old woman to set another plate." He skirted the bar and went out the batwings. Owen heard him lead the bay up a side alley, evidently to a stable in the rear.

He took his drink, hearing stealthy feet mounting stairs above his head. Aware of the drifter pair's suspicious glances, Owen walked around the bar and went announced through the back door, halting on its threshold. A slatternly, tired-looking woman was turning sizzling steaks in a skillet; she said without looking up, "Want sump'n?"

Owen looked bleakly at the oilcloth-covered table, seeing the tin plate with a half-eaten steak and the half-empty coffee cup. He looked at the woman, watching him now with a faint uneasiness.

"Supper," he said.

Her thin reddened hand touched the bosom of her soiled dress and pushed back a straggle of lank hair from her face. "Sit yourself. Ready in a minute." She picked up the dirty dishes and clattered them into a wreckpan.

Bayliss came in, then the drifters, and the four of them hunched in rickety chairs around the small table, wolfing down beefsteak, fried potatoes, and scalding black coffee. The wordless silence was somehow deadly. Behind his famished concentration on the food, Owen felt the directed hostility of them all, and since his own rough appearance should have passed him without suspicion, he knew that word had come ahead . . . there was Bayliss's overt signal, that half-eaten meal, the quick footsteps ascending the staircase which he now saw through a doorway to his right. He sized the situation, and did not like it, and thought: *The drifters won't buy in. But Bayliss'll back McVey; wait a while . . . watch him.*

Afterward he went back to the barroom and poured another drink while the drifters started a stud game, squatting over a barrelhead in the corner. Beyond the fly-blown windows night had salved over the sun-blistered buildings. Bayliss entered from the kitchen, his frayed carpet slippers slap-slapping, bearing an armload of cedar stove lengths which he dumped by the blackened fieldstone fireplace. He stoked up a fire, then came to stand behind the bar, not looking at Owen.

The spreading tawny glow beat back the high-country night chill, pleasantly thawed Owen's numbing body, and his thoughts drifted; he caught himself nodding, uneasily aware of a creeping drowsiness reminding him that he'd gone more than thirty hours without sleep—and prospect of a sleepless night ahead. His hand rasped over his short beard, rubbed his eyes. Thirty-five hours . . . since he and Abner had broken camp with North and Missou Holbrook two days ago. All that had happened since seemed unreal, a confused drift of nightmare scenes, and he knew this too was the dead weariness of mind and body.

He looked suddenly at Bayliss, seeing him watching with a crafty calculation, and he thought stolidly, *No, you beady-eyed bastard, I won't sleep, but you'll think otherwise, and that's fine*. He said aloud: "How about that bed?"

"Come along," Bayliss grated almost pleasantly. He lifted a lantern from a nail, lighted it, and led the way through the kitchen and up the narrow stairs. The lantern danced wavering shadows along the grimy walls and shafted through the murky corridor above. Owen glanced at the doors they passed, knowing McVey was behind one . . . listening . . . doubtless with a gun pointed at the door, ready to blast. *I'll wait, and he'll break,* Owen thought. *Sometime tonight he'll break.*

Bayliss halted by a door, saying, "No lock. Keep a shotgun by my bed. Sing out, anyone pesters you." Which was by way of an oblique warning, Owen knew. He waited till Bayliss turned away, then opened the door and went in, closing it.

He tossed his hat on the black shape of the narrow cot, cursed as he barked his shins getting around it to the window through which first moonlight thinly streamed. Holding his breath, he silently forced up the warped sash. He shivered at the inrush of icy air.

He pulled up a stool which, with the bed, constituted

the room's sole furniture. He huddled deeper into his sheepskin, leaned his crossed arms on the sill with the Navy Colt in his lap . . . settled in chilled alertness to wait.

———

NINE

Backing the town on either side rose the mountain-flank and the lava heights. Only a man afoot could tackle either. McVey would not leave afoot. That left the road, and from his window Owen had a clear view of its moon-paled ribbon. Time passed, and his rigid body relaxed to the hypnotic creaking of building timbers in a high wind, the ruffled slap of loose shakes on the roof. Twice he nodded, each time jerked erect, again settled back.

Think of something. He thought of Virginia Gilchrist, remembering her face, her movements and voice with a small, odd excitement that kept him awake a time. But his head bowed slowly against his arms; he dozed, his thread of awareness raveled out exhaustedly without quite letting go. . . .

He jerked upright, suddenly on his feet . . . listening. Above the thin moan of wind, he heard the creak of stairboards. *He's left his room, he's going down.* Owen's muscles jerked with the impulse to follow; he remembered Bayliss and the shotgun. *He's like to cut loose, first sight of you. Wait . . . cover the road.*

Owen sank on his haunches by the window. He heard the swing doors creak open beneath the porch—Bayliss' low voice. The hurried rasp of feet turning up the adjoining alley. Owen waited with an iron patience. Shortly he heard the rapid tattoo of hoofbeats alongside the building, and the wicked tension uncoiled in him. He cocked his revolver.

He leaned from the window as McVey swerved out of

the alley, bent low in his saddle, heels drumming the horse's flanks . . . a big, rangy buckskin, not the horse on which he'd left Blanco, Owen noted detachedly as he braced the Navy Colt across his forearm—fired.

The buckskin shuddered and broke stride. Owen shot again as it came abreast of his window.

Realizing that he had lost all control over the animal, McVey had freed his feet from the stirrups, plunging into the dust in a skidding sprawl. He crawled slowly to his hands and knees, doggedly shaking his head. His gun had fallen from its holster and he looked around for it and floundered over to it. Owen held his fire, thinking coldly, *He knows where Cushing Tierney is. First things first.*

He let out his breath in a shout: "Rutledge here, Sykes . . . throw the gun away!"

McVey pivoted on a hip with incredible swiftness, at the same time palming up his gun from the dust. He fired blindly at the window, then was on his feet racing for the alley. His slug hammered into the weathered clapboards. Owen tilted the Navy gun to bear on McVey's legs. He shot carefully, and missed, and then McVey vanished into the areaway.

With a savage curse Owen spun from the window, wrenched the door open. He pounded through the black corridor and down the stairwell. Veering hard at the midway landing where the stairs turned at a right angle, he ran full into the blaze of a lamp in Bayliss' right hand—shotgun in his left as he huffed up the stairs.

Owen lunged at him without breaking pace, lowering his shoulder to slam full into Bayliss' chest. The fat man arched over backward as though catapulted, somersaulting helplessly down the steep-pitched stairwell. The impact of his fall shook the building. The lamp arced up and down and broke, sending a streamer of oil-fed flame across the bottom landing and Bayliss' legs. Bayliss howled and rolled ponderously, beating wildly at his pants. Owen vaulted the blazing floor and ran across the kitchen and out the back door.

As he flung it open, went through, a purple-orange

tongue of flame licked from the darkness. Owen leaped sideways, out of the framing light. He fired at the gun-flash, heard the pound of retreating feet.

For a moment he crouched against the clapboards, hearing the harsh sweep of his own breathing, accustoming his eyes to the shadows that steeped the deep vale of back yard. He made out a low silhouette of the stables, its wide-thrown double doors from which the shot had come.

He left the wall, legs driving at the clay ground as he went across the compound. He came with an aching slam against the stable wall by the doorframe as from deep in the building, McVey shot again. Owen fired back and then dived inside in a low-running lunge. His head crashed against an unseen stall partition, and his foot slipped and he fell with a grunt on his belly. He lay for a dazed moment in the straw-dung-and-ammoniac reek of the damp dirt floor. Then twisted around to strain his eyes toward the stall cornerpost. He saw nothing but moonlight-jagged cracks in the warped wallboards. A horse whickered and stamped in a stall farther down. There was an on-run of silence beneath the low wail of wind.

Owen pulled himself soundlessly to his hunkers, began shucking out the spent loads in his gun. He fumbled for fresh cartridges and thumbed them into the chambers—cocked the gun.

McVey fired at the sound. His bullet ripped through the stall boards, off-target by a good two feet. Owen crouched and listened. He heard faint noises at the stable rear, and he thrust his gun around the upright and fired. The noises continued—a steady up-moving grate of feet on wood that was baffling. Next a rustle of straw just beneath the roof; then, understanding: *He went up a ladder to the loft.* Straining his eyes, Owen distinguished the two-feet-square outline of the traphole against the lesser gloom of the ceiling. *He'll wait for a good shot—cut down from there.* Owen considered that momentarily. *He's used four loads. Give him his shot.*

Owen rose slowly, steadied himself with a hand on the

partition, stepped into the areaway faintly illumined from the open doors. He took a tentative step forward. At the faintest whisper of sound, he stepped sideways into shadow; McVey's gun bellowed. Owen waited for a half-crouched instant of silence. A reek of powderfumes drifted the air. He guessed that McVey did not know whether he'd made a hit.

"All right, Red John," he said softly. "You were enough of a horseman once to keep your hammer on a dead chamber. Come down or I come after you."

He knew a moment's shock as McVey's bitter curse mingled with the roar of McVey's gun. Unthinkingly he felt the wind of the slug as his own gun tilted to bear, bucked against his palm. McVey let out a choking, hard-hit grunt, his body rolled slackly across the trap-hole and, bent at the middle, fell through.

You shot too fast. Owen numbly sheathed his gun and groped forward till his foot touched McVey's body. He heard the low groan. He breathed almost a merciless prayer: *Stay alive, Red John. Just a while yet.*

He bent and gathered up the motionless form. It was spare and light and limp in his arms. He carried McVey outside and laid him in a patch of moonlight. He rolled McVey's head gently in one big palm. "You hear me, Sykes?"

McVey's head stirred; his eyes rolled open, glittered against the light. He coughed blood. His drained whisper was harsh: "Damn you . . . killed me, Rutledge. You've killed me."

"What I set out to do."

"I know . . . known it a long time. Knew it would catch up sometime. Funny how a man knows. Clean forgot though . . . had live shell . . . under pin." He coughed again, a retching and violent spasm. "You wanted me—alive—awhile?"

"Long enough to learn about Cushing Tierney. That long."

McVey managed a smile of wistful charm. "You big son of a bitch. Now you'll never know."

"Depends," Owen murmured, "on what you hate

more—me, or Tierney getting scot-free. There's still time."

"Why," Charlie McVey whispered smilingly, "That's so, and his name—his name is Reed M'Kandless now."

Owen shook his head soberly. "Won't work. You must have some grudge on him . . . telling me a man like Colonel M'Kandless would give a killer of women and children the protection of his name."

"He did!" It left McVey as a harsh cry. He choked again, sagged against Owen's arm; his breathing shallowed and seemed to thread away. For a moment Owen thought he was gone, then had to bend his head to catch McVey's broken whisper.

Cushing Tierney, he said, was Colonel M'Kandless' brother-in-law. The colonel's wife was still alive when Tierney had fled up from Texas, where Owen lost his trail years ago, evading the federal troops then swarming the country who'd have shot him on sight. In desperation he'd gone to his sister and begged her protection. Cushing had long been a prodigal problem of the highborn Tierneys, and inspired, as prodigals often did, perverse affection and protective loyalty in his clansmen.

Lila M'Kandless had heard stories of her brother's depredations and of course believed none of them. She had conceived the foolproof plan of passing Cushing off as her husband's brother. But even the colonel's almost reverent love for his wife, his inbred loyalty to his own class, his hatred of the Union, his ready admission as an old soldier that the bloody tales of war were largely wild exaggeration and propaganda, could not bring him to stomach this deception.

It was then that Tierney had desperately gambled all on one fact: that the colonel, like all the Southern aristocracy, placed the white females of their own families on a protective pedestal—a point of honor that took precedence over all else. He'd sought the colonel out privately and had threatened to inform the federals that his brother-in-law, the colonel, had already sheltered him for a month in return for the lion's share of the cash loot pillaged by Tierney's Raiders. As an outspoken enemy of the Union, the very least the colonel might expect from a federal judge was a lengthy prison sentence. To leave his child and semi-invalid wife alone and helpless was out of the question. His first alternative reaction was to shoot Tierney on the spot—but the shock would certainly kill his wife. Caught between a Scylla of deceit and a Charybdis of dishonor, the colonel had chosen deceit . . . had told his wife he'd agree.

As McVey talked, Owen's thoughts raced back over the brief battle-glimpse he'd had of Tierney, the man's description, and his leisurely view of Reed M'Kandless. It could be . . . trim off the bushy burnsides of wartime fashion, add a neatly clipped spade beard, pad the tense-wiry body with the flesh and pallor of age and soft living . . . and there emerged a sleek and slothful stranger.

A short time following the wasting death of Mrs. M'Kandless, from consumption, John Sykes, broke and hungry after five years of riding a grubline following his separation from Tierney in Texas, arrived in Blanco Basin. Tierney had sometimes spoken of his sister, Mrs. M'Kandless, and Sykes had come to Lionclaw in hopes of wheedling money from her. Lila was in her grave by then, but Sykes quickly recognized Reed M'Kandless as the man at whose side he'd ridden through the war. A single threat to anonymously notify the Territorial Marshal of Reed's identity had resulted in Reed's introducing Sykes to Blanco Basin as an upstanding young lawyer from his home town in Kentucky. A good suit and a clean-shaven face, a quick and facile mind applied to long study-hours over lawbooks, had filled out the new guise of Charles McVey, attorney-at-law.

McVey's voice broke and sank and his eyes closed. He whispered, "Get me a drink. Whiskey."

Owen swung his head toward the stealthy approach of feet from behind. Bayliss halted flat-footed, a lantern dangling from his hand. It glinted on his shotgun. Owen said harshly, "It's done. Keep that Greener pointed down."

Bayliss vaguely sleeved his slack mouth, uneasy stare

fixing the hard, battered face of the huge man crouching before him. "Sure. All right."

"Bring him a drink."

"Water?"

"No."

Bayliss nodded and shuffled away. Owen watched his back till the kitchen door closed behind him.

"Rutledge?" McVey's whisper was surprisingly strong, faintly mocking. "Glad we got your family," he husked. "Didn't kill your sisters right off, you know . . . Rutledge, you believe there's a Hell?"

There is no regret in him, Owen thought dismally, *even now.* "At times," he said aloud, yet softly, "I can hope so."

McVey's lips stirred in a soundless chuckle. "Ma . . . Ma, all that praying better do some good now . . . you old bat!" His body tensed, breath a dwindling rasp—he was motionless.

The wind rattled skeletons of dead brush against the stable wall. Owen shivered. He looked up as Bayliss, returning, extended the bottle. "Never mind," he said.

TEN

The five men left their horses a good two hundred yards from the Lionclaw outbuildings and went in on foot through the moonlight. At a word from Matthew Claiborne, his four companions halted in the deep shadow of the hay shed. Claiborne let out his breath and sleeved sweat from his face, though the windless night air bit strongly through his duck jacket. At midnight now, bunkhouse and main house lay in sleeping darkness.

Claiborne had already gone over the simple strategy several times; he repeated it now in a grating whisper,

looking hard at each man as though daring him to mis-
understand. "Danny, you and I handle the main house.
Other three take the bunkhouse. Blaize, light your lantern when you reach the bunkhouse, go in quickly, catch
them in its light, order them to lie still. You and Clay will
cover the crew while Lafferty collects their guns. Then
you report to me at the house. And Blaize—I want no
gunplay unless they start it; then, do not shoot to kill.
Understand me?"

Blaize inclined his head patiently. He was a tall, yellow-
haired Texan with cold, bleached eyes. The other three
drifters whom Claiborne had hired for this job were dregs
of the chuckline, caring for nothing but a fast, lazy, reckless dollar. Claiborne had approached them at random
among the saddle bums that drifted in and out of his
saloon. Yesterday he had selected Blaize more purpose-
fully from the same ilk. The Texan was as disreputable
and hardcase as any, but with a cool, efficient head, and
the others would take his orders. Claiborne needed one
man who would smoothly nullify the danger of Lionclaw's twenty-man crew while he himself directly
handled the M'Kandlesses. He wasn't concerned about the
shanty row of Mexican families not far distant; the Mexes
of Blanco Basin had never given more than nominal
loyalty to their American conquerors, caring little or
nothing in their *mañana* thoughts for the disputes of
the alien race they served.

They separated then, Blaize and his two men gliding
through the shadows toward the bunkhouse; Danny, squat
and barrel-built, huffed noisily behind the lofty form of
Claiborne, moving up the shallow, moon-bathed rise toward the big house. Claiborne had made only one visit
here, to show his old Armijo land grant to Colonel
M'Kandless, with the expected result of the colonel's or-
dering him off in rage. It had given Claiborne his chance
to size the layout of house and grounds.

Now as he and Danny skirted the house's west flank
to reach the kitchen door, he had only a bitter hope that
this would come off without a hitch. If Ivy North had succeeded in the one certain stroke that would have cut the

legs from under the opposition—killing Colonel M'Kandless in a street duel—it would have been easy to deal with his daughter and brother by a few bold, brief threats—for Claiborne would stand no chance against the M'Kandless position if he matched his claim against their wealth in the courts. But the colonel's fragile body contained a steel will, and he wouldn't be caught twice by the same trick.

North would have had a sure thing if that damned Rutledge hadn't interfered, Claiborne thought bitterly . . . he shivered and cursed under his breath. If he weren't free of the puerile superstitious fancies of most men, he'd almost believe that Rutledge had the Indian sign on him. Three nights ago in the livery, when he'd let drop a casual taunt to Owen over the body of that *Negra,* he'd been for a moment a hair's breadth from death. Heaven help the man that Rutledge had marked for the Negro's killing. . . . But two days had passed; Rutledge hadn't returned, and Claiborne had breathed more easily. At this of all times, he wanted no outside interference from Rutledge or any other. Four days had passed since North's failure, time to lull the suspicions of Lionclaw people— and Claiborne was ready for the big step. Forcing the colonel off Lionclaw would lay the groundwork for crowding the old man to a compromise.

They had achieved the back door of the hacienda now, and Claiborne halted Danny with a word. He had brought two lanterns from town, given one to Blaize. He lighted the other, cupping his big bony hands to shield its glow. Holding it high, he silently lifted the doorlatch and stepped through. In the narrow pantry opening off the kitchen, the cook came instantly upright on his cot, blinking confusedly at the flare of light.

"Sit quiet, fella," Danny ordered in his deep, ugly voice, his gun leveled on the man. Bloody Matt did not wait for the cook's response; he moved on through the dining room, and from there into a wide corridor. The lantern flickered a murky glow which showed two closed doors on either wall. Bedrooms, one empty, three occupied . . . but which by whom? Claiborne halted for a nonplussed moment. The girl and Reed M'Kandless might offer token resistance . . . but it was the colonel who concerned him.

He stiffened, watching a pencil of light form beneath the near door on his right . . . then the stealthy creak of a floorboard. Someone had caught a sound—lighted a lamp and was coming to the door. Claiborne's heart pounded as he cocked his gun.

The door flung abruptly open. Colonel M'Kandless, his mane of hair rumpled over his thin, intent face, stood there in a dressing gown. He held a heavy pistol, swung it to bear as he saw Claiborne. There was no time for words. With a resigned sigh Claiborne fired.

The colonel's frail body spun against the doorjamb, his pistol and lamp clattering to the floor. The lamp landed upright without breaking, but its chimney cracked as the colonel's body sank down, pressing it against the jamb. Claiborne, watching him twitch a frail hand and become motionless, thought with weary dispassion that he'd just watched his thin hope for a smooth operation die stillborn.

The adjacent door was flung wide and Cissie M'Kandless came out, a wrapper thrown over her nightgown. She looked uncomprehendingly at Claiborne and then at her father, went down on her knees by him with a terrible cry. Reed M'Kandless stepped from his room opposite the colonel's, sleepily scratching his thinning tousled hair. He froze, hand in his hair, for the space of three seconds as he took it all in.

"You stand—" Claiborne began, when the girl came suddenly to her feet with a thin scream and flung herself at him. Claiborne took a backward step, backhanded her across the jaw with the hand that held his gun. She crumpled heavily at his feet without a sound. Claiborne lifted a sultry, wicked gaze to Reed M'Kandless. Reed slowly unfroze, one pudgy hand gently massaging the flannel nightshirt over his plump middle. "Oh no," he said stupidly.

"No," Claiborne said. "Unless you make one move." A muffled shot cracked out on the heel of his words.

From the bunkhouse, he thought, and cocked his head to listen. There was another shot. A long, waiting silence, before he relaxed.

"Now," he said conversationally, "are there keys to these bedrooms?"

Still rubbing his belly, open-mouthed and wide-eyed, Reed M'Kandless mechanically nodded. Then he said tonelessly, "A master key—in the colonel's desk."

"Get it."

Reed shuffled across the hallway, gave the colonel's body a quick shuddering glance as he went into the room and opened the single drawer of a small writing desk. Claiborne watched him from the doorway. "The key," Bloody Matt said gently, as Reed's hand dipped in the drawer. "Bring out just the key."

Reed shuddered again. He held up the key. Claiborne nodded. "Drag the body inside . . . take the girl back to her room. Lock both rooms."

"Then—?"

Claiborne smiled faintly. "Then we make medicine, you and I."

He saw the hall shadows change shape, quickly turned as Blaize came quietly into the hall beside him, lantern in hand. "How did it go?" Claiborne asked.

Blaize did not reply, his cold gaze warming wickedly as it touched the still form of the girl. "You hurt that woman?" he asked softly.

"She's not dead, I had to hit her," Claiborne said irritably, but he knew a brief cold wariness as the Texan's bleach eyes fixed him dispassionately. "Kill a man, take his ranch—but never lay a finger on a woman, eh, Blaize? You Texans—setting anything in calico on a pedestal—"

"You got objections, mister?" Blaize cut in softly. His gaze never left the girl as Reed awkwardly lifted her limp weight.

"Quit it," Claiborne said wearily. "I heard shots—"

"That segundo went after a gun. I powdered him off, Too bad, I made him to be a Texas man."

"Damn you. Is he dead?"

"Unh-unh. Side hit."

"The other shot?"

"Feisty little ranny name of Fitz. Jumped me. Lafferty winged him."

Claiborne slowly exhaled. Still, the colonel's death had fulfilled his pessimism. *That killing will make a very large stink,* he thought coldly. But he could not change what had happened, and it was too late to pull back.

"All right. Get back to the bunkhouse, take Danny and the cook with you. The four of you watch the crew."

Blaize hesitated. "You?"

"The girl will be locked in her room safely beyond my vile clutches," Claiborne answered dryly. "Don't worry . . . I'll conduct the rest of my business with her uncle."

Claiborne lighted a cheroot, took it from his lips and exhaled a fragrant streamer. He regarded Reed M'Kandless through the smoke a speculative moment, sailed the match into the woodbox, and said idly, "I meant to wound your brother. He died too easily."

They were sitting at a kitchen table now, facing each other across it with the slack-poise of two wary tomcats, not yet tensed for battle. Claiborne had searched the house room by room for weapons, had found, besides the colonel's Colt, only a brace of antique dueling pistols above the parlor fireplace mantel. Satisfied that he could parley in safety, he'd ordered Reed into the kitchen.

He'd meant to frighten Reed M'Kandless into submissive agreement under his own terms, but already he was sensing that this stout, slack-bodied man's foppish appearance concealed a latent secretive shrewdness. Bloody Matt decided to walk soft at first and take the full measure of his man. He opened with a casual half-apology that yet held no jot of regret, because he knew Reed wouldn't be fooled.

Already Reed's first shocked paralysis had ebbed; his cool milky eyes made a wary sizing-up of Claiborne. He looked at the cocked revolver by Claiborne's elbow, and again, searchingly, at his enemy. "His doctor told the colonel his heart was going," he said mildly. "Any slight shock. . . ." He shrugged, and was silent.

Claiborne frowned. "You know what I want, M'Kandless. Lionclaw. I'm holding a sure hand—"

"That Armijo grant, yes," Reed interrupted, his tone faintly insolent. "But you set it up badly. I'm guessing that you hadn't counted on killing the colonel or Dirksen . . . just moving them and us all off Lionclaw to help cinch your position. . . . I'm guessing you're on a spot now, Claiborne, and singing soft."

"Not altogether, friend. One dead man—or twenty— tell no tales about another dead man."

"A bluff to back a losing hand," Reed jeered lightly. "Your only chance to get Lionclaw by legal murder was to have the colonel braced by that gunnie in town . . . that failed. Now you've started open murder, you have two choices: commit more murders that can't be concealed long, else make some sort of deal with me. Now —what's your offer?"

"Why, your life, damn you—what else?"

Reed gently shook his head, smiling. "Not enough. You thought to scare me—you're smart enough to see by now that it won't work."

Claiborne slacked back in his chair, studying the man. He said calmly: "All right. What's *your* offer?"

Reed said immediately, "I cover up the colonel's death. He had a heart attack before you came. Died of natural causes. That's the story that'll go out. No inquest, no legal stink. His own brother's word won't be questioned."

"You're forgetting the girl."

"Hardly," Reed murmured.

Claiborne stared at him for a full five seconds of disbelief. "You're willing to . . . your own niece?"

Reed said smilingly, "I'm an adaptable fellow. I've had to re-cast my life before this, adapt quickly to new circumstances. Necessities of survival."

Claiborne was baffled. Reed's easy, cold-blooded suggestions rang somehow true to character. Yet it was unbelievable that this man, reputed as a shiftless, gutless fop, should suddenly array himself in different colors.

Claiborne wondered whether the change was a ruse, whether Reed was merely biding his time through the immediate danger till he could see justice done his brother's killer.

Seeing the doubt harden in his face, Reed swiftly leaned forward across the table, the lamp flickering over his fleshy, pale features. "Claiborne. In the early part of the war, when your forces in the Tennessee border fighting were hard-pressed, you received help from a guerrilla band—Tierney's Raiders. They raided more than one enemy supply train to bring you food and ammunition."

"Yes," Claiborne growled, "for a price—the damned blackguards. Don't tell me you were with Tierney?"

"You met their leader face to face several times," Reed said impatiently. "Look at my face—carefully. Come on, man; it hasn't changed that much—"

"*Cushing Tierney!*" It left Claiborne in an explosive whisper.

Reed nodded and began to talk, quietly and quickly. Inside of five minutes Claiborne understood, but still he was puzzled.

"That's a dangerous secret," he said slowly, "very dangerous to entrust to anyone. Why tell me—Tierney?"

Reed spread his soft hands. "To show my good faith, to show we're birds of one feather. We can trust each other—" he smiled thinly— "to an identical limit."

Claiborne said narrowly, "Go on."

"Listen. I once saw the colonel's will. He left everything to his daughter. Cissie as good as told me in her fresh young way that when she inherited Lionclaw my presence here would no longer be tolerated. *She* made her mother no promise to shield her blacksheep uncle. The colonel's death plainly puts me out in the cold. Unless—" He paused, weighing the obvious.

"Unless," Claiborne said gently, "there were no Cissie?"

"Then," Reed said, "I'd be the only surviving member of the colonel's immediate family. No one to worry about but a few shirttail relatives back in Kentucky whose claims wouldn't hold water . . . especially should we forge a new will. The colonel's present will is locked in the safe in his room."

Claiborne understood now. "We can use each other, eh? Let it be known that you, the colonel's only heir, and I, holding the Armijo grant, agreed on an amicable settlement—share and share alike. Sparing both costly litigation and a too-close scrutiny by others of this whole affair. . . ."

Reed chuckled. "And how the colonel actually died need not go beyond this ranch. If your man Blaize will keep his mouth shut?"

"He will, for the right sum. What about the Lionclaw crew?"

"I'll pay them off in the morning—tell them to drift. They'll scatter far and wide, glad to get out with whole skins. The entire matter contains elements of chance, but the stakes are worth the risk."

"That brings us," Claiborne said heavily, "back to the girl." He paused to isolate his next words, said flatly, "I want no part of woman-killing."

"Squeamish, General?"

"No—sensible; that part's dynamite."

"Leave it to me," Reed said calmly.

"It'll have to be—an accident."

"Leave it to me," Reed repeated. "There's one more thing you probably don't know. . . ." He explained about Virginia Gilchrist's old Spanish charter, how it had passed into the hands of "Red John" Sykes, alias Charles McVey, how Sykes had offered to sell it to him.

Claiborne stroked his great beard a thoughtful moment. "Could this Gilchrist woman and her charter be a fake?"

"The colonel thought so. So did I, until McVey told me he'd verified its authenticity with an old fellow who was a servant in the Rivera family's household. This old Mexican's word is said to be infallible. That's one thing we can be sure of. The other is that this document is dangerous to us."

Claiborne nodded, his gaunt face sober. "After acquiring the Armijo grant, I did a good deal of research on judgments of rival property claims. The New Mexico courts have often decided in favor of the old Spanish grants. This one could supercede both our claims. But it will be useless to anyone except the Gilchrist woman. If it gets back into her hands——"

"We have to see that doesn't happen," Reed said flatly. "Sykes has the charter. We have to catch up with him before Owen Rutledge does."

They talked it over a while, Bloody Matt agreeing that after Reed had gotten rid of the crew, he and his men would go after Sykes alias McVey, while Reed handled the problem of his niece.

As they talked, there came a soft tramp of bootsteps on the back porch. Claiborne barely glanced up as the door opened, expecting to see Blaize. His restless eyes caught and froze on the man in the doorway—a huge man bulking larger in travel-stained clothes, a leveled gun in his fist.

ELEVEN

Searching the dead McVey's pockets, Owen had found an empty gambler's pistol, a canvas bag containing forty gold double-eagles, and a thin, oilcloth-wrapped packet. Removing the oilcloth, he guessed at first glimpse of the faded parchment what it contained. Kneeling in the flickering glow of Bayliss' lantern, he'd carefully spread out and examined the Rivera charter, afterward returning it to the oilcloth and tucking it inside a deep pocket of his sheepskin. He wondered tiredly how happy Virginia Gilchrist would be for its return . . . after she had heard everything. *You killed her man; no woman could help but hate you even after she knows the truth.*

The thought clung and nagged through a dragging weariness of mind and body as he helped Bayliss dig a shallow grave in the old camp cemetery back of the stable. When they had covered the blanket-wrapped body, he went up to his room and collapsed across the sagging cot without removing his coat.

Owen slept the deep, dreamless sleep of exhaustion. When he woke, the sun was high above Sunfire's ramshackle rooftops. He went down to the kitchen where Bayliss' wife heated some leftover steak and potatoes. Afterward he went to the stable. He saddled his bay and then out of curiosity went to where McVey's buckskin was stalled. Puzzled, he studied the Lionclaw brand on its hip. Cissie M'Kandless had said that McVey had not showed at Lionclaw; then McVey must have come in secret to Reed M'Kandless, forced him to turn over a fresh horse and probably the sack of money.

In fifteen minutes Owen was on the downgrade trail to Blanco Basin, leading the buckskin. He had no doubt of his immediate destination: Lionclaw. If Colonel M'-Kandless had shielded his brother-in-law Cushing Tierney while half-deceived as to Tierney's real character, this horse, the money, the charter, and a brief explanation should convince the colonel that Tierney had abetted the escape of an unmistakable thief and murderer. Owen considered, *If he won't turn Tierney over to the federals, you always can.* And hated the thought, hard face becoming iron-set. Tierney was his. He'd have him if. . . . For a detached moment he knew strong self-revulsion. This was what he'd become: little better than Tierney or Sykes or even Matthew Claiborne; men who used death and violence to selfish ends. *All right, don't think about it, shut it off. . . .*

He rode steadily through the rising heat of mid-day, chewing some hardtack and washing it down from his canteen without leaving the saddle. The shadows had lengthened across Lionclaw's immense, rolling grass flats. He rode steadily through the twilight and deep into the darkness, guided by the sawtoothed landmarks of basin-rimming peaks which he'd mentally charted on his first visit to Lionclaw headquarters. A moon-washed sky clearly etched the surrounding country.

Shortly after midnight he saw the black-blocked outbuildings ahead, and he came directly up on the rear of the hay shed. There he dismounted in the cottonwood grove and sidled along the building's flank to a front corner. A light showed from the bunkhouse fifty yards away. Late hours for a working ranch. . . . It added a puzzled note to his mounting apprehension about his reception here.

He was about to step from the shadows to cross the yard when the bunkhouse door opened. A man stepped out, paused in the lamplight to say something jocular over his shoulder, and then lounged across the yard, halting by the shed less than a dozen feet from Owen. He paused to urinate, grunted his relief, and took tobacco and papers from his shirt pocket. He shaped a cigarette leisurely, and Owen leaned forward to see his face in the flare of lamplight. A lean and wolfish face, strange to him. Yet he couldn't be sure he'd seen every Lionclaw crewman.

"Hey," Owen called softly. The man dropped his quirly in his haste to wheel around, claw back his coat. "No gun," Owen warned sharply as he stepped out to the moonlight.

The man said tensely, "Who the hell are you?"

"Man who wants to see the colonel without getting shot for a prowler . . . all right with you?"

The man laughed nervously. "That's all right with me. I'll take you to him."

He swung about as though to lead the way to the house; Owen saw his hand again dip slyly, unobtrusively, beneath the coat. Owen slipped out his Navy gun and took two long strides. The man wheeled, bringing out his gun, jaw falling slack as he saw Owen almost on him. Owen swung his pistol in a brief, savage arc that ended above the man's left ear. With a smothered sigh, he slumped forward and Owen caught him and dragged him inside the hayshed, letting him down in the shadows.

He paused in the doorway, narrowly studying the

lighted buildings. He could only guess blindly at the situation here . . . one way to learn the truth. He went across the yard with a low-running stride and circled the main house. Only the kitchen was lighted. He loped onto the back porch and carefully opened the door, gun palmed and cocked.

Matthew Claiborne's casual lifting glance found him and froze to no expression at all. Owen stepped inside, closed the door, and scooped Claiborne's pistol from the table. He let it off-cock and shoved it into his belt, his circling gaze hardening on the pasty, staring face of Reed M'Kandless.

"General, I will give you five seconds to tell what's happened here," Owen said distinctly. "Then I start shooting."

Claiborne carefully lifted his hand and drew on the cheroot. "I'd call you abrupt, Rutledge, not impulsive." His glance warily fell to the Navy gun. "Steady down now. I've met the enemy, they're mine. That should be evident—"

"The colonel, his daughter?" Owen grated. "Speak up, damn you."

Claiborne drew an unsettled breath. "Steady down," he repeated. "The colonel is dead. Heart attack, I didn't kill him."

"Except indirectly. Cissie . . ."

"In her room, unharmed," Claiborne said jerkily. "Listen, I have four men in the bunkhouse. Guarding the crew. One shot, you'll have them on your back."

Owen ignored him, hard glance slanting again to Reed. Color drained slowly back to the stout man's face where Owen saw the sly, fearful knowledge that Owen had learned his identity. But the ruthless, raw courage that had been Cushing Tierney's held the pale eyes steady now.

Reed said softly: "You caught up with McVey—of course?"

Owen was wordless, his grim stare unchanging. Reed stirred uneasily. "Of course," he murmured, as if to himself.

"He lived long enough to talk, Tierney."

"And you'll kill me, I suppose." Reed shrugged, his round shoulders bracing stiffly beneath his quilted robe. "Well. . . ."

Owen drew Claiborne's gun from his belt, laid it on the edge of the table by Reed's arm.

"My men, Rutledge," Claiborne said softly.

Owen's grim glance shifted. "When they come, you'll be my life insurance." He looked back at Reed, waiting.

Reed's eyes lifted from the gun on the table. He did not stir a muscle. His lips barely moved. "I won't go for it, Rutledge. You've dogged me this far; don't let that stop you."

Owen sheathed his own gun. A nerve-strung stillness threaded away, broken by Claiborne's harsh intake of breath. Reed did not move, did not take his eyes from Owen's face. The ghost of a grin touched his thin lips.

Owen realized that his own body was trembling. *You bastard, you rotten smirking bastard, you know I won't, not this way.* He moved forward, towering above Reed with his great fist closing. He smashed it across Reed's jaw with a savage backhanded blow that toppled the heavy man's chair sideways. Reed fell face down and lay motionless.

"Yes, Rutledge," Matthew Claiborne said, "I'd call you abrupt—in your soft-hearted way."

Owen said wickedly, "Don't be premature, friend. Next time we meet he'll hold a gun if I have to strap it in his hand. This isn't the time. On your feet."

Claiborne didn't move. He said musingly, "If you caught McVey, you must have that very valuable Rivera charter now—eh?" Owen's silence seemed to satisfy him; he smiled. "Don't be an utter fool. We can make a deal. . . ."

Owen picked up the gun on the table and came close to Claiborne. He muzzled it against Claiborne's neck, thumbed back the hammer. "You can leave here one of two ways. Bloody Matt Claiborne should know when a man means it."

Claiborne inhaled slowly, slowly sighed out the breath. ". . . . All right." He placed his palms on the table and shoved to his feet, moved to the door ahead of Owen.

They crossed the moonlit yard at a fast trot, Owen shoving Claiborne ahead and glancing over his shoulder at the bunkhouse. Within moments Claiborne's men would be wondering why their comrade hadn't returned. As they passed the open-sided hayshed, a deep groan came from its darkness.

Claiborne halted. "What's that?"

"Buffaloed one of your poodles, he'll be coming to." Owen drove the pistol hard into Claiborne's ribs. "Get a move on."

They skirted the shed, plowed through its flanking brush into the dark cottonwoods. Owen saw his bay and the buckskin in the moon-dappled glade where he'd tethered them. "Hold it."

Claiborne's great height stiffened, but he stopped dead. Owen swung his gun up and down. Claiborne's hat muffled the blow and he sank heavily. Owen ran to the bay, caught the reins, toed into stirrup and swung up. As he careened the animal through the trees, he heard Bloody Matt's sudden-lifted bawl: "I'll ride you down, Rutledge! By God, I'll—"

Owen twisted in his saddle, shot into the trees. He heard Claiborne's shrill curse, the thrashing of brush as he retreated. Owen felt a bitter inward sinking as he spurred out of the trees and north across the flats. Claiborne's hat had blunted the blow enough to dangerously narrow the safe lead Owen might have had. In minutes they'd be on his trail—unless the necessity of holding the Lionclaw crew delayed them.

But Claiborne had known about the charter. Reed must have told him. That meant the two of them had joined forces, had been reciprocally scheming even as he'd had burst in on them. They had a strong incentive to drop everything and run him down. Owen squeezed the bay to a reckless run, heading for the far foothills to the north.

And slowly he became aware of a fresh danger—the bay's flanks were heaving, it was missing stride. The animal had been ridden for weeks with little rest. He had pushed it at a savage pace in his pursuit of McVey; the sturdy beast was reaching the limit of endurance. *Should have taken the buckskin,* he thought now, too late.

For the next two miles he held the animal in, finally halting on a vast stretch of night-silvered grass. The bay needed a few hours' stop, and he had to hone his thoughts to fresh decision. He threw off saddle and gear, hobbled the bay, spread his ground sheet and sat down, his knees drawn up. He took a stubby blackened briar from his sheepskin, and dug out the hard dottle with his pocket knife. It was the poorly kept pipe of a man who rarely smoked, except when alone with his thoughts. Now he merely put it between his teeth and absently sucked the stem.

Shortly at least five men would be after him on a blood hunt. He did not know the country or its people; there was nobody, no sanctuary, he could turn to. He could keep riding on, across the peaks, gain the safety of distance from Blanco Basin. But Virginia Gilchrist wanted her charter returned, and he wanted Cushing Tierney. He thought, too, of Cissie M'Kandless, alone back there with Claiborne and a treacherous uncle, though for the present she was safer there than she'd be had he taken her away. Any of these things was sufficient to hold him.

Owen squinted at the foothills, still distant across Lionclaw's great acreage. He would have to hole up, evade Claiborne's men till they quit the search. That might consume days, days for which he wasn't properly provisioned. *Jerky and hardtack'll have to stretch,* he thought stoically and settled his chin on his knees, sitting bolt upright so as to easily spot the first sign of pursuit on this open plain.

He nodded off several times through the hours that followed, but restless tension kept him jerking awake. When the first pink belt of dawn tinged the horizon, he rose, stiffly cramped, and unhobbled his horse.

Full dawn found Owen close to the foothills, holding the bay to a controlled pace. Soon he'd be deep in wild, irregular backcountry, with a wide choice of places to lie low. *But one good tracker in Bloody Matt's outfit can make it rough,* he worried, glancing continually over his backtrail. He shucked out of his sheepskin against the lifting heat, tied it behind his cantle.

Then his far-ranging stare picked out the distant specks that were horsemen. *They're coming fast, they've likely got that tracker, fresh horses, too.* He assayed these facts, added to them the miles remaining to the first foothills, totaled them to nothing good. Yet he resumed his held-in pace. The last·thing he could afford was to founder the bay and put himself afoot against mounted men.

The land began to tilt upward, but still rolled out flat as a griddle. In a half-hour he paused to rest the bay. The riders were nearer now, coming on a straightaway course that told Owen he was long-seen. They were closing the margin fast. He shook his head, went on. Soon he rode into a deep cleft between the first shallow lift of hills, there struck the grass-grown ruts of an ancient logging road. It wound up a right-hand slope into tall pine timber. The sooner he penetrated good cover, the better; Owen followed the road.

Coming out on the crest of the wooded rise, he found that it dropped sharply away down a rocky, treeless slope. The road twisted sinuously down over a rotted corduroy base, and beyond lay a maze of gentle hills mantled by meadows interspersed with timber belts. The allover view was too open to suit, but he could not turn back now. He'd have to trust blind luck to take him through. Owen put the bay down the slope and cut northwest in a straight line that he hoped would give him a brief lead. The country was at least rugged enough to give the fresh mounts of the pursuit no advantage; they'd be held to roughly his pace.

He pulled up in the first jag of timber and surveyed his rear. No sign yet . . . he'd know shortly how good their tracker was. Owen crossed several more humpy pastures with their wooded skirmish lines and then topped an abrupt rocky ridge and saw beyond where the mean country began. It looked broken and cruel, studded with monolithic boulders and laced by treacherous slides. But the honeycombing of gorges and deep washes looked promising . . . a man should lose himself there. He looked back, saw the five riders just emerging onto the first meadow.

They were moving swiftly, spreading wide into a ragged line to beat through the timbered places. Then he caught a distant shout, saw them converge back to a bunch and come on. Knowing he was spotted, Owen savagely berated himself for not moving faster.

He nudged the bay down the ridge slope which sheered so steeply toward the bottom that the animal skidded the last few yards on its haunches in an avalanche of dislodged rubble. Owen kicked it up into the nearest canyon and rode steadily for a quarter hour, holding to the main trunk of the gorge against a hunted man's instinct to turn into the first small branch canyon, many of which cross-hatched the high walls. The pursuers would have to pause at each off-stem to make certain he hadn't· turned in. Small delays . . . but every minute was precious now.

Then he swung around a bend and came to a dead stop. He faced a freak limestone ridge that ran to either side far as a man could see, with a vertical wall that reared skyward for a good three hundred feet. The gorge ran solidly against the wall and ended. Owen knew a sinking despair, threaded by fresh hope as he came close enough to see a trail—partly faulted out by geological convulsion, partly hand-chipped painstakingly by people of a forgotten age. It followed the facerock sideways at a comfortable angle to the summit . . . wide enough, he judged, to accommodate a single horseman.

He put the bay up the trail, picking out each hoofhold on a tight rein to which the horse responded well. The trail was literally scored into the rock with a hall-like overhang a bare foot above Owen's head; he couldn't tell what lay more than a few yards ahead. Ancient the trail might be, but still firm, and soon he breathed easily, steadily climbing.

Then he felt a constriction of panic as the ledge began

to narrow down. God . . . what a place to get trapped. He halted, his palms sweaty on the reins, leaning as far as he dared from the saddle. He made the mistake of glancing into the dizzy abyss below, and was careful not to look again. As much as he could see of the trail indicated that it did not quite pinch off, and afterward it widened again. *This'll be ticklish, but you can pass it.*

Owen dismounted and led the bay along the narrowing ledge. Part of the liprock had fallen away; this section of ledge, running perhaps a half-dozen yards, was rotted and crumbling beneath his boots. Again he halted. Here was the worst place. A man afoot would cross it cautiously; a horse's barrel would find it dangerously snug.

Owen flexed his clammy hands, spoke gently to the bay as he edged sideways hugging the cliff. The bay's flank scraped against the rock. One hoof slipped on the rounded ledge lip, sending a rattle of pebbles into the gulf. It stopped with a convulsive tremor of muscles. Owen tugged the reins, talking quietly. The bay came on. The footing widened solidly, and they were safely across.

Owen stood by the bay's head, rubbing its trembling shoulder. "Think you're the only one?" he murmured. Aware of the pressing delay, he mounted and headed up the last hundred feet. He came out on the rimrock and drew a deep breath of relief, seeing the gentle fallaway of the land beyond.

And now again the pursuers were close, turning out of the gorge mouth below. Owen heard their approach before he saw them and he led the bay back from the cliff and threw reins. His face tight, he worked along the rim to a point where the trail below shouldered well out from beneath its protective overhang. Numerous sizable boulders littered the rim. He chose one that was roughly block-shaped and knee-high, tested its weight with his shoulder. It was lodged solidly. He stooped and got his fingers beneath a crevice, braced his great shoulders and heaved. The boulder tilted on edge, grated over to lay poised on the rim.

He rested his hands against it, waiting. The riders

were mounting the trail. He heard voices, the creak of gear, the nearing clatter of iron on rock. He could not see them yet for the overhang. When the drift of noise grew directly beneath, he looked down and saw the first rider draw into view on the bare shoulder.

He gripped the block, lifted—so suddenly that its mass tumbled outward, he lost balance and had to scramble back. He heard it strike; a horse screamed and plunged off the ledge; the thin, wailing cry of its rider died away into the gulf. The boulder made a falling crash that drowned all other sound—a thinning rattle of gravel, silence.

Owen saw none of it. Sweating and shaking, he stood and bawled down, *"Keep your distance, you bastards!"* There was no reply, only a faint murmur of talk and more silence. They would not dare come on for a while.

Owen returned to his horse, gigged it into a trot down the far slope. Memory of the falling man's cry knotted around his guts. *He asked for it, they all did.* They'd hunted him like a beast, now they were cut to four. And Owen could think, *They asked for it,* feeling no better for the thought.

TWELVE

Owen sensed that he'd neatly boxed himself before the fact was confirmed.

A brief scare and the loss of a man would not hold Claiborne long, he'd known after leaving the cliff. Darkness was not many hours away; then he could move on while Clairborne's tracker was held to a standstill, leisurely lose himself on a trail where even an Indian would be baffled. More deep canyons lay beyond the cliff, but all dropped away sharply with no paths down.

He rode along the rim of one for several miles before finding a broken wall slide that formed a ramp to its base. It was a good six hundred feet to the bottom, and afterward the sheer walls held for many miles. Owen had no choice but to follow the twisting canyon floor.

It was thus that he came abruptly into a wide cove, a tiny grassed and wooded valley, around all sides of which, so far as he could tell, rose insurmountable walls.

To turn back to the slide area would cut it too fine; Clairborne's men must be nearly there. Unless he could find an exit here, he'd have to make a last-ditch stand.

Owen began a slow circuit of the walls, pushing the bay through deep brush, hoping for a chance fissure or tunnel concealed by overgrowth. Then he smelled wood-smoke, pungent on a shifting breeze.

Someone living here? he thought unbelievingly. Perhaps a maverick Indian . . . or a man hunted like himself. Owen slipped his gun from its holster and pushed on, skirting masses of fallen rock and rotted deadfalls, ramming the bay through tangles of vine-grown brush. He caught the smoke-smell now and again, each time stronger. Then he rounded a boulder the size of a small house and came on the camp.

The fire was smoking badly, evidently untended. The camper had picked out his approach some time ago, and was back in hiding—watching. *And with a ready gun; go easy,* Owen thought. Making no sudden move he sheathed his pistol and rode into camp with reins held at chest-level, hands in unmistakable view. A sizzling frying pan and steaming coffeepot were propped on stones close by the fire. Owen swung down and stood away from his horse.

"Grub's burning," he said quietly, clearly.

He did not turn immediately as boots scraped over rocks somewhere behind him. Then he did swing slowly on his heel. Missou Holbrook came at a light trot around the great boulder, rifle slacked loosely in the crotch of his arm.

"Man can't get off by himself nowheres," Missou murmured, walking to the fire. But a near-cheerful note to it let Owen guess how thin his own company had begun to wear. He laid his rifle down, wrapped a rag around his fist and lifted the frypan and coffee pot away from the fire, setting both on a low slab of rock. Owen tramped over and squatted down by him. Missou poured a tin cup of coffee which he silently extended. Owen accepted it, aware of a belly-knotting hunger; he grimaced, swore softly as he scalded his tongue.

Missou smiled faintly. "Take it easy, dig in." He speared a strip of sizzling bacon on his Barlow knife.

"No time." Owen set down the cup, his eyes fixing the slim youth. "There's a bunch set to nail my hide, coming fast. If you know a way out of this box, better tell it now."

Missou slowly lowered the bacon, frowning. "Only way out's way you came in. Who's coming fast?"

"Major Claiborne, three others."

"After you?"

"No time to tell it," Owen said flatly. "You lay low— keep out of sight when they come. Don't buy in."

Missou's smile broadened. "Won't be happy about taking on two, will they? Relax, grub up." Seeing the exasperated impatience on Owen's face, he added, "I heard your horse's iron hitting rocks when you were a half mile away. Canyon carries sound to beat all hell. You'll hear 'em plenty of time. . . . Those there fish are good."

Owen's glance fell to the skillet. "Fish?" He still wondered at Missou's half-calm, half-eager acceptance of the situation; the kid was likely champing at the bit with inactivity and solitude . . . and ready, so he guessed, to tackle wolves barehanded.

"Brook trout, sure. There's a stream rushes under the walls, full of 'em. I use shirt ravelings, a bent pin, some fat grubs. Fifteen minutes, I got my supper."

Owen wrapped a strip of bacon around a chunk of trout, began to eat—and found himself devouring ravenously. His appetite was scarcely blunted by the savory morsel. But Missou gave a faint, smiling nod at the food, sat back on his haunches to build a cigarette while

Owen cleaned up the skillet. He mopped up the last of the grease with a cold sourdough biscuit, swallowed it. He looked up to see Missou watching him through a furl of smoke, his expression quizzical and musing and faintly bitter.

"Nice here," the boy said quietly.

Owen glanced around, at the dark-aisled pine groves, the late sun mellowing an old-gold patina along the cliff summit. A not-distant brook made its muted, musical gurgle, and the wind soughed murmurously through the pine tops. It stirred a primitive, timeless spell through a man, this wildness and silence and solitude.

"Yeah," he said. Knowing that wasn't all Missou meant to say.

"I had it nice before you came," the boy went on softly. "That hassle in Blanco mixed me up. Had to get away off from things, think it all out. I found this place. Nothing like it. A man can sort things out, place like this."

"Sure."

"You've sort of busted it up."

Owen sensed with sudden insight that the sullen discontent marring the boy's words rose from a deeper dissatisfaction. Missou Holbrook hadn't yet sorted matters out as neatly as he desired. *You can't pigeonhole life, in your mind, you have to learn by living,* he wanted to tell the boy, but aloud he said only: "Sorry."

Missou's quick grin flashed. "Hell, don't matter. Time gets heavy on a man's hands here. I was cravin' a little excitement, you sure as all hell brought it. . . . Figured you and Claiborne would tangle again, after that hassle. What's it all about?"

Very briefly Owen told him. Missou was silent afterward, looking at the dead cigarette between his fingers, not seeing it. He said at last: "Sorry. About your friend. That big—Negro."

Owen said nothing, and then Missou spoke hesitantly: "Got underholts on a real wildcat, ain't you?"

Owen said quietly: "What I said before stands. When

the shooting starts, you lay low back in this brush. They'll never see you. . . ."

Missou was already shaking his head. "Why?" Owen demanded angrily. "My fight, mine alone. You admit you got some long living to sort out. Why throw it away to side someone you hardly know?"

That flashing grin again. "Four of them, two of us. About even odds, good chance we both live through. There's food here, berries, fish, clear water. Two men could hole up against an army, one standin' guard at the canyon mouth while the other sleeps, fixes grub, so on."

Owen nodded, unsmiling and patient. "That doesn't answer the question."

Missou flung his cigarette into the fire with a swift, irritated gesture. "Damn it, I took a liking to you. Want to question that, too?"

"No," Owen said, now smiling a little. "But you're feeling raunchy, too; you want to take a crack at something. Or someone."

"All right," Missou snapped, and then he laughed shortly. "All right, but I meant what I said." He looked into the fire a moment, arms folded on his knees. Owen watched the young face shift mood, a return of that musing bitterness. *How can a man get through to him?* Owen wondered, knowing that he could tell the kid nothing that Missou was not ready to hear, to learn for himself.

And then Missou opened the way, beginning to talk, hesitantly at first, but soon eagerly, spilling the rush of bitter memories. From this Owen pieced the riddle of the boy—his disillusionment, his easy fearlessness, his search for a goal worth a man's loyalty. The war had taken Missou's father and four brothers; and his mother, bearing too much grief, had died soon afterward. Missou was only thirteen when Appomattox came, and afterward had drifted around the homes of his shirttail relatives, who happened to include the infamous clans of the Daltons, the Youngers, the Jameses.

Though they'd ridden with Quantrill's butchers and were outlawed by a hated Union, the James boys were protected as modern Robin Hoods by the people of their native Clay County. Young Holbrook, glowing with hero worship, had spent his adolesdence hobnobbing with Frank and Jesse and Cole Younger in their own households. The gradual realization that his heroes were common thieves and murderers was the second crushing blow in his vulnerable youth.

Desperately seeking anew, he'd followed the great American dream that was moving westward, and found only a brawling, dog-eat-dog frontier. And Owen understood the unspoken yearnings for something better behind the search that had hardened a sensitive boy into a conviction that only top dogs like Ivy North won a violence-pocked place in the frontier jungle. These were the ones to follow and emulate. Only, the shiny-eyed streak of boyhood he'd never lost had suddenly caviled at the murder of an old man. On this pivot of decision Missou had rebelled. *But easy as not he could slip back,* Owen thought. *Unless.*

As Missou sat then in a shamed, angry silence, plainly feeling he'd . said too much, Owen prodded mildly: "So you came here to think things over."

"Why not? It's peaceful here, clean, no dirty damned people. Should have thought of this before."

Owen said immediately, flatly, "It's selfish."

"What?"

"You can't stay here forever. Be nice if a man could wall himself off . . . from all that out there. But he can't. Sooner or later he has to go back."

"Damn fine thing if he didn't have to, though!"

"No. It's selfish. And it's wrong. Fine for a man to get off by himself sometimes, one thing a man can't do around other people is think clear. But a man always has to go back. Because he's part of it, boy, part of the human race. The whole brawling slew of it, good or bad. And if he doesn't find a meaning, a reason, then he's got to make one for himself. Otherwise . . ." Owen hesitated . . . "he's a damned vegetable, rooted in his own muck."

"Know it all, don't you?"

"Damned little. I try to learn . . . a few things."

"Then you tell me where," Missou said savagely, "I can find a few reasons. Even one."

"I'll give you two," Owen said steadily. "Two women who need help. And nobody to help them but us. If you're willing to try."

Missou toyed with a twig, snapped it in two, frowning. "You mean this Eastern lady you was talking about, Miss Gilchrist—and Colonel M'Kandless' girl?"

"If you're willing to try," Owen repeated, very slowly. "This is no job for a wet-eared, thrill-seeking kid. Nothing to be gained except maybe a bullet. Maybe something else, like growing up a little."

Missou watched him steadily, was about to speak. Owen lifted a quick hand—listening. He'd caught the distant, thin-echoed clank of iron on rock. . . .

Missou stood up, his rifle in hand. "Well," he said quietly, "you waiting for something?"

THIRTEEN

Massive chunks of rimrock had long crumbled from the surrounding heights and fallen to the cliff base. Owen and Missou took positions behind two of these just within the canyon where it debouched into the valley. Both had '66 Model Springfields in .50 caliber; they divided their cartridges evenly, lined them in convenient rows in rock niches, and waited, stationed on either side of the canyon mouth.

Missou said softly, "How we take 'em?"

"No killing."

Missou gave a low, wry whistle.

"You ever blood a man, kid?"

"Not yet. Bluffed a few."

"We can bluff here. Place your shots close, pin them down."

"This canyon runs pretty wide," Missou pointed out. "They could rush us all abreast."

"If it comes to that," Owen said wearily, and fell silent. If Claiborne led a mounted attack, there would be no choice: shoot to kill. *You've had enough of that, way too much.* The coming darkness might point a way out. Two of them could pin back the pursuers till then.

He could pick out plainly the sounds of Claiborne's approach. He set his rifle across the rock, bearing down on the gorge's first sharp bend. Claiborne and one of his riders swung into view, coming on easy. Owen glanced at Missou who nodded, waiting his cue. Owen laid his shot at the feet of Claiborne's mount. The pie-bald fiddlefooted, and Claiborne held him in, and then Missou's rifle roared, the slug flailing gravel against the other horse's legs. The animal reared as his rider fought for control. Owen was already thumbing a fresh load into his gun-breech, but Claiborne abruptly spun his mount back around the bend, and his rider followed.

A full minute passed; voices murmured consultation downcanyon. Then Claiborne's voice raised with an angry, harried note. "Rutledge? Rutledge, who you got there?"

"Six Apaches armed to the teeth," Owen called.

Claiborne gave a strained laugh. "I thought I saw his face . . . that kid who was with North?"

"And five Apaches."

Missou couldn't control a spasm of laughter. Claiborne cursed them both blisteringly. Missou grinned at Owen. "You got him going." The kid looked swiftly back at the bend as the blued muzzle of a rifle tilted warily around the rock. Missou took quick aim, waited till the man's eye lifted along the sights, and fired. Rock fragments showered the man's face and he dropped back with a howl.

They settled to a long, wary vigil. Through the hours that followed, as sunset muted the canyon walls to a pale blue, Claiborne made no move. After a long interval Missou stirred restlessly. "What's he waiting for?"

"Dark, same as us."

"You got an idea for then?"

"I don't know. See what happens."

"Kid!" Claiborne's hail came on the heel of Owen's words. "You, Holbrook. Don't be a young fool. No mix of yours. Ride out of here."

Missou winked at Owen, called soberly, "With how many bullets in my back?"

"I don't want you, damn it! Nor Rutledge for that matter, if he's sensible; what I want is that Rivera charter. Don't be damned altruistic fools!"

Missou and Owen exchanged grim glances, with the tacit common thought that Bloody Matt could not afford to let either of them live only to become hidden enemies somewhere at his back.

"We're not that foolish," Owen called.

"You've had your warning, Rutledge. Several warnings, in fact. And now your last!"

The sunset blurred into twilight. Owen took a packet of jerky from his saddlebag, removed a strip and tossed the rest across to his companion. As he methodically chewed the tough, fibrous beef to a pulp that would slide down his throat, he saw a low beginning flare of firelight from beyond the bend. His jaws stilled, watching the high-leaping glare band the broad canyon from wall to wall, wipe back the shadows that would conceal a trapped man's exit.

"That ties it," Missou whispered. "We don't slip out, they don't slip in."

Owen digested this, his mind running over the situation . . . Claiborne would doubtless name off guard shifts to keep an alert. Unless they proposed to settle into a dragged-out siege, there was one chance out, a thin one. And Owen, thinking of Cissie M'Kandless' scheming uncle and the girl's danger, knew they must not wait. Except till full darkness. . . . In a whisper he told Missou the plan, and the boy soberly agreed, trying unsuccessfully to hide his reckless delight at this calculated risk.

When night had sabled down the valley for several hours and Owen guessed that Claiborne's tired men would be sleeping except for the guard, he and Missou silently retreated to Missou's camp back in the trees. They worked a half-hour, cutting up their ground sheets into four square pieces each and their ropes into four equal lengths apiece. They folded each piece of tarp several times, lifted each of their horses' feet and tied the pieces securely around the hoof just below the hock.

When they'd finished, Owen straightened, turning to the boy. He saw Missou shiver, guessed that like himself the boy's body was tension-sweated beneath his clothes, then chilled by the bitter mountain night. But Missou murmured, "I'm freezing in my guts. I'm scared, really scared."

Owen felt a warmth toward the boy that his previous cold courage hadn't inspired. He squeezed Missou's wiry arm, hard. "Buck fever. Just follow me, hear?"

"I'm damn well not backing out!"

"I know that." Owen repacked his gear, cinched it behind the cantle, and swung on. He paced the stock-inged bay a few yards across a bare rock surface, was satisfied by the muffled hoof-falls, and then they moved slowly down the valley toward the canyon.

They picked their way at a whispered tread down the boulder-littered canyon floor. Owen, watching the fitful blaze wash the walls ahead, listened for telltale sound. There was none. He edged the bay around the bend, halted at the circle of firelight. Three blanketed forms surrounded the centered fire. The guard sat on a rock against one wall, head bent as he fashioned a cigarette. His rifle leaned between his knees.

Owen slammed in his spurs. The bay launched forward like a released arrow, into the space between the fire and the canyon flank opposite the guard. His face bent almost into the mane, Owen heard the guard's yell as he sped abreast of the fire and on past. Then the pain burst along his back—mingling with the report of the guard's rifle.

Owen reeled, knowing in one shocked instant that the

bullet had angled up into his shoulder muscles, that it was a bad hit. Then the crash of Missou's Colt, the guard's pained yell. Owen held leather with a concentrated desperation, guiding the bay at a dangerous unslackened run up the dark gorge. Missou pounded steadily in his lead . . . a drift of frenzied shouts from the camp behind.

A half-hour later the two of them were crouched between two sheltering slabs of rock beyond the canyon, after achieving its top rim from the slide trail. The waning moon shafted enough faint light between the rocks for Missour to examine Owen's wound and apply a hasty bandage of torn-up shirt. Sitting on the ground, Owen bent his head between his knees, sweated with still-searing pain, fighting off the black, dizzy waves that tided rhythmically against his mind with each breath.

He realized that Missou was shaking him by the shoulder. ". . . can't stay here, Owen. They won't track us farther'n the canyon bottom till come daylight. We got to find a safe place before then."

Owen dredged up a whisper. "Hole up . . . hold 'em off."

"No," Missou said sharply. "That's a bad hole, bullet angled in deep. It's got to be cut out, wound swabbed clean. I seen men die of infected ones. You need proper care, proper dressing."

"Town then . . . Blanco. . . ."

"Sure," Missou said anxiously. "But it's a long ways . . . have to ride all night, and no easy pace. Can you make it?"

"Can if you . . . tie me in saddle."

"But where to in Blanco? They'll be on our tail when it's light enough, they'll come fast. If we're lucky enough to beat 'em into Blanco . . . anyone there who'll hide you?"

Missou's words seemed unreal, echoed from a distant, closing fog. Owen nodded dreamily, whispering, "Why sure. . . ."

FOURTEEN

Virginia Gilchrist prepared a lonely breakfast in her little kitchen. Usually she enjoyed a pleasant daily ritual before school began, eating leisurely and reading for a half-hour over two cups of coffee. But this morning, as for the last two, she barely tasted her food, gulped the coffee quickly. It only gave her a dull heartburn, and she shivered, unwarmed, and drew her faded gray wrapper tighter around her shoulders. She looked at the cold food in her plate, grease-marbled now, and pushed it away in revulsion. Her head ached from sleeplessness. She leaned her elbow on the table, hand rubbing her closed eyes.

What's the matter with you? she asked silently, knowing the answer she was reluctant to admit. The story of Abner's killing by Charlie McVey had been all over town the next morning; the stable hostler, who'd witnessed it, had been able to add nothing to the mystery. *It's terrible, terrible,* Virginia thought . . . remembering the look on Owen Rutledge's face as he'd left her house. To find Charlie, of course.

She shuddered . . . Through the three days and nights that had followed, Virginia had worried out every cranny of her mind, seeing in bitter clarity the insulated self-centeredness of her own existence; realizing with a deep uneasiness that it was Owen Rutledge, not McVey, for whom she was worried. Of course she didn't want Charlie's blood on Owen's hands, though Charlie plainly merited punishment . . . but what if Owen, not McVey, were the one to die? This thought she hated to front most, yet it was most persistent, recurring through sleeping and sleepless fantasies. And with this fresh insight, she could concede the suppressed excitement she'd felt

112

at their first meeting, which had lingered with her. Even McVey had hinted at it.

She felt lost, tired, and hopeless here in her cozy kitchen. Warm tears formed against her palm. *I don't care about the stupid charter. Let him come back alive. Please.*

The back door shook with a hard blow. She glanced up, startled. There was a second, violent beat of a hammered fist. She rose quickly and went over, shot back the bolt. The door was pushed roughly wide.

She saw Owen Rutledge, his head tilted on his chest, weight slumped against a thin-faced young man whose light blue eyes were marred with a harried impatience.

"Miss Gilchrist?"

"Yes . . . but—"

The youth pushed unceremoniously past, and nudging the door shut with his toe, almost unbalanced himself under his companion's weight. Owen was held erect by an involuntary bracing of his legs and an arm thrown around the youth's neck. Virginia saw that both were bearded and filthy, that Owen's clothes were stiff with dried blood; she felt a wave of palsied sickness and fought against it.

The boy, she realized, was speaking impatiently: "No time to lose, ma'am. There a doctor in Blanco?"

She nodded, unable to speak.

"You'll have to get him. Just now we need a place to lay Owen down."

Virginia felt an abrupt, sure calm—a relief from the corroding tension. Owen was here, hurt but alive, and she could help him. She nodded briskly, her tone crisp: "Bring him into my room."

She hurried ahead and opened a door off the parlor, circled the small, neatly made cot as the youth laid Owen's weight gently across it, face down. Virginia turned his head, arranged the pillow beneath it, and looked at the boy. "How did this happen?"

He removed his hat, drew his sleeve across his mouth, talked quickly. Virginia studied his young face, seeing it dark and strained, quietly capable without being hard.

Before he'd finished, Owen groaned softly. She told the boy to lift him a little, and she opened his coat and shirt. Her mouth tightened at what she saw—blood-caked bandages which hadn't halted the copious bleeding. They would have to be soaked off.

She looked up at the boy who was silent now, fidgeting with impatience. "Your name is—?"

"Missou Holbrook, ma'am."

"How did you happen to come here, Mr. Holbrook?"

"Had to bring Owen somewhere. Before passin' out he told me how to find your place . . . no place else he could go."

Virginia felt a quick glad warmth, concealed it coolly: "And you say Matthew Claiborne and his men are following you?"

"Yes'm. Had a good lead on 'em coming out of the foothills, while it was still dark. Owen like he is, it took me a good ten hours gettin' here. Claiborne and his boys would have been on our trail long before dawn. One of 'em's a middlin' fair tracker. Once he picked out our tracks cutting straight for town, they'd be comin' fast. No sign as I rode in, but they must be close. Thing is, will they know where to look?"

"They might make a good guess," Virginia said. "Didn't you say that Owen has my charter—that Claiborne wants it?"

"Yes'm. Beg pardon." Missou dipped into a pocket of Owen's sheepskin and handed the familiar oilcloth sheaf across the bed. She turned it meaninglessly in her hands, then laid it on the bedside stand. She looked up to meet Missou's curious, slightly cold gaze. "Hope it was worth it," he said quietly.

"Nearly at the cost of a good man's life, you mean?"

"Not my words, ma'am," Missou answered stiffly.

"But your meaning. You are right, Mr. Holbrook. And what's to be done now?"

She saw his mood shift grimly on the youthful face. "Now we see to keeping him alive. When Claiborne comes, he'll likely force his way into your house. Unless . . ."

"Unless?"

"Maybe I can lead him off." Missou paused, carefully weighing this. "I'll need a fresh horse. Mine's tuckered, Owen's is almost dead on its feet. I left 'em out back. I'll take 'em to the livery, rent a nag, and wait where I can spot Claiborne when he rides in. I'll ride out where he can see me, cut the dust like I was just leaving town, and ran into him by chance. If they think I got your paper, they'll try ridin' me down."

"But—if they don't?"

Missou thought again, rattled swift directions. Together they eased Owen's inert weight off the bed onto the rug beside it. Missou tugged the low cot over his body. "Providin' they don't give a close look, that should hide him."

Wordlessly Virginia pointed at bloodstains on the wrinkled counterpane. Missou threw back the bedclothes and mussed the sheets and pillow. "When they come, they rouse you out of bed, see. . . . What's your work, ma'am?"

"Why, teaching school."

"You were sick today, stayed abed."

She nodded. "You had better hurry, Mr. Holbrook."

She followed him to the kitchen, where he paused to glance at the soiled breakfast dishes. "I'll hide them," Virginia said. "Please hurry . . . take care."

His face warmed with a heat-lightning grin. "Don't you fret, I'll lose them in short order. I'll come back tonight; we'll figure what's to be done."

"Yes, do that."

His smile thinned, and he was plainly troubled. "Sorry I brought you into this. They're mean-dangerous, playing for keeps. Can't be sure they'd not harm a woman. . . ."

"You did what had to be done. I'll be all right. Hurry now."

After he was gone, Virginia shoved the dishes out of sight in a cupboard and returned to the bedroom. She bent to look at Owen . . . eyes closed in his pale, close-bearded face; breathing noisily through his open mouth. Her heart pounded fearfully . . . he needed medical attention. But she couldn't risk going for Dr. Hart until Claiborne had made his appearance . . . and left.

She fetched a basin of hot water, and some clean cloths, pulled the cot from above Owen and set to soaking away his bandages. Virginia removed the bloody tatters, cleansed the wound as best she could. Fresh blood welled at once from the ugly hole, but now that he was still, the bleeding had lessened. She made a clean compress and affixed it with long strips tied around his chest. As she fumbled with the last knot, she heard commotion in the street . . . a body of horsemen thundering by.

Virginia lifted the cot back into place, shoved the basin and dirty bandages beneath it. She ran from the bedroom and through the parlor. She opened the front door a crack and strained her eyes down the dust-moiled street. Claiborne and his men had pulled up two blocks down. Beyond them a lone rider was heading from town. Missou Holbrook. Matthew Caliborne was nonplussed.

She saw his gaunt height swing in the saddle, his angry shouted orders carrying clearly: "Blaize, take Danny and search that small white house yonder, the Gilchrist woman lives there. Clay and I will go after Holbrook. If you don't find Rutledge or the charter, follow us."

Virginia closed the door and hurried back to her room. She sank onto the edge of her cot, heart pounding angrily. She bit her lip, forced her thoughts steady. Realizing that her hair was neatly arranged atop her head, she unpinned and let down the thick black braids. She thought: *This man Blaize . . . you've seen him on the street. He always tipped his hat, even bowed, though he didn't know you. He's a man a woman can handle.*

With this relieving thought came a soft, insistent tapping at the door. She rose, not too quickly, and went to answer it. Blaize stood hat in hand, a tall, yellow-haired man whose usually bleak eyes were shifting and uneasy; beside him was a barrel-shaped man who met her glance with a slack, arrogant grin.

Virginia gave them a wan, sleepy smile. "Yes?"

"Apologies, ma'am," Blaize muttered, "must ask you

to take us through your house. Looking for a man, believe he might have come here."

She opened the door wider. "This is quite irregular. This man . . . ?"

"You'll be knowin' him. Owen Rutledge."

"Certainly," she said evenly. "And do you think that I admitted him . . . in this state?" She drew the robe closer to her throat, giving him an outraged look.

Blaize reddened and stammered something. The man called Danny drawled amusedly, "Look, lady—"

Blaize's elbow drove viciously against his thick middle. Danny doubled with a wheeze of pain. "Take your hat off," Blaize snarled, and to Virginia with sharp impatience: "Ma'am, I must ask you to move aside. We're searching the house."

"I can hardly prevent you," she said coldly.

She followed them through the rooms. Hand on his gun, Blaize catfooted warily from parlor to kitchen. Danny rolled sullenly in his wake. The Texan's face bore a fixed, uneasy scowl, and he was careful not to look at her. Finally he halted in the doorway of her room.

Virginia stepped up beside him—and her breath constricted sharply. In plain sight on the bedside stand was the cloth-wrapped charter. Frozen, she watched Blaize's gaze idly touch different objects in the room. Trying to hide her desperation she asked, casually: "Aren't you Mr. Blaize?"

He looked at her with surprise. "Why, yes'm."

She smiled up at him. "I really don't have to ask. We've met before, and I was curious enough about your wonderful manners to learn your name." She frowned slightly. "You're certainly the last man I should expect to invade my home."

His dusty boots creaked with a shift of weight, his long face unhappier than ever. "See, this Rutledge fellow killed a man. Lawyer named McVey. We're part of a posse. Ain't inferrin'," he added hastily, "that you'd hide a killer, but it's said he was seen talkin' with you. We wounded him, he'll look to lay low. Could of come here, lied to you to get your help."

"I see," she nodded, covering a sharp, regretful pang at the revelation of McVey's death. "However I had heard that McVey murdered Mr. Rutledge's Negro friend. . . ."

"All the same, can't take law into his own hands thataway."

"Of course not," she said primly. "As to Mr. Rutledge's being seen with me, that is correct. I had hired him—for a small errand; that was the limit of our relations." She pressed her fingers to her temples. "I'm sorry; I don't feel well—"

Blaize studied her face mercilessly. "You ain't seen him since?"

"I have not," she lied proudly.

"For crissake," Danny began disgustedly. Blaize's soft tones razored off his speech. "You heard the lady, and we looked."

"There's a dozen places—"

"Danny."

The short man shrank from the unveiled warning in Blaize's look. He said no more. Virginia nodded demurely to the Texan's stumbled apology as she showed them to the door. When it closed behind them, she leaned against it a moment, knees weak and her body trembling wildly. When she had herself under control, she returned to the bedroom and hauled the bed away from Owen.

She'd noticed, with mingled fear and relief when Blaize approached the room, that the hurt man was utterly silent. Bending close now she saw with a flood of thankfulness that he was breathing quietly but evenly. The wound dressings were freshly stained, the bleeding not quite checked. *But Dr. Hart will have to probe for the bullet.*

She steeled her thoughts again, went to her small closet and opened it. She hesitated, feeling a warm flush along her veins as she glanced at the unconscious man. Angry at her shamed modesty, she moved the closet door ajar to cut her off from sight of him. *Mock maiden stupidity,* she berated herself coldly as she let the robe and nightgown slip to the floor.

Irresistibly she felt her eyes drawn to the tall tarnished

mirror above the commode across the room. *Too thin,* she thought critically, even as the reflection mocked her with a small ivory image slender and graceful as a New England birch, yet gentling into soft curves and hollows. She was aware of the man again, now with a hot, quickening excitement that was alien and frightening.

She dressed quickly and almost ran from the room. By the time she reached the street, walking prim and straight-backed toward the doctor's office, her expression was again an ivory-modeled coolness. But her thoughts were a disturbed tumult . . . her ideas of love were of a story-book variety, often read, never experienced. *What is this?* she wondered. *What's happening to me?*

FIFTEEN

Reed M'Kandless stood on the wide front veranda of Lionclaw's main house, one pudgy hand toying with the watchchain on his Marseilles-silken waistcoat, the other stroking his spade beard. His crafty eyes were troubled and faintly baffled.

He had not expected this afterwash of conscience when he'd casually suggested to Matthew Claiborne that his sister's daughter be put out of the way. He hadn't counted on the time-blurred memories that had swarmed back on him later, when he was alone and could fully consider this enormity to which he was now committed. He had remembered Cissie as a child, her chubby little arms circling his neck, or as a baby cooing and gurgling on his knee.

He'd told himself that those memories belonged to another place and time and world, when he was still an amiable young rakehell loafing off his family's bounty. A hundred things had since corroded a warm uncle-niece affection into a mutual, barely tolerating, dislike. Now the girl was only an obstacle to his greed, a danger to his security. Cushing Tierney, guerrilla, would have casually and ruthlessly crushed the irritant. But seven years of ease had softened Cushing Tierney in more than body; he shrank from the notion of arranging this murder that must appear accidental. If only he could personally avoid the sight and touch of her death . . . and then he thought he'd seen a way out.

Before Claiborne had left to run down Owen Rutledge, his men had ordered out the ranch crew at gunpoint with all their belongings—save for one man, Bob Fitz. Fitz's arm had been shattered by the bullet he'd taken resisting the invaders; that was adequate excuse to keep Fitz bedridden awhile. When Claiborne had gone, Reed had personally set Fitz's arm, left him with a bottle of whiskey for his pain.

Reed was not worried that the other crewmen might return. They would drift from the basin, workaday cowhands with no stomach for standing up to Claiborne's gunnies. Loyalty to the colonel might have held them, but the colonel was dead. Of a heart attack, they were told. The shot which had killed him was explained away as a warning slug Claiborne had fired over Reed's head. Only the segundo Paul Dirksen might offer a problem; he was not a man to run. But Dirksen had left with the others, his iron will holding him in the saddle, nursing a wounded side. Dirksen would be no trouble for at least a time.

That, Reed thought now, left Owen Rutledge and Claiborne himself. He'd hoped that Claiborne and Rutledge might kill each other in the ensuing chase. Both were potential dangers not merely to his plans but to his life. He shivered, remembering Rutledge's face; next time there would be no reprieve. As for his forced alliance with Claiborne, he'd as soon have bargained with the devil. In the ex-military careerist was a ruthless greed to match his own, and except for Cissie, Reed alone knew how Colonel M'Kandless had met his death.

Reed had also realized belatedly how Claiborne's coun-

ter-knowledge of his identity might be actually turned to
a weapon in Claiborne's hands. Once they were safely
partnered in secure ownership of Lionclaw, Claiborne's
partner could be shot and his body turned over to the
Territorial Marshal with Claiborne's claim that he'd un-
covered the fact of Reed's true identity, had confronted
him with it—and was forced to shoot.

Reed had considered it all carefully. Claiborne needed
him alive a while yet—but he did not need Matthew Claiborne. Once rid of Claiborne, he must find and destroy
both Virginia Gilchrist's Spanish charter and Claiborne's
Mexican grant. Then his position was secured. Baldly
stated, these objectives were simple. But there were a
hundred complications in the doing. . . .

More than thirty hours had passed since Claiborne
had pursued Owen Rutledge north from Lionclaw.
One or both of them might be dead by now; Rutledge had had the Rivera charter; it might now be
in Claiborne's possession. . . .

Reed shook his head. *Cross your bridges as they come,*
he thought coldly. Just now there was Cissie. . . . If he
handled Fitz properly, that problem was as good as elimi-
nated.

He stepped off the veranda and walked down the gravel
drive toward the bunkhouse. The early sunlight was warm
and bright, the rich lawn still dew-sparkling. *A good time
for someone to die,* he thought ironically.

Nearing the bunkhouse, he heard Cissie's low murmur
within, then Fitz's angry, drink-slurred curse. "Gedadda
here, you overgrowed witch!" Something hit the wall with
a clatter.

Cissie came out, walking fast, her face an angry pink
save where the ugly dark bruise left by Claiborne's fist
mottled her jaw.

"What seems to be the trouble?" Reed asked mildly.

She threw out a hand helplessly. "I only wanted to
make him comfortable. I spent fifteen minutes trying to
reason with him. He was obviously in pain, but wouldn't
let me touch him . . . then he threw a bottle at me."

"Perhaps I can make him listen."

"You?" There was faint contempt in her tone, and he knew she was thinking of how, as they had buried her father in the little cemetery plot by his wife, back of the house, he had counciled passive acceptance of their situation, saying that he'd try to dicker with Claiborne to prevent further violence. She'd passionately replied that since there were no men left on Lionclaw, she would shoot her father's murderer herself when he returned. *Which would solve part of my trouble nicely,* Reed thought now with sour amusement. Looking into her clear, angry hazel eyes, he knew another pang of regret, but a brief one.

"I can try. Prove I'm not wholly the foppish coward you think."

"Well," she said grudgingly, "be careful then. He has a gun, must have had it hidden beneath his bunk." Claiborne had appropriated all the crew's weapons. She ignored Reed's word of thanks, striding past him toward the house.

Reed stepped through the low doorway, and walked casually to Fitz's bunk. The small man was reclining with his head lifted, watching his visitor with bloodshot, pain-filled eyes. His pale bony torso was naked, gleaming with sweat, one arm splinted and fixed in a cloth sling. A heavy Colt lay across his belly.

"Goddamn it," he whispered viciously, "get me a doc, can't you!"

Reed squatted down, rocking back on his heels. "Your arm's fixed as good as any sawbones could do. I set a lot of broken limbs in the war. It's rough, eh, Fitz?"

"God, yes." Fitz's husky whisper was drunkenly slurred. "Got another bottle some'eres?"

"Might be another in the house, I'd have to look," Reed said idly. He was silent a moment, broaching this cautiously: "She bother you any?"

"That overgrowed witch!" The hateful edge returned to Fitz's tone. "She'd of liked to make like she was fussing over me whilst she schemed ways to make me hurt more . . . them big ones is all alike. Mean, rotten stinkin' mean. . . ."

"I know," Reed said sympathetically, but his smile was one of icy satisfaction. He'd noted long ago that Fitz was full of a stupid and lazy man's empty, half-hearted daydreams. Such a man could only fail at whatever he attempted. Over Fitz's life, frustration and failure had become rutted into a single bitter channel which was his excuse for self-failure: his unreasoning, savage hatred of larger people, men and women. Now, after two days of festering in a welter of whiskey and pain and self-pity, he'd be easy handling.

Reed drew a deep breath, plunged with a point-blank query: "Fitz, could you kill someone for a thousand dollars?"

Fitz's thin lips formed a wolfish grin. "Who you want dead that bad, mister?"

"Her. The girl. Cissie."

Fitz's jaw dropped slackly. "Jesus," he said softly. "You mean it, don't you?"

Reed talked very quietly and carefully, repeating himself over and over to etch how it must be done into Fitz's drunken brain. It had to look like an accident ... and here was five hundred in advance. He drew a sheaf of bills from his pocket, money that he'd removed earlier from the colonel's safe.

"Damn," Fitz whispered, his eyes shining feverishly, eagerly. Then they dulled with a flicker of fear. "Woman-killin' ... bad business."

Reed pressed it mercilessly. "I recall your bragging, in one of your sweet tempers, how you once knifed a big Mex girl down in Sonora."

"That bitch," Fitz muttered. "Laughed at me. A cheap crib whore. And she laughed at me ... 'dirty little gringo with a face like a rat,' she called me!" His voice rose to an agonized frenzy.

"You'll never be anything but a little man, Fitz," Reed went on brutally. He slapped his hand across the Colt's as Fitz tried feebly to bring it up. "A little man trying to play a big one. That's if you continue to play it like a big man. But a man with money can be anything he wants. He can have the big girls crawling at his feet."

Reed's voice lowered to a hiss. "Think of that, Fitz . . . a thousand dollars at one time is more than you'll ever see as a thirty-and-found cownurse. Properly invested in a small ranch, a business, that thousand could carry you to anything you want to be. And handled as I told you, the girl's death will never be considered other than an unfortunate accident."

Fitz stared at him open-mouthed. If he was small on brain, he had more than his share of cocky ego. "Why sure," he whispered. "All I ever needed was a chance. Nobody never give me a decent chance. . . ."

A half-hour later Reed stood on the veranda, thumbs tucked in his waistcoat pockets, smiling his self-content as he watched Fitz and Cissie ride down the ranch road toward town. Fitz, he'd told Cissie, had regretted his behavior, and he had persuaded the little man to go to town and have Dr. Hart look at his arm. As Fitz was in a bad way, it would be kindly of Cissie to see that he made the nine-mile ride all right. Impressed by her uncle's tactful handling of the vicious little man, Cissie had readily agreed.

And that is the end of Cissie, Reed thought contentedly, watching the pair grow smaller on the long road . . . relieved that a dirty job had passed out of his hands. Of course sooner or later, in one of his drunken stupors, Fitz would brag how he'd been hired by Reed M'Kandless to murder his own niece. But Fitz must return to collect the balance of his pay; one bullet, and the body safely disposed of, would eradicate future danger. Nobody would think twice of the disappearance of a dirty, disagreeable little saddle tramp.

Reed turned his attention to the problem of Matthew Claiborne. He decided to wait here the rest of the day; if Claiborne hadn't appeared by then, he'd go into Blanco. Claiborne might have returned there for some reason. Once their leader was taken care of, his hired gunnies would not take up the fight.

SIXTEEN

When he spurred out of Blanco, Missou Holbrook had
less than a hundred yard lead on Matthew Claiborne.
Still he wasn't greatly worried. On a fresh livery mount,
he should easily out-distance the pursuit.

He let his nag out at an easy lope, pacing them at first
and holding to open country to lead them on. He looked
back and saw only two riders in his wake. The other pair
would be searching Virginia Gilchrist's house. Though
he'd half-expected as much, swift uneasiness touched
Missou; would their thin preparations fool Claiborne's
toughs? Bloody Matt himself would not be easily misled.
But Missou couldn't tell at this distance whether the leader
was one of the pair on his trail.

To the north Missou saw a lift of broken formations,
and he veered that way in an all-out run. The livery
horse was an ugly jug-headed brute who fought the bit,
but he was long-limbed, rangy and powerful. The mile-
eating pace pulled them quickly near the broken area,
which Missou now identified as a single formation composed of barren granite ridges, cut by winding gorges and
littered with jumbled boulders. He headed up a narrow
trail which brought him quickly to the crest of a ridge.
He pulled in to scan his backtrail.

The two riders had not only fallen behind, but had
pulled to a halt. The other two were coming from town
at a hard gallop. They reached the waiting pair, merged
into a brief, tight group to confer. Then all of them
spurred on toward the ridges. An exuberant lift of relief
drew Missou's quick grin. If they'd found Owen and the
charter, they'd not be resuming a fruitless chase; now he
meant to lose them in short order.

He came off the ridge, descended into a winding gorge, cut off into the first cross-canyon. Here it was all sheer travel over naked rock that left no sign. Missou worked roughly east through a tortured labyrinth of gorges, holding his bearings between the steep walls by the sun. Finally he emerged into an off-tapering of gentle sand hills. Confident that he'd shaken pursuit for good, he continued to swing west, now in a wide circle which he judged should bring him out on the straight road connecting town and Lionclaw headquarters.

He had ridden out the previous weary night getting Owen Rutledge, lashed to his saddle, safely into Blanco. Most of that time Owen had slumped unconscious or babbled in first delirium, but Missou remembered vividly his last rational words: "You see to Cissie M'Kandless; help her."

Missou had seen the girl only briefly on that day when Owen had braced Ivy North to save her father; he had taken away a swift impression of her youth and shyness and inexperience. If her uncle was all Owen had said, she'd need help badly. But Reed M'Kandless had had many hours to plan his move, and Missou could command only a near-despairing hope that he wasn't too late.

An hour's hard-driven pace across rolling country brought Missou out on the well-rutted Lionclaw main road. He promptly turned due west, guessing he wasn't more than three miles from the ranch headquarters.

The road was heavily bordered with tangled clumps of ocotillo and ironwood. Missou came to a dead halt at a strange, low sound from a thicket. He cantered his mount across the road and down a brushy aisle, hand on gunbutt and ready for anything. He caught the sound again and distinctly: a low, pain-tight voice little more than a broken whisper.

"Over here, son—over here."

Missou turned his head and saw him not twenty feet distant—a lean, long-faced man lying on his back beneath the thicket's edge. His head was raised, face twisted with pain. Missou dismounted, snatching his canteen from the saddle, and ran to the man. He stooped, lifted his head.

The man drank, leaned his head back with a sigh against Missou's supporting hand.

"Heard your horse. Too weak to look—but had to take chance you was a friend."

"My name's Holbrook." Missou frowned at the man's blood-soaked shirt.

"Dirksen . . . Paul Dirksen. Segundo at Lionclaw." Dirksen's hand clamped with a startling reservoir of strength on Missou's shoulder. "Boy, you got to save her . . . got to. . . ."

"Take it easy. You mean Miss M'Kandless by chance?"

"How—you know?"

Missou busied himself opening Dirksen's shirt as he answered. He undid the blood-plastered cloth tied around the body, winced at sight of the undressed wound beneath a wadded bandanna. Then he held Dirksen half-erect to ease off the man's shirt and tear it into strips for a fresh compress and bandage. Again Dirksen's hand caught his shoulder. "No time—for that. I got the strength to see to it. Say you're Owen Rutledge's friend?"

"That's right." Missou added as he carefully drew Dirksen deeper into brushy shade, "What's this about Miss M'Kandless?"

With jerky haste Dirksen told how, after leaving Lionclaw with his crew, he had deliberately fallen behind the others halfway to town, headed back for the ranch. Never having trusted the colonel's brother, he had anticipated Cissie M'Kandless' danger. But with a not-then serious wound pumping blood at each movement, he'd shortly been forced to dismount and rest. In so doing, he had lost a stirrup and fallen heavily. While he lay stunned, the animal had drifted away. Dirksen had tried to walk, but passed out from the effort. Coming to, he had crawled into the roadside brush and waited through half-conscious intervals for someone to come by.

About a quarter hour ago, he'd heard the approach of riders. He had fought to his knees to peer through the brush screen. He'd made out Fitz—an injured crewman who hadn't left Lionclaw with the others—and Cissie

M'Kandless coming along the road toward town. Abruptly Fitz had halted and pulled a gun. They were still too
distant for Dirksen to hear their speech, but Fitz had
forced Cissie off the road at gunpoint. The two were
soon lost to sight across the wild range to the south.

"Fitz's a mean 'un," Dirksen whispered. "I make it
he was hired by her uncle to do away with the girl. Don't
know what Reed has brewin', but. . . ." His voice sank
and trailed away.

Missou rose, studied the man on the ground. "You're
one tough old rawhider. Held out this long. Think you
can make it a while longer?"

"Never mind . . . you find them. Stop Fitz. But take
care. Mean 'un. . . ."

"Be back soon's I can."

Without more words, Missou went to his horse, leaving his canteen by Dirksen. For the segundo's sake as
well as the girl's, Missou prayed that Fitz hadn't gotten far.

He quickly found where they had left the road, and
he followed up, tracking easily from the saddle. Their
mounts' hoofs had left deep conical depressions in the
sandy ground amidst the desert vegetation that laced
this desolate, unused strip of Lionclaw range. A perfect
place to murder a young girl. . . . Once he had picked
out the line of trail, Missou moved fast.

He heard the gurgling flow of a creek before he came
on it. Cutting east and west across the heart of Lionclaw,
it was a swift deep current which no horse would ford.
The tracks turned east along the steep cutbank, which
Missou followed. He drew in hard at the first sound of
voices ahead. They came from a clump of young willow
trees lining the cutbank.

Missou swung down and slid on his hunkers down the
cutbank. Its high slope would cut him off from an
above view. He loped crouching, gun in hand, along the
water's edge, and sank down a few yards from the voices,
listening with held breath.

"Fitz," the girl was pleading softly, "let me go. I'll

leave Blanco Basin. My uncle will never know what happened, and you'll still get your money."

"You'd talk, you big bitch, blab it all over. . . ." The man's voice was slurred with pain and liquor and weakness, and Missou thought: *He's out of his head and about on his last legs.*

She said desperately, "But I swear—!"

"Girly," Fitz interrupted in a husky, wicked whisper, "What makes you think old Fitz don't *want* to kill you?"

Missou's palms were clammy with the knowledge that his first shot must be accurate, clear of the willows fringing the bank. He had to get almost beneath Fitz. He rose to edge farther up the bank. He saw Fitz's head and upper back, but not the girl.

"Accident, girly," Fitz went on, almost crooning it. "I'll jis' bust your neck with a few good stiff swings of this here gun . . . throw your carcass over the bank. Hoss threw you, see? Accident. . . ."

Missou suddenly straightened, bringing his gun up. The shift of weight to his heel crumpled the moist earth; to keep his footing Missou floundered back into the water. His foot plunged from the shallows into a drop-off and he fought for balance, caught it with a wild splashing.

Fitz was already turning, his six-gun arcing tightly around with this body. Missou flung forward and down as Fitz's gun roared. Missou lay on his belly with his upper body clear of the water and now he lifted his gun at the end of his extended arm as Fitz, cursing, stepped to the edge of the cutbank to shoot down. His narrow, vicious features cleared the rim, Missou gently moved his arm to fix the sights, firing on the instant.

Fitz's head rocked with the impact which flung him back from sight. Missou scrambled to his feet and up the cutbank. He half-climbed, half-fell over it—and stopped on his knees, sheathing his gun. The slug had taken Fitz, asprawl on his back, under the jaw and ranged up through the top of his skull. Missou felt his stomach lurch, set his teeth, and got to his feet.

The girl leaned against a willow tree, hands covering her face, shoulders shaking. With a soft moan she turned against him, burying her face in his shoulder. And Missou let a solicitous question die unspoken, and held her, wordlessly and awkwardly.

SEVENTEEN

Tempered to hard times, Owen's bull-like constitution needed only a few hours of sleep and rest to begin the healing. He was jarred to a few fuzzy, pain-filled rational moments when the doctor went after the bullet embedded in his shoulder, and then he passed out. He came achingly awake to the distant voices of Virginia and the doctor conferring by his bedside, afterward slept again, soundly.

It was full dark when he blinked awake once more and became drowsily aware of where he was. He saw a lamplit crack beneath the bedroom door. "Miss Gilchrist."

His voice came as a parched whisper; he cleared his throat and called again. Virginia's quick footsteps came and she opened the door, paused there slimly silhouetted against the parlor light before moving to the cot. Her cool fingers touched his cheek. "You're feverish, try to rest some more. . . ."

"No." His voice was strong, his mind fought against the pain that throbbed afresh at his first movement. "Where's Missou?"

She was silent and he could not make out her face, but guessed that she was debating how much to tell him. Then she did speak, clearly relating how Missou had brought him here, hidden him and then tolled Claiborne out of town, though she'd had to bluff off two of his men. When she lapsed to silence, he said impatiently, "Well?"

Her shake of head was a weary little gesture. "I don't know. He promised to come back tonight. He hasn't come. But neither have Claiborne and his men returned . . . and your friend had a fresh horse. That's all I know, honestly."

"He tell you what happened before?"

She nodded mutely.

Owen dropped his head against the pillow, not looking at her, coldly berating himself for telling Missou to bring him here, placing her in this danger. A hurt and hunted animal's first instinct was sanctuary; in that same instinct he must have felt that no one but Virginia Gilchrist would give him sanctuary. Yet why turn to this prim and sheltered girl when only impersonal or bitter words had passed between them? And there was McVey, he reminded himself wearily.

"You know . . . I caught up with your friend?"

"Charlie?" she said in a small voice. "Yes. I know." Even as his lips formed apology, regret, she spoke quickly, yet painfully. "Don't, please. I know what your reason was—yet there must have been more to it—than Abner."

He stirred his head in a nod, looked back at the dark ceiling.

"I made arrangement for Abner's burial," she went on gently. "But listen, Owen . . . there was nothing more than casual friendship between Charlie and me. Not that, perhaps. We quarreled before you came—that night."

His gaze sought her half-seen face. "You want to hear why I was after him, why he killed Ab?"

"Yes—very much."

When he had finished, Virginia spoke quickly with a warm glad note to it. "I knew you had to have a reason, a just reason. I don't know how, but I knew." She sobered then. "But a terrible reason too . . . to follow three men all these years—"

Owen felt a hot lift of wrath. "They deserved it. And more. I wish I could make them pay all over. A hundred times over—"

"I don't mean that!" Her vehemence matched his own. ". . . What this has done to you—dedicating your life to a thing of hate. That isn't right. You can't go on this way forever!"

"Don't intend to," he muttered. "No longer'n it takes to get Cushing Tierney."

Virginia abruptly knelt by the cot. "Let him go, Owen." The angry response that trembled on his lips was dissipated by wonder for the desperate, pleading intensity of her. "Somewhere you have to make an end of it. Why not here? Let the authorities have him. If you don't . . . you're lost."

He wanted to snap that she was talking nonsense, but somewhere in his mind a nagging voice had long been telling him the same thing. He would kill Tierney, the last of the five who had murdered his family—and what then? The single purpose that had motivated his life for seven years would be finished, done. He would be, as Virginia said, a man lost, without hope or anchor. He had given Missou Holbrook good advice—*a man needs a reason*—and now in bitter clarity reared the stunted ugliness of his own central purpose, the reason he'd almost used up.

If there was a forked road in a man's life where only sheer will power could stay him from a wrong turn, he, Owen Rutledge, had reached it. He had to change before he lost even the will to change. Like young Holbrook, he was the kind of man who needed more than workaday existence and creature comforts to go on living; Virginia had seen this clearly. For a moment he almost hated her for that clear insight that made him face himself. It prompted him to lash out bitterly.

"What do you know of life? Even out here you've lived like a hothouse flower, insulating yourself in your comfortable past. And feelings? You don't have any. Except to get something for nothing, like that Rivera grant—"

Even as he spoke Owen felt a lurch of shame; if not for Virginia's instant courage, he'd be dead now. But he wasn't prepared for the stinging lash of her reply:

"What do *you* know of my past? You, born into a well-to-do family, good society, attending fine schools. You had every chance, now see yourself—rotted out with hate and revenge. *My* people were already bankrupt when I was born . . . oh, but a man wouldn't understand, men like to rough it. They leave the women to weep over the worn-out clothes they have to sew and re-sew, the family possessions they have to sell to keep a small larder filled, the drunken whining fathers they have to support. But then my father was sick—that was always his excuse—"

She bent her face against the cot, sobbing quietly. Owen touched her shoulder, murmuring tiredly that he hadn't known and fervently wishing he were elsewhere.

Her voice came muffled and broken: "You were right —about my feelings. I'm cold. Even Charlie McVey had said so. I don't want to be that way—I don't!"

"It's all right."

"No, it isn't!" She raised her tear-streaked face. Dimly seen, it looked wide-eyed and lost, like a little girl's. "I —I suppose everyone who's known nothing but poverty dreams of being rich. But most of them outgrow it—find happiness in what they have, like those poor people in Mextown. But that silly charter gave me a hope that made me shut out everything else."

"Times in some people's lives," Owen said gently, "when they've used up everything but hope. You had that right, Virginia."

"And what has my hope done? Brought a blood-thirsty gang after you and that boy, forced you to kill a man, almost got you killed. And God knows where that boy is, what's happened to him—"

Owen moved his hand gently, absently, on her shoulder, thinking grimly of Missou. Of Cissie M'Kandless too. If Missou had eluded Claiborne, he'd probably head for Lionclaw to help the girl, as Owen remembered telling him. The boy and girl both were in danger . . . and he and Virginia, too.

"We'll have to get out of here."

"But you're—"

"Now," he said inexorably. "This place isn't safe. Claiborne'll be back. You won't bluff him as you did his men."

"Can you walk?" she asked anxiously.

"I've got to." With the support of her arms and shoulder, he heaved to a sitting position, teeth set against the pain, and next to his feet. He closed his eyes against a wave of gray dizziness, took a few steps. "Let go," he told Virginia, and as she stepped away he started walking, setting his weight with infinite care on each step.

He moved out to the little kitchen while Virginia went ahead to light a candle on the kitchen table. Owen surveyed the pantry shelves, said, "Pack a grubsack. Some blankets. We'll make a camp a ways out of town. I'll get the horses, come back here for you." He smiled. "And don't forget your charter."

"Maybe if we left the charter for Claiborne—"

"Too late for that. He'll be like a mad wolf on the trail by this time. Nothing less than our lives'll satisfy him. If he finds us—"

"Can you make it to the stable?" She came nearer to him, watching his face worriedly.

"Sure." He took a careless step to prove it, at once lost his balance. Virginia caught at him and they swayed together off balance. His arms went around her as his hip struck the table edge painfully, and, "Oh Lord," Virginia gasped.

A current of air from the open window guttered the candle flame. As it sank and died, his head tipped down and in the dark his lips found hers. Unbelievingly he felt the firm small body melt against him without resistance, her mouth clung to his with a seeking, desperate passion.

He moved her away at last, breathing heavily. He touched her face lightly, awkwardly let his hand fall. "I'll be back fast as I can," he said huskily. "Now don't think about this, just hurry, get your things together."

EIGHTEEN

Owen moved carefully down the main street boardwalk toward the livery stable, holding to the gallery shadows, pausing often to rest his good shoulder against a building façade as his eyes raked up and down the near-deserted street. His wound blazed astir from its throbbing ache to flashes of wrenching pain that made him swallow against nausea. The night held a chill. His sheepskin was thrown over his shoulders; even that slight weight was an added discomfort. He kept his hand on his gun, grateful for a good right arm.

He reached the livery, turned into its wide archway, and paused to scan the lighted runway, seeing nothing of the hostler. He opened his mouth to hail the man, but stopped at the first sound of grouped horsemen moving upstreet from the north end of town.

He gave the street only a fleeting glance—saw the four riders coming abreast—stumbled deeper into the stable, his heart racing hammerblows against his injured shoulder. Claiborne had returned, and his first stop would be the stable.

Owen lurched into an empty stall piled with loose hay. He shrank between the stall partitions and hastily arranged a mound of straw over his legs and body. Lying prone, he drew more above his face, not enough to obscure his vision. He eased out his pistol and cocked it.

Motionless and scarcely breathing, Owen watched the four drooping riders, Claiborne in the lead, file past not two yards distant. They moved out of his sight; he heard their leather-creaking dismount. Claiborne roughly called for the hostler. Owen heard the man emerge from the rear office, begin a surly complaint which he swiftly choked off. Owen had only glimpsed the four but they were plainly hard-ridden, tired, and angry. He heard the hostler lead off the horses, then the men's low-voiced conversation.

". . . wasted too much time trying to find the kid," Claiborne said between his teeth. "Then got separated in those canyons, didn't find each other till nearly dark. Meanwhile that girl and Rutledge are probably laughing up their sleeves at us . . . with good reason."

"I told you—" began one man in a low, edged drawl, but Bloody Matt cut him off savagely.

"Just shut up, Blaize. I should have thought before sending *you* to search her place . . . but I've had time to think—most of a dirty sweaty day crawling through heat and brush and rocks. Rutledge was seen going with the Gilchrist girl to her house the very day he arrived in Blanco. I hazard that she hired him to find out who stole her precious charter. And we know that Clay wounded Rutledge when he and the kid broke past us last night. Of course the kid took Rutledge to her house! Where else would they go?"

"Blaize wouldn't make no kind of real search of the place this mornin'," rasped a vindictive voice.

"Of course, Danny," Claiborne murmured. "That's my point exactly."

"If that's so," Blaize drawled softly, "waste of time goin' back there. They've had time to clear out, go into hidin'."

"Maybe. Maybe not."

"Maybe not," Blaize echoed gently. "But you so much as touch that lady . . ."

There was a hiss of gunmetal clearing leather. "I've had about enough of your misguided chivalry, my friend," Claiborne declared harshly. "Now—we are going to pay a call on the lady. My gun will be trained on you the while. Move out!"

Owen watched the four move past toward the archway, Blaize tramping sullenly ahead of Claiborne's leveled pistol. Owen waited till they reached the street. He sheathed his gun and raised his good hand to grasp the stall partition. With a steady tugging pull he inched to his feet, stepped into the archway, his gun palmed again. A twist of his shoulders shed the bulky sheepskin.

There was no choice now. Half-dead on his feet, he couldn't skirt the rear of the buildings and reach Virginia's before they did. But could he take four of them?

It could be done. It had been done. In Wichita a year ago, he'd seen a half-dozen toughs choose a youth named Masterson. When the smoke had cleared, the six sprawled dead or wounded; Masterson walked away unhit. Afterward Owen had bought him a drink, asked him a question. *I had an edge*, Masterson had said. *A desperate man has got an edge.*

And now Owen could understand the cold truth of those words. There was no time to think of odds . . . no time to wonder whether his pain-wracked body could take the slam of his pistol's recoil.

He moved carefully erect to the archway, paused in its wide embrasure. The four were heading down the street. One favored his right leg, doubtless the man who'd wounded Owen and was in turn shot by Missou. The thickset man glanced idly back at Owen's steps. . . .

His shrill warning word halted the others, and they came about. Perhaps ten yards distant.

"Rutledge?" Claiborne called around the bobbing cherry-glow of his cheroot.

"All right," Owen said between his teeth. *Take Claiborne out first, the others may fold.*

"I feel generous, Rutledge . . . one final warning. You can't take all of us."

"I'll take you, then." Owen swung the cocked pistol up.

Claiborne flung himself sideways bellowing: "Scatter—spread out!" as his hand streaked for his gun. He hit the dirt on his side as Owen's weapon roared. It was a high miss; a store window behind Bloody Matt collapsed in a glassy jangle.

Owen lunged for shelter of the archway jamb, realizing in a cold detached relief that his body was numbly responding to the moment's desperate demand, awkwardly but painlessly. Claiborne was on his feet, running for a watertrough across the street. He lunged behind it as Owen fired again. The slug gouted a sparkling jet of water from the trough.

Blaize, too, faded back to the shelter of the watertrough, firing as he went. The small man called Clay limped toward another alley. The thick-bodied one, Danny, doggedly stood his ground with his short legs wide-braced, pumping bullets at the archway. Owen sank down in a tight crouch, hugging the wall. Slugs ripped through above his head, others furrowed into the clay floor. He heard Clay shout at Danny to take cover.

Owen stuck his head out for an instant, bore down and fired. Danny was lumbering toward Clay's alley, and now he pitched a few stumbling steps and fell across a tie rail. It split explosively beneath his bulk and dumped him in the dirt. He didn't move.

Claiborne and Blaize and Clay opened a concerted fire. Owen flattened out along the clay floor a second before the flimsy wall where he'd crouched was torn and riddled with slugs.

"Hold fire," Blaize called. "That must've got him. . . ."

Owen heard footsteps pound across the opposite boardwalk. He peered out and saw Blaize coming. The Texan caught Owen's movement and veered in his run, still coming on across the street. But toward a side alley.

Claiborne's exultant yell: "That's it, Blaize . . . get to the rear stable door, get behind him—"

Owen's arm jolted as he pulled trigger. And knew he'd missed; now Blaize was safely across, and cut off from his view.

Then farther downstreet another gun spoke. Blaize stumbled out to view again. He was hit, trying to bring his gun to bear on Owen's sudden ally, whom Owen in his prone position could not see. Blaize's shot merged with the unseen gun's second roar, and Blaize spun and went down on a knee—sprawled on his face soddenly. Saw the rider pulling up a fiddlefooting horse in the center of the street.

It was Missou Holbrook.

Owen did not wait now. He stepped out of the stable,

took two steps, and stopped as Matthew Claiborne reared up from the sheltering trough with a single baffled cry. He began firing at Owen, lifting his arm each time and bringing it down as though trying to throw each shot with a crazed violence. Owen's arm lifted and the sights hung steady and then he shot. Claiborne seemed to topple backward with slow trance-like grace. His gun clattered on the sidewalk boards. He fell out of sight behind the trough.

Owen only glanced at Clay as the small man threw his gun away and stepped out, hands high in mute token. Owen crossed to Claiborne and turned the body over with his foot. Paper crackled inside the dead man's bloody vest. Owen stooped and drew it out. Old and faded paper, the Armijo grant. Owen stuffed it in his pocket and trudged back to Missou who was off · his horse and bending over Blaize's crumpled form. The boy glanced up, shook his head, and only then sheathed his gun.

· "Something . . . this blooding of a man," he said shakily.

Owen said nothing, only shook his head and looked at Clay on his knees by Danny. The little man's ferret face lifted, meeting their stares with a bitter cold defiance.

"Danny's still alive. You'll finish it, I reckon. Go ahead. Make it both of us."

"He your partner?" Owen asked tonelessly.

Clay nodded.

"All right," Owen said very quietly and distinctly. "Get him to the doctor's. On your own, weasel-face. When he can ride, the two of you ride out."

Clay spat in his direction with one long look of unrelenting hate, and bent back to his friend. Owen's numb attention was pulled around by the rattle of a buckboard merging out of the lower street's darkness. He recognized Cissie M'Kandless on the high seat. Missou went to help her down. The girl was pale and exhausted, but unhurt, Owen saw with relief.

He stood nodding wearily as he listened to Missou tell what had happened. Townspeople began gathering about timidly in murmuring groups.

". . . went back to Lionclaw and got the buckboard
to pick up Dirksen on our way in," Missou concluded.
"He's in the wagon bed. Bad off, but alive."

Owen frowned, trying sluggishly to recall the question
he wanted to frame. "Oh . . . you didn't see Reed M'Kandless—Tierney?"

"No sign of him on the place," Missou stated flatly. "No
time to really look though, he might've seen us coming,
lit out. . . ." He paused, peering anxiously into Owen's
face. "Can you make it to Miss Gilchrist's?"

"I'm all right." Owen forced strength into the words.
"You and Miss Cissie get Dirksen to Doc Hart's. Come on
to the house after . . ." He felt the energy reserve that had
sustained him swim away in a gray blur—felt the hot
wetness crawl down his back. His wound had opened
again.

Holding himself stiffly erect, he turned on a heel and
went up the street. He saw a slim figure running toward
him . . . her light dress a pale blur against the night.
"Owen, Owen!" she sobbed. . . .

She had almost reached him when the shot came. Gun-
flame blazed from an alley to Owen's right. Owen felt a
slug's whistling breath and turned with its sound, his gun
out. There was a rush of retreating feet within the black
areaway. Owen yelled hoarsely for Virginia to keep back.
Again his mind swung back to urgent focus, held it
tightly.

He went up the alley, walking fast. He blundered
against a trash can, moved around it and reached the
yard at the other end, drenched in window light from
the adjacent buildings.

He came stock-still. Reed M'Kandless, the breath sobbing wildly in his throat, stood on a box by the high
board fence that enclosed the yard, trying clumsily to
heave his stout body over it. The box buckled beneath
his weight and he dropped his gun to grab wildly at the
fence top. Its splintered edge gouged his fingers and he
cried out and went down in a quivering heap. All his
nerve was gone; he stared with a hypnotic fascination
at the man towering above him.

Owen kicked his gun out of reach. "Wait long, Tierney?"

"I wasn't waiting for you," Reed whispered huskily. ". . . For Claiborne."

"The bargain went sour, eh? But you'd settle for me. Well . . . doesn't matter now, does it?"

"Owen."

Virginia's hushed, pleading voice behind him did not make him turn. He reached down and fisted a handful of Cushing Tierney's coat, dragging the sagging bulk upright against the fence. He jammed his gun against the man's soft throat.

In the back of his mind he was waiting for Virginia to object again. Her skirt rustled faintly and he heard her quick breathing—nothing more. She was leaving it in his hands now. The moment for which he'd prayed was here, crowding him to decision. Kill Tierney or have him turned over to the law. What was the law?—a cold and dispassionate machine, man-made authority that could not sit in judgment on this moment for which he'd waited these long years. He was the judge here, and the jury . . . and yet he hesitated and the verdict could not wait. It must be now. Or never.

"All right, Virginia. . . ." His breath sighed from his lungs and his fist unclenched, and Cushing Tierney sank down in a sobbing heap at his feet.

Somehow Missou Holbrook was standing by him, taking the gun from his hand; Owen turned and took one long step and felt himself falling, never seeming to hit the ground. And endless vault of blackness caught him up and bore him away.

There was a pinpoint of light at the end of that black tunnel and his mind climbed doggedly toward it, and his eyes fought open. He knew Virginia's room, and the small cot where he lay, and a familiar face hovering above him. It was all a little dizzy and remote, yet clear enough.

"Coming along, old-timer?" Missou asked cheerfully.

The light hurt Owen's eyes, and he stiffly turned his

head on the pillow and saw with amazement high sunlight streaming mote-hazed through the east window.

"Lucky dog got his sleep," Missou observed with mock envy. "Doc Hart fixed you up . . . we-all have been waiting on you. Oh, Doc says Paul Dirksen'll pull through. Close thing with him."

His voice brought quick footsteps from the parlor; Virginia and Cissie entered. There was open relief and thankfulness in Virginia's face as she knelt by the cot, her eyes never leaving his face.

"Hope you settled that damnfool property by now," Owen whispered light-headedly.

Virginia's smile was tender and tolerant. "We have, sir. I'd be happy to tear up the charter—but Cissie insists that the four of us share alike."

"Four . . . us?"

"Well—we found the Armijo grant in your pocket . . . couldn't think who else it might belong to. There's my grant, too, and Cissie, as the colonel's only heir, also has a valid claim." She spoke lightly, yet with a deep and sure meaning. "With three valid claims around, Cissie thinks it'll be simplest, and certainly most just, considering all that we owe you and Mr. Holbrook, if she has partnership papers drawn up to include the four of us in Lionclaw ownership. Then we could destroy those two old grants . . . they have caused enough trouble."

Owen looked at Cissie, seeing the still-numb grief behind her quiet smile. In these few days she'd come quickly beyond girlhood. Yet he saw her sideglance touch Missou with a kindling warmth.

"Boy," she said softly, "you do want in on this?"

"Boy, eh," Missou said grimly. "I make I got a good three years over you."

"But you never did say your name," Cissie murmured contritely. "That silly Missou, that's no name."

Owen chuckled. Missou swallowed, his face flushing and faintly outraged. "Martin. Martin Holbrook. And I don't need any presents."

So Missou had found his reason and had renewed his young dreams into a reality. And Cissie had a shining new knight to whom she might look up. It was as well, Owen thought wryly; his own armor felt fairly tarnished. Cissie looked at him and at Virginia, and she took Missou's arm. "Come along, Martin, and we'll argue about presents."

When they had gone, Virginia was silent for a time, her hand absently stroking his forehead. She said at last, almost reluctantly, "Missou locked Tierney in a warehouse down the street . . . he's taking him to the Territorial Marshal's office at Santa Fe." Her eyes held dark and uncertain on his. "Owen, you did mean to let him live, didn't you? It was no mistake."

"Head was clear enough, I knew what I was doing," he answered gruffly.

Her face, warm and glowing, leaned close to his. "You did fight him, didn't you? And won?"

"His nerve gave out. No credit of mine."

"I didn't mean Tierney. Owen Rutledge was the man you had to fight. I had to know," she said gently, "that you had beat him," and her lips came to his in a soft rush.

RAMROD
RIDER

CHAPTER 1

A GRAY, STEADY RAIN FELL FAR INTO THE MORNING. IT streamed in silvery torrents off rocks and ledges, and lashed a tight grove of young aspen which stood like glistening specters beyond the cave mouth. Standing under a granite overhang which shelved the low entrance, Wes Trevannon thought, *This is the day for sure*.

He leaned a shoulder against the rock, hands jammed in his pockets, a tall and big-boned man of thirty-five. Broad in no part of his body, he wore soft faded denims which emphasized an all-over rawhide leanness. His bony face was long and somber, not quite homely. His sun-bleached yellow hair was shaggy and untrimmed, eyes deep-set and of a slatey off-gray, eyes that held a sort of alert and positive self-certainty mingled with an indifferent cynicism. When a gust of wind-lashed rain matted his hair against his bare head, he shook himself and turned back into the cave which briefly bisected a steep hillside.

Two horses were hobbled at the rear of the cave. Trevannon's own sugans were neatly rolled and lay by his saddle; on the other side of the dead fire, Cal Kittredge snored on in his blankets. Trevannon went to him, bent and shook him by the shoulder.

Kittredge groaned and sat blearily upright. Ran his long pale hands over dark thinning hair and yawned. He was a slight and graying man of fifty whose once fine and aquiline features were mercilessly highlighted by the dead-gray

daylight, showing deeply incised lines of dissipation, folds
of slack flesh below the chin. He started to speak, this single
effort setting off a violent fit of coughing. He reached
beneath his blankets and drew out a square flask. Uncapped
it and pulled deeply.

Trevannon watched this familiar ritual with a neutral
patience. He said with no reproof, "Better wait till after."

Kittredge lowered the flask. Ruddy fever spots glowed in
his sallow cheeks. "You're right." He grinned. "Some
medicine, though." His hand dipped into a waistcoat pocket
of his shabby, sleep-wrinkled black suit, and drew out a
gold watch on a tarnished chain. "Ten to eight, eh?" He
heaved to his feet and hobbled in his sock feet to the cave
mouth, squinting out at the dreary morning. "By God.
This'll be it. Our day, man. When did it start?"

"Storm broke about midnight. Slackened off some now,
but it's holding steady."

"Perfect so far. Now if the bank opens punctually at
eight . . ."

Travannon nodded. "Let's get started."

He went to a rock shelf running along the cave wall,
lifted down twin bundles, and tossed one to Kittredge. No
words were necessary, for they had rehearsed the details two
days ago. The bundles contained identical patched and well-
worn slickers, battered hats, run-down half boots, and faded
red bandannas. When each had donned his outfit, they made
two anonymously similar figures, the long, shapeless
slickers concealing them from neck to boot-tops, except that
Trevannon was a head taller. They saddled their horses,
packed on their gear and rode out from the cave, immediately swinging southeast.

They rode steadily for a quarter of an hour, crossing a
range of brush-clogged hills hazily cloaked in the smoky
downpour of rain. They descended the steep switchbacks of
a final slope and rode down into the town of Cedar Wells.

Collars turned high and hats tugged low, the slicker-
shrouded pair headed down the sweep of rain-pocked mud
that was the main street. Misty rows of ramshackle false

fronts flanked its wagon-channeled length. Trevannon gave the first building, a fairly new brick structure, a brief attention because it housed the sheriff's office.

His straight mouth formed a smile. *Square under the nose of that damned Dutchman,* he thought, with no personal malice to it. He knew of Sheriff Jans Vandermeer only what he'd heard, and that was enough. Covering this great, sprawling New Mexico county of his jurisdiction, with its broken wilderness and mountain terrain, was no cinch, but Vandermeer, with his handful of deputies, was said to do so with dogged efficiency.

Trevannon had dryly observed as much to Cal Kittredge when the consumptive little gambler had approached him with the scheme. Kittredge dealt faro at the Lucky Angel Casino and daily banked the house winnings. Fall round-up on this plateau range was over, and the cattle buyers had already left, leaving the town bank bulging with the local cattlemen's cash proceeds. Kittredge had taken careful note of the bank safe. A ponderous, old-fashioned affair, ill-suited to handle the flush of prosperity the local ranches had suddenly known after many lean years . . . a few good ones had added up to a small fortune in that battered old safe.

Cal Kittredge meant to take it. But he needed a companion who could handle trouble. He watched the men who came and went. Chose Wes Trevannon, an out-at-the-heels drifter with a ready-worn gun, who came in one night for a quiet game. Kittredge had played as he'd never played, till Trevannon's small stack of chips was heaped at his own elbow. Then he'd leaned across the table.

"Trying to build up your stake, eh, friend?"

"Was," Trevannon said dryly.

"No offense, but you're puny odds in this game. Just now I'm thinking of another kind. Something in your looks says that you're the man I want." He'd paused deliberately. "Run to the law with it, and I'll name you a liar."

"What law?" Trevannon had murmured, and then: "I'm listening."

When Kittredge had outlined the job, Trevannon voiced his doubts—first, about going up against the iron-stubborn tenacity of a sheriff whom lawbreakers might outwit for a time but could rarely lose. Secondly, about the slim chances of only two men pulling a daylight holdup. Kittredge had the answer: the rainy fall weather was moving in. He, Kittredge, would quit his job here, buy up food supplies, and pack them up to a cave he had found a mile north of town. Later Trevannon would join him. So far as the townsfolk would know, both would have ridden on separately.

They would set up camp and wait for a day of bad weather, when few or no citizens would be stirring abroad in Cedar Wells. Even on ordinary days, the bank's business was generally poor for an hour after it opened. Heavy rain would minimize the likelihood of interruption during the few minutes they'd need, would help them pass unnoticed in and out of town, and would quickly obliterate their trail. Even Jans Vandermeer would be baffled, especially if they swiftly lost themselves in the brushy hills above Cedar Wells. They would line out in a due southerly route toward Mexico; in a few days they'd be well beyond Cedar Wells County and its dogged sheriff. . . .

Trevannon felt the cold fist of tension close around his guts as they cantered diagonally across to the bank tie rail midway down the street. Swinging down, he fought back the feeling, looped his reins around the crosspole.

Standing by their horses, the two men swiftly opened their slickers enough to be able to reach their guns easily. They drew up their bandannas to cover noses and mouths. Kittredge ducked beneath the tie rail and crossed the rain-slick sidewalk to the bank entrance, Trevannon at his heels. They palmed out their guns as they went through the double doors.

A young clerk stood behind the half-partition that enclosed his cage, leaning his elbows on his window counter, his thin, precise mouth touched by a smile at something the other clerk had said. He casually turned his head as the doors opened, then his tall thin body froze and his smile went wooden. The other was a slight, gray-haired man who was sweeping the floor, his back to them. He turned with gouty unhaste at the other's sudden silence. "Dave, what the—" The old man broke off, seeing the masks and guns, let the broom clatter to the floor as he raised his hands.

Kittredge crossed the room and thrust his gun across the counter. "Open the safe. Fast and no tricks. Fill that, large bills only—I'll be watching." He shoved a grain sack under the bars.

The young clerk stood dumbfounded. His mouth worked a little, like a fish's out of water.

"Fast, I said!"

The clerk did move then, scurrying down on his knees by the bulky old safe. His thin fingers twirled the dial. Trevannon had remained by the door, dividing his attention between the street outside and the elderly clerk, who hadn't stirred a muscle.

Kittredge shifted his feet, the creak of a floorboard very loud in a stillness broken only by the blind ticking of the square-faced wall clock. He snapped, "Shag into it."

"Missed a turn," the young clerk whispered, not looking up. His sweating brow gleamed palely.

Wes felt a nervous pulse begin its drumroll against his temples; he could only guess at Kittredge's state of mind. But the combination was suddenly completed; the cashier turned the handle. The door swung wide. A grate of steel on steel as a drawer was pulled out, and another. The slicker was a roasting, air-tight confinement, and sweat drops broke out on Trevannon's face and ran in a stinging wash into his eyes. He blinked them away.

The clerk held up the bulging sack. Kittredge said, "On your feet and bring it over. Do it slowly. . . ."

The clerk carefully obeyed, sliding the bag across the counter. Kittredge blindly snatched it up and swung for the doors. At once the clerk's hand slashed down beneath the

counter, came up with a small-caliber pistol. Trevannon's
gun lifted chest-high and he shot. The clerk gave a howl of
pain. Kittredge pivoted back as the young man slumped
across the counter, clutching his arm.

Kittredge started to bring up his gun; Trevannon stepped
forward and batted his arm down. "That shot'll bring half
the town," he grated. "Come on—move!"

He sprinted out the door with Kittredge at his heels. They
were on their horses and reining about within seconds, but
already Trevannon was dimly aware of shouting men
pouring from doorways along the street. Trevannon raked
the flanks of his bright bay gelding, and Kittredge numbly
followed his lead. They lined out down the street at a hard
run, leaning low in their saddles. Some fugitive shots
bellowed in their wake as one or two armed townsmen
rallied enough to open up.

They reached street's end and careened their horses
around the last building, cutting off from the street. Wes
reined aside to let Kittredge take the lead, and the gambler
blindly spurred his horse into a heavy thicket. Branches
backlashed wetly against their faces and bodies. Kittredge
burst through onto a grassy slope and spurred savagely to its
crest. Trevannon was directly behind as they rode down the
other side into a timbered vale, and then he hauled up beside
Kittredge and grasped his reins, bringing him to a halt.

"Let go, you damned fool!"

Trevannon's acid speech ate coldly into the man's terror.
"Get a hold on yourself! Said you had a route figured out
that'd take us up into the back country off the beaten way.
You're running blind—get on it!"

Kittredge rubbed a shaky palm over his wet face. "Sorry.
Yes. All right. We strike up south along that hogback
ridge." He pointed. "It'll take us five miles away from
town and we'll never hit a road or a house."

Fifteen minutes later they were riding the summit of the
long ridge. They would have been skylined here, save for
the thick pine cover; needle-fall made a springy carpet that
left no sign beneath their horses' hoofs. Kittredge breathed

easier, now free of his clutching panic that had almost wrecked the operation.

He said mildly, "I owe you a vote of thanks. Lost my head."

"Damnfool thing, turning your back on a man you just robbed."

"I was lucky. You were there. Paid your way for sure."

The grain sack slung from his saddlehorn brushed Kittredge's knee; he reached down and touched its papery contents with a soft, sly smile. Trevannon had seen the smile before; it had come to him strongly that Cal Kittredge was no man to trust—a consideration which hadn't worried him then. But now they were two men alone with a grain sack containing a small fortune, and Kittredge no longer needed him.

The thin smile held on Kittredge's face as he studied Trevannon's impassive one. "Man, no wonder you didn't do well at faro; you're a poker player."

"But I don't gamble with stakes this high," Trevannon said softly, flatly. "Don't fall behind me, Cal."

Kittredge chuckled; it set off a retching spasm of coughing that doubled his frail frame. He straightened, gasping for breath. He nodded at the old game trail that followed the ridge summit, winding between two pine boles. "Well, it's a fine broad patch . . . and I've no particular disposition to trust you either, m'lad. We'll ride abreast."

Together they gigged their animals into motion, watching one another from the tails of their eyes. Trevannon observed narrowly that the trail just ahead began to pinch down; a bit farther, a huge pine grew from its center, dividing it. His muscles pulled tense as he neck-reined his mount toward the right to pass on that side of the pine. As the tree's bulk passed between them, he dropped his hand to brush back his slicker skirt and expose his holstered gun.

Even so, the quickness of Kittredge's maneuver caught him by surprise. In the brief instant that the treetrunk concealed him, Kittredge magically produced a gun. As their horses moved past the tree, the little weapon barked in his fist. Trevannon was already half-twisted in the saddle to face his companion, at the same time lifting his Colt from leather, when the gambler fired. Wes felt the wrenching blow in his side. Then the Colt came up in a tight arc and bellowed close to his body, beneath his half-raised left arm.

Kittredge's body rose and tilted sidelong. A thin hand fumbled at his pommel in a dying effort to brace himself. He coughed once and rolled slackly from his saddle. His horse bolted and dragged its rider, foot hung in the stirrup, a half dozen yards before pulling to a halt.

Trevannon sheathed his gun. He looked at Kittredge's still body as it swayed grotesquely to a slight motion of his mount. *He had to have it all. The poor bastard. He had to have all the money, and it got rougher'n ever he dreamed.*

CHAPTER 2

HE STEADIED HIS FIDDLE-FOOTING ANIMAL BEFORE DIS-
mounting to check his wound. He stripped off his slicker,
tattered denim jacket, and calico shirt, and dropped them to
the ground. He had to crane his head over his shoulder to
see where the bullet had entered; it had cut cleanly through
the fleshy part high in his left underarm. Kittredge had shot
point-blank but hastily; the hurt was not serious, though
bleeding copiously from back and front. As the numbness
of the bullet's impact receded, the wound burned like fire.

Trevannon unknotted his neckerchief and, catching an
end in his teeth, passed it around the triceps muscle tight
against the wound, tied it tightly. He didn't judge the hurt
grave enough to cause immediate concern, though it needed
better attention.

Aware of the wet chill biting to his bones, Wes quickly
picked up his clothes and shrugged gingerly into them. He
tramped over to Kittredge's horse and it shied away, skittish
with the smell of blood. He quieted it with a hand on the
reins and the good quiet words that men use to animals.
Loosened Kittredge's hung-up foot from the stirrup and let it
thud soddenly to the ground. Threw the worn saddle gear
off the horse and cut it across the rump with the bridle. It
bolted back down the trail.

Trevannon knelt by Kittredge to search his clothing. The
gun caught his eye—a silver-mounted English pocket pistol

that hugged the dead man's wrist, concealed by the sleeve, held there by a slender length of elastic which would stretch with a snap of the forearm, dropping it smoothly into the palm. Trevannon's lips tightened as he went through the pockets. There was only the watch, a fine, well-worn piece with an inscription on its inner case: *To Calvin on His Sixteenth Birthday, from Father;* and a flat wallet containing, except for a few silver dollars, only an old and faded daguerreotype of a young and sweet-faced girl.

For a moment Trevannon pondered over these slender tokens of a gentle upbringing that yet summed up a wasted lifetime. Then, decisively, returned them to the dead man's pockets. He gathered up the body and carried it into a deep thicket, laid it out on the bare ground in an awkward semblance of sleeping dignity. He returned for the saddle and bridle and left these by the corpse. To dig a permanent grave and rock-shore it against scavengers would take hours; he had neither the time nor the strength for the job. The brief exertion blazed abrupt pain into his wound, which had settled to a throbbing ache.

He returned to his horse carrying the sack of money, looped it over the horn. Stood a moment with an arm slung across the saddle swell, thinking. . . . Sheriff Vandermeer would be especially incensed by this daylight holdup pulled nearly under his nose, and wouldn't rest till he'd found the men. That meant, Trevannon thought, that he must waste no time in getting beyond the range of posses, holding the while to deep cover away from roads and human habitations. And he was handicapped, as Vandermeer was not, by his ignorance of this country to which his scattered driftings hadn't previously taken him.

He had depended on asking directions of Kittredge before they parted. During idle talks in their cave, the gambler had mentioned only that the ridge tapered off five miles south. What lay beyond, Wes had no inkling. Still, the ridge would take him that much farther from Cedar Wells; then he'd play the tune by ear. They had covered perhaps a mile when

Kittredge had made his treacherous move. Trevannon wondered whether the shots might have been heard by a tracking posse; Jans Vandermeer would be swiftly on the trail, and no telling how far or near he was at this moment. . . .

The thought galvanized him to movement. He toed into the stirrup, swung stiffly astride, and kicked the bay gelding forward. His animal was unusually big and rangy, long-legged and sound of wind, a stayer. That much was in his favor. In a chase he should hold an easy lead on his pursuers.

Riding the game path between the monotonous walls of dark, flanking pines, Wes Trevannon's mind was drained to numb tiredness by the flurry of violence; his thoughts drifted.

Lucy, Lucy, if you had only lived. . . . That's right, Trevannon, make her your excuse; blame the dead. All right, all right; it wasn't just Lucy or the boy dying, there were plenty of other things. . . .

When had he really stopped giving a damn? A ranch, a wife, a son, self-respect. A poor man slaved for years, drove himself on a shoestring and a dream, to win such things. Then one by one the shorings of his life were stripped away. First four bloody years of war that shattered a man's ideals and human illusions. Returning to Texas to find his wife and five-year-old son living in poverty, his cattle running wild with no market in prospect. Two years of barest existence. Mortgaging finally to the hilt for the means to round up his wild longhorns and drive them north to Abilene, booming new railroad mecca for the impoverished Texas cattlemen. Two weeks later seeing his herd, dead and dying of Texas Fever, strewn for miles along the banks of the Red River. Returning home in the wake of a sudden typhus epidemic to find his son dead, his wife nearly gone.

Remember the good we had together, Wes. Forget the rest. Almost Lucy's last words, those. Only later, when grief had dulled, had he realized how she'd been telling him to draw strength from that part of memory which framed their life together, the strength that he would need alone. And he'd failed. . . . Self-respect was the last mooring he'd lost, and to his shame it had been easily swept away.

First the penny-ante brand-blotting to restock his range. Soon irate neighbors had come with the law; he'd cleared out ahead of them. Threw in with a wild bunch of ex-jayhawkers who were raiding the northbound trail herds. Quick, crooked money, quickly thrown away in company with trigger-wild companions . . . hard-drinking nights and bloody brawls in the wide-open Kansas trail towns. Always in the background the hurts he wanted to forget, till he was past caring even of forgetfulness. And the driftings, always aimless, to keep ahead of the memories you couldn't outride.

Odd though; all those other things, the brand-blotting, the rustling, brawlings and shootings, had been wild and spontaneous, part of a savage outpour of grief. Years had passed since he had buried his family. Strangely, when he'd ridden into Cedar Wells a couple of days ago, it was as though the blunted edge of that grief, his very indifference, had been in itself a healing, or a start of healing. He had been obscurely and drunkenly toying with that thought over his cards and whiskey when Kittredge had announced his plan. This planned holdup had been his first truly calculated act of crime. Why, if he'd begun to feel his way back to manhood?

Maybe that was it. Maybe he had needed to hit rock-bottom before he was ripe for a change. That, Wes realized wryly, didn't make sense; but neither did this sudden keen and lifting exultance in him, in spite of the danger he faced. An hour ago he hadn't cared whether he lived or died. Now he wanted to taste what life held next. It was as though in casting over the past, worrying out each dreary fact, he'd opened a sore and flushed it clean.

A half-hour later he left the ridge at its southern off-tapering tip and continued to push blindly south, aligning landmarks to hold a straight route. No other way to get direction, but it made for long delays, pushing through alternate bands of heavy timber and brush that pummeled and punished horse and rider. The rain was increasing again, belching windlashed gust against their leaning bodies. Chill and dampness worked beneath the collar and skirt of Trevannon's slicker till he was drenched and shivering. Impatience drove him like a galling spur.

When he broke from the forest onto a stretch of wagon road that evidently belonged to an outlying ranch, he didn't hesitate to follow its twisting, muddy ribbon southeast. The anvil-blows of thunder mounted with the flicker of lightning, drowning all other sound. And so he paced the bay around a sharp turn and ran almost head-on into a tight group of coming riders before he heard them.

Trevannon yanked his horse around so swiftly the animal reared, nearly unseating him. He had only that glimpse of the dark shapes of horses and men in the beating rain, and then he spurred headlong into the flanking forest, hearing a heavily accented voice boom an order from bellows-like lungs. Vandermeer of course . . . the old law-dog knew the fugitives must cross the roads, doubtless had his posses distributed at every strategic point. He'd had the bad fortune to run into the sheriff's own group. . . .

Wes heard the crash of brush in his wake as the posse men followed into the timber. There was an outbreak of scattered shots, this ceasing at another bull-roared order by the sheriff. The men were milling disconcertedly through the trees; stray or ricocheting slugs could find anyone.

Trevannon tight-reined his first panicked reaction, forced himself to maneuver at a discreet pace through the wood. He didn't want to fight these men, nor would he be taken alive if he could avoid it; the bank job plus other blots on his backtrail would add to years in prison.

He cut suddenly from a straight flight into a right-angle turn and plunged across a glade into dripping underbrush. Dismounted in the dense foliage, held a hand over his horse's muzzle and waited. The sound of nearing pursuers grew; he caught sight of several through the trees; then they were past and the sounds of their going drifted away.

Trevannon rubbed a hand over his clammy face, his heart pounding painfully in his chest. Too close. Only cover of the storm's murk and noise had spared him certain capture. Now Vandermeer would concentrate his full effort on this area, infiltrate it and cordon it with men. Already a pale blaze along the horizon indicated a clearing sky as the storm clouds rocketed on toward the west. There were yet hours of daylight ahead.

One thing—he thinks you're pushing south now. But when he don't find your trail, he'll come back. Gives you a breathing space. Use it.

Trevannon turned due east and held to the timber till it became sparse and patchy. He could be easily spotted on these open flats, but for now he must think only of gaining distance. He lost track of time as the sky disgorged its final volley of wind and rain, as the steady rocking pace of his horse, held in to conserve its strength, became a monotonous cadence.

Leaving the last trees, he was puzzled to see a vast sweep of gray distance open before him and soon, a little farther on, he understood. This was a high tableland, and now he remembered hearing that its eastern edge ended above the rich grasslands of the lower county. From here the land dropped steeply away in rocky terraces to a distant valley floor. The first terrace slopes looked treacherous, but appeared to taper at a gentler grade toward the bottom. This would be tricky to negotiate, but he wanted to get off the flats; to turn back would almost certainly blunder him into another posse—of men who knew the terrain, who would harry him and drive his back to a wall.

He rode paralleling the rimrock, scanning its fallaway to the first terrace. It wasn't too steep at this point, but plainly laced with treacherous slides and potholes. A man afoot could traverse it easily, but a mounted man would be forced to dismount and lead his horse slowly and painstakingly to its base, repeating this pattern for the next several terraces.

Trevannon halted on the bank of a deep, broad wash, ordinarily dry, but now become a boiling torrent confined by its steep walls. Over ages of beating out a storm-fed track, the wash had scored deep into the rimrock and had worn a fairly easy slant down through the sharp upper terraces. In dry weather it might afford easy passage; to tackle it now would be to risk death by drowning, by being crushed with the flood's resistless force against the rocky banks.

He reined back from the wash, only to iron-hand his bay to a dead halt. Riders were leaving the fringe of timber he'd quitted, coming on without haste. Still perhaps a hundred yards distant, they'd have spotted him at once on the bare rim. Vandermeer had quickly divined his crude ruse, and had backtracked to simply follow out his broken trail through the brush.

They were in no hurry, fanning out in a broad line as they closed the gap. Trevannon made out the glint of drawn weapons, but they could afford to hold fire. Caught between the rim and a line of riders, he could only surrender, make a hopeless fight, or . . .

Wes made his decision. And savagely rammed steel into the bay's sides, launching it like an arrow toward the flooded gully. He heard a posse man's yell as he plunged down the bank. The bay's braced legs skidded stiffly against crumbling talus, then hit the current.

Feeling the animal's powerful surge of muscles as it fought for footing on the slick pebbly stream-bed, Trevannon was tensed for immediate disaster. And found to his surprise that the muddy flow swirled little more than fetlock-deep at this point.

He kicked the bay downstream. Directly ahead the banks pinched narrow and rose to form a wide, steep-walled gorge. The water deepened as it neared this increased confinement. Trevannon hesitated, was swiftly decided by the nearing drift of shouts as the posse swarmed toward the wash. He drove recklessly into the gorge, was quickly lost in its winding turns. The walls heightened; sharp twists cut off view ahead beyond a few yards. And now he knew a trapped and primitive panic as the walls continued to narrow and the flood gained depth and fury, threatening to sweep horse and rider like corks before it.

Suddenly the bay plunged to its knees in a hidden drop, then rolled ponderously sidelong. Trevannon kicked free of his stirrups, flung himself outward, and was immediately drenched. He staggered to his feet, choking and sputtering, grabbed the reins as the bay floundered to its feet. For a moment he faced down-gorge and his heart sank—the walls tapered to a crevice only a couple of yards wide into which the flood roared darkly.

The bay would be rushed off its feet if they went on . . . but the rain-fed waters were piling up swiftly behind. Ride it out to the bottom or be drowned . . . hope the gorge would peter out and widen on the lower levels. With this thought he toed into the stirrup, savagely squeezing the horse forward before he was securely in leather. The bay shied, but then lunged down the turgid channel. The walls closed about them with a solid, oppressive gloom, and the roar of water was a shattering echo.

As he felt the horse lose its fight for sound footing, Trevannon left the saddle and clung with a deathlike grip to his pommel. The horse churned frantically to avoid the flinty walls. An unseen abutment battered Trevannon's hurt shoulder, numbing it and his whole arm. He clung desperately to the horn with his good hand.

Suddenly the watery corridor widened; daylight showed a wide break ahead. At once the water lost force; Trevannon felt the bay's iron shoes grate as it clambered to solid rock underfoot. Again the walls tapered down to low banks. With a last rallied effort of his bruised and aching body, Trevannon heaved himself across the saddle and reined out of the shallowing flow, climbing a low hillock.

He reeled from his saddle and fell face down. Breathed into the wet earth and grass against his face and realized fully what he'd nearly forgotten so long ago . . . that life was a very good thing.

When he had regained his breath he rolled to a squatting position, took his bearings. He was on a midway terrace, past the worst of the steep upper heights. The lower terraces sloping gradually to the valley floor were covered by a heavy growth of trees and thickets that would cut him off from the plateau rim, and he could make his easy way to the bottom.

The pursuers would not follow, he felt certain; he doubted that even Vandermeer could rally any of the counterjumpers who composed his posse to continue the search. Their quarry had slipped through their grasp; they'd be wet, tired, disgusted, and busily convincing each other that he was a goner. Of course the sheriff himself would take no chance; when the gully ran dry, he'd search for the body.

Trevannon eased carefully to his feet. His upper body was a mass of bruises; pain tore savagely at his shoulder. He rubbed his right hip and then stiffened, frowning. He ripped open the slicker and found his pistol gone. Doubtless slipped from his holster when he'd flung himself from his falling horse up the gully.

He released an unsettled breath. At least he had killed any immediate pursuit. He could pick up another gun later—if he needed it. He hoped not; his decision from the dark road he'd forged out had been no whim. *Don't make yourself any promises outside that,* he cautioned himself now. *Life don't let a man deal his own hand. Pick up your cards as they fall.*

Wes mounted up again and took his way through the brush cover of the lower terraces, emerging onto the flats below which rolled gently away to gray-dim meadows and forests. He hit up a southeasterly route at a brisk clip, holding to belts of woodland till he was well beyond the plateau wall, and then struck out across rolling graze. A

slight fever throbbed behind his temples and a burning thirst
drove him to drain his canteen.

Shortly he hit a twisting, low-banked creek, but the water
was roiled and muddy from the rains. He came down off the
bay to kneel down and bathe his hot face, then noted that the
last black clouds were drifting on; the storm was over. He
paused long enough to shed his slicker and tie it behind his
cantle. He emptied a saddlebag and transferred the sack of
money to it, also his gunbelt and empty holster, cramming
his belongings back on top and belting down the flap.
Afterward he followed the stream, hoping it would bring
him to a ranch headquarters or a settler's cabin. A hot meal
and a night's sleep would put him back in shape, and he
could secretly apply a decent dressing to his wound.

Time and again he spooked up bunches of shorthorn
cattle grazing along the stream bottom. They were fat and
moved sluggishly, and he noted the brand—KC. This, then,
was the giant Kaysee ranch, actually a small cattle empire
renowned throughout the territory, as was its owner, Kilrain
Carter. His realm might be small as compared to John
Chisum's, but his name was legendary in cattle country
fame.

As he was wondering how near was the closest lineshack
on this farflung range, Trevannon crested the brow of a rise
and saw spread out below a vast labyrinth of corrals and
buildings—Kaysee headquarters. He smiled wryly as he
gigged the bay down the long slope, thinking that his brief
visit here would add a minor tidbit to the campfire yarns
spun about Kilrain Carter . . . of how a wounded bankrobber took advantage of the rancher's hospitality and rode
on undetected.

Wes saw a wedge of mounted men, evidently the crew,
splitting off from the working part of the layout on the side
opposite to that where he was riding in. Evidently the crew
was leaving their home base now the storm had passed.

Minutes later he cantered his horse across the deserted

compound between two big haysheds, intending to head for
the cookshack which he'd spotted from the slope. Then he
reined sharply in, at once nerve-strung and wary, as a
shotgun bellowed, its single blast beating down the afternoon stillness.

CHAPTER 3

As THE BLACK CLOUDS DROVE ON TO THE EAST AND breaking sunlight swept away the iron pallor of their shadows before it, Andrea Carter stepped onto the roofed front veranda of Kaysee's big, jerry-built main house and breathed deeply of the sharp sweet air. She gave her husband a glance and an absent smile.

"A fine day after all, Kil."

Kilrain Carter glanced at his young wife with heavy-handed irony, grunted dryly, "Fine, now we get in a half day's work," and stomped off the veranda to head across to the corrals.

Andrea watched him go, feeling as she always did that sense of childish awe she might have felt for a stern grandparent. It wasn't only the more than thirty years' difference in their ages. Kilrain Carter was still a giant unbent by the time and trials that marked his harsh, rugged face. Imposing in leather *chaparejos,* a white broadcloth shirt with string tie, and a flat-crowned black Stetson with a sun-glittering hatband of silver conches, he looked what he was: a man who'd pulled himself by his bootstraps to solid power and prosperity. Andrea no longer thought much of the disparity in their ages, the lack of romance in their union, or even Kil's half-tolerant, half-disdainful treatment of her; she had come to lean on his solid, rooted-in-the-earth strength.

Her attention now strayed lightly to the small commotion

over by the breaking corral. The crew had already trooped up from the bunkhouse; it looked as though Tige would tackle that blue mustang today after all.

With a sense of eager thrill, Andrea hurried across the drenched yard. She automatically avoided the puddles, the skirt of her dark blue dress of watered silk lifted a few discreet inches. It fitted her poised slimness perfectly, and the shining auburn coils of her hair contrasted with the faultless ivory of her complexion which sun and wind never seemed to touch. Andrea knew exactly how she looked, was attentive to every detail in her surface thoughts, and didn't really care in the least.

She felt a certain naughty amusement at the way the hands nudged each other as she approached—*keep the talk clean, boys*. Kilrain Carter stood by with hands on hips, looking on with thin patience; he wanted the crew on range, but he always shrewdly gauged their moods. Push them to the limit, but never tamper with their small pleasures; all hands had looked forward to watching Tige Menefee break the blue. Kil gave her an irritable glance, disliking her presence here, but he said nothing—as though he read her mood equally well. Andrea loved such spectacles.

She felt a man move to her side, identifying his rank, sweat-sour smell before she glanced at him.

"Ought to be a great scrap, missus," Bill Treat observed, his sly, milky stare flickering over her before settling on her face.

Treat was a solid block of a man, not tall, in his early forties. His cuffed-back Stetson showed a tight cluster of flaxen-white hair above a broad and brutal face. That curly forelock, Andrea always thought, completed the man's likeness to a ringy bull. Yet his secretive ways confused her; the blunt hungers he barely held in leash made her uneasy.

She started to reach for her heliotrope-scented handkerchief, checked the gesture, and smiled graciously. She murmured, "I'm sure it will be, Mr. Treat," before moving a step away from the stocky foreman. Mostly she considered him a minor unpleasantness which she avoided when she could. Kilrain boasted of the man, called him the best damned ramrod in the territory, so she couldn't easily snub him. Treat showed his small icy grin and moved off.

Tige Menefee, the wrangler, stepped with fluid grace between the corral poles and walked to the snubbing post where a stable hand was holding the blue. Menefee was a white-Ute breed, a wiry, cat-flanked man whose mahogany-colored face was scored by a deep scar which pulled his mouth into a perpetual ugly grimace. Andrea felt his opaque eyes, like pools of shiny tar, swing briefly to rest on her, eyes that flickered for a moment with more than an Indian inscrutability. Andrea felt a quick warmth, as she might for an adoring pup. Tige's awed worship was much nicer than the attitude of that damned smelly foreman.

The big blue stood quietly, though every muscle in his body quivered with a wonderful activity beneath the shimmering, steel-blue coat. Tige cinched on a double-rigged Porter hull, adjusted a braided hackamore with its knot against the tender part of the horse's jaw. Tige could be cruel of necessity, but he had a sixth sense for horseflesh; as he worked, he spoke quietly to the animal in a silvery, flowing Indian dialect unlike his harsh, rarely-used English gutturals. Andrea could see how the animal steadied to his sensitive hands and voice; getting saddle and bridle on an unbroken horse could be a savage chore in itself. Tige had hardly bothered to condition the blue to the gear perviously, yet he had it on in seconds.

Tige was in the saddle with a graceful twist; he nodded to the stable hand, who whipped off the blindfold, let the horse go, and raced for the safety of the fence. . . .

It was a magnificent thing to watch, the blue starting off with a bucking so savage that for the first minute he hardly touched the ground. Then he sunfished and reared high, almost going over backward; but Tige, as though reading his bluff, held the saddle. Then he lunged against the fence, would have crushed Tige's leg to a pulp if the half-breed hadn't unstirruped his right foot in easy anticipation and swung it high out of danger.

Andrea watched wide-eyed, lips parted. Bitter dust stung her nostrils. She felt the craze-paced excitement of the duel race like a fiery torrent through her blood. She could know for these moments exactly the unleashed emotions that her mother had always warned her to keep in check. For an instant, one shocked thought poured through her naked mind, sloughed of her usual restless, shifting surface moods—*is this what a woman is supposed to feel for a man?*

Even the iron-constitutioned Tige began to show the strain of battle, but so did the blue. It was wheezing savagely, coat lathered with dirty froth, as it fought its final token plays against a burrlike rider who outmaneuvered it at every turn. When it came to a shivering standstill, Tige slipped to the ground, ignoring the crew's wild cheers as he tended to the jaded animal, at once throwing off the saddle and bridle, always talking to it in silvery Ute.

Andrea walked slowly up to the house, put her back against a fluted porch column. The tense tumult still held within her. She watched Kilrain give brisk orders to Bill Treat, and the crew dispersed to saddle their horses. Kilrain swung about and tramped up to the house, paused by the veranda to remove his hat and swipe a broad fist across his graying cowlick. For a moment they stood in silence, watching the crew ride out. A silence broken by the low, imploring call of Andrea's mother from the front parlor:

"Andrea, dear—"

"The old lady's calling you," Kilrain said without looking at her.

Andrea shrugged carelessly. "Let her call. It'll be 'Andrea, bring my shawl,' or some other silly triviality. . . ."

He did look at her then, slowly and appraisingly. "I can remember when you jumped every time your old lady breathed hard. Not so long ago, either."

Andrea's dark violet eyes met his softly. "People do change, my dear."

He snorted, clamping his hat back on. "Not your mother. By God, she's a real princess."

"After all," Andrea remonstrated sweetly, "when you married me—"

"I didn't marry your rattler-tongued mama," he observed harshly. "Damned if she wouldn't make a regiment of mother-in-laws."

"Oh, Kil, really . . ."

"All right, all right," Kilrain Carter said wearily. "She's a cripple, a proud one too—no fault of hers. And you're a pretty little showpiece of a wife; I never bargained for more; at my age, a man's earned a right to make a fool of himself. Still, I ain't a patient man, particular for her high-falutin' ways."

He added dryly, "Pass the word."

Andrea nodded mechanically, caught up always by the blunt force of her husband's personality. She didn't suppose she'd ever love him as a woman should, but it was so easy to cling to his strength. . . .

She leaned toward him glowingly. "Kilrain—"

He made a brusque gesture that cut her off; she followed his glance across the yard. A strange figure of a man had come into view from around a hayshed, shambling afoot toward the house. Kilrain grunted his contempt. "That fool half-wit, Bodie Teece."

"What does he want?" Andrea wondered.

Kilrain laughed sourly. "To tell me again how I'm damned to eternal perdition. Make more threats he ain't got the sand to follow through. Hell, you heard him before."

"Yes"—Andrea shivered, though the humid air was already warm—"but he always . . . frightens me. What a strange little man!"

She knew the story—of how, six months ago, some of the Kaysee cowboys on a Saturday night whoop-up had hoo-rawed a revivalist meeting presided over by Bodiah Teece, a fiery evangelist belonging to the strange sect who called themselves the Canaanites. In frenzied rage, Teece had tried

to drag a rider from his horse. A flailing hoof had
accidentally caught the little man in the head. He'd lain
between life and death for a month, and when he'd regained
a semblance of his senses, had blamed Kilrain Carter, the
cowboys' boss, for the disorder. It must have been his last
clear thought before he was struck in the head, and
afterward it had obsessed him always. He visited the ranch
periodically to rail at the rancher, swearing that the Lord
would exact vengeance for the blasphemy against his
servant, which always vastly amused Kilrain Carter.

Now Teece halted a few paces away, a wiry runt in a
greasy elkhide coat and pants which flapped in tatters
around his skinny shanks. The sun polished his saintly ruff
of cloudy white hair to a golden nimbus around his hawk-
lean head. Over one arm he carried a heavy shotgun; this
wasn't part of his customary appearance when he was "out
to raid Hell," as Kilrain put it.

"Hello, Bodie," Kilrain drawled now, humorously. "Get
Satan in your sights lately?"

Teece pointed a bony, trembling finger at him. "Devil's
spawn! Citizen of Gomorrah! I have finally learned how you
mock the Lord and make league with His Enemy . . . and
now may He have mercy on your black soul."

He spoke with a cold, quiet fervor unlike his usual
raving; some note in it made Andrea shiver. Kilrain also
recognized it; his voice hardened. "Get out, you old
lunatic. Come back again, I'll have you horsewhipped off
the place."

Teece didn't move. His vague and watery eyes blazed
with the hot zeal that gripped him. The shotgun rose to
center on Kilrain's broad chest. The rancher's fist knotted,
and he took a step forward.

Teece did not hesitate. The buckshot charge took Kilrain
Carter full in the chest and smashed him backward. A porch
column caught him in the back, and he slid down in a sitting
position. He looked bewilderedly at Andrea and his lips
moved, then he pitched sideward and was motionless.

Andrea's trancelike stare moved to Bodie Teece. The little madman's attention was already fixing her with its crazed intensity. "Woman, the wrath of the living God is a dreadful thing . . . there is no getting out of His mighty hand!" The twin muzzles of the shotgun veered a little to bear on her. "I know you, wanton. All the evil of the world is bound into your nature—Delilah, Salome, *Jezebel*!"

Andrea heard the frightened voice of her mother. "Andrea! Andrea, what is it?" She tried to speak, but her throat worked soundlessly.

Teece took a long step and the shotgun muzzles touched her breast. She recoiled a little, looking down at the sooty smudge left on her bodice. It seemed to release her voice. Her scream hung like a bright keen blade in the warm air.

As the shotgun shattered the ranchyard quiet, Trevannon reined in to place the sound, at once wishing he had his gun. A man might be shooting at quail or rabbit, but his was the taut wariness of a hunted man, even knowing as he did that no word could have yet gone ahead. . . .

Then a woman's scream, holding a note of pure terror. At once he spurred hard past the barns, veered around a carriage shed, and pulled his mount up in a long yard fronting a big, rambling house. For an instant the scene froze him . . . a man sprawled face down by the veranda, another man with a shotgun pointed at a young woman.

The ragged little fellow came instantly about, the shotgun arcing with his turn, training on Trevannon. "Tryin' to sneak up on old Teece, eh, bucko!" he cackled.

Trevannon did not twitch a muscle, not missing the hair-trigger wildness in the man's ravaged face or the shotgun with one hammer back-eared and ready.

"Easy, Pop," he counseled softly. "Stranger. Looking for food and a bed."

The faded, wicked gaze swept him. "Ahh . . . stranger. But this is no Christian place, man; in it you'll find scant rest and sour eating. Turn your animal and leave, before its godless taint touches you."

Baffled by Teece's evangelizing pulpit manner, Trevannon nodded at the man on the ground, saying, "He hurt, or—?"

Instantly the little man's half-mollified gaze flamed; his bony fists white-knuckled around the shotgun. "He has felt the mailed fist of God; vengeance is mine, saith the Lord!"

From within the house came a woman's voice, quavering plaintively, "Andrea . . . Andrea, what is it, what's wrong?" The girl said nothing, staring blankly at Trevannon, her face sheet-white.

Trevannon felt the alien chill a man knows on finding himself face to face with madness. With a maniac whose crazed impulses were plainly dancing on the edge of new violence. And at this range that heavy-guage weapon would cut him from the saddle like a rag doll. Through a dry throat, he forced drawling calm into his words. "Sounds like he was the devil's hairpin, sure enough. Obliged to you for the good word, Reverend."

At once the edged danger in Teece's expression faded, replaced by a childish pleasure. He even lowered the shotgun. "Your eyes are clear . . . God-fearing eyes. They know His spokesman!" The crafty care of a madman marked his next words. "Good, but now leave—wait. You have a gun?"

"Saddle gun."

"Drop it to the ground."

Under that watchful and glinting eye, Trevannon slowly slipped his carbine from its scabbard, let it fall.

Teece motioned jerkily with his weapon. "Now leave. The Lord's justice is not complete."

Wes started to quarter his animal around, lifting the reins, and Teece at once swung back toward the girl, the shotgun leveled.

"Now your reckoning, woman!"

Trevannon cantered the bay a few paces away, reaching down to unfix his lariat from the pommel. Silently he shook out the coils. With dexterous ease he whirled out a loop, at the same time boot-nudging the bay around.

Warned by the sudden break in the horse's pace, Teece

glanced over his shoulder. Shrilled a gibbered curse and began to swing around. Trevannon had already made his cast; as the noose cleared Teece's hatbrim he slammed in the spurs, lunging the bay away.

Teece was bringing the shotgun to bear as the rope snapped taut; there was a sickening sound as his light frame was yanked from its feet. The shotgun's second barrel went off, pointing down; a geyser of mud erupted from the yard. Teece's body mucked out a furrow five yards long before Trevannon could drag the bay to a halt.

Wes swung down and ran to the crumpled form. He started to bend over, then straightened, swallowing against a hot sourness boiling into his throat. Teece's neck was bent at a grotesque, impossible angle.

Dimly he heard the woman in the house moaning weakly, "Andrea . . . Andrea, please." The girl stood rooted, her eyes fixed on Trevannon and beyond him. Suddenly she began to laugh, quietly and almost bemusedly.

Trevannon tramped across to her, intending to shake her out of it. Before he reached her, the laughter ceased as abruptly as it had begun. Her violet eyes focused on his with a cool innocence that reminded him of a child's shocking inability to comprehend tragedy. Her voice was as light and calm as a summer day.

"Thank you, sir. You saved my life."

CHAPTER 4

"**R**ECKON KAYSEE'LL BE HERS NOW."

"And that'll be the end. The Old Man was hard-headed as a ten-penny spike, but her and the old lady . . . The crazy Congreves. It'll run through their fingers like sand."

"I dunno . . . reckon I'd take odds on the old lady Give her a free hand, she'll be hell on wheels."

"Hell, yes! She damn near shoved the girl into Kil's bed to marry into the ranch. Only Kil wasn't as much of an old fool as she guessed. Kept the both of 'em in their place. Well, the Old Man's gone to his Maker, that gives Old Lady Congreve the free hand you mentioned. The girl'll be owner in name only."

"Still, took a lot of *hombre* to hold together a spread like the Kaysee. Old Kil was the man. Lord. Who'd ever thought he'd go like that, crazy sky pilot busting him in two with a load of double-ought buck?"

"Like I said . . . I'll take odds on the old lady."

"Be trouble for sure, shooting trouble, when the word gets out. Our open range'll go up for grabs. For a plugged nickel, I'd take my time, quit."

"What the hell, job's a job. I'll stick. . . ."

Trevannon stood outside the bunkhouse, leaning against the trunk of a big cottonwood whose spreading boughs shadowed him. Staring at the lamplit rectangle of the open bunkhouse doorway and listening to the crew's low voices. Frowning, he drew on his cigarette, felt it scorch his fingers and pinched it out. He swung restlessly away from the tree and lounged across the yard, widely skirting the house beneath its parklike canopy of cottonwoods.

Casting back on this long, violence-crowded day, Trevannon found little to cheer about. A damned poor new beginning for a man, with a robbery and two killings on his conscience. Yet he'd killed once in self-defense, then to save a girl from being murdered in cold blood. . . . No man could choose the hand that was dealt him, and in these circumstances regret was a futile kind of self-pity.

He was more than a little puzzled by Andrea Carter. Her beauty was that of a diamond, cold and hard and unattainable. Even in cowtown bordellos you met such women, frozen behind their own glacial beauty, using their bodies and faces like tools. Yet, he thought, this wasn't Andrea's trouble, or at best only part of it. He remembered how when he'd roped and dragged Teece, she had begun a whimpered hysteria as though she'd wholly lost her grip, only to assume an instant later a polite composure that would have been ice-blooded, except for the complete and genuine innocence of it. As if several people inhabited her body at once, any one of these coming to the fore at an instant's notice. . . . Damned strange.

Though no reason to concern himself, Trevannon thought; at first dawn he'd be on his way south. He had rolled into an empty bunk in the bunkhouse for a spell, but his charged thoughts had kept him awake. Maybe he could sleep after he had worried it all out.

The shotgun blasts had brought back the crew on the gallop, and Wes had noted how the ramrod, Bill Treat, had at once commandeered the situation. Behind the man's sober regret had lurked a sly, expanding pleasure that hadn't escaped Trevannon. A man who'd risen to ramrod an outfit like this one certainly lacked neither competence nor ambition, but while Kilrain Carter had lived, there would have been only one voice of authority on Kaysee. Obviously Treat saw himself liberated by the rancher's death, perhaps, judging by the drift of his attentions, as a comforter of the grieving widow.

Trevannon smiled faintly; he had met Andrea Carter's mother. Treat was likely due for a rude check on his rocketing designs. Kaysee would doubtless need Bill Treat, now more than ever, but as to any bargain achieved when that old lady and the blustering, officious foreman locked wills . . . like the odds-taking puncher, he'd bet on Mrs. Congreve. Treat had gone up to the big house directly from the cookshack after supper, and they were likely debating the situation now . . . with the body of Kaysee's late owner beneath the same roof, not yet stiff in death.

A strange lot, these Kaysee people, Wes decided with only faint repugnance; he had met all kinds. He stirred his shoulders in a faint shrug, winced as his wound throbbed to fresh life. He had got off by himself long enough to clean it with a whiskey-soaked swab and apply a better bandage. It would do for a hurt so slight; he'd received less care for old war lead he still carried.

His slow pacing had brought him to the west fringe of the grove and he paused there, facing the open yard that sided the big house. Heard voices that brought his gaze to the fancy French windows from which warm lampglow spilled onto a broad stone patio. He saw Andrea Carter step outside with her easy, statuesque grace—Bill Treat's powerful, bull-built form moving close to her elbow. Their words carried clearly through the windless, still darkness.

"Whyn't you call me Bill, Miz Carter? You been here nigh a year, this thing sort of pulls us Kaysee people together, if you see what I mean."

Andrea paused and fanned herself with a handkerchief, the tilt of her head abstracted as she looked out into the night, hardly paying attention to Treat's crude solicitude.

"Miz Carter?" Treat said softly, an irritated note to it.

"Oh—oh, pardon me. Yes, that will be fine."

Treat moved around the girl and half-faced her to get her attention. "Now, ma'am, I ain't likin' to right off intrude on your sorrow with business, but it's sorta necessary. Outfit like Kaysee can't afford takin' even a day off for mournin'. Hard fact, but that's so."

"Yes, I suppose so," Andrea said distantly.

"Good. Sensible of you." Treat spoke more briskly. "Let's get to cases. The old gray wolf is dead, and the coyotes'll be circlin' in shortly to divide the spoils."

Andrea did look at him now, aroused from her indifference. "I don't understand. . . ."

"I mean them sodbusters over on the East Bench," Treat said harshly. "This spring they tried to homestead some choice range of ourn. We batted their ears down. Burned their shacks, drove 'em off. They were dead leary of our outfit afterward. . . . But ma'am, Kilrain Carter *was* Kaysee, and the whole territory knew it. With him gone, I make it them sodders'll try to push back, try hard."

"I see," she said slowly. "Well . . . what do you think?"

"I think we should hit them before they hit us. Show 'em nothin's changed. I'll hand-pick a bunch of the crew tomorrow, boys who know this kind of fight. Take 'em over to the Bench, push the sodders around a little, enough to give 'em the idea."

"Oh," she faltered. "Do you think you should?"

"Ma'am," Treat said in a soft, positive way, "it occur to you that Mr. Carter's death might not have been no accident—that it was planned?"

"Oh no," Andrea protested emphatically. "You didn't see that old man before Mr. Trevannon stopped him. He was *crazy*, clear out of his mind. Nobody could have planned that—"

"Think a minute. Them sodders are Canaanites, that religious bunch old Bodie was always preachin' for. Their leader is Ephraim Waybeck, and his wife is Bodie Teece's sister. Sure, Bodie's grudge agin Mr. Carter was never more'n crazy talk—but if someone close to Bodie worked on him long enough, talked some guts into him—he'd've been pushed to this killin'. Be perfect. Old Bodie and his crazy grudge would get blamed, and whoever egged him on would be in the clear. Like I say—Kilrain Carter was Kaysee. You tell me who had better reason for wantin' him dead so's they could grab that chunk of Kaysee range."

"Oh . . . there *was* something that Teece said before he—but I didn't think. . . . Do you really believe that the Canaanites would—"

"Sure, sure," Treat snapped impatiently. "I know. They're always talkin' peace an' brotherhood, stuff like that. That's nothin' but talk, believe me. You seen what that religion done to old Teece. Why, lady, they're a pack of blood-mad dogs; you muzzle your mad dogs before they bite you. Or shoot them." He paused. "Then there's old Cass McQuayle, the lawyer. He's the one who talked Ephraim Waybeck's people into filing homesteads on a chunk of the Kaysee. I always made it he had some private reason for wantin' 'em on that land. Maybe enough reason to want Mr. Carter dead as much as them."

"I don't think that's right. Mr. McQuayle seems like a very nice old man."

"All right," Treat said exasperatedly. "But someone talked up a storm to Bodie Teece to make him gun your husband. McQuayle and the Canaanites had the motive—I say hit 'em before they hit us!"

Andrea pressed a hand to her temple. "I—I don't know," she said helplessly. "This has all happened so quickly. . . ."

Listening, Trevannon grudgingly gave Treat a point: the foreman was shrewd enough to work on the girl rather than on her mother. He'd succeeded in arousing her from her apathy of indecision; now he quickly pressed the advantage, speaking with an air of great sincerity.

"I know, Miz Carter. I know, believe me. Rough, sure, but it's for the best." He paused, his glinting stare intent on her face; his tongue flicked his lips. "They got to know who's boss, you see. Got to know a man has stepped into Kilrain Carter's boots. That man can be me. Just say the word."

Trevannon recognized the double meaning behind the

foreman's words, the lust half-spoken. Treat was too crude, too full of huge, uncomplicated appetites that were driving him further than he'd intended. Andrea only stared at him wordlessly. Her sophisticated way of dress and speech were but surface details of her nature, and she wasn't so much shocked as naïvely surprised.

Not reading her silence correctly, Treat reached and caught her by the upper arms, his face slack with primal hunger he could no longer conceal. He said hoarsely, "It can be, ma'am. Just say the word—"

"No!" Andrea twisted out of his grasp. "Go away—get back to the bunkhouse. Don't ever touch me again."

As it did in men like Treat, desire blazed into a feral rage. "Why you—damned little teaser—"

Andrea thrust out her arms as though to hold him off, backing fearfully away. A stone bench caught her behind the knees and she sat down, Treat hulking above her. Trevannon had already left the grove and was loping across the yard in long strides. As his boots grated on the patio flagstones, Treat came about to face him. The foreman's great shoulders were hunched, his pale eyes burnished with bright, wild fury.

"No mix of yours, saddle bum!"

"You're a pig," Trevannon said quietly. "Back to your sty."

With a throat-deep snarl, Treat moved in toward him. Trevannon had several inches of reach on the thickset foreman and he used it, stepping easily back from Treat's first wild swing, then driving a straight hard right into the man's mouth. Treat backpedaled; blood broke darkly from his split lip. He touched it and his blind rage drained away, replaced by a cold, calculated urge to kill. Trevannon saw it in his face, stepped back as Treat stooped and tugged at his boot.

His hand came up with eight inches of gleaming steel yanked from a concealed boot-sheath—one of the slim, straight-edged knives called an Arkansas Toothpick. Dexterously Treat flipped it in his palm so that the blade pointed outward. Trevannon sank to a crouch and pivoted slowly to keep facing the foreman as Treat began a slow circling of him. Andrea Carter shrank against the stone bench, a hand at her throat.

Treat lunged. Instead of leaping back, Trevannon stepped lightly aside, let the knife pass between his body and left arm, then clamped that arm tight to his side, pinning Treat's at the elbow. Treat slammed into him with a grunt, bounded back from Trevannon's spraddle-legged stance; Wes brought his right fist up between them, a pile-driver that rocked Treat's head back on his short neck. Treat's knees melted, but Trevannon held him upright, caught Treat's knife-arm at the wrist and slammed it across his own lifted knee. The foreman howled with pain; the knife clattered to the flagstones. Trevannon set a palm against his chest and shoved. Treat pitched backward into the bushes that hedged the patio, thrashed frantically there as he cursed in his rage and pain.

Trevannon bent and picked up the knife, drove it into the interstice between two flagstones and pushed it sideways. The blade snapped off an inch below the cross-guard. Wes tossed the handle away and straightened as Treat disentangled himself from the shrubbery.

He faced the tall, gaunt drifter, panting and rubbing his mouth. His eyes blazed undiluted hatred.

"Another time, bum," he whispered. "You got me by surprise. Another time."

"Keep telling yourself that."

The foreman spun on a heel and stalked from the patio, heading for the bunkhouse. Timidly the girl touched Trevannon's arm, but drew back as he looked at her.

"I owe you for twice now," she said softly. For a moment her eyes glowed with a womanly fullness. Then they sparked with a little-girl petulance. "That Bill Treat. He's so smelly and dirty. I hate men who are like that."

CHAPTER 5

As Andrea stepped back through the French doors into the big parlor, her mother's wheel chair propelled silently into the room from the hallway that branched off between the bedrooms.

"Help me to the divan, please, Andrea," Mrs. Congreve said crisply. Her hands, clawed over the iron wheels of the chair, now reached tremblingly for the hickory cane that lay across her lap. With its aid, and Andrea's, she slowly stood and limped to the leather divan, settling onto its worn cushions.

She remained bolt upright, her hands still gripping the cane, her black, fiercely snapping eyes surveying her daughter with a grave and merciless attention. Mrs. Congreve was still in her mid-forties, but so far as Andrea could remember she had always been a miniature and withered woman with dead white hair in a tight bun, had always affected the black prim gowns she wore. She was delicately boned with skin like transparent parchment. Her thin, autocratic face was ravaged by pain that was no sham; Andrea had seen the misshapen horror of her twisted legs only once, as a child—a memory that had haunted her dreams for years.

"There was trouble?" she asked in the brittle, toneless manner that always put a listener on the defensive.

"That nasty foreman," Andrea said with a shudder. "I don't know why you left me alone with him."

"Very simple. He had something on his mind, and he was too shrewd to let it be known while I was present. So I left you alone."

"Oh . . . well, why don't we get up a party now? We can dance around Kilrain's coffin. Poor Mother, you can't dance."

"Irony does not become you, my dear," Mrs. Congreve said calmly. "Bill Treat is a belligerent, unwashed animal—but not a fool. He was right about one thing. That old lunatic could have been goaded into murdering your husband."

"You were listening in the hallway," Andrea accused sulkily.

Her mother ignored the interruption and went on musingly, "And you, my poor blind child, never saw what Treat and I see clearly . . . that Lawyer McQuayle's benevolent airs and mock mantle of righteousness are nothing but a pose. A benefactor of mankind, eh? Bah. I met him when we lived in Coldbrook. The man's a scheming opportunist. I think he got to Bodie Teece— Please pay attention, dear—"

"Mother!" Andrea screamed softly. *"Will* you stop treating me like a child?"

"You are a child, my sweet—a little girl in a woman's body. What do you expect—Andrea!"

Andrea had angrily turned her back and walked to the oak liquor cabinet; she took out a decanter of Kilrain's French brandy. She filled a tumbler, spilling some liquor in her haste, and drank it facing her mother, meeting her eyes defiantly across the glass rim.

Mrs. Congreve waited till Andrea had lowered the tumbler, gasping from the raw burning that scoured her throat and stomach, then said imperturbably, "Exactly what I mean. The act of a bellicose brat. It proves nothing. Come here and sit down."

Andrea did not move, but her gaze faltered away. "You have gotten out of hand since your marriage to Kilrain Carter," Mrs. Congreve went on softly. Andrea shut her eyes tightly, wishing she could silence that calm and hateful

voice. "Because you had him to lean on, you proceeded to
ignore my natural authority—as your mother." *Shut up,
Mother, will you shut up!* ". . . . Kilrain is dead, you
little fool. And you can no more stand alone than you can
fly. A woman, a real woman, would have Bill Treat
crawling at her feet. God knows what would have happened
a minute ago if that drifter hadn't interceded. If you can't
handle an elemental brute like Treat, what chance would
you stand with a man wise in the ways of women? You're
now legal mistress of Kaysee. For how long? Very briefly—
unless I tell you what to do." She rapped her cane on the
floor. *"Come here to me, Andrea."*

As though in a trance, Andrea moved to the divan and
sank slowly onto it, staring at her hands in her lap. Her
mother was silent now, evidently ferreting out the situation
in her mind, and Andrea scarcely noticed. . . .

It had been this way between them as far as Andrea's
memory reached. Her childhood was a dim and shadowy
thing, with scant remembrance of a father. Of him, she had
only her mother's iron judgment: that marrying Curt
Congreve was the single great mistake of her life. Martha
Godwin had come of a fine Boston family; at eighteen she
had run off to the West with a poor dockhand whose ne'er-
do-well ways had seemed romantic to a young girl—then.
Only when the couple had settled down to raise cattle on the
south end of this valley had the shiftless stupidity of Curt's
bedrock nature become apparent. He was a "born failure"—the cardinal sin in Martha's book. The ranch ran
down, the cattle ran wild, Curt never got around to building
a permanent house in place of the soddy where their infant
daughter was born.

And Curt started drinking; Andrea could guess why,
knowing her mother's cool, deadly way of making you feel
abysmally guilty. Curt was drunk the night he drove his wife
to the nearby settlement of Coldbrook when she felt her
time coming again. He missed a turn in the badly rutted
road, careened the buckboard into a deep gully, and crawled
unhurt from its wreckage while Martha Congreve lay

screaming with her lower body pinned beneath a kicking tangle of horses and harness. The bones were splintered beyond proper mending, though the nerves were miraculously intact—enough to insure Martha a lifetime of agony, as the doctor said later in town. Just before he operated to deliver her dead child . . . But not before Curt Congreve walked out into the alley and shot himself in the head. Thus sparing, as Martha Congreve often put it, a great deal of unpleasantness all around. . . .

Dr. MacKinnon—Doctor Mack—was a gruff bachelor who hated matrimony but loved children. He gladly took in four-year-old Andrea, and her mother became an efficient light housekeeper for the doctor after she learned to maneuver a wheel chair. Doctor Mack was rarely home, spending much of his time at his office or on house calls, leaving Martha Congreve a free hand with her daughter. Dimly Andrea saw how her mother had carefully kept her a child, teaching her to rely always on Mother, warning her against the pitfalls into which foolishly independent people fall. *Always stay close to Mother; be safe.* And later: *Andrea, never trust a man. If he offers you gifts, take them; it's no more than he owes for the heartbreak his kind causes all women. When he speaks of love, he means he wants your body. Therefore give him only your body, not your heart—or he will break it.*

Carefully shielded from every experience of awakening womanhood, Andrea was well set in the pattern by the time she was eighteen. During this time she was also carefully instructed by her mother in walking, grammar, dress and all the expected accomplishments of a Boston debutante. These were thoroughly ingrained, with her mother's other teachings, when the old doctor suddenly died. For a time they lived off the small legacy of his savings. In the evenings, they enjoyed mother-and-daughter chats:

"I saw you talking on the sidewalk today with Kilrain Carter, Andrea. What did he say?"

"Oh, Mother, he's such an old man."

"A wealthy old man . . . and not too old. I want you to

watch for him when he comes to town . . . make it your business to encounter him."

"But Mother. . . ."

"I'll tell you what to say. A woman's conversation, gracious and poised."

"But Mother, all he wants to talk about is cattle and horses."

"Little idiot, that's a rough, bluff bachelor's way of approaching you. He's fended off marriage these many years; he feels immune. But no man is immune. He'll expect an easy conquest of a starry-eyed girl. They all do. But you'll settle for nothing less than marriage; *I'll* see to that. First, get him to talk about himself. . . ."

It was six months in the doing—a hundred teasing offensives which Andrea performed by rote, a mechanically perfected wedding trap into which Kilrain Carter walked stolidly—and not so blindly. As he later told Andrea in his roughly mocking way, "Honey, nobody had me fooled. If I couldn't get you no other way, this suited me. Besides . . . got to thinking I'll need a son to carry on. Man thinks about those things at my age. And I'm a great believer in breedin'—horses, cattle, or people. That Boston blood of yours'll add a little sugar to the starch. I'm even endowin' thee with all my worldly goods to hold for the kid, case I pass on before he gets of age. . . ."

But there had been no son . . . there would be no son. And now, glancing sidelong at her mother and seeing the musing calculation unmasked in her face, Andrea realized in a rare moment of insight how Martha Congreve must have hoped for something like this. While Kil's driving personality had dominated Kaysee, she could never be more than a crippled and helpless object of Kilrain Carter's charity. And she had lost her hold on Andrea. The pressure of a maniac's finger on a shotgun trigger had given her back her daughter and all the old dreams of wealth and position, the birthright she had foolishly discarded.

A shocking thought came on the heels of that insight: *You don't have to do anything she says. Why, you own Kaysee now, you can send her away.* The thought brought a crushing fright from which Andrea shrank. . . .

"Andrea!"

Her mother's voice was brittle-sharp and Andrea looked at her quickly. Saw the satisfaction in her mother's seldom shown half-smile, and knew she'd reached some decision. "This man, Andrea—the saddle tramp, Wes Trevannon—I took a careful look at him this afternoon. I liked what I saw."

Andrea's thoughts veered warmly to the tall drifter. "Oh, I liked him too!" she said impulsively. "He looked so terrible when he was helping me—twice, you know—but then he was so quiet and kind you wouldn't think he was the same—"

"Andrea!" Mrs. Congreve snapped. "I am not interested in his gentle qualities—nor do I want you to be. Do you understand me?"

Andrea nodded wearily.

"What interested me," Mrs. Congreve went on thoughtfully, "was a sense of confidence, of quiet strength you could actually feel in the man. A sense of tragedy, too. But that in no way impairs a conviction he lends of being able to handle any physical or strategical situation. Which he certainly did, first saving your life with quick thinking, and then handling Bill Treat like a child in his arms. And he's a cowman; his whole appearance says as much. . . . Yes, I think that no man could easily outmaneuver Mr. Trevannon. A woman," she added softly, "might."

"What?"

"It's very simple. Shortly Kaysee's enemies will be circling in for the kill, as Bill Treat said. Not only the farmers, but small ranchers who were roughly treated by Kilrain over the years. Now Treat might be good enough to stop them, or he might not. He had, I think, a handy notion when he advised roughing up the squatters on the East Bench. If cowardly pacifists like the Canaanites could move in on us and get away with it—and I've little doubt they'll try—how can we stop the others?" Mrs. Congreve paused significantly. "There is obviously a better man than Treat to block this thing before it starts."

"Oh no," Andrea began to protest.

"Oh yes. Wes Trevannon will be Kaysee's new foreman." Mrs. Congreve stated it flatly, leaving not a jot of doubt.

"But—he might not want the job."

"Money is always a good argument. Reinforced by your charms, it should be a most telling one. The grieving, lovely widow who needs help . . . a few pleading tears shed . . . and you can tell he's a man who was raised to respect women. A rare sort, I might add. You could win Bill Treat over by earthier means—but you are a respectable widow now, my dear, and my plans for you do not include letting that swine paw you."

Of course not, Andrea thought dully, *damaged goods can't be used again*. Vaguely she wondered how she could be aware that she was her mother's pawn and yet lack the strength to break away. . . .

"Look outside," Martha Congreve commanded. "Is he still out there?"

Andrea walked to the French windows and looked out toward the grove. She saw the red firefly of a cigarette coal, and, by straining her eyes, made out Trevannon's tall form.

"He's just standing—smoking. Over by the trees."

"Good. Listen carefully, and I'll tell you exactly what to say. How to act."

CHAPTER 6

BREAKFAST IN THE COOKSHACK WAS A LONG-DRAWN AFFAIR because Bill Treat ate very slowly, forcing each mouthful between swollen, sausage-thick lips. He cursed once when he tried his coffee, left the scalding brew untouched. Afterward he held a black silence. The crew dawdled over their food and matched the foreman's taciturnity, carefully not looking at him. Though not troubling to conceal shuttling glances of curiosity at the unmarked face of the man who'd whipped him.

Wes Trevannon sat at the foot of the table with his long legs crossed, slumped in his chair, an arm slung over its back. His other hand held a cigarette which he'd absently rolled and lighted while brooding into his wiped-up plate. He mulled over his situation, ignored Treat and the crew.

Last evening Andrea Carter's offer of the job had caught him off-balance. She had approached him with a cool and decisive poise which contrasted to her previous childishly shifting moods. He couldn't tell whether that poise was real or simulated. If her mother had primed the girl, she'd done a remarkably convincing job. Andrea had mingled the offer of a breathtaking wage with a soft appeal to her defenseless womanhood that had touched him in spite of its probable calculation. Also his reaction was tempered by his new-found facing of himself . . . there was nothing sorrier than human putty warped by a bad mold. That girl needed help far beyond having a ranch saved. He couldn't frame this impression too well, even to himself, but one fact stood out strongly: these were two near-helpless women in a man's world, and he was a Texan and a Southerner. Every instinct of his upbringing swayed him.

Yet, almost curtly, he'd told her he would sleep on it, and then had headed for the bunkhouse. He had slept poorly enough, but by morning he'd made his decision.

He had to stop running sometime, had to make a start somewhere; why not here, where there was a need? A fugitive's first instinct had prompted him to put miles between himself and the mule-tenacious sheriff of Cedar Wells County. But during the night he had considered it out carefully. His face had been masked during the holdup; he was certain that no posse man had had a clear sight of him in the storm meeting. Even his horse, a solid-color bay with no distinctive markings, could not be certainly identified, and he could ride a different animal for a time. Word of how Kaysee had acquired a new foreman could not fail to reach Vandermeer and trigger his suspicion—but a lawman like Vandermeer would arrest no man without scrupulous evidence.

And evidence hinged solely on that grain sack of bank money. This Trevannon had buried beneath the clay floor in a corner of the harness shed when he had left his saddle there yesterday. That was a safe hiding place till he found a way to anonymously return the money to its bank. A man won no self-respect by halfway measures; if there were any guts to his reforming, he must make it clear-cut and decisive. The money was not his, and it would be returned.

With that decision he had to wryly remind himself against his first smug satisfaction: *You're no saint, never were, never will be. But you can look at yourself in a shaving mirror again of a morning. And that, by God, is something. . . .*

"Stayin' on a spell, mister?"

The casual question from the man at his elbow broke the

near silence. Trevannon glanced up, as did every man in the room. The questioner was a wolf-lean and grizzled man with a be-damned-to-you spunk in his faded eyes that Trevannon had noted and liked. If part of these oak-tough men's discreet silence was due to the shadowy wariness of their squat, brutal foreman, this old man didn't share it.

Bill Treat had paused in the act of lifting a forkful of griddlecake to his mouth. Trevannon met his hating stare a moment and thought coldly then, *No point putting it off.* There would be trouble for certain, but he guessed that it would come from Treat alone. Since it couldn't be side-stepped, it would do the crew good to watch it. A soft and evasive authority would never impress such men.

"Expect to be around quite a time." Trevannon ground out the cigarette in his plate as he spoke, met Treat's look squarely.

Treat set his thick, hairy hands on the table and half rose. He grinned frostily. "Wrong. You'll drift, bum. Now. Or be carried off after a sound horsewhippin'—"

"Why, Bill," the old man broke in with whimsical dryness, "that's plumb poor return for what this fella did. Put Carter's killer dead to rights—"

"Shut up, you old fool," Treat snapped.

He reached a hand to his hip, apparently remembered he wasn't packing a gun, and wiped his hand on his pants to cover the gesture.

"I'll be around a while, Treat," Trevannon said quietly. "You won't be. Unless it's pounding leather for thirty and found. Mrs. Carter don't like you. Neither do I, but I'll leave you a choice. Only you'll keep in mind that I'm rodding this outfit, starting now."

"You're a liar!"

Trevannon didn't stir a muscle." Ask Mrs. Carter."

Treat's swarthy face had shaded down palely at Trevannon's words; now it ruddied with savage feeling. "That's it, eh? Got to the bitch, did you? Big hero-man—"

As he spoke Treat vaulted the bench and started his

plowing lunge around the table to reach Trevannon at its foot. The drifter came to his feet and straddled the bench to meet Treat's rush. The thought flashed across his mind to end this quickly. Near to hand was the heavy coal-oil lamp, off-center of the table toward his end. Trevannon scooped it up and swung full-armed, crashing its base against Treat's bull head. The chimney shattered with the jangling shock and lamp oil sprayed over Treat's face and clothes. Carried on by his own lunge, he crashed headlong into the cold potbellied stove in the corner before plunging on his face. The light stove rocked loosely against the wall, tipped and fell on its side. Disjointed stovepipes clattered down and a black torrent of soot sifted over Treat's inert form.

Trevannon slung his other leg free of the bench and stepped away from it, facing the whole room. "Gentlemen," he said softly, "I do not aim to argue this with any one of you."

"Son," the old man said mildly, "you don't give a man much leeway for argument."

"Not any," Trevannon said flatly. "What's your name?"

"Gabe Morrow, *segundo* here."

The fat cook had waddled in from the kitchen, a cleaver in his hand. He halted, looked down at Bill Treat, and scratched his head foolishly. "Hear you say you're new foreman?"

Trevannon nodded. "Throw some water on him. Where's the wrangler?"

A lean, Indian-looking man grunted. Trevannon glanced at him. "Cut a horse out for Treat. Load him on, with his warsack. If he's got pay coming, get it from Mrs. Carter." His gaze swept the crew and came back to Gabe Morrow. "We'll step outside."

The two men walked off a distance from the bunkhouse before Trevannon asked, "How'd you take your orders, Mr. Morrow?"

"From Kilrain Carter through Treat."

"But you know the routine."

Old Gabe smiled. "I top-handed for some sizable outfits when Bill Treat was in knee-britches. Only there's them thinks when a man passes sixty he loses his grip." His shrewd old eyes glinted. "Kilrain Carter's boots were more'n man-sized, mister."

It was a direct and wholly reasonable challenge; a brief smile flickered Trevannon's lips. "I trail-bossed to New Orleans before the war—for Eli Lapham's Double Bar X in West Texas."

Old Gabe's lips pursed in a soundless whistle. "Heard of the outfit. Hell of a drive, too, that one. You couldn't of been much more'n a kid then." He chuckled. "I didn't ask no question, but you sure as hell answered it."

"I'll answer the other you didn't ask. Man's as good as he proves himself at any age." Trevannon paused deliberately. "I don't know Kaysee or this valley yet. Till I get the feel, I'll need a man to give orders. That man could make my way a lot smoother or a hell of a lot rougher. Got a feeling the men'll follow your lead. How's it to be?"

Old Gabe's shrewd gaze sized the tall, still-faced man before him. "Like the way you sink your stakes, son. Hard, straight. I'll go along."

He extended a hard-calloused hand, and Trevannon took it, saying then, "This homesteader business, Gabe. It sounds like trouble. I want to hear what you think."

"How much you know?" When Trevannon had told him, Gabe Morrow said, "About sums it up. This side of Elk Crick is all patented land. Kil Carter bought out a flock of small outfits years ago. But east of the crick is the big bulk of our graze, and that's all open range. Anyone who's a mind to can homestead over there. That does gravel an oldtimer." Gabe tugged his lower lip embarrassedly. "Still . . . them Canaanites ain't near black as Treat and the Old Man always painted 'em. Either of 'em would of skun us alive if they'd knowed, but fact is the boys and I often dropped in on them people when our work took us over that way. Notwithstandin' that we roughed 'em up that time, even accidentally killed one of their menfolk, those folks're friendly, and forgivin' as all get-out. Make a man plumb ashamed. . . ."

"Was or was not this Bodie Teece a Canaanite?"

Old Gabe's sun-wrinkled face crinkled into a sober frown. "Crazy in the head, that one. Can't judge the rest by him. Good people. Got their odd ways; too Holy Joe for my taste. But what the hell, man's beliefs is his own affair. Still, it's a fact they want a chunk of our open range almighty bad. . . . Look, you want my opinion, here it is: before you do anything else, ride over and talk to old Ephraim Waybeck. He's their leader. Talks over my head, but I cottoned to him."

"I got it," Wes observed dryly, "that this Teece was Waybeck's brother-in-law. Should make me something less than welcome there."

"You don't know Eph Waybeck," Gabe Morrow said quietly. "He'll hear you out and never lift a hand agin you. Take my advice, you'll hear *him* out."

Trevannon scrubbed his stubbled chin with a flat palm, slowly nodded. "All right. I'll do that, Gabe. Now's as good a time as any . . . you give the crew their orders."

"They'll want a time off for the buryin'. No one liked Kilrain Carter much—but every manjack respected him."

"I'll ask Mrs. Carter about that."

Gabe nodded, and Trevannon turned on his heel and headed for the main house. He passed the dark-faced wrangler returning from the house, asked him if he had gotten Treat's pay, and the man gave a bare nod and went on.

As Wes neared the veranda, Andrea Carter stepped out onto it. She was immaculate in a black riding habit with a matching tricorne hat perched on her high-coiled hair. *Colors of the grieving widow,* Trevannon thought ironically, seeing the bright, griefless smile that touched her lips at his approach.

He halted with a foot on the bottom step, touched his hat. "Morning, ma'am."

"Good morning." Andrea's restless gaze wandered to the bunkhouse from which the wrangler had just emerged, helping a stumbling, slack-legged Bill Treat toward the corrals. "Tige Menefee told me. Well, I'm glad *he's* leaving. I suppose when he learned—"

"Yes, ma'am," Wes said dryly, "he didn't like it a little bit. . . . Reckon you'll want town services and a funeral for Mr. Carter?"

"Well," she said uncertainly, "Kilrain was hardly religious. . . ."

"If you like," Trevannon said patiently, "we can bury him here. Might be more fitting. Someone can say a few words. And the crew'll want to attend. Tomorrow be all right?"

She nodded with obvious relief that a problem of irritating decisions was taken off her hands. "I think that will be fine."

He hesitated, weighing his next words. "You'd better hear this, Mrs. Carter. I'm going to ride out to the Canaanite settlement, talk with their head man. Might be we can reach some sort of agreement. Worth a try, to settle any trouble without shooting."

"I—don't think that would be wise."

"You don't," Trevannon murmured with mild irony. To his surprise, she retorted instantly, "You read people very well, don't you, sir? But you're wrong this time. I meant exactly what I said: *I* don't think it's wise for you to go there alone." Her eyes darkened, lifting toward an empty shed in which Bodie Teece's body lay, covered by a piece of canvas. "Before he shot Kilrain, he said something about learning that Kilrain was in league with—with the Devil. Somebody must have put such a notion in his head."

Trevannon's grave nod was his apology, concealing his startled realization of a fresh side of her many-faceted nature: a mature instinct that was at times aware of her own

childish dependency. He told her then what Gabe Morrow
had said, and she listened attentively.

"If that is so," she said calmly, "then we certainly
should avoid needless violence, if possible. Anyway, you
are the general, as well as foreman, here; the decision is
yours." Her violet eyes lightened, softened. "But be
careful—please."

He nodded, looking away in embarrassment. Whatever
her state of mind, she was a damned alluring woman by any
standards; her expression could unsettle a man without
conveying a hint of boldness that would be unseeming in a
newly-made widow.

His gaze absently strayed toward the corrals where Treat
now sat his horse, clutching the pommel. His face was slack
and sick, but even from here Trevannon could see the naked
hate burning in his face. This burly and unwashed man
might be a slave to his own lusts, but he had a definite
animal cunning, and no man who'd risen to foremanship of
Kaysee was incompetent in practical matters. He, Trevannon, had twice beaten and humiliated a brawling bully by
cool thinking and faster reflexes, but Treat's cunning and
competence, backed by brute strength and his raw pride,
made him a dangerous enemy.

The wrangler, after assisting Treat to mount, had gone to
the bunkhouse. Now he returned at his flowing, catlike
walk, carrying a warsack and a bedroll. He lashed the gear
to Treat's saddle. Treat slashed his quirt across his horse's
flank with a sudden viciousness. The animal squealed and
leaped, and would have knocked Tige Menefee sprawling if
he hadn't leaped back with a pantherish quickness. Treat
spurred across the yard, his arm flailing up and down, until
horse and rider were lost to sight around the far outbuildings.

Andrea released a held breath. "I'm glad he's gone. You
hurt him. Now you'll really have to be careful. . . ."

Trevannon nodded, his curious gaze veering back to the
wrangler. The man's murky stare had settled on the two of

them. It held briefly on Andrea, then found Trevannon with
a dead, cold flatness. Menefee's scarred lips twitched. That
intensity of look, Trevannon realized, was inspired by his
own closeness to the girl. *Why,* he thought amazedly, *the
man's crazy jealous.* . . .

Andrea followed his gaze and smiled. "That Tige, such a
funny one."

Almost as funny as dying, Trevannon thought grimly,
watching the half-breed turn and head back to the corrals
where the crew was saddling up. It was like this girl to take
a man's affection for granted with a child's thoughtless
acceptance of a gift it felt was only its just due. Yet, he
realized, in Tige Menefee's case she was safe in doing so;
this man's was dumb, selfless adoration of a pure goddess.
Only Andrea was no goddess, but a creature of sudden-
shifting moods, and Wes had the cold thought: *If she so
much as stamped her foot at a man, that Indian would likely
kill him.*

Glancing then at the fresh innocence of her face, he felt
almost ashamed of the thought. He said, "There any law in
this valley?"

"Oh . . ." Andrea tapped the rawhide quirt thonged to
her wrist against a smooth cheek, frowning. "You mean we
should report Kilrain's death?"

"And Teece's. Sheriff'll find out anyway. Better if he gets
it straight from us how it happened. If this thing comes to
trouble, best the law has no black marks against us."

"Yes, that's true. Well, the sheriff has his office over in
Cedar Wells—that's the county seat. But it's way up on the
plateau there"—she pointed westward with the quirt—"not
too far as the crow flies, but the escarpment is so high on
this side, all the good trails from the valley to the plateau
swing way around north—a good two days' ride." Her
wonderfully guileless gaze held on him. "By the way, how
did you come into the valley?"

"From the south," lied Wes. "Was heading straight
through, riding the grubline. Came here by chance."

"Oh. Anyway, there is a deputy sheriff at Coldbrook,

here in the valley. That's Job Bell. I can fetch him, I suppose. . . . I was going for a ride anyhow."

"I'll saddle up for both of us," Trevannon said. "No point putting off that talk with Ephraim Waybeck."

"You don't have to for me," Andrea said smiling. "Tige has my horse all ready, see?"

CHAPTER 7

AS AN AFTERTHOUGHT BEFORE THE CREW LEFT, TREVANNON borrowed a gun and shellbelt from one of them. In spite of Gabe Morrow's optimism, he intended to ride into nothing blind. With like caution, he did not take his bay gelding; he roped out a blaze-face sorrel with the KC brand. Andrea had given him rough directions for reaching the East Bench where the Canaanites had their small settlement. Leaving Kaysee's headquarters, he held due east on its rolling acreage by the sun, which climbed into mid-morning as he rode.

Within an hour he began to hit areas where the rich graze faded to sparseness, and weeds and broad-leaved shrubs had moved in. Here and there the earth was stripped of vegetation, eroded by gullies. Trevannon's brows drew to a fixed scowl as he studied the terrain. The cattle had not been properly scattered here; first, concentrated overgrazing had taken its toll, then numerous sharp hoofs had trampled the grass to extinction . . . and now this area was significantly abandoned.

Wes dismounted by a scalped hillock, squatted down and sifted a handful of the remaining topsoil between his fingers. Loose and sandy, the kind that absorbed a lot of water but didn't hold it. This wasn't farming country, and even grazing should be carefully balanced. Once that topmost layer of virgin sod, accumulated by ages of nonuse, was gone, the undersoil became a plaything for wind and water. He'd seen the disastrous pattern this had followed on the Great Plains. The cattlemen started the process; the plowmen finished it. Drought and dust followed, and abandoned ranches and farms.

Trevannon had worked cattle all his life, but he was honest enough to admit that if the sodbusters were the worst offenders, it was only by chance; his own kind was equally blind. Only a few alert men appeared concerned about the long-range effects of the prodigal waste left by the white man in his westward rape of the continent. John Wesley Powell, a government geologist, had recorded an outline of the process, what must be done now if the Western lands were to be saved from the disaster that would come, but Powell's findings were gathering dust in Congressional archives. So Trevannon had heard. But the vast majority, he knew, were greedy enough to say, in effect, to hell with the future. . . .

Still it was a cattleman's gorge of anger that now rose hot and angry in Trevannon's chest. After talking with Gabe Morrow he'd felt strong doubts about the rightness of Kaysee's position, and now knew in a cold corner of his mind the unfairness of this sudden partisan feeling. Though this country should be restricted to grazing, Kaysee had itself misused the land. Yet an uncompromising half-hostility seeded in his mind, as he rode on across heightening land, ridge-broken and dotted with timber stands.

It was in this mood that he topped a ridge and faced across the wide-sweeping Bench where a nucleus of many farm buildings centered a vast swath of tilled fields. The worst of his expectations were fulfilled as he frowned across the scraggly plots of corn and beans. Nearly harvest time, and damned poor returns there'd be. As usual too, the damned sodbusters had indiscriminately felled trees that would have broken the soil-tearing winds and provided moisture-storing roots. He put the sorrel down the slope till he hit some wagon ruts between two fields, followed these toward the buildings.

A man who was hoeing out weeds between pathetic corn

rows near the roadside looked up, removed his hat and sleeved his forehead. He wore linsey-woolsey homespuns of a drab neutral color.

Trevannon cantered the sorrel to a halt as the man, with a pleasant smile and nod, said, "Morning, neighbor."

Trevannon nodded, saying shortly, "Where can I find Ephraim Waybeck?"

Apparently unaffected by a grim response, the man said affably, "First house to your right. But here, friend . . . you look hot and dry—" He tramped over to a waterjug sitting in the tall grass by the road.

Trevannon abruptly put the gelding into motion, throwing a curt, "No thanks," over his shoulder. By the time he reached the first house, he was enough ashamed of his rudeness to grin down at the small boy who was building a mud castle in the yard.

"Hi there, carpenter. Is this where Mr. Waybeck lives?"

"I am Ephraim Waybeck."

The voice was deep and gentle, and Trevannon lifted his gaze to its owner, seeing a man tall as himself now descending the rickety stoop to cross the yard. He was old, yet walked with a swinging, youthful stride. Trevannon couldn't help the awed fascination he felt at this barrel-chested man, who had a muscled, fatless girth of body to match his height, and a mane of hair that flowed into the great snowy beard spilling over his chest like fresh hoarfrost. His blue eyes seemed to burn from gentleness to fiery fervor and back again, yet always mirroring a great, calm certainty. An Old Testament patriarch, Trevannon thought, stepped from a bygone age. . . .

"Come down, sir, come down. You look hot and thirsty." His white brows flew together in a stormy frown. "You passed Elia in the fields; didn't he offer you a drink?"

Trevannon nodded reservedly, instinctively holding himself on guard against the warm, tremendous magnetism of the man.

Ephraim Waybeck studied his face a moment as though

reading his thoughts; the quick eyes suddenly twinkled. "I see. But of course you'll rest and sup with us . . . I beg you." With his last words came the faint and rueful smile of a man who knew that even his invitations sounded like commands.

Wes swung to the ground, glancing at the tow-headed boy. He was about ten and he was eyeing the gun at Trevannon's hip with grave fascination.

"Jerry," Ephraim Waybeck said sharply, and the boy jerked from his trance.

"Yes, Grandpa."

"Take the gentleman's horse to the stable; water and grain it. See you take care now; the animal looks heated. . . . We'll go inside now, sir. Your pleasure is ours, Mister—?"

"Trevannon, Wesley Trevannon."

He braced his hand to meet this venerable giant's clasp, but Waybeck's horny hand was as gentle as it was firm. They crossed the yard to the house, which was more like an oversize lean-to shack. It was unpainted, with not even a tarpaper layer to cover the warped and weathered sheathing. This retempered his mood to cold disapproval. *The usual damn nester's sloppiness,* he thought.

Noting his bleak study, old Ephraim said gently, "Paint and trim, sir, are vanity of vanities."

"And humble pie is hell on good lumber," Trevannon growled under his breath; Ephraim, hearing the tone if not the words, only smiled. . . .

They stepped into a single large room that was combination kitchen, parlor and dining room, with wooden double bunks at either end. The hand-carved furniture was crude and meager. An elderly woman moved slowly back and forth in a rocking chair, a large Bible spread open on her knees. Her gaze was distantly vacant in a thin face with its tightly bound frame of silvery hair.

"My wife, sir," said Ephraim Waybeck, his deep voice very gentle. "This is Mister Trevannon, Mother. He'll stay for dinner. . . ."

The old woman's eyes riveted, as had the boy's, on Trevannon's holstered Colt. Her thin fingers trembled on the Book; a little moan left her tight and bloodless lips. Ephraim Waybeck's hand dropped lightly to her shoulder, an infinite sadness and affection in the gesture that made Trevannon look uneasily away.

Through the heavy steam and cooking odors that filled the room he now saw another woman bent down by a fieldstone fireplace. Food utensils were set on the glowing embers, and a large iron pot hung from an iron rod set in the stones. The woman was stirring a stew with a long-handled ladle, and though she was stooping with back turned, Trevannon knew that she was young.

Waybeck raised his voice. "Calla, come meet our guest . . . my daughter-in-law, Mr. Trevannon. You've met her son—which completes immediate introductions."

The young woman wiped her hands on her ragged apron, crossed the room with a quick trim stride. Her finely molded face and strong, full-breasted body were scarcely marked by the hard drudgery that was plainly her lot, though he judged her age as not quite thirty. Her fair hair was drawn to a prim knot at the back of her head. Her eyes, of a dark, clear gray, held Trevannon's attention. They mirrored a serene and full acceptance of life that awed him, the same iron-gentle quality he'd felt in Ephraim. Yet Calla Waybeck's smile was quick and shy, and she hesitantly moved her right hand upward and then dropped it. Trevannon put out his hand and held it there till she took it, and her smile warmed.

Trevannon caught himself grinning; he forced his mouth to a sober line, said formally, "How do you do?"

With a pleased chuckle, Ephraim Waybeck boomed, "Is the food ready, Calla . . . and a pitcher of cold water for our guest?"

She nodded, still smiling, and bustled back and forth between the fireplace and the crude puncheon table. Ephraim assisted his wife to a bench on one side. The old woman moved very slowly and stiffly, hardly taking her eyes off the stranger, rather, his gun. Trevannon skirted the table, taking the opposite bench where he could face the door. He waited till Calla had summoned Jerry and the family was seated, old Ephraim at the head, before sliding onto the bench beside the boy.

Trevannon half-reached for the pitcher of water, withdrew his hand as he saw the family bowing their heads, and sat stiffly through old Waybeck's lengthy grace. But he did listen. Remembering the rote-droned and hellfire prayers and sermons he'd heard as a boy, he contrasted them to the simple, moving speech of this man. Ephraim Waybeck was plainly a man full of the love of the earth and the things known by the earth, and this feeling chorded powerfully through his words of thanks.

Finished, Ephraim at once reached for the dish of stew and ladled a generous portion onto his guest's plate. He cocked a brow as he served, saying mildly, "A cowman such as you obviously are could only be among us on business, sir; but I trust you'll wait till we've eaten? Too, if you'll yield an old man the privilege of bluntness, a visitor of relaxed suspicion would not so hastily have chosen a seat facing the door."

Trevannon felt embarrassed heat rise to his face. "That's right." He hesitated, added, "Your son won't be joining us?"

"My son James—my only son—has been dead these many months," Ephraim Waybeck said quietly. Trevannon glanced quickly at Calla, saw her hands still momentarily on a dish. She drew a quick breath, then reached the dish across to her son, her face wholly composed.

"The only family member not present is my wife's brother, Bodiah Teece. He has been gone several days, not unusual as he travels always on foot. He is," Ephraim added wryly, "something of a preacher."

A mouthful of stew soured on Trevannon; he swallowed with an effort. He'd half-forgotten, in the warm hospitality here, the little fanatic who had died by his hand. He could not go on with this; better to have it out now. He cleared his throat to speak, shifting his weight on the bench. His

holstered gun bumped loudly against the bench. The old
woman jerked sharply at the sound, lifted her head and fixed
on his face with a terribly intensity. Her lips moved almost
soundlessly, yet he caught the words clearly:

*"And another horse came forth, a red horse: and to him
that sat thereon it was given to take peace from the earth,
and that they should slay one another: and there was given
to him a great sword. . . ."*

Ephraim Waybeck got up and came around the table,
helped his wife slowly to her feet. "Come, Mother . . .
you'd best lie down."

As docile as a child, the old woman permitted herself to
be led to one of the bunks. Ephraim eased her back on the
blankets, touched her face lightly with a great hand, and the
tension seemed to flow from her. She relaxed, hands folded
on her breast, and stared vacantly upward.

Calla Waybeck leaned forward, saying softly, "We don't
apologize for my mother-in-law, Mr. Trevannon. She is not
responsible . . . her mind has not been right since Jim
was killed."

"Killed?"

"Yes. Evidently you're a stranger to the valley, or you'd
have heard the story. When we first came here, we filed our
homesteads on land claimed by the Kaysee ranch. Legally it
was public domain—but one night their riders raided us,
burned our dwellings one by one, and drove us all, men,
women and children, toward this Bench—herding us like
beasts. Violent resistance is against our teachings . . . but
Jim—my husband—lost his temper. He dragged one of the
riders from his saddle . . . another shot him. He lived for
a week in pain and delirium. His mother watched it all,
never leaving his side—but she could not save him. She was
never a strong woman, and it left her as you see her. . . ."

Ephraim Waybeck took his seat again, and Trevannon
gave him a sharp glance. "Let 'em get away with it, eh?"

"Sir," Ephraim said softly, "our creed is simple but firm.
As we hold the hereafter to be an unanswerable mystery, we
emphasize rather peace among men and the good life on this
earth."

"Peace," Trevannon said harshly. "Much peace you'll find in this world. . . ."

Ephraim smiled sadly. "Indeed, at times it has seemed so. . . . In Ohio, I was a common farmer, though with an advantage of considerable formal education, a man as venial, lusting, and profane as any. Then, a few years ago, I felt the Command . . . directing me to take my household and such friends as would follow me and seek a new country where we might abide in peace and friendship and live that which we professed. Like Israel of old we set our faces toward the wilderness and sought Canaan. Hence our name—the Canaanites. It is not important, except to give us a sense of solidarity. A long search led us to this valley, and again came the Command, clear and unmistakable. This is our home; we shall not be driven from it. Yet, we're farmers, and this Bench is poor land; that claimed by Kaysee ranch is rich. As we cannot meet force with force, it seems we must wait . . . hope that God and time will soften Kilrain Carter's heart."

Trevannon scowled. "I don't get it. As government homesteaders, you're entitled to government protection. All you had to do was get the sheriff to send for a U.S. Marshal or a Land Office agent. . . ."

Ephraim said steadily, "Our sanction to that land is not by the word of man, but by a law far higher. We will observe man-made laws, but we do not appeal to them. To force ethical behavior upon others is wrong; moreover, to appeal to such law would be to show a tragic weakness of faith. Our good friend the lawyer McQuayle who recommended the land we homesteaded did not approve of my stand in this—but so it must be."

Trevannon said slowly, "That's why you didn't take the murder of your son to the sheriff—why you didn't try to—"

"Avenge his death? God knows I had the impulse; I wanted to seek out Kilrain Carter—but I restrained myself. And sought God's help . . . to find a reason."

Trevannon started to shake his head in resignation, then

checked the gesture. But Ephraim caught it; a tolerant light sparkled in his eyes. "I hardly expected a miracle, Mr. Trevannon. But the answer came in my heart—wait, be patient."

Their religion, Trevannon thought sardonically. Even to a uniform: the drab, linsey-woolsey dresses and identical prim hairdos of the women; the similar frayed and oft-patched shirts and trousers and round-crowned black hats worn by the men and boys. But inward ridicule couldn't still the sense of awe he knew before the tremendous serenity and quiet happiness of these people, making itself felt through the sense of tragedy that lingered over this household.

"Mr. Waybeck," he said uneasily, "there's a thing you'll have to hear. In private."

Ephraim gave the barely touched food a glance, nodded. "Something in your tone suggests that it cannot wait. Come then, we'll step outside."

They stood up and Wes preceded Ephraim Waybeck, both men ducking their lofty heights beneath the low lintel. Trevannon paced off from the house a half-dozen yards, swung to face Ephraim Waybeck.

"Your brother-in-law, Bodie Teece, won't be coming back. He's dead. That's part of what I came to tell you."

"Ah, Lord. . . ." Ephraim raised a stunned hand, dropped it helplessly. "I had thought Bodiah's madness to be a harmless thing . . . and now this. What happened?"

Trevannon spoke for five minutes, and Ephraim Waybeck's expression did not alter, except for a deepening sadness. At last he said, "Little wonder that you faced the door, held yourself tensely as though among enemies . . . but you had nothing to fear, son."

"Know that now."

Ephraim turned his head to stare across the parched fields, musing aloud. "My teachings became, in Bodiah, a malignant obsession. He perverted my central doctrine, evangelized it with the savor of brimstone. My teachings were never to be exhorted by such means. . . . We'll send a wagon to Kaysee for Boliah's body. I will tell my wife he met his death by accident; a lie will be kindest. Perhaps he has found peace. Kilrain Carter too. . . ."

Trevannon toed at a clod of earth, said nothing.

"You did what had to be done," Ephraim said gently, "to save that young woman's life." His voice gained a brisk note. "There's another thing you came to tell me?"

Trevannon drew a deep breath, let it out. "I'm the new foreman of Kaysee."

"I see. . . . Mr. Trevannon, coming here as you did was very difficult for you—a very fine thing."

"You may not think so when you hear the rest."

"Perhaps then you've come to renew Kilrain Carter's old ultimatum to us . . . to stay off the land your ranch claims?"

"Look," Trevannon said roughly, "I'm not unreasonable. This isn't farming country, Mr. Waybeck. The soil's bad, the growing season's way too short in this high-up country. Start plowing it up, you'll only ruin it for everyone." He shook his head impatiently as Ephraim started to reply. "I heard your argument, the Lord's willed it you settle here. I don't know about things like that. Me, I just know cattle; I know the land. I think you got that feeling, maybe in a different way. And you got to understand one thing—you can't farm this valley."

"But we cannot leave," Ephraim declared passionately.

"Look . . . why crop the land? Other valley people raise cattle."

"You mean—change an entire way of life to which all of us here were born?" Ephraim shook his shaggy head—yet with indecision. "I do not know. This would take time, and pain."

"Sir," Wes said softly, "I'm almighty hopeful you make the right choice. There's times when faith and good intentions just ain't enough. There's plain facts, too. One of which is that for you to plow up Kaysee range would be a damnfool and wasteful thing—and if you try it, I'll stop you."

"You butcher."

Calla Waybeck's voice struck out with a controlled passion that was startling. Trevannon looked around, saw her standing in the doorway with her hands on little Jerry's shoulders, hugging him against her skirt.

"Haven't you done enough?" she whispered. "You and your kind . . . you murdered this boy's father, put his grandmother out of her mind. And so easily propose to do the same thing again. But why wait?" She pushed the boy forward a step. "Here he is. You have a gun. Finish your dirty work, Mr. Trevannon! Nobody will try to stop you; it's against our—"

"Calla." Old Ephraim spoke very quietly, no less firmly for that. "Why don't you clear the table?"

She stood proud and straight, her eyes blazing. But she said nothing, only stepped back inside, pulling her son with her. A moment later there was an angry clatter of dishes.

"Another point of my belief," Ephraim murmured, "is that our evil impulses are part of us, with the good. Better to turn the bad energy into useful work. Which is the reason for our lack of what folk regard as necessary comfort. We keep poor and busy—and out of mischief's way." A faint smile touched his bearded lips. "Calla does not take kindly to some of my beliefs. Certainly she has never forgiven her husband's unpunished murder. For all her quiet ways, she's a strong-minded woman, and when she marries again, I think it will be outside of our group." He paused thoughtfully. "Actually she's quite like you, Mr. Trevannon."

"Me?"

"Why, yes. I should say that you are one of those rare and fortunate people who carry their religion about as a part of them. With your obvious courage and principles, I've sensed also a self-reliance that is not arrogance, but only a great completeness as natural to you as breathing. You are not, I think, wholly at peace with yourself, but there is another reason for that." His white brows climbed a notch. "Sometimes a man needs someone else—"

"I'll be going," Trevannon growled. "And Mr. Waybeck, I meant what I said. You think it over, think on it hard. Make the right choice, I'll do what I can for you."

"You've given me much food for thought." Ephraim sighed profoundly, "Now give me a little time. . . ."

"All you want. But no Kaysee range for plowing."

"Come again, my friend. Soon." With this farewell, old Waybeck turned back toward the house, slowly shaking his head.

Wes got his horse from the little stable behind the house, cantered across the yard and swung down the road. Then he heard young Mrs. Waybeck call, "Wait . . . wait a minute, please."

She came swiftly across the yard, holding her skirts, stopped breathlessly by his stirrup and pushed a fine wisp of fair hair back from her forehead. "I'm sorry," she said simply. "You're not like that other Kaysee foreman. A fool could see that."

Trevannon nodded acceptance of the apology, said shortly, "Bill Treat's already through at Kaysee." Hesitating, he then added, "I didn't say it, but I was sorry too. About Bodie Teece."

"Yes, I heard that part. Forgive me for listening. So little news comes to us here." Calla Waybeck paused, frowning lightly. "What I don't understand is what drove Uncle Bodie . . . to do what he did. He was not a man who was easy to know, and he was rarely home. . . . I—I can't say that his death truly touches me. But I could have sworn that he was harmless—for all his bluster. Something we didn't know about must have driven him. . . ."

Trevannon leaned forward, crossing his arms on his pommel. "That seems to be the general opinion. . . . Mrs. Waybeck, there's a name that keeps cropping up in this affair: Cassius McQuayle. Like to hear your opinion of him. He have an ax to grind?"

"Why, Grandpa Ephraim considers Mr. McQuayle our great friend. And he does seem a kindly, grandfatherly sort of man—yet . . . somehow, I always felt he was almost too good to be true. He talks of justice, of the rights of the downtrodden. But I'll never forget how he looked when Grandpa refused to file charges against Kaysee, after those cowboys drove us from our homestead claims. He'd been strangely insistent that we settle where *he* told us . . . that once, at least, he seemed to wear a different face . . . an ugly one."

Trevannon smiled gravely. "Woman's got a knack for sizing up such things. Still, by my lights, McQuayle was right. A man should fight for what's his."

"My husband—did." A bitter remembering darkened Calla Waybeck's eyes. "At least I can tell Jerry that his father died like a man, defending his family and home."

Trevannon was silent to this plain renunciation of Ephraim Waybeck's pacifistic stand. Ephraim, he reflected, had shown his people how to live with simple goodness and charity in a dog-eat-dog society . . . but in the world as it was, such people inevitably suffered. Calla had too much sharp spirit not to revolt against that fact; he liked her better for it. His gaze lifted to the boy Jerry who was standing in the yard, toeing at the earth while he regarded the man on horseback with childhood's wondering reserve.

"Kid's too old to be building mud houses," Wes observed.

"He should be with a father now," Calla agreed. "Hunting, perhaps. But Grandpa Ephraim permits no guns to be kept here." She added smilingly, "You like children, Mr. Trevannon."

"My boy would have been about his age," Wes said musingly. "I guess—"

"Oh . . . you had a family?"

"A wife. Son. Dead now. Typhus."

"And I prattled of my troubles," she said softly. "Again—I'm sorry."

Trevannon shrugged brusquely, straightened in the saddle and caught up his reins. "I'll be going. One thing I wish you'd do . . . tell me where it was on Kaysee range you made your homesteading try. I'd like to ride there and look it over."

"Gladly." She stepped back from his stirrup, studying his face in her quiet way. "Grandpa Ephraim asked you to come again. Will you?"

Wes hesitated, in that moment felt something electric pass between their locked glances. He couldn't deny the way he'd felt drawn to this woman from first sight, and yet he was baffled. *You could make too much out of this,* he warned himself, and then said in a neutral tone, "Yes'm. I'll want to hear what he decides to do."

CHAPTER 8

The town of Coldbrook was no more than a few weathered frame buildings sprawling slapdash on either side of a wagon-rutted trail in a creek-bend of the lower valley. Its only excuse for being was a supply center for Kaysee and the smaller valley outfits; goods were freighted in monthly from Cedar Wells, the county seat. Kilrain Carter, as the valley's first settler, had set up the general trade store to service his ranch hands, and later a couple of saloons, a feed company, a blacksmith shop, a hotel, and a professional building had grown up around it.

At high noon Bill Treat sat on the porch of the small Coldbrook Hotel, his loafer's chair back-tilted against the building's clapboarded front. Picking his teeth after a meal in the hotel dining room, a meal which he'd barely tasted.

Seven good years as foreman of a great ranch . . . shot to hell. The best damned ramrod in the territory booted out of his job as casually as you'd snap your fingers. He couldn't quite believe it still. Kaysee had become Treat's life. The stolid routine of his job suited his nature; the tough authority of it was an obsessive need in him. At first a dozen wild schemes for regaining his post had swarmed in his mind, but the hopeless futility of each was soon apparent. Now he felt empty and a little sick, wondering where he could go from here and not really caring.

He was sure of one thing: a cold hatred of Trevannon that

cankered in him so strongly he could taste it. He gingerly
rubbed the base of his thick neck where Trevannon had
clubbed him with the lamp. Paying Trevannon back was a
thing he could damned definitely do. Catch the drifter
alone, nail him from ambush, bury the body in a ravine
where it would never be found. With Trevannon out of the
way, he might even regain his old job.

Yet it was risky, damned risky. If Trevannon suddenly
disappeared, suspicion would logically center on Bill Treat.
Even though nothing could be proved without a body,
murder was an appalling step . . . especially inside the
jurisdiction of that law-leech Sheriff Vandermeer. Treat's
younger, wilder days were past; the caution of an older man
warned him to consider every angle carefully. . . .

He drew a cheap cigar from his vest pocket, snapped a
match alight on his thumbnail, touched it to his cigar and
tossed the wisp-furling match away. His eyes narrowed
against the smoke as he saw a woman on horseback swing
onto the street and dismount by the jail. It was Andrea
Carter. He leaned forward, elbows on his thighs as he
watched her graceful motions of dismounting, feeling the
hungry frustration that boiled in him at every sight of her.
That simple little bitch parading in front of his eyes daily
always set up this crazy gnawing in his guts. Acting so
damned high and untouchable. Too good for him . . . *like
hell she is!* Still, she was a lost cause as far as he was
concerned, he admitted bitterly.

She entered the jail where its office fronted on the
street—probably to report her husband's killing to Bell, the
deputy sheriff. In about five minutes, she emerged, Job Bell
at her heels looking red-faced and flustered as he assisted
her to her sidesaddle. Treat, with cynical insight and dour
amusement, guessed that the young deputy, who'd always
had a serious case on Kilrain Carter's beautiful bride, was
already seeing a chance for himself with the freshly
widowed girl and was remorsefully ashamed of the thought.

Bell went downstreet to the livery stable, giving Treat a bare nod in passing, and shortly rode out on his horse, joined Andrea and the two of them jogged out of town. Bell probably planned to question the Canaanites, Treat thought cynically; it was damned well certain that he'd get no satisfaction from them. If they did know why Bodie Teece had been driven from empty threats against Kilrain Carter to a killing, they'd say nothing, hanging together like leeches as always. . . .

Treat glanced idly toward the north end of town. Tensed in his chair as he recognized the hulking, bear-huge man astride a paint horse just riding in. *Well, I'm damned. Jans Vandermeer. What brings him down here?*

Curious, Treat lounged to his feet and stepped to the edge of the porch, leaning his shoulder against a gallery post. He lazily hailed the sheriff as he came abreast of the hotel.

"How, Dutchy."

"Hello, Bill."

Vandermeer paced his mount sideward to the hotel steps, then removed his dusty hat and produced a handkerchief. He ran it around the sweatband of his hat, passed it over his pale, sweat-matted hair. He did this methodically, then glanced up at Treat with a broad, ruddy face crinkled by the friendly smile that never reached his cold, china-blue eyes. Eyes that never relaxed their chill alertness, mirroring the dogged, single-minded patience of a career that also was Vandermeer's religion: catching lawbreakers.

"So now," the sheriff chided mildly, "the foreman of Kaysee loafs in town on a weekday. It is not like you, Bill."

Treat grunted. "Off-pasture yourself, ain't you? You generally make the rounds of the county towns once a month. Wasn't you down here just a week ago?—Hoss looks like you been pushing hard."

Vandermeer gave a slow and ponderous nod, saddle leather creaking with a shift of his massive weight, of which hardly an ounce was fat. "Yesterday the bank in Cedar

Wells was robbed. Two men, both masked. With a posse I trailed them on the ridge running south from town.''

"Huh. How much they get?"

"Twenty thousand and odd dollars, Bill."

Treat whistled.

"Considerable loot, eh? They must have quarreled over it, for we found the body of one in a thicket by the ridge trail. Shot through the heart. The other we followed to the eastern edge of the plateau, where he eluded us by plunging his horse into a wash swollen by the storm. We were not foolhardy enough to follow, judging that he would drown. My posse returned to Cedar Wells, but I stayed."

Treat grinned. "Yeah, *you'd* want to be sure."

Another heavy, humorless nod. "Yes. When the storm passed, and the water had died to a trickle, I entered the wash and followed it down through the terraces to the bottom. I found no body. But this—" The sheriff's hamlike hand dipped into a saddlebag; he held up a cedar-butted Colt's. "His gun. He somehow lost it in the gully. But made his way safely to the base of the plateau and this valley of yours. I spent till dark looking for sign, but the rain had wiped out his trail. I camped the night and searched again this morning, again found nothing. So I rode to Coldbrook to enlist the help of Deputy Bell. If the robber is still in the valley, we must find him." His glacial-blue gaze studied Treat. "If he continued to head east, he might have come to Kaysee headquarters. I thought perhaps you might have seen him, Bill."

Treat's mind had skipped with immediate suspicion to Trevannon, ferreting out the possibilities with a rising excitement. *By God, it might be!* He rubbed his chin, saying slowly, "Well, now, hard to say. There *was* a saddle bum rode into Kaysee late yesterday, named of Wes Trevannon—"

"Did he ride a bay gelding horse?" Vandermeer demanded swiftly. "Did he wear a gun—or not?"

"Hold your horses, Dutchy," Treat said. "Wait'll you hear the rest of it. . . ." He launched into his narrative rapidly; the sheriff listened in a mounting amazement he couldn't quite hide.

When Treat had finished, Vandermeer said gently, "That is my man for sure. A bay gelding horse. And he wore no gun, eh? What is greatly surprising to me is that a man of this stripe risks his life to save Ms. Carter from that little madman."

Treat shrugged. "Dunno about that. Hellfire, though, man's one smooth talker, that's sure . . . he talked Miz Carter into firing me, puttin' him in as foreman. Seems he's one of them there confidence men. O' course, Miz Carter was grateful to him and all—but I put in a lot of good years for old Kilrain. Man, man; don't seem nohow fair. . . ."

Vandermeer nodded thoughtfully. "It is hard to believe that Kilrain Carter is gone. He was like part of the land itself." He added with token sympathy, "A cruel break for you, Bill."

Treat drew on his cigar, frowning at its tip. "I'm a direct man, Dutchy. A woman favors them smooth talkers." He paused momentarily. "Look, you riding out to arrest this Trevannon?"

"I will talk to the man, you may be sure."

"Couldn't make it stick, eh?"

"This is doubtful," Vandermeer admitted. "He was masked, and so the clerks of the bank did not see his face. And of course he has probably hidden the money by now. I am sure this man is our guilty one, but our courts proceed on the assumption of a man's innocence. It is for the prosecution to prove guilt. And this is very little proof, Bill—the horse, the lost gun which I cannot show is his, the time of his providential arrival at Kaysee. Thinly circumstantial, do you see?"

"Suppose," Treat said gently, "you could turn up the twenty thousand. It figures he's hid it by now. You'd likely find it on Kaysee headquarters or close by. . . ."

Vandermeer smiled grimly. "The money found on Kaysee, where only one arrival, Trevannon, could have brought it, should be very convincing to any judge and jury. But shall we then overturn every square foot of earth on the ranch?"

"No. But look, Dutchy. Suppose you hold off on the arrest. Sort of lull his suspicions. Meantime I'll ride back to Kaysee and hire on. Trevannon offered me a job on the crew. Tell him I changed my mind, I'll take it. Then I'll scout around, scour every likely place. Know that spread like the palm o' my hand. There's a good chance I could turn up the loot. If I do"—he spread his hands—"you can take your man on a charge that'll stick."

"That is good thinking, and a most generous offer, Bill."

"For strictly selfish reasons, Dutchy. I want my old job."

Vandermeer returned Treat's wide grin. "That is so. Good. You go on to Kaysee, Bill, and I will stay with Deputy Bell in town till you bring me word of success or of failure. . . ."

"Bell, he left town just before you rode in. Miz Carter fetched him. Reckon he's out investigatin' the killin's."

Vandermeer said approvingly, "Young Bell has the makings of a good officer. I will wait at the jail for his return. And I will be waiting on news from you."

He raised a hand in parting, cantered his mount toward the livery stable, and Treat watched him go, narrow eyes burning with satisfaction. His shoulders shook with silent laughter. He was pretty certain that his old position would be returned if he were to appeal to Andrea Carter's mother rather than the girl. Mrs. Congreve would have the sense to see that only he, with Trevannon out of the running, could fill the foremanship of Kaysee.

Best of all, a robber convicted of so sizable a theft should collect a lengthy sentence. A bullet from ambush would mean too easy, too quick a death for the man he hated. A proud, independent hardcase like Trevannon would die slowly behind prison walls. Treat's cigar had gone cold, and he snapped another match alight to fire it up. But an exultant chuckle escaped him, and the explosion of breath blew out the match.

CHAPTER 9

On his way back to Kaysee, Trevannon swung wide to the north to see for himself the tract of land recommended by Cassius McQuayle to his Canaanite friends. Following Calla Waybeck's directions, he found it easily, a pocket of bottom land easily comprising two sections along the northeast boundary. The many-branched creek that supplied fertility to Kaysee's sprawling acreage cut through it running north and south. Trevannon halted the sorrel on a rise and studied it over. It was a typical chunk of rangeland with no more to recommend it for money crops than the rest of this cattle valley. From here he could pick out the charred remains that marked one homestead of the Canaanites' aborted claims.

What, he wondered, was this lawyer McQuayle's angle? Bill Treat had thought the man had one, a possibility echoed by Calla Waybeck. Why should the lawyer have been insistent about the Canaanites' filing on this particular parcel of land, apparently no different, better or worse, than any other quarter section on this vast, grass-covered valley floor? Was McQuayle beating some private drum? Only one man could answer this, and Wes grimly resolved to call on Cassius McQuayle soon. A peaceful settlement of this range feud could be undermined by someone working in the background for his own hidden reasons. If someone had really incited Bodie Teece to facilitate the seizing of this land, it surely hadn't been the Canaanites themselves, he was now certain.

Pondering, Trevannon turned the sorrel southeast toward Kaysee headquarters, following a creek tributary. An hour later he hauled up to let his horse drink from the rushing brook. His keen-ranging eyes idly quested the wind-rippled grass. Halted and tensed on a black dot moving across the neutral greens and tans of this flat plain. He had to squint to make out a horse with its rider crouched against its mane. A runaway. A second rider pounded behind, evidently trying to overtake it. But the far-stretching gait of the first animal held an easy lead.

The runaway was angling generally his way, so Trevannon set the sorrel to an unhurried lope to head it off. Coming nearer, he felt a thin shock of recognition. This was the big black he'd seen Tige Menefee saddle for Andrea Carter that morning. And now he made out the girl's face, white with exultance rather than fear, he thought, then knew he must be mistaken. The black was out of control; a fall at this pace could kill her.

Trevannon started to rein around hard, spurring to bring his horse into stride with Andrea's so he could grab her rein. Then the black plunged sideward into a ground dip; its hoofs flailed away its footing, and momentum sent it into a skidding plunge on its side. Andrea was thrown clear of her sidesaddle, rolling to a stop a couple of yards away.

Trevannon pulled up the sorrel and left his saddle, running as his feet hit the ground. She was already sitting up when he reached her side. Her little hat sat askew on the broken tumble of her hair, one cheek smudged and skinned. She rubbed her nose with a grubby palm, giving him a gaminlike grin, and extended her hand. He pulled her to her feet, thinking unbelievingly, *She started that crazy run apurpose!*

The second rider thundered to a halt, threw himself from horseback, breathing heavily. Andrea met the heavy disapproval in their looks with a little frown. "Well, really, can't a girl have any fun?"

"Wonder you weren't killed!" the youth gasped. Trevannon now noted the star glinting above his shirt pocket. He wasn't over twenty-one, a lean and wiry youth with a blond cowlick, not yet filled out by maturity . . . or, Trevannon guessed, by experience.

Andrea, her face gay and flushed, said, "Job Bell, deputy sheriff . . . Mr. Trevannon, new Kaysee foreman."

Young Bell didn't offer to shake hands. He gave Andrea a brief, sultry glance before fixing his attention on Trevannon. His fists flexed once; a dark scowl muddied his stare. Another of her jealous victims, Trevannon knew wearily . . . Treat, Menefee, and now Job Bell. Each with his own brand of lust, devotion, or romantic dreams revolving around this widowed girl who'd been molded into a neat and attractive package of woman purged of every womanly feeling.

"We just came from Kaysee," Bell announced. "I looked at the bodies. Seems to have happened as Mrs. Carter said."

"That mean I pass?" Trevannon murmured.

Job Bell flushed. "No offense," he said coldly. "My job. You're a stranger, mister. A double murder—killing," he amended without haste, "isn't so usual."

"To say the least," Trevannon agreed soberly. "Heading out to question the Canaanites now, are you?"

"Seems sensible. I talked to Mrs. Carter's mother; she thinks they may have goaded Teece into attacking Mr. Carter." He gave Trevannon a narrow regard. "Mrs. Carter says you had intended riding out to see them?"

Wes inclined his head briefly. "I have."

Bell said with obvious reluctance, "And your opinion?"

"That they're poor and honest people trying like the devil to mind their own business."

"There was Bodie Teece, though," Bell observed with a thin, triumphant smile.

"Exception that proves the rule. I won't try to advise you, Mr. Bell." Because Bell's smug, surly manner was irritating, Trevannon added, "Man should be entirely free to make his own mistakes."

Bell grated his teeth, a trick Trevannon guessed he'd developed to master a quick-flaring temper. "That's right," Bell snapped. "Except I reserve one piece of advice for nosy greenhorns: let the law handle its own mad dogs. We don't need help!"

"Why, certainly," Trevannon agreed gravely. He touched his hat to Andrea and started to rein past them.

"Wait a bit, Wes," Andrea said brightly. "It was a very nice ride, Job. But I must go home now." A scowl flicked Bell's face, and she smiled sweetly. "It's a long ride to the Canaanites', Job. You won't be starting back before nightfall. Propriety, you know . . ."

Propriety! Trevannon nearly snorted aloud . . . one day a widow, and she was playing fire between men with a little-girl coquetry. If a couple of more killings didn't come out of this, it would be a damned miracle. . . .

Job Bell swallowed hard, fashioned a weak grin. "Sure. That's right. Well, be seeing you." To Trevannon he gave a totally unfriendly nod, mounted up and spurred savagely across the shallow creek and eastward.

Trevannon set his horse apace alongside the girl's, and they rode in silence. Aware of her frank, intent sideglances at him, he grimly said nothing. Andrea was used to men's attentions. When she at last spoke, a faint pique marred her tone.

"I think it's marvelous how you've taken hold at the ranch." She seemed to linger thoughtfully on that casual remark. "In some ways, you're very like Kilrain—was."

He didn't reply.

"Oh, I don't mean outwardly," she went on obliviously, caught up in this notion as with a new toy. "Even in manner, you're very different. But I feel that same sense of *strength*, do you know?"

"Job there, now," Trevannon deliberately veered the subject, "he don't look like any kind of weakling."

"Physically, of course not," she said impatiently, "but Job and I practically grew up together. His father was the former deputy in Coldbrook. When he retired, Job sort of succeeded him. But honestly—Job is still a *boy!*"

To that Trevannon carefully said nothing, and there was another silence. Andrea's profile was a cameo of restless discontent as they reached a point at which the creek suddenly broadened into a wide bowl. Here the water gathered deep and placid before taking up its narrow course again.

Andrea abruptly halted her black on the grassy bank, staring across the wind-riffled pond surface where sunlight caught as fractured chains of mobile gold.

Wes broke the silence. "It looks deep."

"It's deep enough," she said. "Dark and deep." Her teeth caught her lower lip; she shivered, though hot sunlight westered against their backs.

"Goose walk over your grave?"

Her glance was quick and dark. "Why did you say that?"

Wes shrugged. Her gaze dragged back to the pool in brooding fascination, voice toneless and low as though she'd retreated far into herself. "We used to steal off from town on hot summer days when we were children. Job and I. It was a long ride, but there was no other place we could swim. The water was always cold, no matter what the weather. Job tried to dive to the bottom once. He was under a long time. And he couldn't reach bottom. . . . I—was always afraid to try. I guess it joins with an underground stream down there. . . ." Her voice trailed off.

Trevannon squinted into the water, aligning his gaze with a deep-shafting ray of sunlight. "A deep one, all right."

"Come on!" Her tone was sharp and querulous with the savage rein-around of her Appaloosa's head, and she kicked it into a hard trot. Repeatedly baffled by this girl's moods till he became resigned to them, Trevannon shook his head and followed.

When he'd ranged up beside her, he commented briefly, "Good way to ruin a good horse's mouth, that."

"I know," she said complacently. "What's cruelty? Just the other day, I saw Tige kick a horse in the stomach."

"Not meanly, I'll wager you didn't," Trevannon told her. "Sometimes a balky one can be cured by a kick in the belly." He had noted Tige Menefee's miraculous touch with animals that morning, and he added, "That Tige, he's half horse himself."

"He can be led like one, that's for sure," Andrea observed.

A man, Trevannon thought, gave his loyalty, his guts and soul, to her, and it meant less to her than a new toy would. And oddly, perhaps, she was neither stupid nor cruel—rather, oversensitive, in a way that had made her easily receptive to whatever warping forces had stunted her growing mind till there wasn't an honest feeling left in her. Likely her mother's doing.

Reminded of Mrs. Congreve, he said grimly, "I'll want to talk to your mother when we get back."

The big, lofty parlor of the Kaysee main house was a man's room, with its plain furniture, massive fieldstone fireplace, smoke-blackened ceiling rafters, and walls hung with bright Navajo blankets, antique rifles, crossed sabers, dueling pistols and trophy heads of grizzly, bighorn, and mule deer. Trevannon noticed Mrs. Congreve's cold and disapproving appraisal of the room as Andrea pushed her wheel chair into the parlor. Guessed that she was already planning a refurnishing that would erase the impact of Kilrain Carter's dominant personality from the house.

Mrs. Congreve adjusted a laprobe that covered her knees; her thin, arthritic fingers gripped the cane across her lap, tapping it impatiently on one chair wheel. "Well, Mr. Trevannon? You wish to tell me something?"

Trevannon was slacked in a leather-covered chair, his long legs crossed. "Yes'm." The chair creaked heavily as he leaned forward, elbows on knees and revolving his hatbrim between his hands. His ordinary courtesy to women was instinctive, but he knew there would be no mincing of words with this woman; physically helpless, she had an inner, driving ruthlessness that must be met by a tight rein.

"Mrs. Congreve," he said bluntly, "when your daughter hired me last night, she hinted that I'd be expected to keep Kaysee clear of any and all settlers."

"Andrea has already told me.that you bothered reasoning with the Canaanites," she replied brittlely. "I must say, sir, that I consider this an utter waste of breath and time."

"Then," Trevannon observed flatly, "driving 'em off by force *was* your idea."

Mrs. Congreve said coolly, "Treat's, first . . . and I agreed. Hardly an original procedure; Kilrain Carter believed it was the only way to handle that trash. Evidently you believe otherwise?"

"I do. And told Ephraim Waybeck he could homestead that strip along the upper creek he wants with no interference."

The crippled woman was utterly motionless except for the slight flare of her fine nostrils. "I see. Exactly what kind of a cattleman do you consider yourself, sir?"

"An old-time one, like Carter was. But one with sense enough to know the day of open range is going . . . fast. Time's past when ranches were few enough to grab all the land they could hold. The Homestead Act ain't new, but the little people're beginning to see what it can mean for them . . . taking advantage of it. The law stands with them." He hesitated, tasting the strangeness of his next words. "I stand with the law."

She laid down her reply flatly and coldly. "You were hired principally to handle those farmers. For the reason that you seemed to be the man who could hold Kaysee intact—*for us.*"

Trevannon's tone matched hers. "I'll give it to you straight, way I did to Ephraim Waybeck. I'll have all of

Kaysee's patented land properly surveyed, the boundaries
marked off. I'll even hold Kaysee's open range against
everyone who's got no more legal claim than us. But I'll
make no move to stop the Canaanites or anyone else from
proving up government homesteads on any open range. I
told Waybeck he could stake out where he wants, provided
he switches to cattle—no cropping this valley. If I can solve
this thing without shedding blood, I mean to. That's my
way. Take it or leave it."

Mrs. Congreve's ravaged face framed the thinnest smile.
"Tell me why you came to me with this—not to my
daughter."

"Sized you as the real power here."

"You are observant. Do you hear well, too? Because you
are through here, Mr. Trevannon. Get your things and get
out."

"No," Andrea said very gently. Her lips were touched by
a faint, speculative smile; her dark violet gaze did not leave
Trevannon.

Mrs. Congreve snapped imperiously, "What? What did
you say?"

"I said no, Mother. Wes isn't fired." Andrea's smile
held, and she did not even glance at her mother. "Aren't I
the owner of Kaysee? With the right to hire or fire as I
choose? Wes stays."

Mrs. Congreve drew a shuddering breath, let it out.
"Darling," she faltered, "are you going to start behaving
badly again? Mother knows what's best for us—"

"Kilrain never cared what you thought, Mother," Andrea
said softly. "Here is another man who doesn't." She gave
Trevannon a full and dazzling smile. "Do whatever you
think is best, Wes."

Trevannon rose with a nod at Mrs. Congreve's sudden
and deathly paleness. He said quietly, "Better take care of
your mother." He walked softly from the room, stepping
out onto the veranda. The dying sun slanted thinly against
his eyes before he clamped on his hat. He hadn't realized it

was this late, and now aware of belly-gnawings of hunger, he swung toward the cookshack. Wondering what had prompted Andrea's newest whim, even to defying her mother's will. . . .

He halted just within its doorway, feeling a wary shock at sight of Bill Treat seated at the foot of the table, eating with the crew. Treat's coffeecup stopped halfway to his lips and he set it down carefully, breaking the crew's sudden watching silence.

"That offer of a job still open?"

"You had your choice this morning, Treat. You made it."

Treat slowly settled his scarred hands to the table. His murky glance lifted with no surliness. He said heavily, "A man works an outfit best years of his life, raises himself to foreman. Then a younger buck whips him and throws him out on his ear. Hard thing to take. Maybe I earned that. But I earned my job too, took a lot of sweat, a lot out of me. Ain't so young I can start from scratch again, ain't so old I can't still make a top hand in this or any damn outfit you can name. Besides, man grubs and sleeps at a place that long, it gets in his bones. Wasn't easy for me to come back after this mornin'. And I won't beg from no man. But I'm askin', mister."

The silence hung again as he concluded; Trevannon's glance shuttled from one face to the next. Expressionless each, yet in each a kindred emotion reflected. Not a man of them liked Bill Treat, but it wasn't Treat as an individual that concerned them. Each man saw himself in another man whose life was his, who had sweated and frozen by his side in a grueling job, who had shared the barren dwellings of cookshack and bunkhouse that were their only homes. A man who had known his job and done it well for many years. You might overthrow such a man if you were strong enough and he deserved it, as Treat richly had, but you didn't kick him out like a dog. Treat was too proud to beg, humble enough to return, and this, too, impressed them.

Trevannon's first reaction was instant suspicion. What the hell was Treat up to? *Go slow now,* he cautioned himself;

this wasn't what he had expected of the deposed foreman, but men could change. Or adapt to changed circumstances, anyway. Old Gabe Morrow's eyes mirrored the same steady question as the others', and this decided Trevannon.

He nodded wearily, saying, "Hang up your hat, Treat," as he skirted the table to take his seat.

CHAPTER 10

KILRAIN CARTER WAS TO BE BURIED THE AFTERNOON following Treat's return to Kaysee. A mile from the ranch was an old Indian burial ground which had also served over the years for the interment of men who had died in the service of the ranch. Bill Treat knew that Carter had been anything but a sentimentalist, but long observation had told him that men worked harder and better for that of which they felt themselves an integral part; his consideration for the dead was one of various provisions by which he bound his men to loyal service.

The crew invariably got a day off for the burial; the corpse got a fine casket and a long eulogy given by the parson of Coldbrook's single community church; the parson got a generous fee. Carter would have scorned the final rites, and the words that Gabe Morrow, longest in Kaysee service, would speak would be brief and blunt; a wooden marker and the pine coffin containing the Old Man's mortal remains were fashioned by the crew in a couple of hours that morning.

The men, togged out in their somber best, followed in mounted file the jolting wagon holding the pine box. Bill Treat waited till the slow-pacing procession was a brief distance from the ranch. Then he began to cant forward in his saddle, rubbing his stomach, his face tight and wry.

Old Gabe Morrow, his toil-bent and desiccated frame looking incongruous in the neat, ancient suit he wore, glanced at him. He asked, with no sympathy, "Somethin' you ate, Bill?"

"Guess so," Treat grimaced. "Gut was actin' up all morning."

For the next quarter mile he continued to grimace and grunt till Wes Trevonnon, riding up behind the wagon with Andrea Carter, fell back beside him, told him curtly, "If you're sick, get on back to the ranch."

Treat swallowed as if against nausea, gave a painful nod and swung his mount out of the column. He put his horse slowly down the backtrail till they were out of sight. Then quirted the animal savagely. . . .

He was filled with calm certainty as he turned his piebald into the corral. He knew every nook and cranny of this layout in his mind's eye. Logically, he guessed, Trevannon would have buried the bank loot. The first thing to look for was freshly turned dirt. The funeral party had been moving slowly, and he had plenty of time. He toted his saddle and bridle to the harness shed, toed open the door and went through. He slung his hull and blankets over a saddle pole, tossed his bridle over a peg, then turned to survey the dark interior of the shed. He meant to cover the inside of each dirt-floored building with special care; here a man would have time to bury an object without likelihood of discovery; the heavy shadows that filled this windowless shed made it especially choice.

Treat lifted a bull's-eye lantern from a peg, lighted it, and began a slow circuit of the walls, carefully scanning the ground by low-held lanternlight. Almost at once he found the telltale freshness in a rear corner where the clay floor had been boot-stamped and smoothed to restore its hard-packed texture. He stooped and touched it. Still moist . . . freshly dug not over a day earlier. He set the lantern down, hunted for and found a shovel hanging from a nail. Eagerly he attacked the stubborn hardpan.

Five perspiring minutes later he hit a yielding bundle. Feverishly he cleared the dirt away and hauled up the filthy grain sack. Struggled with its knotted mouth, cursing and sweating. Finally he spilled out the neat, clean packets of greenbacks in their brown half-wrappers.

He knelt in the flickering lantern glow, thumbing through the large-denomination bills: sweat broke out afresh on Treat's face. His hands trembled. Far more money than he'd ever seen at one time, even on cattle-buying trips. Temptation threaded his insides like a boring worm, but he put it aside. Kaysee was the central stake in his life, and this money would buy back the position that was his meat and drink.

He returned the money to its sack, jammed it in the pocket of his cheap suitcoat, and skirted a barn as he headed up for the main house. Best to establish an understanding with the old lady right now. She'd always quietly despised him for a thick brute, and he'd cordially hated her for it. But his hate was tempered by a certain awed respect for her cold gentility, her ruthless immorality which he'd sensed, and she was nobody's fool either. . . . Get on her good side, make her see how far they could go together, and maybe even . . . Andrea. By God, he might even stand a chance there.

He tramped onto the veranda and tapped diffidently on the door. Mrs. Congreve's brittle invitation to enter came at once. Treat halted just inside the door. She turned her wheel chair slowly from the window, her usual icy regard at his presence lessened by a distant but definite curiosity.

"Good afternoon, Mr. Treat."

"Wanted to talk to you alone, ma'am. If you can spare a minute."

"A crippled woman's time, sir, is hardly that valuable to her or to anyone else." There was an acrid bitterness to her tone that alerted Treat. Trouble between her and Andrea? Maybe. "You seem," she went on, "to have wanted this talk badly enough to desert the funeral cortege. Please sit down."

Treat settled his bulk on a leather chair facing her, his hat dangling between his fingers, certain now that there were cross-currents he'd missed. He'd half expected a sharp rebuff at first; instead she was almost cordial. Confidently he told what he'd learned from Sheriff Vandermeer, that all signs pointed to Wes Trevannon as the bank robber. That he'd agreed to search Kaysee for the stolen money. He dipped into his bulging pocket and lifted out the grain sack.

"You—found the money then?"

Treat hefted the sack lightly in a thick palm. "Twenty thousand dollars, ma'am."

Only Mrs. Congreve's eyes betrayed her sharp exultance. "Ah-h," she breathed. "That puts you in a bargaining position, Mr. Treat."

Treat frowned. "I figured—"

"That I would be unhappy at this intelligence? On the contrary. It's true that I first endorsed discharging you . . . giving Mr. Trevannon your place. That was before he decided to handle the Canaanites with a light hand. He proposes to let them take up their former homesteads, provided that they raise cattle." Mrs. Congreve's fingers taloned whitely around the arms of her chair; she leaned forward in her intensity. "You know what this will mean; our open range is the richest in the valley. The breakthrough of a few successful homesteaders will bring in a flood. I did not—" She hesitated. "I will not mince words; I believe that you and I understand each other. I did not manipulate my daughter's marriage into Kaysee so that I could fritter out my days as a confined, unwanted invalid. But Kilrain Carter was a hard man; he wielded the only whip on Kaysee. His death gave me a reason for hope.

"I had thought I could control Andrea, and, through her, Trevannon . . . whom I will not deny I thought a better man than you. But she is becoming soft on that drifter; my hold on her is weakening. I fired him, and she countermanded it—to my face." Her voice softened to a faint hiss. "Kaysee without its open range is nothing. I, without a whiphand here, am nothing. *Now* do you understand why I will not grieve if this Trevannon is removed?"

Treat stared. *By God, she's a hungry one!* Power-hungry . . . He'd sensed it before, but hadn't realized the intensity of her need. "Yes, ma'am," he said softly, "I surely do . . . and how do we stand?"

Mrs. Congreve leaned back, her eyes half-closed. "I think I can safely promise—you'll have your old job back . . . once I have back my daughter. Removing Trevannon's influence will insure that."

Treat gently cuffed the grain sack against his hat and said nothing.

Her eyes widened sharply. "That's what you want, isn't it?"

"Yes'm, partly."

"Partly? Oh-h." Her fragile lips formed a faint, ironic smile that made Treat stir uneasily. "You haven't relinquished your designs on my daughter, eh? I see. How very primitive. Might those designs include, perhaps—marriage?"

Treat swallowed hard, disciplined his single-minded lust, plunged with a muttered, "Yes'm. If she'll have me."

Mrs. Congreve's soft laugh was paper-dry. "You mean, if *I'll* have you."

"Ma'am," Treat said, anger carrying him to boldness, "this ranch is my life. I'd die before seein' it tore to pieces by a pack of cropper dogs. Reckon you know that. Kaysee'll need a man like that at the reins. Long's your daughter holds the only authority here, how can you be sure she won't overrule me? As her husband, I could damn well assure you there'd be no soft-pedalin' on any sodders!"

"I have no doubt of it," Mrs. Congreve said evenly. "I have no doubt either that if you had a legal hold on Kaysee, my own position would be relegated to precisely that which I held when Kilrain Carter was alive—a helpless nonentity. Also, whatever you may have thought, I am not without gentler feelings. My daughter means a great deal to me— and I will not see her bedded in a sty."

Treat's fists knotted in black, bitter fury; he set his jaw to control its tremor. "Think that over, lady. Just now I'm a pig you happen to need."

"Quite so. But I believe your vaunted love for Kaysee is enough to hold you."

"Listen, I can get up now and walk out that—"

"Can you, Mr. Treat? Can you really?"

For a moment they locked stares till Treat's fell sullenly from that bright, mocking contempt. *The old bitch has me by the heels and she knows it,* he raged silently. With an effort he achieved self-control, said very softly, "There'd be nothing that'd change your mind?"

"Money," she said at once and flatly.

Treat blinked.

"Money," she repeated gently. "For two reasons. First— a man can change, even you. I'm not deceived about blue blood and gentle breeding, that sort of rot. I come from one of Boston's oldest families, the Godwins. Do you know how my ancestors came by their wealth? The original Godwin was a London guttersnipe who rose as a pirate freebooter, raiding Spanish merchantmen, pillaging and murdering. His sons became New England merchants who augmented their ill-gotten inheritance as crooked and cut-throat pirates of the business world. You see, money does work wonders, even on swine. Even you, Mr. Treat, could become bathed, broadclothed, mannered, and perfectly respectable . . . in time, for stupidity is not one of your undesirable characteristics. A man like that could win my daughter—with my help."

"Two reasons for money, you said," Treat declared harshly.

"Just so. The next man to marry Andrea will have to pay her mother a very sizable dowry. I do not share your great love of Kaysee ranch, Mr. Treat, nor of your raw, brawling West. I would much prefer power on my own terms, in my own society. That society is Beacon Hill of Boston, the circle of snobs who disowned me when I married a weak, ne'er-do-well, Curt Congreve. I would like to return there with the means to buy back—position. And the pleasure of watching certain people crawl for me. It really is amazing what a universal language money speaks."

Treat licked his dry lips. The deadly and disillusioned cynicism of this woman made a man's spine crawl. "Sort of lets me out," he muttered gloomily.

Mrs. Congreve's pale lips formed her thin, wicked smile. "Cheer up, Mr. Treat. You will have your old sty back, after all. . . ."

It was well toward evening before the funeral party had returned to the ranch that afternoon. The crew off-saddled and straggled toward the bunkhouse, talking in hushed voices. Trevannon, as he unsaddled the sorrel, reflected soberly that it was as though a giant pine had crashed to earth, leaving an empty space against the sky. He remembered the stories of Kilrain Carter, a legendary giant, he'd heard over the years, and today he had helped lay that legend to rest.

He was conscious of Andrea Carter standing at his elbow, impatiently tapping a horsehair quirt against her palm. She wore a black riding habit and hat with a dark veil . . . fashionable widows' weeds that set off her slender fullness. Part of the travesty of her mourning, Trevannon thought wearily as he turned to her horse and uncinched the sidesaddle. He began to swing it off, only to find it held in an iron grasp, and he looked across the saddle swell into the murky hatred of Tige Menefee's eyes. With a sigh he let go of the saddle, and Tige took it and stalked silently from the corral. Wes picked up his own saddle and swung to face Andrea.

Her eyes glowed innocently through the veil. "Tige always takes care of my riding gear. He's very jealous about that, you know. But he's a dear, really. . . . I was thinking that you must be tired of cookshack grub. Why don't you have supper with Mother and me?"

"That an order?" he asked unsmilingly.

She did smile, quite archly. "I can make it one."

He shook his head. "Better not."

"Why, that sounds like an ultimatum."

"You could say that."

Andrea kept smiling, tilting her head a little to regard him. "Nobody tells you your way, do they?" she murmured. "That's what I like most about you."

There was a deep softening in her face that made Wes uneasy. He had believed that her flying in the face of her mother's will by refusing to fire him had been a typical whim; now he wasn't so sure. She had openly flirted with him before the crew, which had accounted for the sullen, subdued air that hung over the whole proceeding. The simple ethics of these men were his own, running counter to the whole behavior of this capricious, moody girl. True, they'd all made a joke of the patent farce of the Old Man marrying a woman little more than a third his age, but in their eyes, aberrant behavior in a "respectable" woman was shocking. . . .

But Trevannon's concern went deeper. Not missing the wealth of hidden meaning behind her light words and looks, he was left perplexed and worried. In a way he liked this girl for all her unpredictable moods; he wanted to help her, but hadn't anticipated that she might want something of him he couldn't give. He couldn't deny the strange attraction of her childlike innocence and womanly beauty; it had possessed other men, could engulf him too unless he kept on his guard. . . .

"I'll be going," he growled and walked off, with the silver trill of her laughter following. He left his saddle at the harness shed and tramped to the bunkhouse, met Gabe Morrow halfway there.

"Treat ain't in the bunkhouse," the old puncher told him. "Thought at first he might've strayed off the trail on his way back, sick as he was—"

"He made it back—that piebald horse of his is in the corral."

"Thought of that." Gabe paused worriedly. "Sick man should be in his bunk. Where'n hell—?"

"You look around the cookshack, corrals, stables. I'll try the house. You find him, sing out."

Gabe nodded and headed goutily for a haybarn. Wes

headed toward the main house and its outbuildings, set off from the working part of the ranch. He started with the big carriage shed which faced away from the house. Stepped through its big double doors and halted there to accustom his eyes to the musty gloom.

A boot whispered against the clay floor.

"Treat?"

Moving toward Trevannon, the bull-shouldered hulk of the ex-foreman took sudden shape in the half-darkness. The uptilted gun in his fist glinted against the late-westering daylight. There was something bulky in his other hand.

"What is—"

"Shut up," Treat rasped. He took two more steps to squarely front the taller man. His breathing was a harsh sweep. "I've been waitin' for this. . . . You looking for something, maybe?" He lifted the bulky object from his side. "Like this?"

As Trevannon's eyes flicked down, widened on the grain sack, Treat struck, savagely and without warning. His gun barrel slashed along Trevannon's temple, staggering him. He hit again, driving the drifter to his hands and knees.

Through a swimming blur Trevannon saw Treat's legs and tried to grab them. Treat stepped back and drove a boot into his side. He tried to flinch away from the knife-like pain, gagging. A second kick snapped his chin back, drove him sprawling on his side. He saw Treat loom above, saw the shining arc the gun made coming down again, and helplessly awaited it. He felt it explode against the top of his skull; his dizzy senses pinwheeled off into blackness.

CHAPTER 11

CONSCIOUSNESS REACHED FOR HIS MIND LIKE A GRAY AND flickering pulse before it riptided fully back in shattering pain. Dried blood crusted his eyelids; he forced them open.

Tied across the saddle with his legs on one side, his head and arms swinging on the other, his body rocked limply to his horse's gait. He saw the rutted dust of a road moving beneath, and nausea boiled into his throat and he retched into the dust. Gasping, painfully he turned his head to see Bill Treat's bulky silhouette riding ahead, a lead rope in his fist fastened to the bridle of Trevannon's own bay gelding. Treat, looking back over his shoulder, gave a dry chuckle.

Trevannon squirmed and fought the ropes till his body began to slip free; Treat, with a curse, halted and swung down. Unfastened the ropes and gave a yank on Trevannon's belt that dumped him to the ground.

"I make it you're feisty enough to sit a saddle," he oberved.

Wes shut his eyes against the throbbing fire in his skull, lay motionless awhile till sense and feeling flowed back.

Treat rooted him viciously in the side with a boot. "Come on, get up there!"

With an effort he pulled himself to a sitting position, caught a stirrup and hauled his body upright. He leaned a panting moment against the bay's flank, toed into stirrup and heaved himself astride, leaning his face sickly against its neck.

Treat unfastened the lead rope and handed up his bridle. "You ride ahead." Treat's palm slashed across the bay's rump, started it moving. He mounted his piebald and fell in behind.

For a full five minutes, Trevannon let the bay pick its way without guidance, his face bowed into the mane. He set his teeth then and half-lifted his head. The landscape dizzily swam, settled to firm outlines.

Sunset's final flush was dying against the black-toothed rim of horizon. It was not quite full twilight, but the sunglare had softened bright hues to old-rose and gray. His eyes hurt, and he was grateful for the muted light and the coming coolness. He place landmarks and judged that they were several miles west of the ranch. He had never been to the valley settlement of Coldbrook, but had no doubt that was their destination; the wagon road beneath was well-marked by ranch traffic. He glanced at the dipping sun and decided he had been unconscious for over an hour. Andrea Carter had mentioned that Coldbrook was ten miles from Kaysee. They might have covered half the distance by this time. . . .

Without turning he spoke, shocked at the broken croak his voice made: "You got a warrant, Treat?"

"Citizen's arrest," Treat answered amusedly. "Man who steals twenty thousand dollars makes himself free game in an open field."

"So you talked to the sheriff, put two and two together. I had you all wrong."

"Outsmarted you, eh? Never occur to you why I really came back?"

"That," Wes said softly, now looking back. "Also I figured you'd crowd your chance harder . . . like putting a bullet in me, claiming self-defense."

"Man," Treat laughed, "you bought yourself free room and board on the territory—maybe twenty years of it—when you took that money. Now why should I spoil that?"

Trevannon nodded weakly, dropped his head back to the horse's mane as though he'd given it all up.

Actually his mind was racing desperately over his situation, assessing it. That backward glance had shown him Treat comfortably slack in his saddle, his gun in holster. Contemptuously careless, and not without cause. Even should his prisoner try a break, he could easily put a bullet in his back; the country was flat and open, only thinly stippled with blocks of timber. Without moving his bowed head, Trevannon's questing gaze took in a dense stand of young trees whose lower aisles were crowded with heavy brush . . . just ahead, the road cutting through its center.

It was a long chance, but it might be his last one. He could never have pulled it off in full daylight; the thickening twilight gave him a bare edge. And Treat had read him aright: a man for whom freedom was the breath of life would die a thousand lingering deaths behind prison walls. Better to take the slender gamble, he thought bleakly. If it went wrong, he'd still lose less in the long run.

They reached the timber and rode between its dark flanks. The air was breathless and still except for the hushed *clop* of shod hoofs in the soft road dust. Without stirring his body, Trevannon flexed his sweating hands before him, tightly gripped his bridle. Smoothly coordinated the sideward wrench on his horse's head with the jab of spurs. Launched the bay hard and sideways into the brush. Crashed solidly through it and broke at once into an open glade, not halting.

Treat's shrilled curse had come even as he left the road, but he was already inside dim cover when the first shot came. It whipped foliage somewhere at his back. Trevannon spurred across the glade, saw another thicket loom darkly to his right and threw himself from the saddle into its springy top branches even as he heard Treat's crashing advance into the brush behind. His balled body plunged through the bare lower boughs and he made himself small amidst their tangle as his horse bolted on into the trees beyond.

At once Treat hauled up his mount in the little glade not three yards from where Trevannon crouched. He hoped achingly that Treat would judge his position by where his horse had stopped. Treat slowly dismounted, stood for a moment listening. Wes heard his heavy breathing, saw his body tense-postured, the steely twinkle of his drawn gun through the screening leaves.

Slowly Treat tramped forward—moving past the thicket not a yard distant, but swallowed almost at once by the close-set tree boles. With infinite care Trevannon broke off a limber branch and noiselessly detached himself from the thicket, took several long strides to reach Treat's horse. He quartered it around to face the road and slashed the switch across its rump.

The piebald squealed and plunged away toward the road. Trevannon faded back into the trees, listening to the fast-diminishing tattoo of hoofbeats as Treat, squalling curses, crashed back through the wood toward the road. He'd guess that the fugitive's ruse had involved taking his horse, which was what Trevannon wanted him to think—giving Wes a chance to reach his bay, with Treat left afoot halfway between town and the ranch. The piebald probably wouldn't stop till he reached his home corral, and the time it took Treat to get back and fork a fresh horse would give Trevannon a wide lead.

Quickly he groped through the timber till he found the bay standing quietly almost at its far end. Once in leather, he nudged through the remaining grove and hit up an easy lope. . . .

Now, he knew bitterly, there was no choice left him. Treat's uncovering of the money would pin the identity of the bank robber squarely on him, the only stranger at Kaysee. That was the price he'd paid for underestimating the squat foreman. He must keep riding, clear of the valley, far out of the territory, before he could draw another safe breath. Something else he hadn't expected was that this

knowledge really hurt. A man had to exonerate himself in
his own eyes, and he'd made a good start here. Now he
must drop everything and run, and every fiber of his being
rebelled against the fact.

He thought of the Canaanites . . . and mostly of Calla
Waybeck. That made it harder, for she had stayed in his
mind after their brief talk. He wanted to see her again before
he went on . . . *But what then?* he wondered bleakly.
What good would it do, for you or her? He considered that
more thoughtfully. Just maybe he could do her and the
others one bit of good. There was still Cassius McQuayle,
the man he hadn't met, whose name had cropped up
repeatedly and who might be using the Canaanites for a
hidden purpose, something that might hurt Kaysee too.

If he could offer Ephraim Waybeck proof of the perfidy of
a man he trusted, put him on guard, he could still bring
some good out of his own brief part in this affair. Too, partly
at least, it was a kind of last gesture, like a damnfool kid
showing off for his girl. He wanted very much not to leave
Calla Waybeck thinking ill of him, as she must if he simply
vanished without explanation.

Meantime the broad head start he had on Treat would
give him time. He didn't know Cassius McQuayle; the man
might be an iron ramrod or a fragile reed, easily broken.
You can find out fast enough, Trevannon though grimly.
. . . Without hesitation he swung his horse back toward
the wagon road.

It was full dark when the black-blocked buildings of town
grew into view. Trevannon rode down Coldbrook's single
avenue, through the long rectangles of saffron glow out-
thrown by street windows. He spotted the general trade
store and tied his horse at the rail and went in.

The proprietor was about to close up, but his first
resentment faded at the sizable order of grub staples
Trevannon gave him against the trail ahead, when he
expected to hole up and sleep by day, travel by night and

avoid towns till he was out of the territory. The storekeeper was brisk and officious; it didn't take him long to assemble Trevannon's wants, dump them in a flour sack. As Trevannon paid, he asked casually where Lawyer McQuayle lived.

"In his hotel room where he's always lived," the proprietor snapped. "Always works late in his office, though. Want to see him now, suggest you try there; professional building across the street."

Trevannon thanked him and left, lingering at the tie rail to tie the sack of supplies to his saddle horn. Then he cut across to the professional building where he saw a single light burning in a second-story window.

Wes paused at the entrance to scan the street, a mechanical precaution. His gaze narrowed down on the adobe jail across the way a block down. His mouth went dry. No mistaking the broad, towering outline of the man lounging in the doorway . . . Jans Vandermeer. Cal Kittredge had impressively described the sheriff: ". . . built like a mountain . . . man you couldn't miss." So Vandermeer's search for the robber had brought him to Coldbrook . . . Of course; it was Vandermeer who'd tipped off Bill Treat.

Just now the sheriff's head turned; he was talking over his shoulder to someone in the office. Trevannon let out a long-held breath and went lightly up the staircase, taking the steps three at a time. The second-floor corridor was dark, but he saw a fine slit of lamplight beneath a door halfway down. He catfooted to it, gently palmed the doorknob and turned it, an instant later closed the door behind him.

Sallow lamplight profiled a man sitting at a rolltop desk, hunched over it busily. A swivel chair creaked under his slight weight as he swung about. He was a frail specter of a man in his mid-sixties whose wispy white hair framed a slack-wrinkled and benign face. His blue eyes held a tired but facile kindliness, and his age-rusty black suit lent an air of honorable poverty. He tossed his pencil onto a scattering of legal-looking documents and removed his iron-rimmed spectacles with a genial smile. "Can I do—"

Cassius McQuayle dropped his statement in mid-air and let it hang unfinished. Trevannon's face reflected his mood. Sudden alarm washed across McQuayle's; he reached slowly for a desk drawer by his knee.

"Better if you didn't," Trevannon said gently.

"Wh—what?"

"Just some talk." Wes walked to the desk, slung a hip over its corner. Warily eying him, McQuayle picked up a tobacco plug by his elbow, with palsied fingers sheared off a wad with a penknife and stowed it in the pouch of his cheek. He cudded it slowly and uneasily. Trevannon ignored the nervous ritual, staring stonily into McQuayle's eyes.

"I got some question. You better have the answers."

McQuayle's benign blandness drained away, baring a cold slyness. Calla Waybeck had been right about him, Trevannon thought then. "Who are you?" MacQuayle asked in a genial tone.

"Mister, you don't ask, just answer. Why you really want that land you got the Canaanites to homestead?"

"I don't know what you—" McQuayle began, and Trevannon's big hand shot out, fisted a handful of his shirt front and dragged his frail body from the chair. He forced the lawyer to his knees, twisting the high, stiff collar cruelly against the scrawny neck. Trevannon had already sized up this shyster as nothing but an oil-tongued confidence man, and he was out of patience.

"Don't waste my time," he told McQuayle. "I haven't any to spare."

"God's sake, mister—ease off—I got a bad heart—"

"Then you got good reason not to tax it. I haven't. Remember that." Trevannon let up his grip enough for the lawyer to drag air into his bruised throat. It had been far easier than he'd expected . . . a single threat, a brief show of force, and this bland little man was reduced to a quivering bundle of fright.

McQuayle now babbled out a story whose main outlines Trevannon had half-guessed. With the Homestead Act had come a host of elaborate land swindles that took ruthless legal advantage of the honor code of an earlier West, where a man's handshake was his sworn bond. Against the new land pirates, every cattleman had learned to be on his guard. Like much large-scale chincanery, McQuayle's scheme was wholly within the law. He'd seen the uselessness of this valley for other than forage crop purposes. He also knew that the federal government had forced a treaty on some nomadic Navajos which had deprived them of a large chunk of their southern stamping grounds, including most of this valley, which Kilrain Carter had tacked onto his Kaysee ranch years ago by burning out a Navajo camp. The new treaty had made the valley public domain.

McQuayle wanted a sizable strip along Kaysee's east boundary. To get it, he'd gone to the newly arrived Canaanites, and after ingratiating himself into friendship with Ephraim Waybeck, had persuaded him that this was the tract he wanted, Ephraim half-believing that McQuayle's persuasive manner was part of the Providence that had guided him here. The Canaanites were diehard farmers. Within two years at the most, they would see the futility of trying to crop this land, even with the sanction of divine guidance. Rather than starve to death, they would sell their proved-up homesteads to McQuayle for next to nothing.

McQuayle's eyes flickered slyly. "And I'd have a nice piece of grass to speculate with. . . ."

"You're a liar," Trevannon said flatly. "Why that particular piece? I make it you got a get-rich-quick joker up your sleeve. Your kind never cares about slow returns, and you're an old man, too old to wait. There's something else about that land. . . ."

He reached for MacQuayle's throat again; the lawyer made a thin, bleating sound, flinched away.

"For God's sake, don't hurt me! I'll tell you!" He rubbed a shaking hand over his sagging, putty-tinged face. "I know

quite a bit—about mining and mines. Used to hang around
'em a lot—"

"Selling useless stock in 'em?"

McQuayle paused uneasily. "Anyway, I was riding over
that way a year ago, found gold in the beds of some creek
branches on that tract. Enough to make me interested."

Trevannon said grimly, "A lot of streambeds are filled
with heavy color. Don't mean a damn thing. When I was a
kid, I wasted a year panning streams. Took most of my pay
in an aching back."

"I spotted some auriferous outcrops," McQuayle sighed.
"Like they say, gold's where you find it. Auriferous rock,
though, can mean rich deposits. I spent several days digging
shallow test pits . . . and carefully covering them up
again. Time and again, I hit solid veins, pockets of the
stuff." He paused; his face in the lamplight had a sick,
yellowish cast. "That whole boundary strip is filthy with the
stuff . . . placer deposits, A man who owned the land
could set up mining equipment, large-scale operations.
Chance of a lifetime. . . ." His voice trailed; his chin
dropped to his chest.

Trevannon took him by the shoulder, gave a hard shake.
"Anyone plowin' that land'd be sure to run into some gold
pockets."

"Know that," McQuayle said wearily. "That's why the
Canaanites were ideal for my purpose. They believe wealth,
the wordly pleasures it buys, is the worst curse under the
sun. Unlike most people, they don't turn their backs on their
beliefs when it's convenient. And they wouldn't let word of
the gold get out, knowing that everybody in the country
would swarm in to stake a claim if they did."

"And you think they'd ever sell out to you, when they
found out what you was after?"

Cassius McQuayle smiled feebly. "It was admittedly a
gamble—but I think it would go something like this: I know
Ephraim Waybeck well. He's no fool in his way, but that
childlike faith of his will always betray him. He reads the

real good in people like a printed page—his big weakness is, he also reads good into people when there is none, simply because he wants to believe it. Then too—while I have no illusions about myself, I can create a most convincing illusion of myself for all except folk with a streak of—shall we say, honest cynicism—like yourself. And like old Ephraim's daughter-in-law Calla, a perceptive young woman who does not think in the same terms as her compatriots. She plainly distrusts me. Fortunately, a woman's opinions carry small weight. . . .

"Now—I would go to Ephraim Waybeck wearing a contrite face, with many apologies for recommending this property that turned out so badly for them. And offer to make amends by buying it up. Despite the bad state of my finances, I would feel I must make what small atonement I can afford. Ephraim would be most touched—and gladly sell me the land with its riches which are useless to him, but which in my benevolent hands would be used judiciously and wisely as a force for good."

Trevannon was silent, regarding the old con man with a kind of reluctant admiration for a born scoundrel's elaborate foresight. "That's long-range guessing," he said.

"I told you it was a gamble," McQuayle whispered. "God knows I've no physical courage. But a confidence man without confidence—what's that? These were the stakes which would climax—and justify—these many years of petty schemes, mostly failures. I was casting all my experience and a few thousand dollars I'd saved into one magnificent pot." He glanced up with a faint, sly hope. "I wonder—how many people will believe this story?"

"Calla Waybeck," Trevannon said promptly. "And likely Ephraim, if it comes from me. I met him; he sort of took a fancy to me. He won't be particularly happy, either, about you stampedin' his crazy brother-in-law into cutting Kilrain Carter in half with a shotgun. . . ."

McQuayle's eyes jerked wildly. "Who said I did?"

"One or two people who figure Bodie Teece was no

killer, for all his ranting. They figure somebody put a bug in his ear—something Teece said before he shot Carter points that way. They think you're a likely candidate. After meetin' you, so do I. You're the kind could talk a rattler out of his fangs."

"Now I ask you . . . do I look like a man who'd plan a murder?"

"Not directly, no. But if the stakes was high enough, and you could push it along with no danger to yourself. . . . why not? This way you couldn't be touched, no matter what anybody suspected."

McQuayle was too defeated to argue. "Ah-h . . . what's the difference? Bodie hated the Devil even above Kilrain Carter. I told him Carter was known to hold Black Masses . . . that he was gathering the forces of darkness to crush the Canaanites. Old fool was ready to believe anything bad about Carter. I didn't think he'd bother to mention to anyone where he picked up the notion." His eyes narrowed. "That might have turned the trick—or possibly something else did. You see, you can't prove a thing one way or the other. Now, damn you," with a sudden flare of spirit, "will you get off my back?"

McQuayle settled himself in his chair, with movements like those of a very old and tired man. "I had the idea, anyway," he murmured. "The glorious taste of it. The one thing you can't take away."

Suddenly this little man and his office were very shabby and unimpressive, and Trevannon, scowling down at him, could find no words small enough to waste on him. He stood and walked quietly to the door. All he could do now was tell Andrea Carter and Ephraim Waybeck what he had learned. It would not solve all their troubles, he knew bleakly; those were only beginning, but cutting the ground from under McQuayle would end a lot of grief before it got started. In any case, he couldn't do more. . . .

He palmed open the door and stepped into the murky hallway. Instantly froze as the bobbing flare of a lantern appeared in the stairwell, filling the corridor with its diffused glare. Trevannon's hand brushed his holster, reaching for the gun Treat had taken, before he remembered. He stopped dead, facing the stone-faced giant coming up the stairs with a lantern in one hamlike fist, a leveled gun in the other. Jans Vandermeer had caught up at last. And crowding behind the sheriff's bulk was the grinning face of Bill Treat.

CHAPTER 12

SHERIFF VANDERMEER'S STOLID GRIMNESS HARDLY RELAXED with the taking of Wes Travannon and the recovery of the twenty thousand in bank loot which Bill Treat has turned over to him. It was all in the day's work; his ready smile never touched the other lines of his craggy face. When he'd gotten Cassius McQuayle's assurance that he was unhurt, though badly shaken, he glanced at the small heavy safe in one corner of McQuayle's dingy office and said that tomorrow he'd start back for Cedar Wells with his prisoner; Lawyer McQuayle's safe looked to be a sturdy one, and might he leave the twenty thousand dollars there overnight?

McQuayle apathetically agreed, and the sheriff watched him dial open his safe, place the grain sack of money inside, and close it. The sheriff then thanked Bill Treat for his help, said a stolid goodnight, and left with his prisoner, headed for the jail.

Bill Treat lingered in McQuayle's office, slacking into the visitor's chair, feeling elatedly expansive as he fired up a cheap cigar. Enjoying McQuayle's trembling reaction as the shyster sat hunched in his swivel chair. "Put a scare into you, did he, old man?" Treat asked with mock sympathy.

McQuayle stirred a hand feebly, only now glancing at Treat. "I don't understand how you—the sheriff—happened to come here."

Treat was feeling ebullient and boastful. He told how he'd arranged with the sheriff to capture Trevannon, whom

251

they'd deduced was the Cedar Wells bank robber. When he'd turned up the necessary evidence—the bank loot—he was to bring Trevannon in for arrest. On the way Trevannon had escaped and set him afoot, hoorawing off his horse.

"What he didn't know, I raised that piebald from a colt," Treat concluded, chuckling. "He don't go far from old Bill even when he's stampeded. . . . I whistled him up and hustled on to Coldbrook. Figured Trevannon might cut for here first to pick up some grub. Sure enough, found his horse hitched in front of the general store, sack of grub tied on. Old Murfree was just closin' up. I give him Trevannon's description. Said he'd asked about Cassius McQuayle. Well, your window was still lighted—that cinched it. So I fetched Dutchy Vandermeer on the double." He leaned forward curiously, lacing his thick fingers together. "What did he want with you anyhow?"

"None of your business."

Treat's gaze narrowed. "Wouldn't have to do with the Canaanites, would it?"

A sudden wariness flickered in McQuayle's faded eyes before he covered it.

Treat laughed. "Hell, man, you can play Father Christmas to them simple-minded sodders; a man who's been around can see through you like glass. That bastard Trevannon's no fool, neither am I. Don't know what your game is, 'cept that eggin' plowmen onto a couple sections of graze that wa'n't made for plowin' don't make sense on the face of it. . . ."

McQuayle shaped a strange, hopeless smile. "What's the difference now? Trevannon knows anyway. About the gold."

"Gold!" It left Treat in an explosive grunt. He came out of his chair and took three long strides to McQuayle's side, set his fists on his hips and glowered down at the smaller man. "Cass, you got some medicine to make. And it better be straight talk."

A part of Treat's mind hung avidly on McQuayle's

droned, dull-spoken explanation, while his thoughts leaped ahead with a mounting exultation. . . .

Till a few hours ago, when he had reached a dissatisfying agreement with Mrs. Congreve, two passions had centered Bill Treat's life. Driving passions, yet limited both, for he wasn't by nature a complex man. One was Kaysee, the other was Kilrain Carter's beautiful widow. Previously he had been satisfied with foremanship of the great ranch he'd help make; a savage lust had filled out his desire for Andrea.

Whether she'd so intended or not, Mrs. Congreve had caused Treat's ambitions to vault sky-high. The possibilities she had suggested—marriage to Andrea, coming into full control of Kaysee—had left him breathless with the sight of shining new vistas, even while he realized the hopelessness of these goals. Money was the huge drawback, the root of his frustrations. With money, he'd have Mrs. Congreve's cooperation—and then Kaysee and Andrea—and finally Mrs. Congreve herself sent back East and out of his hair for good.

He was puffing his cigar with wild excitement now . . . *gold on Kaysee!* Treat's emotional demands were simple, but his sly mind was handy at mulling over ideas, if they weren't too abstract. It busied itself at once. Rather, there was gold on public domain, a fortune waiting in the earth, unstaked and unclaimed. Even unknown, as yet, save to Cass McQuayle and now himself. *And Trevannon,* he thought viciously. . . .

McQuayle had good reason to be upset. There would be a mighty claim-rush on that land if word got out. And Trevannon, now prison-bound, had no reason to keep quiet, had good reason to reveal the lawyer's scheme to use his friends the Canaanites.

If Trevannon were somehow silenced, the scheme could go ahead as McQuayle had planned. Around this simple fact revolved the key to the wealth Treat desperately needed. Except that, instead of keeping the Canaanites off that land as he'd vowed to Mrs. Congreve, he'd be committed to insuring their successful settlement . . . at least till their homesteads were proved up and they could sell out to McQuayle.

Somehow he must trick that shrew of a Congreve woman. There were ways. If he couldn't keep her in ignorance, he'd explain that he judged Trevannon to be right on one point: that land wasn't fit for farming; the land itself would defeat them, and they'd abandon it, their failure a warning to all future sodbusters. It would be more effective than throwing them off. Yet if they took Trevannon's advice and raised cattle instead, he'd have to wait till they'd proved up their homesteads before driving them off. That could make him a lot of trouble. By God, it was all chancy enough, and no mistake. But he'd cross his bridges when they came up; the important thing was, this was his main chance and he had to grab it.

His hand dropped to McQuayle's frail shoulder, shaking it roughly. "Listen, Cass," he said with a wintry grin. "How bad you want that land? Enough to split whatever you get from it down the middle?"

McQuayle was staring vacuously at the papers on his desk, kneading his lower lip between thumb and forefinger. He glanced up wearily. "What's the difference now?"

Treat's hand tightened. "Do you?"

McQuayle winced. "Yes, damn you, I'd settle for half! But what—"

"You remember," Treat pressed, "what Trevannon said a few minutes ago when the sheriff asked him if he had anything to say?"

The lawyer frowned. "He said, 'Nothing you'd listen to.' I surmise that he's smart enough not to say anything till he gets his day in court. Then," McQuayle added bitterly, "he'll tear my idea wide open by springing it dramatically in public. . . . What's on your mind, Treat?"

"Something," Treat murmured, "that a shaky, rabbity old gent like you couldn't pull off by his lonesome. All right—Trevannon ain't about to talk. Gives us time. Not that we need a hell of a lot. Just a few hours, till the town's asleep. And then, old man, for the cost of a bullet you and I'll have our fingers in a fortune . . . not a bad trade, eh?"

The Coldbrook jail was a small stone building with the deputy's office constituting its front half; a door opened into the cell block behind where a short corridor, illumined by a lamp in a wall bracket, divided two large cells. In one, a drunk was snoring it off. Wes Trevannon stepped into the other, and Deputy Bell clanged the door shut and turned the key. Trevannon slacked onto the narrow wooden cot, crossed his legs and pillowed his folded arms behind his head.

Sheriff Vandermeer stepped close to the bars, frowning in at him. "Mr. Trevannon," he said deliberately, "I confess that you have me buffaloed. With twenty thousand stolen dollars it makes sense that you would ride far from this country with all possible haste. It does not make sense that a fleeing criminal would risk his life to save another, as you did for Mrs. Carter—but granted that he might, why should he then remain for any purpose? You are a very rash and foolish man, Mr. Trevannon, or a very complicated and clever one . . . perhaps something of both. This I don't know. Wish you now would explain yourself."

Trevannon shook his head very slightly.

Job Bell tossed the key ring up and down in his hand, glaring through the bars. "You want my opinion, he used a saddle tramp's gall to run a sandy on Mrs. Carter, then finagled himself into that foreman's job. Figured if nobody found the money, they couldn't do anything. That's simple enough."

Vandermeer shook his massive head reprovingly. "You tend to oversimplify always, Job. This is not a good thing in a man of law. It makes you overlook what else there may be under your very nose. But it is so with young men. See now: a man afraid of the law, smart or stupid, his first instinct is to run far away; he does not reason so closely as

all that. No, there is something to this man that remains
unsaid. Why does he visit Lawyer McQuayle? McQuayle
says he comes in and demands money. For the getaway?
Perhaps. But why pick on a poor attorney? Why did he not
rob this thriving store where grub he buys?"

Trevannon smiled faintly, looked away from them and
tilted his hat over his eyes.

Vandermeer snorted gently. "Get your sleep then. We
start for Cedar Wells early tomorrow."

When the door to the office closed behind the two
lawmen, Trevannon swung at once to his feet. Stoically he
did not curse his bad luck, wasting time in futile regrets.
You couldn't plan life; when a situation soured, you had to
make the best of it. He felt the solidly mortared stones of the
walls, stood on his cot to test the bars of the single high
window, and calmly accepted the impregnable sturdiness of
his prison. He sat on the bunk and without haste or panic
pondered the problem. Only wit could help him now
. . . and Vandermeer would know every jail breaker's
dodge in the book. On the other hand, and as the sheriff
himself had hinted, young Job's mule-set way narrowed his
thinking; in a prosaic situation he'd be cautious enough, but
caught off-guard by an unfamiliar one, he'd more likely act
on confused impulse.

Trevannon thoughtfully studied a knothole punched
through one of the two-by-eight ceiling joists overhead.
Then cocked his head, listening to the drift of voices beyond
the door.

". . . should get some sleep at my pa's house if you
want an early start," Bell was saying. "If you think best,
I'll stay the night here—he's a slippery customer."

"That would be best," Vandermeer assented, hesitating
then as if for a special word of caution. Which, since he'd
already criticized Bell, he didn't voice, only saying quietly,
"Watch sharp, Job."

The outer office door closed behind the sheriff. Trevannon heard Bell's swivel chair creak with his settled weight. . . . Then he set quietly to work. He'd picked up not a few useful tricks during his law-dodging interlude. One was the handleless blade of a straight-edged razor, hidden in a deep slit of one of his run-down half boots. Filed very thin and lying flat within the thick, stiff leather, it had escaped even Vandermeer's practiced search of his clothing. It took five minutes to work it free of the boot. Then he took the single coarse blanket from his cot and cut three lengthwise strips from it. Working quickly, he braided the blanket strands into a tough, crude rope. He stood on his cot and stretched his height on tiptoe, straining his arms upward to poke an end of his rope through the beam knothole. He anchored it with a tight knot and then swung his full weight off the cot to test it.

The improvised length held. Trevannon climbed back to the cot and stripped off his denim jacket, bound the free end of the rope around his torso and beneath his arms, straining to take up all the slack possible. He pulled his jacket on again, buttoned it to his throat and turned up the collar. He hinged his knees and let his inert weight swing off the cot and hang suspended, slowly turning, in the center of the cell. Extended his legs and found with satisfaction that his toes swung clear of the floor. The rope ran down the back of his neck, hidden by the jacket; the razor lay concealed in his right hand, flat against the palm.

Now you look like gallows' fruit, you better act the part, ran his wry thought. He raised his voice in a strangled yell, wildly churning his arms and legs. At once Job Bell flung open the door and lunged into the corridor, halted with his jaw falling slack. "Godalmighty," he breathed, and frantically snatched the key ring from his belt.

As Bell lunged through the door, Trevannon's leg kicked back as if by painful reflex. Then he drove it savagely forward into the pit of the deputy's stomach. Bell simply melted to the floor. Crumpled there in doubled-up agony, he gagged soundlessly. Trevannon reached above his head and slashed the rope with a stroke of his razor, dropped to the floor.

He bent over Bell and jerked his gun from its holster. Said between his teeth, "Sorry, boy, you learn the hard way," as he brought the barrel down in a stiff, chopping arc behind Bell's ear. The young deputy's muscles strung hard, then he went quickly limp.

Trevannon removed Bell's gunbelt, caught him beneath the arms and hoisted him onto the bunk. Stretched him with his face to the wall and spread the blanket over him. His hard blow had been carefully placed; it would lay a man out cold for an hour or so and leave him with no worse than a bad headache and some painfully acquired wisdom.

Wes buckled on Bell's gun, locked the door behind him, glanced at the man in the other cell who snored soddenly on, and then went out to the office. He tossed the keys on Bell's desk and stepped to the door, opened it a crack to scan the street. The hitch-rack by the general store was empty; Vandermeer must have taken his horse to the livery. A tinny piano was banging away in a saloon, and a couple of men came out arm in arm, drunkenly weaving and bawling tunelessly,

> "We cleared up all the Indians,
> Drank all the alkali,
> And it's whack the cattle on, boys—
> Root hog or die. . . ."

Trevannon tugged his hatbrim low and went out, closing the door. He headed unhurried down the sidewalk, skirting the two drunks, and turned in at the livery stable. A lantern hung over a spike driven into a stall post burned dimly. No sign of the hostler . . . catching a drink, likely.

Trevannon quickly located his bay in an end stall and saddled up. But he rode out from town as though he had all the time in the world, drawling, "Howdy," to the casual greeting of an incoming rider he passed.

Beyond the last building, he lined onto the wagon road toward Kaysee, his bitter impatience set like a hot coal in his belly.

CHAPTER 13

Aᴳᴬᴵᴺˢᵀ ᴛʜᴀᴛ ɪᴍᴘᴀᴛɪᴇɴᴄᴇ, Tʀᴇᴠᴀɴɴᴏɴ ʜᴇʟᴅ ʜɪs ʜᴏʀsᴇ ɪɴ to conserve its strength, and it was two hours before he came in sight of ranch headquarters. From the road he could see the bunkhouse and main house were darkened, but wary of being picked up by the ranch dog he tethered his horse a good fifty yards from the buildings and hiked in, circling wide to come up on the house from the nearby grove. He'd been unconscious when Treat had taken him away; he had to assume for safety's sake that the other Kaysee people knew by now that he was a wanted fugitive. His two days' foremanship here had hardly been enough to command the crew's loyalty—of them, he'd gotten close only to Gabe Morrow. He couldn't get to Gabe without arousing the others. That left Andrea, and he wasn't sure which room was hers, knowing only that the bedroom windows opened on this side of the house.

But emerging from the grove and trotting across the yard, he found himself in luck. Lamplight filled a rectangle of a window, beyond which he glimpsed Andrea's bright crown of auburn hair. He ran silently to the window and tapped on a pane.

She was sitting on her bed, wearing a red quilted wrapper, head tilted as she brushed out her hair; it crumpled softly across the shirred collar of her robe, a darkly burnished mass shot with red-gold highlights. She quickly

260

turned her head, lowered the hand that held her silver-chased brush. Wide-eyed, she rose and came quickly to the window, wrestled the lower sash up a couple of inches. Trevannon got his fingers beneath and shoved it higher.

Andrea went down on her knees, her fingers grasping the sill. "What happened?" she said.

"You don't know?"

Her hair stirred softly with a negative motion of her head. "I went to the bunkhouse to ask you again if you'd come to supper. You were gone and the crew said you and Bill Treat went to town together. Said they didn't know why . . . they sounded uneasy and evasive." Her ripe underlip formed a petulant shape. "Nobody tells me anything . . . always treating me like a child—"

"Now," Trevannon said quietly, "you'll have to act the woman. I'm in trouble, bad trouble."

Her eyes dilated darkly; she said swiftly, "Come in. Quick, before you're seen."

She moved back, and Trevannon wormed sideways between sash and sill, stepped inside. Andrea drew the shade down and turned to face him. "What is it, Wes?"

Trevannon breathed more easily; she was responding maturely and sensibly now. *But she changes like the wind,* he reminded himself, *so go easy.* He began to talk, studying her face closely, and as he spoke he saw her first resolution falter. Yet she said nothing, only stood unmoving, hardly breathing. Wes felt a cold uneasiness; the girl was a complete enigma—how would she react? Still he had to see out this thing he'd begun, and he kept talking, quietly and reasonably.

When he'd finished she said very softly, "But you can't just go away like this, Wes. What will I do?"

"I told you," Trevannon said patiently. "I gave you the facts about Treat and McQuayle. Use 'em."

"But Mother told me that Bill Treat will be foreman again," she said, half-whimpering. "That was just after you disappeared with Treat. I didn't understand then—but she sounded so smug, so sure—"

"Look, Andrea .. . ." Trevannon drew a deep breath. "It sounds to me like your ma and Treat are dealing behind your back—listen to me, dammit!" he added savagely as her attention listlessly strayed. "You're mistress of Kaysee. Get that through your head! You got the say-so here; when you say cricket, they chirp. But you got to start believing it. Here's my advice. Get rid of Treat and make your peace with the Canaanites. They're good people and understanding, and you'll need friends like that—"

"But what about you?"

"I told you, the law's breathing on my neck. I'll be lucky to get shed of this valley a jump ahead of Jans Vandermeer. Bell's likely come to, roused him by now. And he won't wait. I got to cut out now, no choice. Girl, you got to brace up, face life like it is. For your sake, for your ma's—"

She seized on that straw. "Oh, but I can't trust her. She does things behind my back, you know that."

Wes nodded coldly. "She's part of what you'll have to handle—by yourself."

"But I can't run Kaysee!" she wailed.

"Gabe Morrow's a man can be trusted. Make him foreman, he'll handle the ranch end."

Andrea's slender shafts of argument were used up. She faced him mutely, her face deathly white. And Trevannon realized amazedly that she was frightened—actually terrified. This baffled him, till she moved closer and her hands reached blindly, caught his arms. She came against him, her head bowed on his chest. Her low voice was a muffled sound.

He bent his head. "What?"

"I said, I love you."

Trevannon felt the shock of it, was strongly aware of her firmly rounded body trembling against him like a scared child's, and the fragrance of her hair. A sum of heady temptation that he forced from him; he stepped back, his hands on her shoulders holding her at arm's length. Her tear-streaked face tilted up, and seeing it he felt only pity then and a deep sadness.

"Child, you don't know what you're saying."

Sudden anger sparked her violet eyes. She stamped her foot. "I do so! You're just like the rest—" she broke off with a tremulous smile. "Just like a man, too blind to see what's under his very nose. But you do understand now, don't you, Wes?"

"Sure," he said hollowly. "I understand."

A fierce joy blazed in her face. "Oh, good. That solves everything, don't you see? I only argued about those other things to make you stay. And you know why I really wanted you to stay. I don't give a damn about this silly old ranch or Mother either!" Her mouth twisted in a brief, ugly way. "I hate her. I'm tired of her nagging and her orders. If I stayed, it would only be more of the same." Again her bright eagerness. "But I don't have to stay, do I?—Not now."

"Look," Trevannon got out, "if you're thinking—"

"But certainly, darling. I'm going with you. See how simple it is?"

Trevannon shook his head slowly. "I can't be your father, Andrea."

"What *are* you talking about?" she said exasperatedly, and then laughed. "Wait till you learn what I can be, for you."

"I don't want to find out," he said doggedly. "That's what I'm telling you, girl. No good arguing about it." She raised her arms and came to him, but he caught her wrists and thrust her roughly away. "Now quit that! I'm leaving now, and you're staying here. Understand?"

She flinched from his harsh anger as from a slap, and a flush of abrupt rage beat into her face. Swiftly it mounted beyond rage, ugly and chilling. For Trevannon, there was something coldly familiar in the varnished blankness of her stare, and then he knew. He's seen it in Bodie Teece only a few days ago, that one state of mind with which nobody can argue. He stepped back to the window, warily watching her.

"You won't take me with you," she murmured tensely. "So you won't take me with you. Well, Tige will fix you. Tige!" She screamed the name. *"Tige, come here!"*

Trevannon slung his leg over the sill and ducked out, sprinting for the grove. He tore through it at a run, cut wide around the outbuildings to reach his horse. As he hit the saddle he looked back, saw a lantern bobbing from the bunkhouse as somebody exited on the run, headed for the main house. Faint screams still throbbed in his ears, and Trevannon found himself shaking, sickened by what he had witnessed. God alone knew how long it had been building in her, to this . . . a thing before which he, like all men, was powerless.

He could not help Andrea Carter. His thoughts veered to the Canaanites. Nothing left but to warn them of McQuayle. And there was Calla Waybeck; suddenly he wanted to be with her and be touched by her full serenity, the gentle reserve that glided over calm strength. He seized on that like a drowning man in a sea of shadows. Nothing else made sense any longer. This he could accept with relief, without question.

He turned roughly south for the Canaanite settlement. The night was black and moonless, and the stars were overcast, lending only a faint silvery complexion to the oceanic roll of grassland. He did not know this country well, and with landmarks and stars hidden, even his lifetime plainsman's instinct was baffled. It would be too easy to head wrong. And he needed rest and sleep badly. The strain of these last hours had been fierce; his head and body ached from the brutal beating Treat had administered.

Accordingly he pulled into the lee of an outcrop, hobbled the bay and settled himself into a crotch of rock, propped half upright with his gun in his lap. Sleepily he mapped out his future moves . . . catch a few hours' sleep and be on his way at first light. He'd lose no margin of safety, for the thick darkness would hold back pursuers till then. See the Canaanites and ride on from the valley without delay, as fast and far as possible. He felt a numb pang of regret, thinking of Calla. A hell of a time for two years of loneliness to catch up, he thought distantly, as if he hadn't enough barbs working in his hide already. A minute later his exhausted mind mercifully let go, and he slept like a log.

Kilrain Carter had had a fine oaken four-poster bed freighted in before he'd brought his new bride to Kaysee a year ago. She had been tense and frightened that first night: this was one thing for which her mother hadn't prepared her. And it had been fully as terrible as she'd expected, for Kilrain Carter was never a gentle man, with men or horses or with a woman, and finally he had turned in disgust from her pain and fear and sobbing. Later it hadn't been so bad, but the sick knowledge that she was only a plaything for an aging man's last brittle fling at lust had stayed with her. She'd found relief in his masculine domination, except for this shameful stain that she couldn't wipe from memory. . . .

It kept coming back to Andrea now as she lay alone in her vast bed, while the dreary, pre-dawn light filtered through the east window. But the remembrance was muddy and inchoate, broken by other thoughts which moved in and out of her mind like patches of light and shadow. Her head hurt so that she wanted to scream aloud. But she only lay quietly, wide eyes fixed on the gray frame of ceiling, her bosom hardly stirring with her breathing. Vaguely it occurred to her once or twice that every warped circumstance of her life was funneling at last into a breaking point, but this single thrust toward sanity, like a warning bell in her mind, flickered and drifted and was lost in her tattered thoughts.

Suddenly she began to shiver uncontrollably though the graying darkness was warm and close, and she clutched the blankets to her, feeling small and lost and afraid. If only Trevannon had not left her. For a moment her thoughts held warmly on the tall man, and she was sorry she had sent Tige after him. Then she thought spitefully, *He had it coming. Leaving me all alone. I hope Tige hurts him good.* Anyway, she still had Mother. *Oh, no,* she thought with abrupt stark hatred, *it was all Mother's fault.* Strangely she was no longer sure exactly how, but only that her mother was somehow to blame. . . .

She did remember clearly how her outcries had brought the crew boiling over to the main house in a body, with Tige Menefee loping in the lead. She had met them on the veranda and screamed at them, "What are you staring at? Go on, get back to the bunkhouse, all of you—no, Tige, stay here." She remembered their startled, sleep-drugged stares, and then they had filed sheepishly back to the bunkhouse, except for Menefee. Still trembling with anger, she had given him his orders in a low, strangled hiss. Tige had responded instantly, without surprise or question; he'd nodded and was gone in the night.

Andrea had turned back into the dark parlor to hear her mother's voice calling for an explanation. In the darkness Andrea had reached out and grasped the empty wheel chair, and its hard feel had steadied her. She'd even smiled then. Nightly she helped her mother to bed, leaving the wheel chair in the parlor. Her mother insisted on this, to enforce obedience . . . but she could not leave her bed without help. *"Andrea, Andrea, you wicked girl, come here at once!"* And Andrea had only stood, smiling and listening, as the peremptory tone became an imploring wail . . . finally died into silence.

Andrea had returned quietly to her room. But sleep had not come. The stillness grew oppressive . . . frightening. It was all very well to make this token rejection of her mother, but Kilrain was gone, Trevannon was gone, Daddy was gone, and there was no one to turn to but Mother.

Dimly now, she knew that hours had gone by as she lay there; her fists clenched in the folds of the coverlet. *No no no, I hate her! I won't go back to her, I won't!* The core of pain swelled till she thought her head would burst, and she couldn't lie still any longer.

She flung herself out of bed and ran to the commode, fumbling blindly for the lamp there. She found a match and lifted the sooted chimney. Her hands were trembling wildly and after she struck the match she could not steady it to the wick. Desperately she clasped the lamp to her breast and bit her lip intently as she lighted the wick. At that moment the match scorched her fingers, and she cried out and flung the lamp from her to nurse her thumb.

The lamp hit the floor and broke, sending a spray of coal oil across the carpet. It caught at once, a sheet of flame whipping along the floor. "Oh," Andrea said aloud, "I've got to stop it." She began to stoop and pick up an edge of the carpet; she straightened, watching wide-eyed the progress of the flames as they licked avidly at the log walls.

She would not stop the fire, and it would serve Mother right. The thought began as a momentary and shocking impulse, against which she briefly recoiled. But as she continued to watch the out-fanning flames with fascination, it came back forcefully, and with it a great sense of relief. The tension and fear vanished, and she laughed joyfully aloud. She let her nightgown slip to the floor and paused, liking the sensual glow of rosy heat against her body. But she would have to leave the house now. Almost reluctantly she began to dress. Her movements were automatic; her mind danced like a gay moth, glorying in this forbidden fruit.

Dressed, she ran from the house with her hair streaming out behind. Reached the narrow areaway between the carriage house and a tool shed, sank breathlessly down between the walls. She watched awhile as the flames tongued through the windows and peeled up the outside walls, mounting swiftly to the roof. The logs were old and almost tinder-dry, and the whole east wing had caught now. Mother usually slept the sleep of the dead. Andrea grinned at the thought, hugging her knees and rocking back and forth.

It seemed a long time before the loudening crackle of the fire brought a faint shout from the bunkhouse. Soon the dark shapes of men were pounding past her shelter, and she scrooched deeper into the shadows, making herself small between the shed walls. If she were found she would be punished, and she didn't want that. Once at Doctor Mack's, she had got a whole box of lucifers off the pantry shelf and set them afire. *"Andrea, you naughty girl! Do you want to burn down the house?" "But the fire is so pretty, and I made it for you, Mama."* Andrea bit her thumb gleefully, watching a roaring torrent of flame belch across the dry roof shakes. *If only Daddy could see the fire, too.*

The shouts of the men forming a bucket line to the creek hurt her ears, and the leaping flames hurt her eyes; she rubbed grimy knuckles against her lids and looked away. She did not remember Daddy very well. He was a thin, tired man in bib overalls, and Mommy called him Curt . . . or no, was that someone else? Maybe Daddy was the big, gray-haired man with the silvery wheels on the band on his black hat . . . Kilrain. There was another man mixed in somewhere too, a tall, homely man with yellow hair who had left her alone, and try as she might, she couldn't remember his name at all. Anyway, they were all gone now, all except Mama.

"Where are you, Mama?" she whimpered, beginning to feel afraid again. Only the crackle of flames answered her. She felt sleepy and confused and scared, and here she was all alone, and it wasn't fair. Maybe . . . if you could go back and start all over again, maybe you could make it come out right. If you could go way down deep into the darkness where it all began, you could start over. Why, that was the answer, she thought excitedly. And she was not at all surprised that she knew; it seemed that she'd always known.

She got to her feet and slipped out at the back of the areaway, running to the shed for her bridle, and then to the corral for her black horse. She did this without thinking about it. All the men were fighting the fire on the far side of the ranch layout, and nobody saw her leave.

CHAPTER 14

TREVANNON HAD ALWAYS HAD THE LUCKY FACULTY OF clockwork slumber, waking almost to a minute of his choosing. He came awake and alert all at once, and though it seemed he'd dozed off minutes ago, he saw gray false dawn now belting the eastern sky, picking out the land in shadowy outline . . . time to travel.

He rode straight northeast, retracing the route he'd followed two days ago. He hit a branch of the creek and followed it for a time, forded it at a shallow crossing, and shortly left the rich grasslands of Kaysee open range for the scrubby country to the east, where ridge and flatland, meadow and forest, merged helter-skelter.

The first pink flush of true dawn was dissipating the last murkiness when he left a belt of timber and headed across a badly eroded roll of flats, with its scalped hummocks and deep-worn gullies. . . .

He felt the heavy thud of a long rifle slug slam sickeningly into the bay's flank behind the left forehock. Felt the beast's convulsive dying shudder beneath him even as the rifle's bark whipcracked brittle echoes across the clear, still air.

As the bay's weight sloughed sideways, he kicked from the stirrups and left the saddle, saw the brown earth cant wildly toward him, and lit on his shoulder and hip with a grinding impact that drove the breath from his body. He rolled in blind panic from the falling horse and stopped

269

face-down when he heard the hard cantle crunch against the ground. He got his hands beneath him and pushed his body a foot upward before the second shot thudded into the horse. It twitched with a final muscular spasm, and was still. Trevannon flattened out again as two more shots came, one laid so near it flung dust against his legs.

He squirmed around on his belly and floundered an awkward yard to the shelter of his dead mount. He hugged the saddle and rump with his body, buried his face in the mane. The rifleman deliberately and unhurriedly sent three more shots into the carcass, held fire then.

Five minutes dragged by and Trevannon did not move, his heart thudding painfully against his cramped ribs. He had caught only a confused glimpse of powder smoke laying a pale smudge against the dark lift of timber high on a looming ridge off to his right. A fact of no value whatever. Even if the ambusher weren't completely hidden, he was out of pistol range, and Trevannon's saddle boot was empty; Treat had taken his rifle. Here he was nailed securely, pocketed precariously behind an inert carcass. For ten feet in any direction was no other cover. He might make it to his feet, but he'd be a dead man before he took a second step. . . .

This he knew from the deadly accuracy with which the first bullet had been placed, directly to the bay's heart. Baffled ignorance of the rifleman's identity was an added goad to his sense of utter helplessness. He gripped hard on his nerves then and reasoned three things: the man was full of unrelenting hatred, enough to play cat-and-rat with a certain victim; he had iron, self-possessed patience that had enabled him to wait till he could drop his victim in this open trap; he was an uncanny woodsman who could trail in bad light, follow unseen while matching Trevannon's own pace, and even work ahead of his quarry to pick a likely spot.

For Trevannon had no doubt that this deadfall was by anything but chance; he'd left all his enemies behind. One had followed. . . .

He took off his hat, raised his head till his eyes just

cleared shelter, straining his vision against the black timber. He caught a flicker of neutral color which moved, became a horse and rider shifting across a break in the timber. He recognized Tige Menefee's big blue mustang and the half-breed's easy saddle slouch, before the trees swallowed him a second later. Tige was working downhill, coming in closer. Trevannon held his breath, wondering if this might not be the time to run. He got a knee under him and half-rose and was answered by the instant crash of the rifle. He dived flat again, his sweating face pressed to the dirt.

Tige Menefee . . . of course. Tige, seething with all the jealous, single-minded hatred of his savage blood . . . set on his trail by the girl Menefee blindly worshipped. A girl who'd strike out in the only way she knew . . . like a hurt child, without thought, without regard for the consequences. And Tige would play this dragged-out game which could have only one end to the last drop of torment he could wring from his prey.

Trevannon twisted on his belly, eyeing longingly a patch of trees fifty feet to his right. If he could achieve that, he could work around into the timber cover of the ridge. There he could move freely on somewhat equal terms, where Tige's rifle would give him no edge.

A morning breeze rose off the flats and whipped along the level ground, stirring the long hair which had fallen lankly over his forehead. He tossed it back out of his face and gripped the dusty sod in his frustration, twisting the sere grass in his hands.

Wind and grass . . . *fire!* The idea grenaded into his consciousness. He tore a handful of the dry graze from its weak rooting. The breeze was strengthening, blowing toward the ridge. Erosion had done its dirty work here, and a dry summer had finished the job. A stretch of dead grass rolled sparsely to the foot of the ridge. Enough of it to carry a line of fire to the dying brush that heavily mantled the lower ridge.

He began tearing up all the grass within his reach, fisting a half-dozen bunches around small pebbles for weight. Tige

had now settled into a fresh position, and he laid a few
desultory shots fairly close, evidently amusing himself.
Trevannon unbuttoned the breast pocket of his jacket to get
out an oilcloth-wrapped packet of matches which he laid out
by the grass bunches. Methodically he struck a match and
touched it to each bunch, the dry blades flaring at once with
a clean hot blaze. He squirmed onto his back and tossed
them out one by one, roughly spacing his throws across a
line thirty feet long. Then he flattened hard against the
ground and the carcass, knowing that Tige would now begin
firing in earnest.

Menefee pumped his magazine empty with a haste that
told of his first alarm that his quarry might escape. Bullets
hammered into the horse, into the earth, scattering dust and
pebbles over Trevannon's clothes. The half-breed's long
pause to reload . . . while crawling flames spread and
joined into a blazing line which ate toward the ridge. Fine
banners of smoke wisped up, not yet enough to lend cover.

And then, as Tige resumed firing, the flames reached the
first tangles of vine-covered brush and crackled avidly
upward with a terrifying speed. Masses of vegetation
exploded into fireballs; where dead brush merged with
green wood, dark smoke billowed thickly and was wind-
borne up the ridge face. Menefee was in sudden danger, and
Trevannon heard his racked coughing and afterward the
crash of brush as he plunged up the slope.

Trevannon lunged to his feet, long legs driving him
toward that clump of timber. Hit the fringe of trees and kept
running, cutting a semi-circle to come up on the flank of the
ridge. He heard Tige's mettlesome, half-broken blue,
panicked at the first smell of smoke, come bursting blindly
through the heavy brush straight for him. Trevannon
breasted the brush savagely, his hard-driven breath searing
his lungs, to head off the blue.

He plunged into a small clearing and across it as the blue
came tearing through the last impeding undergrowth. Wes
leaped in recklessly to grab for its bridle. He caught it as the
startled brute reared, then pivoted to avoid the flailing

hoofs. He iron-handed the brute down and got astride with a leaping twist of his body before it could wheel to avoid him.

The mustang fought, piledriving savagely, with Trevannon's spine catching every crushing downjolt. He knew a bleak flash of horseman's admiration for Menefee, whose uncanny sense for horseflesh had mastered this surging power so easily.

And Menefee was coming; Trevannon heard his loping bounds through the underbrush. Tige could hear the struggle but must have mistaken its real nature, for he whistled shrilly. Amazingly and at once the blue stopped fighting; his laid-back ears pricked up and he only snorted and sidled uneasily beneath his alien rider.

At the same time Menefee plowed through the last growth, his head bent behind his flailing arms. Trevannon knew sinkingly that now there would be no avoiding a showdown, as he'd hoped; he slid out his Colt as Menefee broke into the clearing.

The breed's inky eyes flared with the upswing of his head, absorbing the situation in an instant. He whipped up the rifle across his body, bringing it to bear . . . too late, for Trevannon's pistol was already trained. But the half-breed's sudden movement set off the blue again; he careened wildly as Trevannon fired—missed. Tige brought the rifle to his shoulder, sighting carefully to get Trevannon's jolting body in his sights.

And Trevannon clamped a tight and desperate rein on the blue, halting its gyrations for a breath-held instant. The barrel of his six-gun was still braced over the lifted forearm of his bridle-hand. Almost without aiming, he shot.

The shots crashed as one. A smashing blow drove Trevannon sideways from the saddle, and he jerked stirrup-free by instinct, hit the ground rolling and stopped face-down and stunned. He heard the blue bolt from the clearing. Only a powerful effort of panicked will enabled him to roll on his side to face Menefee, wildly wondering why the breed hadn't shot again. . . .

Tige lay on his back with his legs jackknifed grotesquely,

his side-tilted head fixing his sightless stare on Trevannon. The pointblank slug had taken him chest-center. Wes dropped his head into the dirt and closed his eyes, fighting back the black, dizzy waves that engulfed him. Only the blazing pain reaching through the blackness forced him throbbingly awake.

He was hit on the same side where he had caught Kittredge's try a few days ago, but this time it was deep, it was bad; and he knew he must summon strength to move, else die where he was.

Strangling whiffs of smoke, the crackle of flames, warned him that the inferno he'd begun would catch him in its path within minutes. Thus goaded, he pushed himself up on his hands and knees, and then to his feet. He stumbled with slack, dragging steps from the clearing and headed down-ridge.

At the bottom he fell to his knees. Took a few panting seconds to muster fresh strength, feeling the hot wetness plaster across his back and soak his pants. He frowned and focused his rambling thoughts. Ah . . . he hadn't been more than a half-mile from the Canaanite settlement when he ran into this deadfall. It was just beyond the next ridge, outlined by black jagged pinecrests. Surely someone had heard the shooting and would investigate.

But he could not wait, and he tried to stand again—failed. He began to crawl, pausing each few shuffling feet and reaching doggedly for the waning will that would take him a little farther.

CHAPTER 15

In Cassius McQuayle's shabby office, Bill Treat sat with his legs outstretched, staring unseeingly at the slat of early sunlight streaming through the musty window across his cracked boots. His bull head was sunk on his great chest, hands rammed in his pockets, and his eyes brooded sullenly. He scarcely heard Cassius McQuayle's frightened berating of him.

"You utter fool," McQuayle muttered as he frenziedly paced the floor. "Why in hell did I listen to you! Damn your—"

"Enough from you, old man," Treat said heavily, raising his head. His eyes, red-rimmed from lack of sleep, the cold fear that sat him now like an icy hand, made his glance very ugly. "You were ready to tie in with my idea when it looked sure-fire. Now we hit a snag, you ain't backin' out."

McQuayle subsided into his swivel chair, muttering, "All the same, if that boy lives to talk— It was your doing, not mine."

Treat grinned coldly. "Ain't they some shyster lingo to cover that—like accessory before the fact? Man, you're in it to your neck. Take it a step further—suppose Bell lives long enough to talk, then dies? That'd mean the noose for me, not much better for you. You're an old, sick man, Cass; prison 'd finish you in short order."

"And if you're nailed for murder," McQuayle whispered, "you'd incriminate me—out of pure spite?"

275

"Man, that's rank injustice. Wouldn't tell on no one who plays square with me. Thing is"—Treat hunched forward in his chair, gently shaking a meaty finger—"there's no reason either of us should stay around to git caught. Yonder's twenty thousand dollars Vandermeer left stashed in your safe, plus what you was savin' to buy that land off the Canaanites. Enough to take us a hell of a way, buy a sight of good livin' when we get there."

McQuayle picked up his tobacco plug, tore off a chunk with his teeth and crammed it in the pouch of his cheek. He chewed wildly, muttering, "I have a bad heart—can't set a fugitive's pace. And a steal that size will get every lawman in the territory and beyond posted on our descriptions."

"A long shot," Treat agreed. "But it's that or rot in prison for you—hangin' for me. Think it over."

Treat grimly watched McQuayle's scrawny frame seeming to shrink into itself, growing even smaller, and was silent then to let this sink in. . . .

It had seemed so easy, so foolproof last night when the prospect of wealth and fulfilled desires had dazzled Treat into the certainty that Trevannon's mouth must be shut for good. All he had to do was wait till the town was asleep, steal into the alleyway by the jail, stick a gun through the barred window and pull the trigger. A pleasant job done for the price of a bullet, as he'd told McQuayle.

He had gone to the jail shortly after midnight. By standing on tiptoe he was able to angle his vision down into the cell, where a blanket-covered form lay huddled face down on the narrow cot, dimly illuminated by a lantern hanging in the corridor beyond. Good . . . no witnesses, for the man in the other cell was sleeping off a drunk. As he watched, Trevannon had twitched fitfully beneath the blanket and feebly moaned; seeing his enemy's nerve shattered had pleased Treat immensely.

As he'd brought his gun up to the bars and cocked it, he couldn't resist saying aloud, "Man, don't be sad. Here's to endin' your misery." At the sound of his voice the cot's occupant had twisted wildly, and then Treat fired. Saw to his frozen horror that it wasn't Trevannon at all, as the man rolled on his side and he stared into the putty-white face of Job Bell. The deputy strained to sit up, and the blanket fell away. He clutched at his chest and then rolled sideways off the cot, crumpling limply on the floor. The drunk was aroused by the shot, mumbling, "What 'a hell? What 'a hell?"

The sights and sounds of those few seconds were compressed in Treat's brain with crystal clarity. He'd snapped to his senses then and melted swiftly back into the shadows, pounding along the rear of buildings with un-reasoning terror lending wings to his feet. Again and again, during the hours since, he'd cursed himself for leaving the mistaken shooting half-finished; he could have made sure of Bell. In his scared confusion, he'd thought only of flight.

He'd figured it out by now: Trevannon had somehow tricked Bell, knocked him cold, and escaped. Bell had been coming to when Treat had arrived. Lord, if he had only waited till Bell turned his face before he fired. . . . *If—if!* he thought savagely; it was done, and he had to apply his wit to getting out of this with a whole skin . . . had to size up every angle, weigh each with care. Bell had surely recognized his voice, had probably made out his face at the window before he passed out. Bell, if he lived, could pinpoint the man who'd shot him. . . .

When he'd got his trembling panic under control, Treat had hurried to the doctor's house at the end of town. A small crowd was already gathering, including an elderly couple who were Job Bell's parents. And Jans Vandermeer was there, his face rock-grim, wearing only his pants over his woolen underwear. Treat learned that the sheriff, who was staying with Job and his family, had left his bed on the run at the sound of the shot, expecting that one of the Kaysee crowd might have tried to break Trevannon out. Finding his deputy unconscious and bleeding on the floor confirmed his suspicion. Treat had never seen the sheriff's mountainous calm so shattered; his broad face was pale and tight, and his huge fists kept closing and unclosing; he plainly had the thinnest grip on his boiling fury.

Vandermeer had turned to Job's father, who wore a dazed expression as he tried automatically to comfort his weeping wife. "John, you had better take Mrs. Bell home. It will be very bad, the next few hours. . . . And the rest of you leave now. Go back to your homes. No, you stay, Bill."

Treat had wondered with a stab of fear what Vandermeer wanted with him as the onlookers cleared out of the doctor's little waiting room. When the two of them were alone, Vandermeer's final shred of calm had broken. He'd swiped savagely at the air with his fist; his voice shook. "God, Bill, I must be getting old. I am fond of that boy; I was grooming him to fill my boots. Job had much to learn. Ah, Lord, why did I leave him alone with that clever devil?"

"Too hard on yourself, Dutchy," Treat had said uneasily. "How is the kid?"

Vandermeer had jerked a nod toward the closed door to the adjoining room. "Doctor Griffith cannot tell yet; he is now removing the bullet. It went in just under the heart. He must live, Bill; that boy must live. Yet, I'm afraid. . . ."

Treat had weakly cleared his throat. "Ah, you wanted to talk to me—"

"Yes," Vandermeer had said heavily. "You know Trevannon a little. The man is a riddle to me; yet I had not thought this of him. How does his mind work? Where will he go now—what will he do?"

Carefully hiding his vast relief, Treat had given a wry shrug. "Your guess is damned near as good as mine. Still—" Treat had frowned thoughtfully. "Heres a hunch you can play for what it's worth. Mrs. Congreve told me Trevannon was over visitin' them Canaanites—got right friendly with the clan, so she says. Stuck up for 'em agin Kaysee. Now he knows you'd look for him first at Kaysee—he wouldn't stop there. So—"

"Wait, Bill," Vandermeer had scowled impatiently. "I have visited the Canaanites on my rounds. They are fine people, the only ones I can be sure will never make trouble. Ephraim Waybeck is my good friend, the salt of the earth. These people would not harbor criminals. Nor would such a man as this befriend them. Mrs. Congreve was surely mistaken."

Treat's sly thoughts were now functioning swiftly. "Possible. But like you said—that Trevannon's a tough nut to crack; no telling how his mind works. Told you before how he charmed hisself into that foreman's job. Likely he had some reason of his own for makin' up to the Canaanites. And, not meanin' to slight old Waybeck, he is a kinda simple soul. . . . Trevannon'll have one neat story for him, puttin' himself in the right, the law in the wrong. You'll look like a damn ogre before he's finished. And he'll figure like you just did—that the Canaanite settlement is the last place you'd look. Even if you show up, they'll hide him, cover for him. Yessir," Treat finished emphatically, "that's the place to look, mark me."

The sheriff had smiled thinly. "I have always admired your thinking, Bill—if not your tactics so much. Such as throwing the Canaanites off their homesteads."

Treat shrugged. "Took my orders from Kilrain Carter, like always. Anyway . . . they didn't complain, did they?"

"No," Vandermeer said wearily, "they did not complain. Luckily their lack of respect for the law in no way impairs their observance of it." His face hardened again. "I will see them now. If they think to hide Trevannon—they will learn that this was a mistake."

"Man, it's pitch dark." Treat added mildly. "That's why I didn't go back to Kaysee tonight myself."

"Still, I should be able to hold the wagon road as far as Kaysee; I will make certain that Trevannon did not return to the ranch. By then it will be light enough to cut across-country to the Canaanites'." He went on brusquely, being first and always a man of the law, "I cannot wait to learn news of Job. Perhaps then you will do the goodness to wait and follow me later with news of the boy."

When he'd gone, Treat hung around the waiting room, pacing restlessly, staring at that blank hardwood door till the tension threatened to crack his nerves. When he could stand it no longer, he rapped on a panel. "Doc!"

Dr. Griffith had opened the door a crack, his bushy gray hair awry. "Damn it, Treat. I'm fighting for a man's life in here. If you can't pry yourself away, at least keep quiet!"

"He ain't—?"

"I've removed the bullet; he has a fighting chance."

"Dutchy's gone after the killer," Treat had said hastily. "If the kid comes to, I'm supposed to get word—"

"I'll let you know if he does," the doctor had retorted waspishly, and had shut the door.

Treat had remained there in an agony of suspense, afraid that Job's first words on reviving would be to breathe the name of his attacker. John Bell came in several times to ask news of his son, then hurried home to take care of his wife. By sunup, Treat's patience had frayed out . . . also he wanted to make sure of McQuayle. He'd tramped up to the lawyer's office to find him in a funk of pure fright. McQuayle had learned from a citizen what had happened, and was afterward too terrified to leave his office.

Talking to McQuayle had eased Treat's tension enough to let his mind function freely. He hadn't quite dared to consider his next step if Job should talk. Now he did, grimly and methodically.

McQuayle broke the long quiet, his voice taut and shrill. "All right, Bill. I've thought it over; you're right, of course. But may I inquire what in hell you are waiting for? The sooner we leave, the better."

"Old man, shut your mouth, eh? We'll break when I say so, not before."

The distinct wicked edge to it shut McQuayle up. Treat shifted his glowering attention back to his boots. He could not bring himself to accept that his blunder might have wiped out all his grandiose dreams of a few hours ago. If he broke and ran now, only to learn later that Job Bell had died without talking, he'd have thrown away everything for nothing. This possibility gnawed at his insides. He couldn't abandon the fight till he was certain he'd lost. Whatever he had to do, Vandermeer was out of the way for the time being—that was a break.

With his grim course mentally set, he rose and left the office. McQuayle called after him; he didn't reply or glance back. He hit the street, went up the block and turned onto the sidestreet where Dr. Griffith had his house and busines.

Treat entered the waiting room and found it still deserted. He seated himself with automaton stiffness on a sagging couch, dangled his hat between his fingers and stared at the far wall. Long ago, when he was young and reckless, he'd done a stint as teamster for a mining company. He remembered how once, driving a loaded ore wagon with a ten-mule-span hitch down a narrow, twisting road, his brake handle had snapped off short. He felt now the same detached numbness, that of a man caught on a careening vehicle gone out of control on a mountainside, and nothing to do but ride it out clear to the bottom. . . .

The door to the side room opened. Treat steadied down on his raw nerves and met the doctor's tired gaze calmly as the medico stepped out, holding the door open.

"He's awake," Griffith said. "Weak—can't speak above a whisper. Seems to be rational, though. Keeps asking for the sheriff. . . ."

Treat moistened his lips. "Dutchy ain't back."

"Then you can talk to the boy . . . take his message. His condition is still critical, and he needs rest. He won't sleep till he gets this thing off his chest."

Treat nodded as he stood, saying softly, "After you, Doc."

He followed Griffith into the room, was careful to close the door tightly behind them. Bell lay on the narrow operating table with his bony upper body swathed in bandages. His young face was palely drawn; his breath whistled noisily in and out.

"Job," Doctor Griffith said gently.

Job painfully turned his head a little. As his gaze lighted on Treat, his body heaved spasmodically. Griffith caught him by the shoulders and held him down. "Easy, boy . . . for God's sake, easy."

"Doc," Job whispered harshly. "He's the one . . . Treat. One who shot me."

Griffith frowned. "No, Job. Try to think clearly. Don't make a mistaken accusation that could hurt an innocent man. Think back . . . it was another man who shot you. Who was he?"

"Doc . . . got to believe me. Treat . . . was Treat. Trevannon . . . only knocked me out. Come to . . . heard Treat's voice . . . saw his face . . . window. Shot me. . . ."

Job's whisper waned and his eyes flickered and closed. Griffith straightened slowly, removed his glasses and tucked them into his breast pocket as he turned frowningly toward Treat—then stiffened at sight of the gun in the stocky man's fist.

"So you did—"

"Turn around, Doc," Treat said huskily. The doctor did not move, and Treat rasped, "I said turn, damn you!" He grabbed the slender physician by the shoulder and savagely spun him about. Whipped the gun barrel up and down. Dr. Griffith wilted to the floor.

For a long moment Treat intently regarded the man on the table, listening to his harsh breathing. Thinking bitterly, *Sounds like he ain't got long. But Doc knows, damn him!* He looked down at the crumpled medico, and for an instant the wild impulse chased through his mind to shoot, wipe out the valid witness. His thumb eared the gun-hammer to full cock.

But he did not even point it, as the madness of the notion

bore fully home on him. A shot would bring people. Even could he dispose of these two quietly, there'd be others who'd seen him enter the house. And this killing could not be blamed on Trevannon. Too, Trevannon, if he were caught, could give an explanation that would point a convincing finger straight at Bill Treat. And McQuayle would certainly break wide open, admit everything to save his own hide. With all odds stacked against him, there was one way open: flight.

He stirred the limp form of Griffith with his foot; satisfied that the doctor would be out long enough to give him a good start, he let his gun off-cock, sheathed it, and left, headed back to McQuayle's office.

The old con man was hunched against his desk, his face buried in his hands. He came erect as Treat entered and slammed the door. "Bill, what—"

"Bell talked," Treat said tersely. "I laid the Doc out cold. There's time to use. Open that safe. We got to move fast."

McQuayle sat frozen. Treat, out of patience, stalked to the desk, grabbed him by the collar and yanked him to his feet. "Get a hold on yourself, you old fool, and *open that safe!*"

As he spoke, he threw McQuayle stumbling away, and the lawyer's frail form hit solidly against the safe edge. He bowed forward and collapsed across it. Without a sound he rolled slackly sideways and crumpled to the floor.

Treat didn't believe it. He went down on his knees, turned the body over. McQuayle's head lolled back, his mouth fallen open. His wide-blank eyes were sightless.

His goddamn heart! Treat climbed to his feet with a stiff, mechanical effort, his eyes dragging to the safe. Twenty thousand-some dollars a foot away . . . and it might as well have been in China. He thought of rifling McQuayle's desk—the combination might be written down some-where—and knew, even as the thought occurred to him, that McQuayle wouldn't be so careless.

The room tilted dizzily, as though the walls were closing on him. He steadied quickly. Yet in that moment something died hard in Bill Treat, and he forgot about Andrea Carter and Kaysee and twenty thousand dollars. He knew one elemental urge now, to live, beat his way out of a trap, get far away. . . .

He ran from the office, half fell down the stairwell to get outside. His horse was tied at the rail in readiness. He ripped free the reins, vaulted on and kicked into a crazy run.

He'd head eastward, over the mountains; he knew an easy pass out of the valley. He'd stop at Kaysee only long enough to pick up his belongings. Beyond that he had no idea what would happen, and just now, quirting his horse viciously to greater speed, he did not care.

Treat dropped the reins of his lathered, shuddering horse, and took a dazed step toward the smoldering wreckage of the house. Charred timbers projected like black, smoking jackstraws from its collapsed ruin. He was hardly aware of the crewmen standing about, their clothes scorched and sooted, nursing their burns, apathetic after their failure to save the house.

"Looks like you damn close to killed that horse." This cold disapproval from Gabe Morrow.

Treat didn't answer. Something like a sob broke in his thick chest. This house, center of the great ranch that was a sacred monument in his mind . . . the house he'd shared with old Kilrain for years before the Old Man had brought his bride to Kaysee. Burned to the ground, gone forever. It was the crowning blow to all that had happened; it even diverted Treat's rage to get away into a sudden venom of explosive hatred.

"Who done it?"

"Can't say how it started," Gabe muttered dispiritedly. "It was caught on too good by the time we roused out. Couldn't hardly get close enough to toss water, for the heat.

Couple of us tried to git in, git the women out; damn near got burned up before we reached the door, couldn't make it. . . . The old lady couldn't walk, but can't figure why Mrs. Carter didn't clear out. Smoke must've overcome 'em both. . . ." Gabe's voice trailed off, and he shook his head back and forth, back and forth.

"Who done it?" Treat asked again.

"Bill, I tol' you— Where'n hell you going?"

Treat had turned back to his jaded horse. He led it to the corral and stripped off saddle and bridle. Then he plodded doggedly to the bunkhouse, jammed his few belongings in his warsack, and tramped back to the corral. He saddled a rangy, strong-winded pinto and fastened on his warsack. All this he did very methodically, and he rode away from Kaysee headquarters for the last time without looking back.

Treat knew exactly what he was going to do, and hell or high water couldn't stop him. Of course it was Wes Trevannon who'd fired the house. He, Treat, was Kaysee; and Trevannon would pause in his flight to hurt Kaysee out of pure spite. He didn't ask himself whether this explanation made sense. As for Andrea, his reaction was one less of grief than of thwarted fury. Why, dammit, everything that had gone wrong was Trevannon's doing. He seethed over that with a sense of almost joyful relief. Sure as hell . . . if Trevannon hadn't shown up at Kaysee and taken his job, he wouldn't have been drawn on, step by step, to this bind in which he was helplessly caught.

He rode southeast through the bright morning. Ahead lay the Canaanite settlement; directly beyond, the pass he'd follow out of the valley. He wouldn't even have to ride out of his way . . . just pay a brief visit. He hadn't been shamming when he'd told Jans Vandermeer his belief that Trevannon would look for sanctuary with the Canaanites. It figured, all right . . . and if he ran into Vandermeer there—with the death of Bell already scored against him— why stop with Trevannon? Besides, that damned lawman

would be a positive danger, one he'd breathe easier for
cutting down. . . . Yessir, it was figuring better now,
straight as a bullet. Treat found the rough imagery amusing;
he chuckled aloud. Straight as a bullet.

CHAPTER 16

TREVANNON CAME AWAKE SEVERAL TIMES, FIRST, TO FIND himself jogging painfully in an improvised litter made of a ragged greatcoat and two unpeeled poles . . . and then he passed out. He woke next to find himself face down with someone cleaning the wound in his back, his arms and legs thrashing, and himself bellowing in pain; strong hands pinned him back, and he fainted.

The third time he came to, very drowsily and with his shoulder throbbing, he turned his head with an effort to see a window with full dawn staining the sky, and the nimbus of Calla Waybeck's fair hair against it. Knew he wasn't dreaming when her cool fingers touched his face; he smiled and closed his eyes. Slept like the dead. Later on he had the impression that he was being moved, but knew when he woke that he must have dreamed it. . . .

He was lying belly down in the same wooden bunk where he'd last found himself. The single room of the Waybeck cabin was flooded with daylight, and he wondered at once how long he'd slept. He felt a good deal better, only slightly feverish. Though when he tried to move, he found himself weak as a half-drowned cat.

A warm pillow of savory cooking smells hit his face, and he saw Calla bent by the fireplace, as he'd first seen her. And the old woman was there, rocking gently to and fro, looking at him steadily without seeing him. Trevannon lay

287

motionless, letting the pleasant sights and sounds and
smells of this room wash gently through his consciousness,
let its workaday bustle flood him with peace. . . .

The boy Jerry was sitting at the table, his chin in his hand
and tow hair tumbling into his eyes as he frowned over a
school primer. He tossed his hair back with a twist of his
head, and his gaze widened on Trevannon watching him.

"The man's awake," he said softly.

Calla turned quickly from the fireplace and came to the
bunk with her strong, lithe stride.

"Hello," Trevannon said weakly.

She nodded hello, smiling a little as she wiped her hands
on her apron. She turned her head to call, "Grandpa," and
then gave Wes an oddly tender attention.

Ephraim Waybeck bulked through the open doorway, his
venerable face showing only kindly pleasure as he came to
stand by Calla. "Well," he boomed gently, "and how is our
guest feeling?"

"Hungry," Trevannon whispered. "Curious. Hungry
first."

"You Texans are indeed a whang-leather breed," smiled
Ephraim. "In spite of which, I think that a nourishing liquid
is your limit at present. A bowl of broth, Calla. . . . The
wound was not as serious as I first thought. When Elia and I
found you, you were unconscious—I should say, from
shock and blood-loss. A few days' rest will set you up."

"Haven't got . . . few days. Got to ride. . . ."

Ephraim squatted down, elbows on knees, his big, dirt-
soiled hands laced loosely together. "That is out of the
question, friend," he said seriously. "Though I hardly
blame you, considering . . ."

"How much . . . you know?"

"Quite a little. Not enough." Ephraim's falcon eyes were
speculative. "Here is what happened. . . ."

The Canaanites had been up before dawn, as was their
custom; the men were already in the fields when they heard
the shots and saw the smoke of the burning ridge. Ephraim

and Elia had hurried to cover the half-mile on foot. They had found Trevannon unconscious near the base of the ridge, his dead horse nearby. When they had rigged a crude litter and borne Wes to the settlement, Ephraim had sent men back to fight the fire. As the land surrounding the ridge was mostly denuded, they'd easily halted the holocaust by scooping out a few trenches, letting the fire burn itself out on the ridge timber. As Ephraim had guessed that whoever had shot Trevannon might be on his trail, he'd also given orders to have the dead horse dragged off a distance and covered with brush.

"How effectively this might throw off your enemies, I did not know, but should they come, we could not defend you with guns; our only hope was to hide you, erase what sign we could." He paused somberly. "Unless I read you very wrongly the first time, I need not ask you to tell me nothing but the truth."

"Anything I can tell you," Trevannon husked gratefully.

Ephraim smiled and gripped his arm gently. "I know. First, what sign I could make out indicated that you had been shot at from ambush—that you started the fire to thwart your enemy. Who was he?"

Trevannon told him about Tige Menefee, weakly concluding, "His body was on the ridge . . . fire went over it, why you didn't find it . . . and his horse stampeded."

"I understand. How strong do you feel, sir? Strong enough to accept something of—bad news?" At Trevannon's nod of assent, Ephraim said, "I had no sooner finished removing the bullet, cleansing and bandaging your wound, when a horseman came across the Bench at a gallop. At once I anticipated your enemy."

He shifted aside to make room for Calla as she drew up a chair beside him, holding a bowl of steaming broth she had ladled from a pot bubbling over the coals. Ephraim helped Trevannon to maneuver onto his side and propped up his head with a rolled blanket—apparently the Canaanites permitted no luxury of pillows—and Calla spooned the broth into Trevannon's mouth.

He gulped the first spoonful, said impatiently, "Who was it?"

"Sheriff Vandermeer. Before we made out his identity, I knew we must hide you somehow. I was in a quandary. Calla had the solution. We had a couple of minutes, time enough to lift you off the bunk and slide you onto the floor beneath it. A tight squeeze, but we got you in place, spread a blanket over the cot to hang down and conceal you . . ."

Calla said, bringing the spoon back to his lips, "Then we had Grandmother lie down on the bunk. Nothing could have looked more completely innocent."

"That too was Calla's idea," Ephraim observed wryly. "I must own that I was quite shaken, even paralyzed, by this emergency. And I am far too simple a man to follow such devious female thinking." Calla smiled at the fond chiding in his tone. "Even then, I knew some bad moments in what followed. We'd barely gotten the articles of treatment out of sight and settled ourselves about the table with cups of coffee and expressions of casual innocence when the sheriff came barging through yonder doorway like a winter storm.

"He was not his usual placid self—that was at once obvious. We understood when he told his mission . . . of the boy he insisted that you had shot. I was terribly shocked, of course, and then he asked about you." Ephraim frowned sidelong at his daughter-in-law, his fingers gingerly kneading his right knee. "At which point, Calla kicked me—hard."

Calla said serenely, "Grandpa, I didn't want you to say the wrong thing, before you thought."

"The sheriff is a man I highly respect," Ephraim admitted. "Perhaps, had I followed my first impulse, I would have answered with the truth." He sighed. "Bearing false witness, even in the name of justice, isn't a sin that sits lightly afterward."

Trevannon almost smiled, knowing that Ephraim's scant respect for organized law, his pride in his ability to read a man's character, would have influenced his decision. Still, it was Calla whose response had reflected an absolute and unquestioning trust in him; he met her calm gray gaze now with a sense of humble gratitude that awed him. He knew in that moment that this woman would stand first in his thoughts if he lived to a hundred. And this with the knowledge that all along he'd have expected no less from her; he had instinctively headed here with that fact central to his thoughts.

Ephraim said with a faint embarrassment, as though he'd read Trevannon's mind, "To make the story short, I lied like a trooper. I didn't doubt the sheriff's word, but I felt that he'd been somehow misled. As we talked, the details were clarified. My friend Vandermeer granted that certain things puzzled him . . . though he was certain that you could give the answers. Then he asked about the fire on yonder ridge, which I sheepishly informed him we'd started by accident. He sternly reminded me that it had been mostly a dry year, to take more care—and then, speaking of fires, he said the main house of Kaysee ranch had mysteriously caught fire last night . . . burned to the ground."

Trevannon started to jerk upright; with the stab of pain he sank back. Ephraim shook his head sadly to the unspoken query. "Apparently Kilrain Carter's wife and her mother— burned to death. Terrible," he murmured, still wagging his head. "The sheriff had ridden by on his way here. The Kaysee hands had half killed themselves trying to stop it. Hopeless. And none knew how it had started."

God, she went that far, Trevannon thought, stunned. *That far. . . .* "Vandermeer—he left?"

"He went outside, poked about in some sheds a bit. Was evidently satisfied. Gave me a good-day, and rode off. However, I was cautious enough to drift about the fields telling the men to work as though nothing had happened, to betray nothing out of the ordinary. It was well that I did. . . . An hour ago I chanced to look up at the ridge above the Bench—saw sunlight flash off something. I would hazard that the sheriff is up there with an eagle eye— and field glasses—peeled. He evidently believes that we might have concealed you anywhere in the settlement, that the lot of us would conspire to protect you—and that a lone man searching would be baffled. So he's watching for the smallest betraying move on our parts." Ephraim shook his head sorrowfully. "Always, this man took his duty coldly, as a matter of course . . . now, there is a terrible and savage determination in him. He will leave no stone unturned."

"He still up there?"

"I can't say. We must simply continue as we have. And now, my friend, I have spoken my piece . . . what of yours?"

Trevannon tried to keep it brief, but it seemed a long time before he'd told everything. It involved digging far into the past he'd wanted to forget. He was sweating, his voice weak, when he finished.

"Cassius McQuayle," Ephraim murmured. "How I misjudged that man. Yet—judge not—"

"Grandpa," Calla said with deep concern, "don't trouble him now. Let him rest."

Ephraim set his hands on his knees to rise, but Trevannon detained him, clamping a hand on his arm. "Sir, I got to know."

"It's been a long road for you, Wesley Trevannon," old Waybeck said with great gentleness. "One paved with good and bad. More good, I know, than bad. I know too that whatever solution you choose will be yours alone, for that is your way. I will say this: you have reached a forking in the road; you have a grave decision to make. But you know that. Until you decide—we'll shelter and hide you here, if we have to outwit the very devil."

Calla laughed softly, affectionately. "My devious ways . . . Grandpa, I've corrupted you."

Ephraim settled a gentle hand on her shoulder as he stood. "That—never, my dear. And now we'll eat."

Trevannon lay quietly, the muted drone of Ephraim's midday grace touching only the surface of his mind. What had the old man meant? That he must choose whether to run, or to placidly turn himself over to the law? Likely enough. *That last is his way,* Trevannon thought grimly. *Not mine, and not against a stacked deck.* It would be a murder charge now.

But why should anyone shoot Job Bell? He ran his mind back over the night's events. He'd left the unconscious deputy covered with the cot blanket. The killer had probably made his move before the deputy revived, had fired through the cell door or the barred window without getting a close look at the covered form. The bullet had been intended for him, Trevannon. McQuayle had the motive . . . to wipe out Trevannon's knowledge of his plan to put grabs on that gold-bearing land.

Trevannon exhaled slowly; it was a bitter sigh. Try to prove any of this . . . impossible. No way to escape hanging but to run—and with a wound that would lay him low for several days. Even a slight movement tided rhythmic strokes of pain and dizziness through his body. A black bitterness seethed in him. Everything he'd tried to do since hitting this valley had been selflessly done in the best interests of others. He'd netted this for his pains: helplessly waiting for an angry, deadly-dogged lawman to take him off to jail, a guilty verdict, a hangman's noose.

And yet, he reminded himself, Ephraim and his people were unhesitatingly risking a great deal to help him. This fact beaconed strongly among his dark thoughts. You had to believe in human goodness when you saw its evidence with your own eyes, and there wasn't much finer under the sun.

Young Jerry, gulping down a last mouthful, asked to be excused from the table, and ran over to the bunk. Wes met his large gray eyes in surprise, eyes so like his mother's in their grave frankness . . . for the boy had been painfully shy till now.

Jerry touched a fascinated finger to the butt of the heavy Colt, slung by its shellbelt over the back of a chair by the bunk. "That—that's a nice gun, mister. . . ."

"Like to see it?" Trevannon reached out, lifted the gun from holster.

"Jerry!" Ephraim thundered. "Go outside."

"I was about to take out the shells," Trevannon said dryly.

"No matter; the boy will handle no gun beneath my roof."

"A tool, Mr. Waybeck. Like your hoe. You watch the man behind it."

Old Ephraim's bearded lips became a tight line. "There are some things, sir, on which you and I will never see eye to eye." He clamped on his black hat and tramped outside, his lofty back stiff.

Calla paused in the act of clearing away the dishes, and came over to slap Jerry lightly on the rear. "Go help Grandpa. Go along, now."

The boy edged reluctantly from the room, and Calla sat down by the bunk, her work-strong hands clasped in her lap.

Wes growled, "You like letting him raise that kid on a cloud?"

Calla said quietly, "I know. Jerry is at the age where you can't draw a line between boy and man. He should start to know what life is. But as Grandpa said—this *is* his roof."

Trevannon was silent a moment, said then awkwardly, "I haven't thanked you."

She colored faintly, avoiding his eyes to study a pleat in her skirt. "I just—believed in you. Don't ask me why; I can't—"

"You and me," Wes interrupted quietly, "we're too old for pretendin' games."

"There is no sense to this," she said in a voice grave and

low, and then bit her lip to hide a smile. "Two people don't just . . ."

Trevannon grinned a little. "They do, though. Sometimes, anyway. Since we talked the other day. Only it took me a time to catch up with myself. I don't guess feelings are things you can sort out too neat. We both done our share of mourning . . . life goes on. I can't say this very well."

"You do well enough." Her fingers closed over his, tightly.

For a moment they only sat, a sense of wonder and strangeness still holding them. Then he said, low-voiced, "This isn't much good. We can't—"

He broke off, at once alert, as Ephraim came back through the doorway. "The sheriff is returning," he announced quietly. "He must have become impatient with only waiting. He is coming fast. We'll have to—"

"No hiding," Trevannon said with flat finality. He fought up on his elbows.

Calla gasped. "No, Wes . . ."

He picked up the gun which he'd laid on the blanket, its well-worn cedar grips a hard assurance against his palm. "Help me to the window."

"In that," Ephraim said sternly, "I will not oblige you. Let us help—or give yourself up. In either case—put away your weapon."

Trevannon's grin was a mere tightening of lips. "As you're so fond of remindin' a man, sir—my way is my own. Keep out of it, then." He looked a hard question at Calla.

Without hesitation she bent, got both hands beneath his good shoulder, helped him swing his legs to the floor.

"Calla," Ephraim murmured sadly, "you must know this is wrong. His way is—"

"Mine," she said, "mine, now," and did not look at the old man. She caught Trevannon's full weight on her shoulder as he clumsily stood. For a moment they swayed off-balance. Then with Calla's help he took faltering steps to

the single front window. Waves of nausea and pain laid a
punishing rhythm through him as she left him leaning
against the wall. She brought the chair and he settled
heavily onto it. The gun butt was sweat-slick; his hands
shook. He ground down hard on his weakness. A greased
cloth covered the window opening in lieu of glass,
admitting a yellow-murked light. Wes tore it away and laid
his gun barrel across the sill.

Vandermeer was very near, riding hard past the first
ramshackle dwellings. Trevannon filled his lungs, let out a
broken shout: *"That's near enough, Sheriff!"*

Vandermeer saw him and heard him . . . and kept
coming. He brought his mount to a skidding halt in the
dusty road by Waybeck's yard, swung heavily down. He
threw the reins and stood spread-legged, his massive chest
rising and falling with hard breathing. Otherwise he looked
composed. But his eyes were the glacial calm of chipped
ice, his voice bland as iron. "Shoot, you killer, and be
damned!"

He drew and cocked his pistol in an unbroken motion.

Yet neither man fired. Across the few yards of dirt that
separated them tension strained like a fine drawn thread. For
an instant a baffled strangeness filled Vandermeer's broad
face. He shook his head doggedly and and came across the
yard at a hard trot.

Trevannon sank back into the chair, the hand with the gun
dropping limply on his thigh. Resignedly he shut his eyes.
That was it, your decision.

His eyes shot open, startled by the sudden tug on his
hand. His gun was gone. Calla held it double-handed,
thumbs dragging back the hammer. She wheeled at the same
time, running to put her back against the wall opposite the
door. She raised the heavy Colt's at arm's length, pointing it
at the door. Old Mrs. Waybeck let out a high, tremulous
wail.

"No, Calla, no," Trevannon heard himself say—and

then Vandermeer reached the door. A powerful kick sent it swinging inward. The sheriff lunged into the room, stopping his headlong rush even as he pivoted on a heel, his pistol swinging to cover Trevannon. He halted in midmotion, only then seeing Calla with the gun leveled at his chest.

CHAPTER 17

"**Y**OUNG WOMAN," JANS VANDERMEER SAID STOLIDLY, "IF you mean to use that—do so now."

Calla stood tall and stiff, her eyes flashing. She lowered the gun very slowly; when it touched her skirt, she let up the hammer gently, let the gun clatter to the floor.

Vandermeer scooped it up and rammed it in his belt, motioned curtly at Trevannon with his own weapon.

"Get up."

Old Ephraim moved foward, lifting a restraining hand. "Wait, friend Jans. The man is hurt. And there are several things you must hear."

Vandermeer's glacial attention shifted to the old man. "I think you have said enough. You lied to me to shield a murderer. Of all men I know, I had not thought this of you. Shall I listen more to a man who baldly breaches faith?"

"My good friend," Ephraim chided gently, "would I lie to save a man I *believed* was a murderer? Would I?"

Vandermeer scowled. "I had not thought this of you," he repeated. "You lied for this man once; why not again? I am sorry. This thing will go hard for you, Ephraim, and for your family."

"At least listen—"

"I am not disposed to listen where *this* is concerned," Vandermeer said harshly. He made a sweeping motion of his hand toward Trevannon. "The signs were plain. My deputy had been struck over the head before he was shot . . .

298

hard enough to lay him low for hours. To escape, it was not necessary to then put a bullet in him with his own gun." He tapped the butt of Job's weapon in his belt. "Yet this man did so in cold blood."

"Wasn't that gun that did the job, Sheriff," Trevannon whispered.

"You will prove this."

Trevannon slumped against the chairback, rubbing his head between his hands. Fever pulsed hotly behind his temples. He felt weary and sick and disgusted. He could not prove it, not with that gun recently fired and the expended shell still chambered. The bullet that had brought down Tige Menefee. There were other facts, of course . . . Tige's body, his own wounding by Tige. But this bullheaded lawman would not listen now, and he was too dizzy and tired to explain any more. He summoned strength to his voice. "I'm ready, Sheriff. Let's go."

"No, Wes," Calla began, starting toward him. "You can't ride—"

Trevannon lifted a hand sharply to cut her off. A horseman was coming up the road at a hard gallop. He leaned toward the window, winced and bit down on his lip. Leaned his head in his hands and waited for the surge of agony to recede. "Who is it?" he whispered.

He heard Calla's light steps move to the window. "It's that Treat . . . Bill Treat."

He raised his head and stared at her. Heard the slobber of racking breaths from a hard-driven horse, the broken shuffle of its halting. Then Treat's gruff tones, holding a rough note of friendliness. "Howdy, kid. Your Grandpa in?"

Trevannon gritted his teeth and heaved his weight forward. Caught the windowsill and gripped it hard. Treat was standing by his horse, his clothes dusty and sweat-patched. His face was red and shining beneath the shadow of his hatbrim, looking down at young Jerry, who'd evidently been coming back from a neighbor's when Treat had accosted him. Treat glanced up quickly now; his gaze

locked with Trevannon's. *What the hell brings him here?*
Wes wondered.

Treat's hard grin parted his lips; he dropped a thick hand
to the boy's towhead. "Let's go in and see him, eh, bucko?"
He came on across the yard, propelling the boy ahead with a
heavy hand between his shoulders.

The door was ajar, and it creaked thinly as he pushed it
wide, commanding a full view of the room. He halted on
the threshold, hand settled loosely on the boy's thin
shoulder. He grinned widely, but Trevannon saw the wild
glints race through his milky stare.

"Howdy, Dutchy. Folks. Trevannon . . ."

"Bill," the sheriff said urgently, "Bill, you have word of
Job?"

"Man, he's good and dead by now." Treat's right arm
was held close to his body, his hand hidden by the boy, and
now it came up holding his leveled Remington .44 above
Jerry's shoulder. His left forearm shifted, locking brutally
around the boy's throat and pulling him tightly against
Treat's legs.

"Bill!" Vandermeer choked. "What is this?"

"You'd have found out," Treat smiled. "That's why
you'll never know. Better drop them guns. One in your
hand's pointed the wrong way, and I got a dead bead on you.
Big man like yourself might last long enough to get a bullet
in me . . . but I wouldn't try. Not with the boy in line."

Vandermeer's empty hand formed a fist at his side. "I
would make a guess, Bill. You shot Job. I thought I saw fear
in you, there in the doctor's office. But I could not guess
why. Why, then?"

"Dutchy. The boy." Treat said it confidently.

With a hard-wrenched sigh Vandermeer let his gun fall.
He lifted the other weapon from his belt and dropped it; it
bounced at an angle and skidded across the floor.

Now Treat moved deeper into the room, holding the boy
in front of him. "Over against the wall by Trevannon. All of
you." Vandermeer obeyed phlegmatically, tramping over to
stand by Trevannon's chair. Ephraim Waybeck followed

more slowly. Calla was breathing deeply and steadily, her body tense.

"You too, missus. Your boy won't be hurt, 'less one of you moves wrong. Trevannon there, and Dutchy . . . they're my meat."

Calla stepped to Ephraim's side, and the old man took her hand, murmuring, "Be steady now. Be strong."

Treat's irritable glance slid toward Ephraim's wife. "You. Old woman. You don't hear good?"

Mrs. Waybeck was rocking gently in her chair, fixedly watching Treat's gun. Her eyes were vacant, her lips moving. ". . . . *And behold, a pale horse: and he that sat on him, his name was Death; and Hades followed with him. . . ."*

Treat wiped a hand quickly across his mouth, his first betrayal of uneasy tenseness. "What's the matter with her?"

"You ought to know, Mr. Treat," Calla spoke softly. "You did this to her, you and your riders. It must be a relief to forget so easily."

"What'n hell are you talking about?"

"Her son. The man I married. This boy's father. He was killed when you raided our homestead that night, six months ago."

Treat grunted. "Hell, I ain't forgot. Was me that shot that fella. We had orders from Carter to just shoot high and scare you. Me, I figured to serve your sort a sharper lesson . . . pinked your husband square when he tried to drag a Kaysee man off his hoss. Everybody figured a chance slug got to him." Treat wagged his head with mock sorrow. "They was all regretful."

Old Ephraim made a sound deep in his chest and took a step. "No," Calla whispered, holding his arm with all her strength. Slowly the old man stepped back, his stare burning on Treat.

"That's smart, missus," Treat said. "Do beat all what it takes to kill some critters. Trevannon there, he looks half dead awready. Someone use you for a target?"

"Someone," Trevannon said quietly.

"Be a shame to end it so fast then. All right, Dutchy. You stand nice and still—wouldn't want the wrong one gettin' hit. . . ."

Wes dropped weakly in his chair, his head bowed on his chest. His breathing was a strained rasp, telling of helpless weakness. And so Treat contemptuously ignored him, fixing his decision first on Jans Vandermeer. Trevannon's eyes had already flicked sidelong, marking the distance to Job's gun which, when the sheriff dropped it, had bounded to within a few feet of the wall. It lay in a dust-hazed sunshaft a yard from Ephraim's boots.

The move had to be his; Treat had already discounted him, but was wary of the others. Did he have the strength left, the speed? He would have to dive for the floor, endangering Ephraim and Calla who would be standing directly behind him. And Jerry. The crown of the boy's head just reached Treat's breastbone.

Aim high, Trevannon thought, *and careful, for God's sake* . . . and then there was no time to think more, for Treat was raising the Remington to arm's length, sighting carefully down on Vandermeer's broad chest.

Trevannon was sitting sideways, his knees bent, his toes firm against the clay floor. With a mighty effort he straightened his legs and launched his body hard and low, his shoulder powering into Vandermeer's hip. The impact drove the sheriff piling into Ephraim and Calla, as Treat's gun bellowed deafeningly in the room. Trevannon twisted his shoulder upward as it struck the sheriff so that it slid off without slowing his sideward lunge, and he rolled as he fell. He hit the floor at the others' feet, squarely on his back, his left hand flinging out with straining haste for Job's gun even as the painful impact smashed through his body. It was a blind reach, but his hand closed true over the butt; and thumbed the hammer as he brought the gun up.

Though it happened in the space of a quick breath, he had the agonizing sense that he was moving with a trancelike deliberation. Though he didn't remember that till afterward.

His maneuver might yet have failed if Jerry hadn't suddenly writhed and kicked in Treat's grasp. The boy had stood quietly till now, only moving when he saw Trevannon move. Treat had his hands full. He made the mistake of trying to hold the kid, and then, with a curse, flung him aside and aimed quickly down at Trevannon.

The Colt arced around at the end of Trevannon's extended arm, and he saw the ruddy patch of Treat's face blur beyond the sights, and then he shot. Treat's heavy shape was dissolving toward the floor before his gun went off by reflex.

Blinded by powder fumes, Trevannon shrank instinctively against the floor as Treat's shot roared deafeningly between the confining walls. Then he saw Treat sprawled with one arm flung out, the other bent and pillowing his head. Wes tried to raise himself on a hand, grunted in pain and slipped back. The room swam; black shadows rocked in his vision.

Then Calla's strong arms went around him, and with Ephraim's assistance she got him to the bunk. She was already loosening his blood-soaked bandages as Vandermeer bent down by Treat and turned his head.

Not wanting to see, Trevannon looked as Vandermeer curtly asked Ephraim for something to cover the body. The old man was speaking quietly to his wife, and when her soft moaning had ceased, he tramped from the room, taking the boy with him. Trevannon watched Calla's face, the shadings of concerned emotions that colored its still calm as she removed the last of the bandages and began to clean his wound.

He set his teeth and bore the pain through a silence that held, unbroken by Vandermeer who stood stolidly by, his arms folded, his eyes chill as a winter sky. Ephraim returned with a piece of ragged tarp. A minute later, he and the sheriff bore it from the room, hammocked around the dead weight of Treat.

Trevannon closed his eyes. This time there was no way out. Coming to grips with this fact had smothered his last spark of resistance. He couldn't have run had he wished to; to this he was fatalistically resigned.

Vandermeer returned shortly and indicated his wish to hear the whole thing from the beginning. Trevannon tried to speak, but Calla hushed him and with impassioned defiance told Wes's story. Vandermeer's few spare, cold-eyed comments were merely questions.

When she'd concluded, Calla observed acidly, "You'll be wanting to take the man who saved your life on to prison now, I've no doubt—though the trip will certainly kill him."

"I am not in such a hurry," Vandermeer observed with ponderous gravity. "Neither do I want to risk his escaping again. I have no haste for another lengthy chase. First, Ephraim, I wish you to take me to the burned hill yonder where you say Tige Menefee's body is. I wish to see if that happened as you said—"

"Certainly," gibed Calla. "We wouldn't expect you to take our word."

"Calla," Ephraim said wearily, and to the sheriff, with a nod: "I will do that."

"I will also ask for the loan of a wagon to take the bodies of Treat and Menefee back to Kaysee. I think there will be no need for a coroner's investigation. Tomorrow I return, and then wait till you are well enough to be moved."

Trevannon stared at him, this man of iron, wondering if the brain behind that stolid face ever knew a subtle flicker of indecision, of uncertainty, as to its course. "You're too damned kind."

Vandermeer grunted without even a twitch of his lips. "I give you thanks. That for saving my life. What more does a breaker of laws expect—"

"From you? Nothing. Not a damned thing. Don't lose any sleep."

"From a man dedicated to keeping the law," Vandermeer went on imperturbably. And, with a touch of unexpected irony: "I am thankful for your understanding."

He pivoted and walked from the room. Shortly Trevannon heard the sheriff hooraw a team into motion as he and Ephraim rode out. He looked at Calla and tried to speak, but her fingers touched his mouth and her lips formed, "Rest."

Gratefully he closed his eyes. And slept. A restless, nightmarish sleep, and when he awoke with a start, he was feverish and bathed in sweat. It was hours later, and the windows were dark. The lamp on the table flickered a sallow glow, picking out the mounded shaped of Ephraim and his wife in their bunks, the quiet, deep breathing of the boy in the bunk above Trevannon.

Calla's back was toward him, and she was hanging a blanket to a pair of nails in the rafters by a far wall where she'd improvised a pallet of straw for her own bed. She slipped behind the screening blanket, and he heard the sliding whisper of cloth. He knew a lonely man's foolish embarrassment at the intimate sounds of her undressing, and then the sensation ebbed quickly. There should not be, could never be, a withholding, a false reticence, where she was concerned. The feeling had grown between them till it was as strong and certain as Calla herself . . . and, he thought bleakly, ended before it had begun.

She stepped out wearing a long gray nightgown, and moved to the table to turn up the lamp, afterward coming across to his bunk. Briefly her body cut sideways between his vision and the light, and the glow diffused through the gown to profile the sturdy fullness of breasts and hips and thighs beneath its loose folds. Above his weakness and sickness, he felt the quick stir of his blood. She bent at his side, the pale rope of her unbound hair crumpling softly on his shoulder. She felt his forehead, and his hand went out and caught hers.

"Oh . . . Wes, you're awake."

His hands on her shoulders guided her firm weight down against him, and her lips were full and giving. It was a moment of urgent hunger that was a desperate protest against the injustice, the hopelessness, of their situation. The shattering pain of his wound jarred him back to sanity;

with his recoiling wince, Calla drew back, her breathing
deep and ragged.

"Nothing," she whispered hopelessly. "We'll be apart
soon . . . and we can't even have the time that's left."

Wes drew her face to his and stroked her head, talking
quietly. Giving her a comfort he didn't feel, with tomorrow
laying its bleak certainty across his thoughts.

CHAPTER 18

Trevannon slept fitfully, then more soundly as his fever cooled, and when he awoke late the following morning he felt better, even refreshed. Calla was preparing the noon meal, busily stirring about the kitchen as she had been the first day he'd come here. From the yard echoed the bite of Ephraim's ax as he tussled with a stubborn chunk of cordwood, and the old woman creaked to and fro in her rocking chair, her gnarled fingers moving over the pages of her Bible.

But now there was something automatic and unreal in the workaday bustle, and the bright-blocked sunlight that fell on his blankets held a brittle and cheerless warmth.

Young Jerry moped in the doorway, and he was the first to see Trevannon awake. He came to the bunk, saying gravely, "Are you going away?"

Calla turned, brushing a strand of hair from her eyes. She made a movement as though to shoo the boy away, but Trevannon's eyes met hers in a wordless communion so natural he knew a painful irony in it, and he shook his head.

He ruffled the boy's hair. "Not for a while, anyway."

Jerry's eyes were very direct and sober. "You don't have to, ever. We can hide you. I know a cave over by the hills. Like Jesse James and all them have. Specky Burdick and me play outlaw and Injuns over there."

Calla remarked with only faint censure, "What did Grandfather tell you about that?"

"Said he'd whup both of us if we played at shooting people again. Even tol' Specky's pa to keep us apart so's we'd stay out of mischief."

"Well, then."

"Aw, Ma."

"So long as we live with Grandpa, we must do as he says."

"Sure, I know . . . but Mr. Trevannon don't. Do you?"

"No," Trevannon said slowly. "Only there's a thing you got to understand. When you stop taking orders from other folks, you got to start taking them from yourself."

Jerry considered this carefully, then said, "I don't get that."

"Well . . ." Trevannon eased himself up on an elbow, frowning gently. "Grown folks don't have to take orders from anyone if they've a mind not to. But that don't mean they can step on other folks' feet when they feel like it."

"Sure, everyone knows that."

"That's why there's rules they make to keep each other in line. Everyone knows the rules—laws—and mostly they keep them. When they don't, other people have to see they do."

"Like that old sheriff," Jerry nodded, and then: "Did you break a law?"

"I took money that other people earned. I thought I was put on sore enough to justify it. I did some other wrong things too, which came first. You do wrong things long enough, you start telling yourself they're right. Pretty soon you're breaking a lot of rules and a lot of people get hurt. That's why the rules got to be kept—even when you can't help thinking they're wrong. Understand me?"

Jerry nodded, but a little sulkily, and then he burst out, "But if you *know* you done bad and you're sorry, you don't do wrong again, do you?"

"Some do. I'd say no, though."

"Then you don't have to let that sheriff take you away," he pointed out triumphantly.

Trevannon was mustering his thoughts for his own benefit as much as the boy's, and he wondered wryly whether he would have sounded so self-righteous if he were unhurt now, capable of escape. Still, a man made his road rocky with his own mistakes; the boy had to see that. "A man has to pay up, Jerry. You see—"

He broke off at the sound of a wagon coming, and then he heard Vandermeer's phlegmatic greeting, Ephraim's cold reply. In a moment, the sheriff's formidable bulk filled the doorway. He sank onto the chair by Trevannon's bunk, elbows on knees, his big hands laced together, and quietly spoke.

Vandermeer's contained calm had returned. Trevannon learned why: Job Bell would live. Cassius McQuayle had been found dead in his office, apparently of a heart attack. Bill Treat had been seen by several citizens leaving McQuayle's office on the run, then riding from town at a furious pace. Vandermeer had concluded that McQuayle and Treat had thrown in together to carry through McQuayle's scheme to get the gold-bearing tract. Treat's part was to kill Trevannon before he let out word of the gold. This explanation made sense, at least . . . and McQuayle's heart had given out when he'd learned that Job Bell had named Treat as the would-be killer, which would include McQuayle as accomplice . . . or he and Treat had quarreled. The details were not important, and Jans Vandermeer had other matters weighing his mind.

Concerning the burning of the Kaysee main house, he said, an unexpected development had come to light. Yesterday afternoon, when Vandermeer was returning with the wagon containing the bodies of Treat and Menefee, he'd followed the relatively level slopes of the creek bottom-lands. In a wide, deep pond which broke the onrushing

stream at a low point, he had found the body of Andrea
Carter floating face down. Evidently Mrs. Carter had
herself fired the house, then had ridden to this pool and
drowned herself. . . .

Vandermeer had taken the three bodies to Kaysee, where
he'd consulted with Gabe Morrow. Gabe had given it as his
opinion that Mrs. Carter's actions were precipitated by grief
for her late husband. Trevannon silently guessed that old
Gabe had shrewdly sized up the real truth, but would never
speculate aloud on it. And that was best, Trevannon
thought . . . best that this strange tormented girl's secret
die with her. Even the sad pity he now felt belonged to
memory. It was as though the few days he'd spent at Kaysee
had been lived in another world, and he no longer cared
about the ranch or its ultimate fate. There was here and now,
and there was Calla—yes, and the boy. He had to give the
future a realistic eye; if there was even a chance. . . .

"Sheriff—I shot a clerk on that holdup. I reckoned he
wasn't much hurt, but I wonder if you know—"

"When I returned to Coldbrook last night, I found a man
from Cedar Wells waiting. Sent by my wife to get word of
me. Among other things, he said the young clerk is already
back on the job." The sheriff paused, weighing his next
words. "I told him I was still working on the holdup. That
is all I have told anyone, except Gabe Morrow—yet."

With puzzled alertness, yet not daring to hope, Trevannon said slowly, "You stalling, Sheriff?"

Vandermeer rose brusquely, restlessly paced a circle.
Then he faced him, growling, "Damn it all. Damn you,
Trevannon. It is a hell of a debt for a lawman to owe a
bankrobber."

"Sorry," Trevannon said patiently, and waited.

"You are sorry!" Vandermeer snorted explosively. "Is a
man to forget so easily that you saved his life?"

"Try harder," Trevannon advised him coldly.

Vandermeer dropped his bristling front and sank onto the

chair. He stirred a great paw in an aimless, weary gesture. "That is not what I mean. You understand? I am a man of law; this comes first. It is myself who angers me. My very father I could bring to justice if the matter demanded."

"Sounds more like you, Sheriff."

Vandermeer's merciless gaze seemed to probe the root nature of the man on the bunk. "So. You think you know much. Well, you are not a fool. And maybe, if you had come as an orphan to a strange country, when you have nothing, when you look for something . . . if you had studied long to master a strange language and had found with relief a thing in which to believe . . . a system of laws which promises justice for all men and punishment for those who laugh at justice . . . if you spend days and nights struggling with great books to find the heart and meaning of this thing called law, this thing to which you have dedicated yourself. . . . Maybe, Mr. Trevannon, when you have done all this which sounds so easy in the saying, then you will know what I have tried to learn."

He scowled, looked down at his hands and massaged them, scowling slightly. Trevannon was faintly embarrassed, that this iron man was trying with difficulty to express the creed which centered his life.

Vandermeer continued slowly, "I live by the law, but I see it in my own terms. It must be a human thing, for it was made for humans. So. Ephraim Waybeck is my great friend. And this sharp-tongued lady," he motioned toward Calla, "is a fine woman. They know right and wrong well. It is not the law they fight, but a thing they think is wrong. But the law should always do right, eh? So I see it . . . justice wears a blindfold, but justice must not be blind. Punishment is to balance wrong, to prevent more wrong. Now . . . a man has suffered for wrong. He has tried to atone. Even when he could have watched the man of law who has come to take him shot down, he throws himself across the way of a bullet to save that man."

Trevannon raised himself on his elbows, frowning. "Don't get me wrong—"

"I do not; that is my point," the Dutchman said sternly. "And do not interrupt, please. Punishment is for a reason. When this reason is gone, there must be an end of punishment. Otherwise there is not justice." He set his hands on his knees and rose with ponderous gravity, his frosty eyes meeting Trevannon's with decision. A decision hadn't been easy, but once made, it was set in this iron-principled man's stubborn mind with the weighted certainty of a giant ridgepole timber lowered into place. "You are a man who has learned his own worth by a bitter road. Now live by that worth."

Phlegmatically he clamped on his hat and walked with his stolid, sweeping stride from the room. Trevannon lay unmoving, listening to the creak of leather as the sheriff mounted his horse, hearing his gruff farewell to Ephraim, the dying away of brisk hoofbeats. Jans Vandermeer was riding off, turning his back on the fugitive he had grimly bloodhounded. The money would be returned to its bank, accompanied by a small lie that reflected a bigger truth as this strange man of law saw it. . . .

Ephraim Waybeck came to the doorway, his seamed and bearded face alight, and he looked on them all and was wordless. Calla came to Trevannon and he held her hand tightly. For the moment there was nothing to say.

The old woman gave a little murmuring sound and then she stood and made her slow, groping way to the bunk. Her trembling fingers went out and traced lightly over Trevannon's brow. A little smile touched her soundlessly moving lips as she glided slowly back to her chair.

"She understands something of all that's happened," Calla said softly. "She was trying to tell you that. Perhaps she may even recover now. We've wanted that so much. This could be a beginning."

The boy scrambled to his feet and ran over to stand between them, leaning on his mother's arm where it reached to touch Trevannon's. His gray eyes were serious and hopeful. "Is Mr. Trevannon staying, Ma?"

Trevannon had not heard Calla's laugh before, and now it brimmed with her quiet strength. "Yes, Mr. Trevannon will stay now."

T.V. Olsen was born in Rhinelander, Wisconsin. "My childhood was unremarkable except for an inordinate preoccupation with Zane Grey and Edgar Rice Burroughs." He had originally planned to be a comic-strip artist, but the stories he came up with proved far more interesting to him than any desire to illustrate them. Having read such accomplished Western authors as Les Savage Jr., Luke Short, and Elmore Leonard, he began writing his first Western novel while a junior in high school. He couldn't find a publisher for it until he rewrote it after graduating from college with a bachelor's degree from the University of Wisconsin at Stevens Point in 1955 and sent it to an agent. It was accepted by Ace Books and was published in 1956 as *Haven Of The Hunted*.

Olsen went on to become one of the most widely respected and widely read authors of Western fiction in the second half of the twentieth century. Even early works such as *High Lawless* and *Gunswift* are brilliantly plotted with involving characters and situations and a simple, powerfully evocative style. Olsen went on to write such important Western novels as *The Stalking Moon* and *Arrow In The Sun*, which were made into classic Western films as well, the former starring Gregory Peck and the latter under the title *Soldier Blue* starring Candice Bergen. His novels have been translated into numerous European languages, including French, Spanish, Italian, Swedish, Serbo-Croatian, and Czech.

The second edition of *Twentieth Century Western Writers* concluded that "with the right press Olsen could command the position currently enjoyed by the late Louis L'Amour as America's most popular and foremost author of traditional Western novels." His novel *The Golden Chance* won the Golden Spur Award from the Western Writers of America in 1993.

Suddenly and unexpectedly, death claimed him in his sleep on the afternoon of July 13, 1993. His work, however, will surely abide. Any Olsen novel is guaranteed to combine drama and memorable characters with an authentic background of historical fact and an accurate portrayal of Western terrain.